Quest for the Source of Darkness

Patricia Perry

PublishAmerica
Baltimore

First printing

ISBN: 1-4137-7427-X
PUBLISHED BY PUBLISHAMERICA, LLLP
www.publishamerica.com
Baltimore

Printed in the United States of America

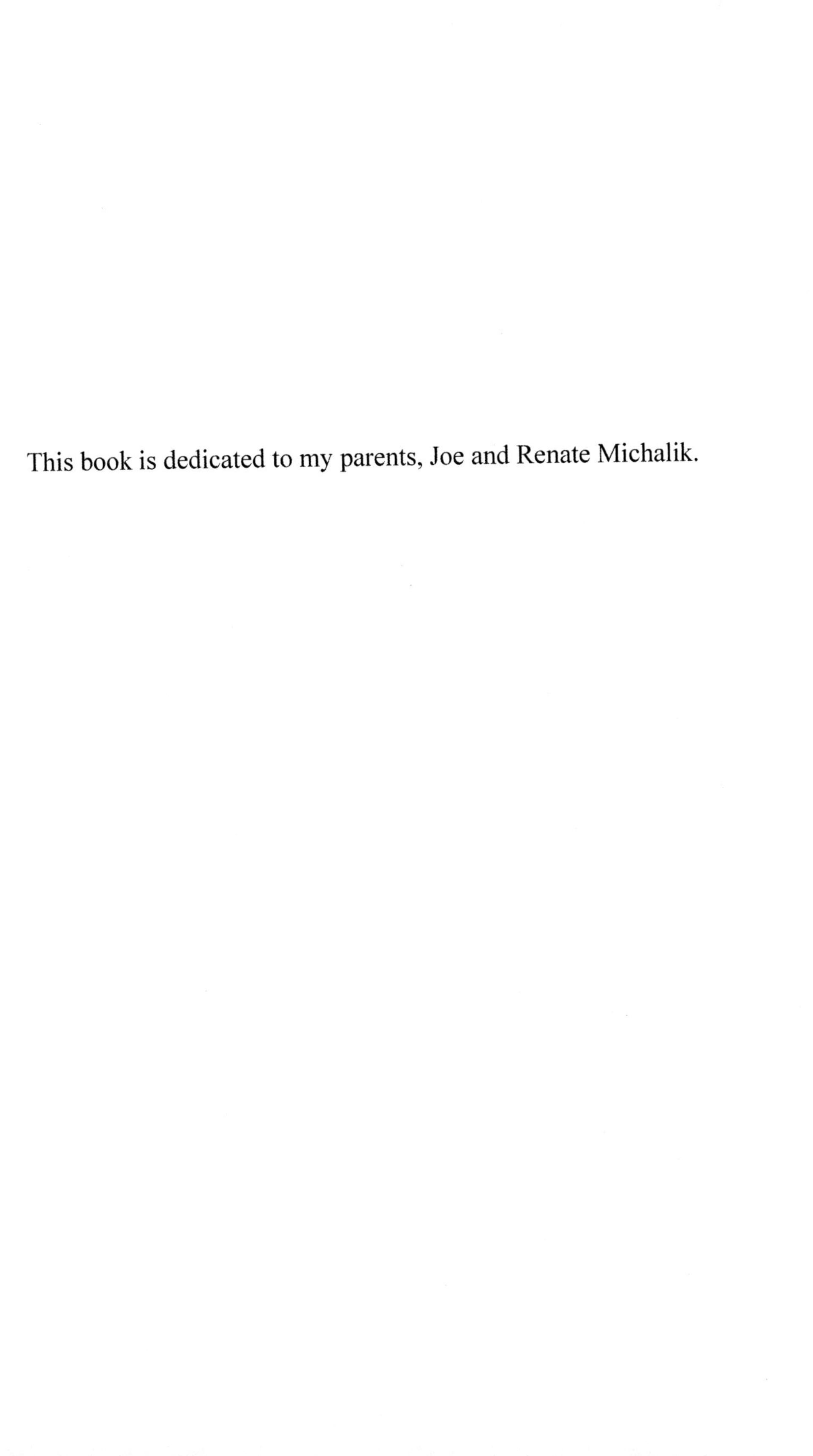

This book is dedicated to my parents, Joe and Renate Michalik.

Special thanks go to Sue for her encouragement, Patricia for her invaluable support, and to "Big Nurse" who helped me during the delivery.

Front cover photo by Sheri Sochor.

Back cover photo by Pamela.

Part 1

-1-

The dunes sparkled like powdered silver beneath the full moon, their undulating shapes stretching away as far as the eye could see. The wind shifted them into rolling forms that changed right before your very eyes, first hiding then exposing that which lay beneath: things mostly forgotten but not quite gone. Nothing ever truly disappeared for the vestiges of what they once were became reformed, sometimes into things that did not resemble their original appearance.

A stain emerged upon the immaculate silver sand and spread outward, appearing like a foul oily sheen floating upon an even fouler blackness. The smudge began to sink into the sands, momentarily disappearing then reappearing, exposing a wide rift from which cries and shrieks issued forth. Screams of bitterness, hatred and torment froze the blood and sent shivers of terror up the spine. A faint sooty haze rose from within the darkness, stretching upward toward the star-encrusted heavens, accompanied by the tortured howls. It blocked the twinkling points of light for a brief moment before falling back to the dunes, where it withdrew back down into its noxious void once more.

A cloaked figure lying prone on the dune to avoid being seen watched with a combination of fascination and horror as the vapor erupted from the sands. This was where the power was imprisoned, but it could never be bound to a master in its raw state: the figure would have to wait until it manifested itself into something that could be controlled. The desert kept its secrets well hidden, allowing them a brief breath of air only when no one could see…but there was always someone who did. The desert's mysteries remained secret no longer as the hooded and cloaked figure crawled backward in fearful apprehension.

She awoke to the sound of a deafening peal of thunder; her heart racing with fright as she bolted upright from her prone position, scanning the area with her saucer-shaped eyes. She found herself in an unfamiliar place with a vicious storm raging just beyond the entrance to the cave. Lightning streaked with a vengeance, illuminating rain intent upon beating the earth into submission. The wind shrieked and moaned as it, too, sought to punish the land for unknown crimes. She shivered, more from the roiling and seething storm than from the cold seeping into her shelter. She pulled her knees up to her chest, struggling to remember what she was doing in such an inhospitable place during such a ferocious tempest. She stared around the cave. The brief flashes of lightning illuminated an area that was not very large but was strewn with boulders, especially near what appeared to be a former rockslide toward the back. The air was relatively fresh and dust free, which told her that the cave-in had occurred long ago. The thought of the mountain being unstable, however, made her uneasy. Could a deafening clap of thunder loosen up more of the rocks, burying her within this stony crypt? She winced as the sounds from without took on a human timbre then slowly realized the throat from which they issued was indeed human.

She cautiously approached the entrance, mindful of the driving rain, and cocked her head to the side. For several long moments all she heard were the noises caused by the storm. Then a faint cry reached her ears. She crawled forward to the very lip of the cave and squinted downward, gasping at the wreckage loosened by the howling winds and rain. Vivid lightning lit up a disturbing scene as boulders, ledges and a variety of unidentifiable clumps lay strewn about, but she could see little else that could have been the source of that faint shout. She was about to edge back into the relative sanctuary when a white-hot bolt briefly exposed a hapless soul desperately clinging to an outcropping of stone several yards away. She immediately headed for the struggling person, her fingers gripping whatever seemed remotely stable as she half-climbed, half-slid down toward the figure. A large chunk of rock skittered past her, seemingly intent on dislodging the desperate figure. It met with a jagged pinnacle on the side of the mountain down which she scampered, deflecting the projectile away at the very last moment. She redoubled her efforts, finally reaching the figure just as he lost his grip and painfully descended down a few more yards. She silently cursed to herself, grabbing his wrist before he could disappear into the black nothingness far below.

The touch seemed to bring the figure back from its acceptance of doom as he lifted his head upward. A burst of light illuminated the man's battered and bruised face. His eyelids drooped and spittle sprayed out of his mouth as he gasped for air. Blood, diluted by the rain, trickled palely down his countenance. She yanked on his hand to catch his attention then pointed her head back up the way she had come. Something registered in his face and he offered her as much help as his exhausted body could give, then clawed and fought his way up the strangely viscous side of the mountain. Both of their hands were raw from the effort, their clothes torn by the sharp objects impeding their upward progress. He began to tire and she realized if she had misjudged the entrance to the cave she would not have the strength to help either of them the rest of the way. She glanced upward, forcing her eyes to stay open against the pounding rain long enough to find the cave, exhaling with relief as she spied it just a few more yards away. She pulled him with a short-lived energy, for a large boulder began to bounce down from somewhere overhead in the darkness. She instinctively pressed herself against her exposed charge and prayed it would somehow be deflected away before crushing them beneath its bulk or sending them careening down the side. It dropped onto the ledge next to them, splintering in half before bits and pieces fell away below, the razor sharp shards biting into their flesh. She groped along the shattered shelf then stared up toward the mouth of the cave: they were almost there. The storm intensified as if it meant to destroy them. Time, she knew, was not on their side. Soaked, pounded by the elements and rife with welts and cuts, she dragged the benumbed man inside and fell in a heap beside him, instantly succumbing to her fatigue.

Her aching and throbbing body forced her awake to face the day. It took a second or two for her to remember another being lay in the cave beside her. Flinching in pain, she propped herself up onto her injured elbow. The faint light that managed to trickle into the cave revealed ugly cuts above the injured man's left eye, along both of his cheeks and across the lower portion of his jaw. Bruises were widening under his skin giving him a misshapen appearance. She worked hard to get his partially wet clothes off then gently poked and prodded at his injuries to check for any broken bones. His injuries, to her relief, looked much worse than they were but needed attention nonetheless. She sighed, then cast about for her few belongings, hopeful she had some items in her pouch that could help them both. She found some dried food, a set of clothes, several small briquettes, ointments, bindings, a small pot and a spoon. She had certainly been prepared for wherever she was going. Necessity compelled her to dig a shallow depression in the dirt floor and light a briquette with some tinder from her pouch. She was both surprised and pleased the small black chunk gave off as much heat as it did: it would take very little time to heat some water. She spread her blanket out then rolled the man onto it before cleansing his wounds and applying the balms, satisfied none of the injuries required binding. She placed her warm cloak over him, tucking the edges all along his body to keep him warm before checking herself for any damage. Other than a few cuts and bruises she was unscathed. She changed into some dry clothes then walked over to the entranceway to view the storm's destruction. Had anyone else had the misfortune of being caught in it?

She gasped out loud at the landscape below her, for it was a mass of uprooted skeletal trees and piles of rocks and boulders covered with a sickly colored reddish mud. Her brow furrowed as parts of animals, some partially buried, others ripped apart by the force of the storm, lay scattered in twisted heaps. She carefully left the cave and maneuvered past the overhanging ledge where she could get a better view but found only more of that same destruction. No, not quite, she thought spotting a large lizard, its tail firmly caught beneath a large rock. She removed a black knife from within her tunic, crawled over to it and beheaded the creature with one deft movement of her hand. She cut off the tail and hefted the dead reptile over her shoulder while noting the ominous sky above. She hurried back into the cave, glancing down at her companion before setting about skinning the lizard then placing it on a makeshift spit over the fire.

The deluge began once more. She placed the pot outside to catch some water then sat down beside the man to study him. He was lean yet strong, his hands bearing calluses, his skin tanned by the sun. He had slightly angular features, gracefully arching brows and elegantly pointed ears, the likes of which she had never before seen. She lightly ran her finger over their curves several times wondering what sort of creature he was as he shifted in his sleep. For a moment he opened his eyes but she could tell by the vacant look he was unable to focus on his surroundings.

"Sleep," she gently advised him, then smiled as his lids slowly closed again.

He drifted off into an uneasy sleep, torn and fragmented images of the time just before the storm's onslaught filling his mind. He and his companions had been patrolling along the Broken Plain when the first dirty gray clouds blotted out the sun. They were caught in the open then separated from each other when the sagging clouds disgorged their contents, leaving nothing but chaos in their wake. He remembered distant shouts and the screaming of horses, but the oozing mud grabbing at his feet kept him from answering those calls. Every heartbeat marked a different memory while he slumbered. Thump-thump. He was climbing the unforgiving mountain scratching and clawing for something, anything that would allow him to ascend to safety. Thump-thump. The remnants of a bush tore his clothing as he passed over it. Thump-thump. He could still feel the burning sensation as the rocks cut his face and hands. Thump-thump. The rain felt like needles as it hit his skin. His mind continued to assault him with the images until he finally drifted off into a fitful sleep.

Unaware of her companion's flood of disjointed memories, she rose and walked over to the entrance, crossing her arms as she leaned against the side. The rain beat down upon the earth as she sought answers to her identity and how she came to be here. Had she been traveling to or from someplace? Was her home nearby or far away? She had some provisions but not enough to last for very long, yet a change of clothes meant she would be away for a few days at least. Other than the stranger who slept behind her, she had been alone. The desolate plain below didn't seem familiar either, nor was the reason for her being in this cave. Had she scaled the mountain seeking refuge from the impending storm? Was this a meeting place? If so, who was she supposed to meet? She shook her head trying to shake the knowledge loose from within the confines of her mind, but it refused to budge. The sizzling lizard broke through her thoughts demanding her attention. She crouched down beside it and poked at it with her knife: it was almost ready.

Her companion slowly roused himself from his slumber grimacing in pain as he attempted to roll over onto his side. She eased over and helped him sit erect, holding him in her arms like a child while he drank a few sips of water.

"Who…who are…you?" he asked in a thick, choking voice.

"A friend," she replied, trying to get as much food into him as possible before he went back to sleep. "What is your name?"

"Danyl…The others…"

"You were alone," she replied quietly.

"Must…find…" He tried to rise but the parts of his body that didn't hurt had no strength left.

"No. You must rest. There are no signs of anyone else out there but that doesn't mean something happened to them." She watched as his body refused to cooperate with his mind, leaving him no choice but to stay put.

The thought of his companions out in that storm troubled him greatly but there was nothing either one of them could do right now. When the weather cleared and he had healed somewhat they could look for survivors. He finished a few more mouthfuls of food before lying down once more, his bleary gaze aimed toward the entrance.

She filled her stomach after he had eaten, licking the grease from her fingers as she stared out into the rain. They had supplies for a few days then she would have to hunt for food, a prospect she did not relish. If he did not get better before then she would have to leave him alone and at the mercy of whatever ventured into the cave. She had noticed the carcasses below and knew it would only be a matter of time before the scavengers, wolves among them, would find their need to eat far outweighed their fear of the storm's fury. The smell of decaying flesh would not long go unheeded. They would, however, be safe for the time being. She lay down beside him, placed her head upon her arm and drifted off to sleep.

The next morning began as the previous one but she was pleased at the progress Danyl was making. He still had difficulty seeing but he had become more active, slowly dressing himself in his dry clothes while she stared out at the plains below.

"Can you see anyone out there?" he asked in a hoarse whisper.

"No."

"Twelve men cannot simply have vanished."

"The storm could have dispersed them."

"What if they are hurt? We have to look for them."

"Not while the storm still rages," she reminded him.

He squinted, willing his eyes to focus long enough to catch any movement below. All he could see were blurry and shadowy forms devoid of color, leaving him feeling disorientated no matter how hard he tried to concentrate. His only reward for his effort was a splitting headache and a queasy stomach. He swayed unsteadily on his feet; one hand gripping her arm while the other rubbed his throbbing forehead. Reason finally took root in his mind, for as badly as he wanted to look for his companions, his body was not strong enough yet for such an undertaking.

"The rains seem to have let up," she said more to herself than to him. "A full day of sun could bake that mud until it's passable."

"I hope it dries soon."

"Why?"

"Wolves. I could hear them…looking for food."

She shuddered. Even though there were plenty of carcasses littering the plains below, the predators still preferred fresh meat. They usually hunted in pairs but would form temporary alliances with other wolves if the situation warranted it. The two of them would eventually be found if they stayed here. He would be easy prey and she would be unable to fight two or more wolves at the same time. They hid during the day, preferring to hunt late in the night. She and Danyl would have to increase their vigilance or become the wolves' next meal. She practically willed the sun to harden the muddy earth below to allow them at least a chance to escape. Danyl lay back down and closed his eyes knowing he would need to conserve as much strength as possible.

That night the wolves did come closer, but they had not yet picked up their scent. It was a small consolation for they both knew they would eventually face those vicious killers. It finally stopped raining. The waterlogged ground placed them in a dire predicament: attempt to cross that sticky red morass or wait one more night and take their chances with the wolves. She had gauged the distance between the cave and the faint green tinge to the east during the day, judging it was perhaps a day's journey taking into consideration Danyl's weakened condition. He had insisted things were safe there, yet who knew how far the wolves would forage for a fresh kill.

They sat huddled together. Neither one of them could sleep, their senses strained as they heard the unmistakable sounds of large paws scrabbling against the loose debris outside the cave. He cautiously reached out and tapped her arm as both looked out of the mouth of the cave at the slowly setting moon. He groped for his short sword, the only object other than his clothes he hadn't lost, while she unsheathed her blades. She eased closer toward the entrance, keeping in the shadows as best as she could, listening for the sounds of death. She heard Danyl shift somewhere behind her as her eyes caught sight of a silhouette just beyond the lip of a long, flat ledge to her right. A pair of wolves was passing by when they suddenly froze. The hair on their backs stood straight up, their ears lay back and the sounds of a low, sinister growling met her ears. She barely breathed, fearful they would turn from their path, but it was already too late. The pair altered direction and slowly skulked toward her, their yellow eyes rife with hunger and anticipation. She watched as the pair suddenly split up and withdrew into the darkness. The hunt was on. The wolves' coarse, gray fur blended in perfectly with the scraggly brush and rocks littering the mountainside; the murky night only added to their invisibility. She started as pads dislodged bits of debris along her left and right, squeezing the hilts, the feel of the cold metal reassuring. Then there was a complete moment of silence, one she recognized as one thing only: attack.

The sound of her pounding heart filled her ears as she anticipated the shadows of death to pounce at her from two different directions to tear her and Danyl apart. Perspiration trickled down her face and neck as she nervously gripped her knives, all the while straining to hear any sound. She detected scraping claws moving across exposed rock and instinctively knew the wolves were close. Growling sounds preceded the charging pair as they lunged at her in unison, their fangs snapping at the air around her with such ferocity she was soon covered in their slobber. Their merciless eyes were mere inches from hers; the thought of their jaws clamping down around her throat propelled her to hack and slice at them with a desperate urgency. She grimaced as one clawed her thigh, an act she rewarded with a cut along its muzzle. Howling in pain, it charged at her with a renewed fury, splattering her with its blood as it thrust itself upon her.

She kept them from entering the cave for as long as she could, but one managed to sneak past, disappearing into the cave behind her. A second later she could hear Danyl grunt and groan as he fought the wolf, the sounds of snarling and snapping sending a shiver of panic up her spine. Would he be able to handle the beast in his debilitated condition, or would it tear him apart? She had her hands full with the wolf trying to force her down and finish her. It was a mistake, one that left it with a nearly decapitated head. She kicked the beast once then turned to help her companion, the eerie silence issuing forth from the darkness grabbing at her innards.

Danyl's keen hearing and the faint light filling the entranceway to the cave offered him some hope as the fuzzy shadow surged toward him. The wolf with the gash across its jaw moved purposefully, yet unsteadily forward, the need to feed outweighing the pain. Although injured, the wolf sorely tested Danyl's weakened condition as it lunged and snapped at him from many directions. Every time he dodged the beast the fetid breath it left in its wake overwhelmed him. He tried to ignore the horrible stench emanating from its foul maw as his short sword cut and stabbed at the beast until he finally brought the blade down into its skull. He dropped to his knees, gulping in air as the remainder of his strength dripped off his body along with the sweat. He could barely hear the woman calling to him from the front of the cave.

"Danyl?" she cried out tentatively at first, then with a sense of panic. "Danyl!"

"I'm fine…the wolf is dead."

She sighed and found him on his knees before the beast, breathing hard as the tip of his sword rested in a pool of blood on the ground beside him. She dropped down, placing her arms around his shoulders.

The thought of being alone again was too much to bear. Danyl's hands let go of the hilt and gripped her tightly with a powerful need for human contact. His keen hearing helped him win the battle but the amount of energy it had cost him was very unsettling. Other wolves would undoubtedly come but he would not have the energy to fight them. As soon as the sun came up they would have no choice but to leave. Would he be able to cross the plains? She certainly would not be able to carry him nor would he be able to outrun the wolves if they were pursued out on the plains.

"We are out of choices, Danyl," she began in hushed tones, fearful of attracting another unwanted visitor into the cave. "We must leave at daybreak or we will die here when night comes. Do you have the strength to get across the plains?"

"Yes," he lied, sitting down to conserve what little energy he had left.

They ate out of need, ignoring the dead wolves she had pulled into the far corner of the cave to limit attracting more the rest of that night. She packed up her few belongings, placing them beside her as they waited for the sun to rise. The hours seemed like days, and they often started at the imaginary sounds of pads dislodging rocks outside of the cave. They managed to find comfort in each other as the night slowly gave way to the morning.

"You never told me your name," he whispered into her ear.

"If we survive then I will tell you," she said, wishing she knew what it was herself and wondering if she would ever remember it.

"Why not now? After all…you did save my life."

"I have only prolonged it, Danyl. We must still cross the plains without getting killed. How is your vision?"

"Blurred. The rest of me is strong enough, I suppose. By the way," he tried to ease both of their fears with a little bit of levity, "did you peek?"

"'Peek'?"

"When you took my clothes off."

"I took no unwarranted liberties, if that's what you mean." She couldn't help but smile. "You shouldn't talk, Danyl. Save all of your strength for the crossing."

They both silently begged the sun to hasten into the sky where it could dry the land and give them a chance to live another day. It did indeed rise but in a way neither could have imagined. The sun began to bake the earth with such intensity, that steam began to rise upward from the abused land. They felt the heat even in the relative coolness of the cave and dreaded having to face it once they left their shelter. It was finally time to leave and so began the difficult descent down the mountain. The storm had spared nothing, forcing the pair to crawl over extracted debris or scamper downhill sliding on their backsides. She was never far from Danyl, guiding him on with not just patience but also with extreme urgency, for the sun was climbing steadily into the cloudless sky. By the time they reached the bottom of the mountain it was already midmorning, leaving them with precious little time to make the crossing to the greenish haven miles away.

Beads of perspiration ran down their faces as the merciless sun cooked the earth. Rifts great and small spread out along the plain making for treacherous footing. Both stumbled more than once as the brittle ground beneath their feet gave way. She ripped her extra tunic into sections and bound their heads for protection. She could do nothing against the nasty black flies appearing out of nowhere once they reached level ground. The insects had been feasting on the rotting carcasses but they, like the wolves, preferred to feed off the living. They proceeded to swarm around them, invading every moist part of their bodies. The pair's sweat attracted the flies even more as they landed and bit at will. It became almost impossible to shoo them away. They adjusted their head coverings, dealing with the constant annoyance as best they could. Within an hour, a reddish dust rose from the tortured earth, intensifying with every step and every puff of wind. The flies hated it and left to harry some other creature, but the pair's relief was soon short lived. The dust infiltrated everything and they could not speak without coughing and gagging. She kept a careful eye on Danyl, touching his hand resting on her arm to confirm he was still able to continue as she led him on toward the soft green line, far in the distance.

The sun began its descent, elongating their shadows until the silhouettes stretched grotesquely ahead of them. Spindly limbs and elliptical heads sprouted from frail torsos, the dark outlines slanting bizarrely as they passed over uneven ground. They did not stop, even when she handed him the canteen. She heard him rinse out his mouth before taking a deep swallow, an act she repeated, grateful to be able to flush some of the dust out of her mouth. They managed to plod on and, near early evening, reached the line of scraggly trees. There was a change in the air as they stepped off the rust-colored plains and entered the greenery. It was much cooler and fresher beneath the unfolding branches, the sound of running water reaching their ears. They both glanced over their shoulders at the nightmare they had left behind and for the first time felt as if they had a chance to survive.

"Do you want to stop and rest, Danyl?"

"No, not here…by the water," was his raspy reply.

They were both exhausted, ready to plunge into the cool water, but they needed to make sure the region was safe first. She settled him onto a fallen log then made a quick search of the surrounding area, finding only groups of small trees, low bushes and the beginnings of grasslands a little farther to the east. Satisfied, she returned and helped him to the stream. The water was fresh and clean, both of them dunking their heads into its refreshing wetness. She shared the last of her food with him, hoping she would be fortunate enough to catch something for dinner. A flash of silver in the stream: fish were swimming to the surface to feed on the flies, and with any luck, one would fry in her pan later on.

"How well do you know this area?"

"Fairly well," he managed to utter, his shoulders stooping and his chin nearly touching his chest. "There are villages to the north and east…patrols use this area to water their horses."

"What kind of patrols?"

"Elves."

"Like you?" she asked after a long pause, glancing at his ears.

"Yes…I thought you knew." He strained to see her features but could only distinguish vague shapes and very little color. He couldn't think of any race that didn't know about the elves, yet this woman was puzzled by their existence.

"I'll search for a safe place for us to spend the night while you catch your breath." With that, she turned and scoured the site for an easily defensible place, the wolves never far from her mind. She found a suitable place about a hundred yards up on a little hill. The foothill was hemmed in by pine trees, its sides steep enough to deter an invader. Pleased, she went back to him, filled her flask with fresh water then led him up to their shelter. She broke off several boughs, placing them on the ground for cushioning, the makeshift bed a vast improvement over the unyielding rock floor of the cave.

"Here," she eased him down, "you are already half asleep so…" She smiled as his eyes closed the moment he lay down, pulling out the blanket to cover him. Sleep did not come easily and more often than not she snapped awake at every sound that drifted close. She curled up against his slumbering form for warmth and security, his nearness offering her some measure of comfort. He shifted in his sleep as if sensing her presence and placed his hand upon her arm.

She rested her hand within his, her mind grappling with the fact that even though she had no clue about her past, her presence in the cave had preserved their future. They were evidently not meant to die on that mountain or while crossing the plains. What fate had in mind for them down the road was unknown, but she hoped their road would not end within this piney hollow.

She awoke at dawn, more tired than refreshed. Danyl too began to stir beneath the blanket and gave her a little smile of encouragement before rising stiffly. He grimaced as he tried to stretch out his cramped muscles, squinting in order to take in his surroundings. She stared at his face, noting that the bruises were slowly turning color and his cuts had begun to scab. The swelling from the fly bites was beginning to diminish, and his eyesight, she surmised, would improve in a few days.

"I'll try to find something to eat," she said while brushing the leaves and dirt off her clothes.

"If you see any low bushes with long slender leaves, you'll find a root that grows underneath...they have frilly tops and a deep reddish color. They require a bit of digging but they are quite good." His eyes remained downcast as he spoke.

"I promise I'll return with an armful of something," she replied.

She began to search the area for the shrubs, keeping alert for any woodland animal she might be able to catch. She never strayed too far from Danyl, occasionally glancing back at the shelter to make sure everything was as it should be. The patrols he spoke about would have been a welcome sight, but as the day grew older she realized they would not be so fortunate. He wanted to be with his people and she needed to learn about herself. Which direction should she travel? Where was her home? What if she had originated from beyond the Broken Plain? She noticed the bush Danyl had described, the leafy clumps clustering beneath the droopy branches.

It took a lot of effort to dislodge the slender tubers but she managed to extract enough for a couple of meals. Meat, she thought, would be a welcome bonus.

She hid behind the bushes and waited. A rabbit appeared to her right, its nervous little nose testing the air before nibbling on the leaves of some underbrush. She withdrew her blade and quickly gauged the distance then let the dagger fly. Her aim was true, the weapon pinning the startled hare to the ground. She pulled the knife from the creature, slit its throat and picked up her prize. She turned to head back to Danyl when the unmistakable sounds of hooves thudded hollowly just beyond a stand of trees ahead of her. She scurried toward a hiding place fearful those approaching were foes instead of friends. She could see nothing, her view blocked by the foliage. She peered over at the shelter, silently pleading for Danyl to remain hidden. The seconds ticked by like hours, the roots and rabbit forgotten as she waited for the strangers to break through the hardwoods. They rode cautiously through scanning the area but unaware she crouched in the thicket in front of them. She absorbed virtually every detail as they came closer, remaining motionless as they dismounted.

They were dressed in greens and browns, riding sleek, lathered horses with reins of braided leather and well-oiled saddles atop plain brown blankets. They were well-armed, with bows, arrows, short swords, and numerous small daggers strapped to their waists, legs and arms. She noted their set expressions, the unmistakable arched brows and pointed ears and realized they were elves. They had come to search for him and take him back to his home. One elf in particular stood out from the rest. His sturdy frame and uncompromising demeanor commanded a great deal of respect. His piercing dark eyes studied everything in the area, leaving her with the impression that little, if anything, escaped their keen scrutiny.

A part of her wanted to break out from her concealment and lead them to Danyl but she resisted. She watched as they split up, each pair searching the area for any danger while calling out his name, their routine precise and well-practiced. The leader moved toward the hill, attracted by the broken twigs and flattened grass, his hand on his weapon as he tried to peer up into the semi-darkness. He shouted an unfamiliar word into the thickly covered hillock then waited for a response. The reply was immediate. She spotted Danyl stumbling down from the hill, smiling as he greeted his companions. She was grateful he was with his own folk but saddened, too. She would now be alone. She watched as two of his companions stayed with him while the others began to look for her, but she remained hidden, unwilling to expose herself. She should have met up with them, told them what had happened, then gone her own way. She could see Danyl arguing with his comrades, gesturing back toward the shelter while they tried to urge him onto a horse. The disagreement finally ended with Danyl mounting the steed and reluctantly following his companions through the trees and out of her line of sight. She waited until they were gone, gradually emerging with roots in one hand and the rabbit in the other. Her eyes never left the point where the riders disappeared from view.

You are a fool! Call out to them!

"Most people would welcome a chance to leave this place…why not you?" an indifferent voice called out to her from behind.

She jumped in shock; dumbfounded, she had failed to see one of the elves sneak around behind her. She dropped her dinner, instinctively drawing her knives in response. She stared at the stocky brown elf with the expressionless face for a moment then slipped the daggers back into her tunic. She scooped up her meal, her eyes locked with the dark ones as they scrutinized her from top to bottom.

"You startled me."

"Answer my question."

"I must go my own way," she replied, the underlying truth in her voice producing a faint nod.

"You have done a great service to my kin by saving Danyl and must be rewarded."

"I need no reward…all I care about is that he is alive."

"I am called Lance. You will be warmly welcomed if you ever travel to Bystyn." He turned to leave but she stopped him.

"Lance? I ask that you keep this between us."

"Why?"

"I don't really know…I just need to take care of a few things first," she replied as candidly as she could.

"If we meet again in Bystyn that might change. What are you called?"

"That's one of the things I need to find out," she stated quietly before heading back to the shelter.

Lance did not pursue her but stared after her for some time. There was nothing in her demeanor to alarm him, but he did have several questions he wanted to ask her. Why was she here? What was she doing along this cursed plain? Did she know whom she had saved? Why did she refuse any sort of recognition for her act? Perhaps Danyl had answers to some of these questions or maybe she would answer them if they ever met again. Lance whistled for his horse, mounted it in a single fluid motion and rode after his men.

She watched him disappear through the trees feeling completely alone for the first time, the hare and roots dangling from her hands. The afternoon light began to wane, lengthening her shadow with every passing minute. She stared around at the now abandoned area. The late day breeze kicked up little puffs of red dirt to the west and stirred the dirty strands of hair hanging in front of her even grubbier face. The sweat of her exertions left little trails along her body, its pungent odor lifting up into her nose. Her gaze remained focused on where Lance had disappeared. Her stomach began to growl, diverting her attention to the details at hand. She made a small depression in the ground, placed a briquette into it then erected a spit for the rabbit. She watched it sizzle as it cooked, absently munching on one of the vegetables, its flavor tangy and sweet at the same time. She ate the entire animal, not bothering to worry about what she would eat tomorrow, then climbed up the hill to sleep. She was about to roll herself up in the blanket when she spotted a pouch a few feet away. Curious, she opened it and smiled: the elves had left enough food to last for many days. She pulled the generous gift up to her body and drifted off into restless sleep.

-2-

She awoke as the sun poked over the horizon, ate, then packed up her things. She headed down to the stream, washing the sleep from her eyes before heading east. She walked through the trees and low brush until the land opened up and offered her a spectacular view. To the north and many leagues away was a dark forest line, one extending to the northern borders of the plains in the west and as far east as far as her eyes could follow. Behind them were the majestic snow-covered peaks that even from this distance seemed to touch the heavens. The southern section of the land appeared to slope away behind a series of small rolling hills while the east lured her with its wide expanse and clusters of budding hardwood trees. The earth was beginning to awaken from its long winter slumber. There would still be a few crisp nights and damp chilly mornings but spring promised those would soon be left behind. She smiled, hiked her provisions over her shoulders and headed east. She'd have plenty of time to think along the way and maybe, just maybe, she'd run into Danyl again.

The road to Bystyn took longer than she had anticipated even though the journey itself was pleasant enough. The farther east she traveled the more people she encountered. Many swept out the dust and gloom of winter from their homes while others began to prepare their fields for planting. She passed on by, absorbing the sights and sounds as the sun's warmth prodded the grasses, flowers and trees into life. She inhaled the fresh aroma of turned earth and reached out to touch branches covered with buds and tiny leaves, their velvety feel and vitality a balm to her travel-weary soul. She slept beneath their protective boughs in the night and hunted among them for fresh food during the day as she continued on her journey. She hadn't been able to recall anything from her past, but the beauty and serenity of the land compensated for the disappointment of not remembering anything. She greeted a farmer and his wife as they crossed in front of her, politely declining their invitation to join them for a meal. The farmer's wife dug into her basket and handed her a loaf of bread and a block of cheese, gifts she gratefully accepted as she placed them into her nearly empty pouch. She waved to the couple as they continued on their way then went on her way.

It had been more than two weeks since she had left the plains, her dirty body and clothes wearing down on her road-weary feet. The land before her spread out, undulating in gentle green waves as the wind blew gently over the knee-high grasses. The stands of ash, oak and maple trees clustered here and there were alive with birdsong and small animals scurrying along the branches. Many patrols had been traveling back and forth, making her wonder if such vigilance was a normal occurrence. Their faces, like those of the group that rescued Danyl, were firmly set.

She crested a small line of hills a few hours later, stopping at the top to gaze down below. Several miles away were groups of stone houses, the yards alive with livestock, people and carts, but beyond them stood a sight she could barely absorb. An expansive and impregnable yet wholly inviting structure rose from the middle of the verdant plain. Its walls were built of gray rocks, its massive front gates thrown open wide to welcome the myriad of wagons, people, and horsemen entering and exiting. Four monumental towers stood at each corner of the solid walls; a series of buttresses leaned out from the battlement at specific intervals in between them. Sentinels walked along the ramparts keeping watch over the steady stream of people coming and going through the main gate, their weapons glinting in the sunlight. A series of low trees encased in pink and white blossoms extended from the eastern wall to a copse of pine trees a few miles away. A silver current wound its way out from near the pines, flowing slightly south then west before meandering east once more. The abundant vegetation growing along the banks of this river could be seen even from her vantage point. Farmlands were visible just beyond the river, the fields' collections of deep browns separated by low rock walls. The snow-covered peaks she had seen from the edge of the Broken Plains towered over the city in the north, their precipitous sides a deterrent to anyone who sought to scale them. Was this Bystyn? She looked up and noticed the sun already beginning to descend. The initial excitement at finding the city gave way to reality as her aching body and growling stomach demanded she appease them. She needed to find a place to eat, sleep and bathe, but had nothing with which to pay for any of those amenities. She decided to take a chance and headed toward the vast complex nestled amid the grassy plain.

The sun hung midway in the late afternoon sky as she neared the gate, feeling overwhelmed by its width and depth as she walked beneath it.

Shadows swallowed her up midway through the gate corridor, the permanent chill seeping out of the stones making her shiver. Two wagons and four horsemen riding abreast passed by each other and still there was plenty of room for at least another cart. Another wall stood just inside the main one where barracks and stables were located. The area in between the walls was bustling with activity. Elves worked several large stones busily sharpening swords, lances and other weapons while blacksmiths banged away on their anvils, the clanging noise reverberating off the thick wall. Horses were being groomed and cartloads of provisions unloaded, the heavy sacks forcing the bearers to walk at an odd angle. She finally entered the city proper, following the main avenue as it ran straight ahead. Shops claimed the prime spots along this road, an occasional inn or tavern sprinkled in between. The cobblestone streets were clean and well-maintained even with the constant traffic of horses, people and wagons. Stoops were swept, and window boxes, already showing some signs of life, were everywhere. The elves took great pride in their homes and city. She passed a bakery and inhaled the aromas wafting out into the street, the distinct fragrance of honey drizzled baked goods somehow eliciting one tiny memory: her name. It came to her as a voiceless whisper from deep within her mind, leaving her grateful that at least she now had something to call her own. She lingered in front of the shop for so long the proprietor waddled out and placed one of the delicacies into her dusty hand.

"The first batch is always the best," he said with a smile.

"I can't pay you for this…"

The baker winked at her then retreated into his sweet realm. She stared at the pastry covering her entire hand, her stomach imploring her to devour it, gurgling with anticipation as she brought it up to her lips. It was still warm, the sugary coating melting in her mouth, the cake still springy to the touch. It was her first bite of food since the previous morning.

She nibbled on the treat scanning the street for inns. She went to all of the inns in the city yet none could offer her any rooms. She had nothing to pay for the lodging, and considering there were already plenty of helping hands, she was turned away. The late afternoon turned to early evening and she had visited every inn in the city. She burped up the treat: it was all she had eaten. The provisions the elves had left for her by the plain were long gone, and the quiet chill sneaking in as the sun descended told her it was going to be a long night. It was time to abandon the city and seek refuge along the riverbank.

Positioned in the middle of the city where the two main streets intersected, she looked around one last time for a place of lodging. No signs greeted her tired eyes but a stair invited her to sit for just a few moments before heading out into the night. She sat down on the broad step, ignoring the trellis and bright green shutters flanking the windows, her body protesting as she rested her arms on her knees. Her head dropped onto her arms and she was immediately asleep. The street sounds diminished; the hardness of the stone stair was forgotten and the distant whisperings in her mind became more and more muffled.

"Excuse me," a voice called out from somewhere beyond the haze of exhaustion, "may I help you?"

Was someone speaking to her? Who would address her? She was a stranger here…looking for shelter and a hot meal…sitting on a step? She was so tired…couldn't she just rest for a few more minutes?

"Young woman," the voice gently persisted.

Sophie looked down upon the dirty bundle of rags with pity, for the woman who wore them was too road worn to even lift her head up. Sleeping on her front steps, however, was out of the question. She watched the woman slowly rouse herself and glance up, the dark circles under her puffy eyes noticeable even through the dust clinging to her skin.

"I'm very sorry, good woman," she managed to say. "I was just resting for a moment." She struggled to stand then sluggishly headed down the avenue toward the gate. Sophie watched her leave, the prospect of finding any lodging nonexistent. People poured into the city this time of year to be with friends and family after the long, dark winter kept them cooped up in their homes. They came to enjoy the spring festival, which would be held in another week. This girl needed a break.

Wait," she called out to her. "You may stay here for a night or two."

"I have no money to pay you, but I will gladly lend my services to you in repayment."

"I do have a few things that need attending to around here…I am Sophie…and you?"

"Ramira."

"Good: first a bath then a change of clothes, some food and sleep. When was the last time you ate or slept in a bed?" The girl's appearance was dull, shades of brown, gray and red covering her from head to toe. Sophie's kindness rejuvenated her a little, the thought of food and a bath chasing away her fatigue.

"A treat from the baker a few hours ago, and I cannot remember the last time I slept in a bed," replied Ramira, following Sophie into the back of the house and into the kitchen. It was cozy here, the smell of freshly baked bread and a simmering stew making her mouth water. She pulled off her cloak, placing it and her things beside the fireplace. Sophie disappeared into a chamber behind the large stone hearth, the sound of running water bringing a smile of relief to her face. Sophie reappeared briefly, nodding for her to sit while she fetched a clean set of clothes from upstairs. Sophie walked back into the kitchen, handed Ramira the clothes then ushered her into the bath chamber.

"There's plenty of hot water, Ramira," she called through the door. "By the looks of you I figure you'll need a bit more than one tubful."

Sophie had been correct in her assessment. Ramira ended up filling the tub twice more, the dirt she had accumulated over the past few weeks stubbornly refusing to yield to the washcloth. The infrequent washings in a river or stream had done little to keep her clean. Her clothes stank and needed mending, too, but she would leave those chores for tomorrow. She remained in the tub for as long as she could then left the tepid waters and dressed. Her demanding appetite could be denied no longer. She combed out her long hair letting it hang loosely down her back. She accepted a mug of tea from Sophie, drinking the dark liquid with great relish. Sophie placed her hands on her hips and studied the girl, amazed at what the absence of filth revealed.

"You are beautiful, Ramira," she stated, her eyes studying Ramira's subtle bronze-hued skin, amethyst eyes and long, red-gold hair. Her brows arched elegantly upwards like the elves but her ears were rounded. Ramira had entered Sophie's home a dirty stray, emerging from the bath a polished young woman.

"I am clean, Sophie, and that is far better."

"Sit." Sophie invited her to the table where bread, cheese and a bowl of stew awaited her. Ramira ate until she thought she would burst, her embarrassed countenance quickly erased by Sophie's words.

"Don't worry, child, you'll have worked that off and more by the time you finish with my list of chores!"

"You are too kind, Sophie."

"Repeat that to me tomorrow," she said with a gentle chuckle, pouring them both a glass of wine. "What brings you to Bystyn?"

Ramira gazed into the ruby red contents of the goblet, the bath and food beginning to sap the last of her strength. Sophie needed to be assured she had not let a dangerous stranger into her home, but Ramira had little information to offer her.

"I'm afraid I cannot tell you too much about myself," began Ramira quietly. "I came from the west but can't remember exactly who I am or where I came from. As to why I ended up in Bystyn…well…it was a destination as good as any other. I was hoping I would be able recall some things along the way but the only thing I could recollect was my name."

"Did you have an accident?" asked Sophie, her brown eyes kind yet scrutinizing at the same time.

"I don't know," she replied honestly.

There were no apparent lies or deceptions in her words or tone of voice. Ramira sat quietly at the table waiting for Sophie's judgement; her hands folded in her lap while she fought to keep her eyelids from closing. Sophie's gaze shifted from Ramira to the darkness gathering outside beyond the patio.

"How long have you been traveling, Ramira?"

"A little more than two weeks." She drained her glass, straining to keep her eyes open. Sophie decided any further questions could wait and suggested she get some rest. Sophie began to lead her up the stairs when Ramira caught her sleeve.

"If you feel uncomfortable with me here…"

"Nonsense, girl. If I thought that I would never have let you into my house." She led her to a room at the end of the narrow hallway and opened the door. "There's a basin, a dresser and a chest with extra blankets. I'll look in on you in the morning…sleep well, Ramira."

"Thank you, Sophie," she replied as the woman left her room. She walked over to the balcony, peering through the curtains at the sleeping garden below and wondered why she kept such a delightful room for guests instead of for herself. She headed over to the bed and slipped between the warm quilt and fresh linens. The memories of the hard ground and damp grasses began to dissolve, chased away by the warmth and softness surrounding her aching body. Ramira shifted once then gave in to her exhaustion.

Sophie did not waken Ramira, letting her sleep out her exhaustion. She washed her clothes and blanket, hanging them out in the fresh spring air then decided to launder her pouch as well. She was surprised to see it was of elven handiwork. Ramira had mentioned she had been on the road for more than two weeks…approximately the time it would take to reach Bystyn on foot from the Broken Plains. There had been bits of caked-on reddish mud in her blanket and cloak—not a significant amount but the only place to find that type of soil was along the plains. Danyl had traces of it on his person as well.

Did she meet up with Danyl and the scouts somewhere along the way? They would have shared supplies with anyone who needed them, especially in that accursed land. Ramira would have encountered dozens of homesteads, villages and patrols along the way, any one of which could have furnished her with the provisions.

Sophie believed Ramira when she confessed she had no memory of her past, but she evidently remembered the last few weeks. Perhaps she should invite Danyl and Lance to her home, pitting their reactions—or lack thereof—against her theory. Sophie suddenly chided herself for meddling in things that were really none of her business. Her days were full enough of things requiring her attention without being sidetracked by this little mystery. She stared at the pouch in her hands then out to the things dangling from the line and back again. She sighed and finished her task, her mind on the mysterious creature sleeping in her house.

Ramira entered the kitchen in the late morning feeling refreshed but upset because she had slept so long. She accepted the strong cup of tea Sophie handed to her, slightly embarrassed as she spotted her belongings draped on the clothesline.

"I would have done that, Sophie," she protested.

"It is done, besides, they were borderline foul," she said with a little laugh.

"I noticed that after I left the bath last night," she confessed, her nose wrinkling up in distaste.

"My daughter, Anci, will be back this afternoon and will take care of her chores but you," she handed Ramira a pair of leather gloves, "…you get to clean out the woodshed. The broom is behind the door and don't waste time…more wood will be delivered early this afternoon."

Ramira nodded, eager to begin repaying Sophie for her kindness. She walked to the side of the house, unlatched the rough-hewn door and entered the little hut. Sunlight squeezed through the cracks, illuminating the dust launched into the air by her deed, the cloud of dirt making her cough and her eyes water. She opened the windows, propping them up with slats of wood to get a better view of the task at hand. Most of the wood had been used up over the course of the winter, leaving her to contend with just a few rows of wood and piles of bark. She finished her task then pulled out enough slivers from her arms to start a roaring fire.

She went into the kitchen and poured herself a glass of water, drinking down the refreshing liquid in just a few gulps before refilling her glass.

Sophie's kitchen was cozy with plants and herbs on the windowsills, bright copper pots and pans hanging from hooks on the wall. A rocking chair rested on a braided rug in front of the hearth, its back bowing slightly outward, the finish on its arms nearly worn away. Sophie appeared weighted down with baskets of food and other items, bunching the plain tablecloth as she pushed the containers toward the middle of the table.

"You seem too content, Ramira. I think you need more work to do!"

"I am at your service," replied Ramira. She helped unload the purchases, wondering how long her good fortune was going to last before Sophie asked her leave.

"You'll have a busy day tomorrow," began Sophie as she put away the stores. "I am sending you to an elderly couple beyond the orchards who need a few things done for them. Jack and Ida will appreciate the help, for their sons are currently out on patrol to the west." *Your absence will also give me a chance to do some snooping*, she thought.

"When do I leave?" asked Ramira with some measure of comfort, the extra work a hopeful sign that she would be able to stay a while.

"At sunrise…no lounging in bed until most of the day has already passed by," she playfully chided her.

"I'll try," she joked.

"Ah…hello, Anci." She greeted her daughter as Anci came into the kitchen, the young girl's glance lingering on the stranger helping her mother. Anci's slim form seemed to get lost within her mother's ample embrace then she brushed back her auburn hair and smiled as Sophie introduced her to Ramira. Anci studied Ramira, her brown eyes glancing questionably at her mother without any hint of discourtesy to their guest. Ramira noted the slightly pointed ears, yet Sophie's were as rounded as hers were. Anci's elven blood flowed more strongly through her veins.

They chatted while finishing up the last of the chores, Anci talking amiably about her day. She was young and spoke of innocent delights, her exuberance bringing smiles to the women's faces. Sophie mended some clothes after supper, keeping a watchful eye on Anci working on her studies. Ramira poured a cup of tea and sat on the terrace behind the kitchen, a wrought iron fence covered in climbing rose vines providing added privacy from the neighbors. Clay pots of varying sizes stood against the wall, the seedlings growing in them ready to be transferred into the ground. The bushes and trees encircling the yard would not get their full complement of leaves for another week or so allowing the sounds and smells from the avenue to waft.

As the evening progressed the noises became muffled then silent as night descended upon the city, its inhabitants settling in their homes. Ramira noticed dark shadows slowly undulating in the gentle breeze and remembered her things were still hanging to dry. She drained her mug then retrieved them, folding the items on the way back to the kitchen. She stifled a yawn, nodded sleepily at Sophie and Anci and went upstairs to bed.

"It's not like you to take in strangers, Mother," Anci stated in a matter-of-fact tone, wondering why Sophie had taken Ramira in.

"She was worn out and I couldn't see her spending all those nights in the woods."

"It's odd that she can't remember much about herself."

"Things happen, Anci. I don't believe she is a bad person or I would never have let her stay; besides, we could really use an extra pair of hands around here."

"True."

"Anyway, I am really looking forward to the spring festival…it's been such a long and dreary winter. It'll be nice to meet up with friends we haven't seen in a while."

Sophie leaned back in the rocking chair, her sewing forgotten, her hands idle and a slight smile touching her mouth. The frigid days and icy nights became distant memories, replaced by gentle breezes and sun-warmed skin. Flowers, not icicles adorned homes and birdsong, not silence greeted them at dawn and dusk.

"It'll be a great way for Ramira to learn more about the city and its people, too," said Anci.

"Perhaps." Her daughter pulled her from her reverie. "Will you be done with your studies before the festival?" Sophie eyed Anci then her books.

Sophie put away her mending, her thoughts on the woman sleeping above them. Maybe the festival would invoke a memory or two but even if it didn't, she was sure Ramira would thoroughly enjoy the celebration's merry atmosphere. She rose from her chair and pulled a few dead leaves off the plants over the fireplace, closing her eyes as she inhaled the fragrant aroma.

Ramira walked down the main avenue at sunrise the next morning, a knapsack full of things for Jack and Ida strapped across her shoulders, eager to explore more of this wonderful place. The only open shop belonged to the baker but lights shone through many of the curtained windows as the elves began to prepare for the day. She reached the gate, the guards acknowledging her as she passed by, and was about to step upon the still sleeping plain when a group of riders exited behind her. Shadows clung to the gray stonework of the tunnel-like gate yet she could still make out the profile of one of the riders. She had spent hours studying it in the semi-darkness, tracing the lines and curves with her fingers while he slept. The empty feeling she had experienced when he rode away with the scouts began to disappear, replaced with contentment and relief. She paused, the subconscious purpose of her trek to Bystyn fulfilled. She dropped her gaze as he started to turn toward her, almost as if he sensed someone was watching, but the horses exited the gate before he could fully turn his head. Ramira stared after him for a few moments, remembering the cave and the urgent trek across that cursed plain. She shivered involuntarily, her mind replaying the death duel with the wolves, grimacing with disgust as she relived the flies and dust. Watching Danyl's dark form pass by made all of those terrible things worthwhile.

She headed east, the low-lying silhouettes in front of her becoming more distinct as the sun hastened the murkiness from the land. The river began to sparkle with life as the first rays of the sun ignited the water until it appeared to be composed of molten silver. Birds and small, furry creatures, freed from the long winter, chirped and scurried beneath the growing light, their cacophonous enthusiasm greeting the promising day. Her eyes absorbed every nuance around her, her spirit reveling in the rebirth of the land, offering her a measure of calm and serenity. Her pack may have been heavy but it certainly could not weigh down her eagerness as she eagerly absorbed every detail of the land. The sun chased away the shadows and mist, exposing a vast orchard to her left and the tree-enclosed river to her right. The bright green grass felt soft beneath her boots, the spring flowers dotting the land adding color to the rich meadow all around her. She spotted the house once she broke through the orchard. The diminutive and gnarled couple greeted her warmly as she stepped up onto the porch, accepting Sophie's gifts as well as Ramira's eagerness to help.

Danyl glanced briefly over his shoulder at the silhouette walking away from the city, a peculiar sensation momentarily washing over him. He shrugged, the indistinct impression fading away the farther he and his companions headed west. He recalled the words spoken at last night's meeting, the strange set of circumstances taking place in the west prompting the elves to increase their vigilance. Cooper, King of the race of man, kept a tepid relationship with Bystyn, usually sending an emissary to at least feign a connection with the elves. His ambassador was four weeks overdue. Elven patrols scouting the land abutting Cooper's city, Kepracarn, had seen no activity, an oddity considering people should be preparing their fields and homes this time of year. Herkahs, the feared desert nomads who have been man's sworn enemy for hundreds of years, were rarely seen by anyone but had been detected along the line of mountains where Danyl nearly died. Their sudden appearance coupled with the absence of man initially drew a grave picture but the Herkahs avoided the Kepracarnians as much as possible, unless forced to retaliate. The probability of the nomads having eradicated man was nonexistent. He pursed his lips, wondering if a Herkah had saved his life that terrible night on the mountain. He wished he could remember more of what had transpired, often trying to will an image, any image, to form in his mind. The only things he could recall were the hungry creatures and the flight over the wretched plains. That and the fact his rescuer was a woman. He owed her a great debt and would forever rue the fact he could not repay her.

He kept his thoughts to himself as they continued to ride on, his preoccupation keeping him silent during most of the journey. They met up with another group of scouts around midmorning, listening to their brief report before sending them on to the city. Everything was now strangely quiet to the west, the elusive black-garbed desert dwellers vanishing without a trace.

"They come and go with purpose," stated Lance.

"Yes...but why? What do they want?" asked Danyl of no one in particular.

"They are not a group of people eager to share such information," replied Lance.

"Perhaps Prince Nyk has learned more."

Danyl nodded hoping his older brother, who had traveled to the northwestern corner of the plains, would bring back more information. He had departed from the city the previous week, following the vast forest that ran along the foothills of the towering mountain range to the north. Nyk and his men had to be cautious as they passed by the farthest section of the forests, for the Khadry, a distantly related group of elves, inhabited that part of the land. There had been little contact with them over the course of the millennium. When they did cross paths it usually ended in an uncomfortable standoff and sometimes even bloodshed. The focal point of their disagreement had become blurred over time but Danyl thought it had something to do with the first elven king's refusal to allow the Lords of the

Houses to build their own domains. The first king wanted to construct one city for them all but the Khadry, afraid of losing their influence, chose to set out on their own rather than accept a ruler not of their choosing. Danyl believed such a split and the ensuing ill will served no purpose whatsoever, especially since the first king had no intentions of stripping the Khadry of their prestige.

They rode on throughout the morning receiving the same reports from different patrols. One group had obtained information from one of Nyk's scouts: the prince and his men had safely progressed past the Khadry without any confrontations. Danyl stared westward after hearing the last bit of news, his mind trying to make sense of the reports. There was no imminent threat looming on the horizon, just a collection of irregularities requiring the elves' attention. It was probably nothing more than a new twist in the Herkah/man conflict, one that the elves would soon learn all about. They always did, especially if Cooper sought the elves' interference with the people he had insulted. He ordered his men to return to the city, knowing as much as he did when they left at dawn. It had been, in his opinion, a wasted trip. They arrived near sunset, grateful to be home as they neared the gate. Danyl glanced down at a passerby, the woman with the long braid illuminated by the torches lining the dark opening. Lance, too, noticed the woman, studying her intently as he rode by. She looked up at Danyl and nodded a greeting then glanced over at the captain. Lance's eyes narrowed, his mouth opening as if he were about to speak then he shut it again as she tilted her head ever so slightly. She silently pleaded with him. Lance's face promised nothing as he propelled Danyl on. She nodded ever so faintly at the captain before heading up the avenue to a hot bath and a warm meal.

Nearly a week had gone by and Ramira was still welcome in Sophie's house, the woman never tiring of giving Ramira things to do. When there was a lull in chores, Sophie sent her to the old couple's house. The three women finished up the last of their tasks then retired to the terrace; they breathed in the fresh evening air, sipping wine and chatting amiably with one another. The topic of conversation turned to the festival. Anci's eyes were sparkling, her hands gesturing in the semi-darkness while she described the spectacle to Ramira.

"Everything is brightly decorated and there are tables of food and drink in front of almost every home." She pushed back a lock of hair that had fallen across her forehead. "There's music and dancing, jugglers and acrobats and...well, you'll see!"

The young girl's enthusiasm was contagious, her breathless account making Ramira wish the celebration would start that very second. Sophie gave Anci a warm hug then winked over at Ramira. How different would her life now be had she found a room at an inn? *Everything happens for a reason*, a faint voice whispered into her ear. Gravel crunched along the side of the house, announcing an unexpected visitor. He walked out of the dark, the lamplight illuminating first his boots then the rest of his body until his face was bathed in its soft, gold glow. It was Danyl.

"Well, well, well," Sophie playfully chided him as he embraced her. "I thought you forgot about us!"

"Hardly." He accepted a hug from Anci then nodded to Ramira. "There's been quite a bit to keep me busy of late."

"Ramira, this is Danyl, the third son of the king." She introduced them, watching Ramira's reaction as she rose to bow to him. Danyl's hand quickly shot up to stop her.

"Please do not do that. Didn't I see you at the gate today?"

"Yes," she replied, the sudden urge to disappear increasing with each passing moment. A prince? She now realized the true meaning of Lance's words when he spoke them near the Broken Plains and understood the truth would eventually be revealed. In the meantime she would continue this innocent deception for as long as she could to avoid any unwanted attention. She had no desire to become the center of attention.

Danyl studied Ramira's face, noting the slight flushing in her cheeks and the subtle shifting in her eyes. She pushed a section of her long hair back over her shoulder then momentarily met his gaze. He thought he saw a glimmer of satisfaction in her eyes but the contact was too brief for him to be sure. Sophie was quick to help others in need but she was not known for taking in strangers. Ramira did not seem to worry either Sophie or Anci, the two women acting as if their guest had lived with them for a long time. He glanced over at Sophie who waved him to one of the seats before disappearing into the kitchen for more refreshments.

"Tell me, Ramira, from where do you hail?" His innocent question evoked a hint of sadness as she focused on her hands clasped in her lap. She remained silent for several moments then took a deep breath. He was about to retract his question when she quietly responded to his query.

"I'm not quite sure, Prince Danyl..."

"Just Danyl," he abruptly corrected her.

"I wish I could tell you but that information seems to have tucked itself away into the far corners of my mind."

"If her mind could extricate as much memory as the dirt I washed away from her clothing she'd be overwhelmed!" Sophie gently reminded her.

"A long and dirty journey?" he asked.

"Long and dirty…" she replied as if from far away. The storm on the mountain and the flight across the plains replayed itself in the air in front of her, the memories of their struggles as potent now as when they occurred. She closed her eyes to erase the scene but not before he saw the dread flickered within them.

"Sometimes life's most treacherous roads lead to the greatest of sanctuaries, Ramira," Sophie reminded her.

"Fortune has smiled down upon me by bringing me to your door, Sophie."

Ramira listened to them speak, the amiable conversation more akin to a family meeting rather than just of friends. A sense of warmth and contentment flowed from one to the other even with Danyl teasing Anci about her latest beau. Ramira smiled as Anci rolled her eyes in mock indignation, claiming he was nothing more than a friend. Ramira glanced over at the elf and remembered how he had appeared weeks ago; the bruises, scrapes and distortions were now gone, revealing his true features. They were strong and finely chiseled, tempered by pride but not arrogance. His eyes sparkled when he laughed and, she recalled, had glittered with cold determination when faced with death. He glanced over at her and she immediately looked away. It was time for her to escape while she could.

Pretending to be tired, Ramira excused herself and disappeared up to her room. Anci followed suit not too long after, leaving Danyl and Sophie alone on the terrace. She refilled their goblets and stared at the prince, waiting for the inevitable questions.

"Why did you to take Ramira in?" he asked, keeping his voice low.

"She was exhausted, filthy and very hungry. Besides," she took a sip before continuing, "there is something about her that intrigues me."

"I know what you mean," he replied, glancing up at the little balcony overlooking the garden.

"No, you don't." Sophie's tone of voice took on a sterner timbre, one forcing Danyl to pay attention.

"Tell me then."

"Her clothes had reddish dust on them and she carried an elven provisions pouch with her. She also confessed it took over two weeks to travel from the west."

"What are you implying, Sophie?" he asked, his eyes narrowing with every passing moment.

"Perhaps she saw you and your rescuer at some point." She watched his features abruptly change, metamorphosing from playful to hopeful in a matter of seconds. His green eyes widened then narrowed at the thought of someone being able to help him fill in the gaps that had plagued him for so long.

"Have you asked her about that?"

"No, for some reason I don't think that's a good idea. I would advise against you prodding her for answers ...not yet anyway. Give her a chance to find herself and I believe she will tell you what, if anything, she might know."

"Everything is still so blurry..." He exhaled a long breath, his eyes becoming unfocused as the faint memories taunted him again.

"What do you remember?"

"Hands reaching out and snatching me from certain death then tending to me even though I was a stranger. That woman had placed her own life in peril, disappearing instead of accompanying us back to Bystyn. What if Ramira was my rescuer, Sophie? How can I ever repay her?"

"Perhaps by honoring her desire to remain anonymous...if she was the one who saved you."

"I wish I could recall what she looked like."

"What do you recollect about her?"

"That she was fearless and caring."

"Everything will sort itself out in the end, Danyl. It always does."

He did not reply as he stared into the night, his mind showing him the fuzzy images and muted sounds from the cave, crossing the plains and collapsing in the leafy bower upon the hill. He faintly remembered her burrowing up against him, a reaction to the chill in the air, the unfamiliarity of their surroundings, or the wolves forcing her to seek contact. It could have been a combination of all of those things or of something else, but he had welcomed the connection, and it remained with him to this day.

Danyl nodded in agreement then bade her a good night. He walked down the avenue greeting the few passersby still about, his attention firmly focused on Ramira. How fortunate would he be if she were his rescuer? If her reluctance to admit to her deed was based on remaining anonymous, he would keep her achievement a secret. All he wanted was to know what happened and, more importantly, to thank her. He was so engrossed in his thoughts that he had passed by the small park and the homes of the nobles abutting the castle without ever seeing them.

"Good evening, Lord Danyl." The sentry acknowledged the prince as he walked up to the gate, the oil lamps dangling from their supports casting a wide pool of light. Danyl waved at him, following the wide walk to the steps leading into his home. An attendant opened the huge oak door for him, the massive iron hinges creaking ever so slightly as they strained to hold the portal.

He headed for the broad staircase in the center of the huge reception hall that led to the royal family's private chambers, vaguely aware of the late hour. He undressed and lay down in bed; his last thoughts before drifting off to sleep were of Ramira.

Ramira tossed and turned trying to shut out the voiceless whispers invading her sleep. They were as elusive as a wind blowing down from a snow encrusted mountain…and just as cold. Their dismal vibrations thrummed into her, chafing at her nerves until they could take no more. She rose and stepped out onto the balcony, breathing in the fresh air while lost in the inky nothingness of the moonless predawn hour. The darkness began to shift before her eyes and for a moment she thought sleep still clouded her vision as the images formed before her. They flashed briefly, vanishing before she had time to make sense of them. They were chaotic and the insidious whispers accompanying them made her hair stand on end. She shivered and went inside, closing the door as if trying to lock them out then sought the comfort of the kitchen. She sat in front of the fire, staring into the flames as they danced and snapped on the logs, eliciting another memory. This one seemed to assuage her apprehensions, for her mind and body began to relax. She must have been a child for she lay curled up in a lap, a pair of hands holding her as she was being rocked back and forth. A soft humming filled her ears, the gentle breath of the singer caressing her cheek. The love emanating from that embrace chased away the bad dreams, leaving her feeling less troubled but still confused. That image faded away, too, until the flames filled her sight once more and she became aware of Sophie carefully watching her from the doorway.

"You're up early," she stated as she poured a mug of tea, a tinge of concern flashing in her brown eyes.

"Couldn't sleep," replied Ramira, rocking in the chair by the hearth.

"That is quite apparent. Anything wrong?"

"No. What needs to be done today?" she asked, intent on changing the subject.

"Not much…actually nothing that can't wait for tomorrow. Today, therefore, is yours to do with as you please."

"Thank you." Ramira decided to explore the land near the river, eager to get as far away from her nightmares as possible. She packed a bit of food, put on her light cloak then headed out into the dawn.

She left the stirring city behind her and headed south, the walk to the Ahltyn River a pleasant one even if the morning mists concealed the waters flowing between the trees. The rising sun burned them away revealing the emerald cocoon enfolding the river and spurring the birds into song. Her short boots were damp with dew as she trod over fallen logs and spongy soil into the stand of trees. It was peaceful here; the sights and sounds of the city were kept at bay by something even older than the elves. She made her way to the edge of the river, dropping her light pack and inhaling the fresh air with closed eyes.

Ramira sat down beside the river and leaned against a willow tree, its long fronds forming a curtain of pale green around her. She purged her mind of the nightmares, letting the soothing sounds of the water and calming lushness of the trees and grasses permeate her being. She felt the disquiet seep away, absorbed by the frilly mosses beneath her. She could understand why the elves chose this place: the fertile land provided them with bountiful food; the river offered them fresh water. There was beauty in the landscape and the elves honored that splendor without competing with it. Bystyn was immense but it stood humbly upon the land in deference to the majestic peaks in the north and the proud stands of trees to the south.

She reached for her water bottle, drinking deeply as she gazed around the emerald enclosure. Deep purple and bright yellow irises crowded beneath flowering bushes along the riverbank, their reflections clear upon the water. A red and black ringed snake sunned itself on a rock, ignoring the iridescent insects flitting around it. A small waterfall spilled into a pool surrounded by sturdy, velvety headed reeds and tall grasses with plumed heads. The sun poked through the growing leaves, dropping little puddles of light onto the ground that shifted as a slight breeze moved the boughs overhead. She sighed and lay back upon the soft grass, seduced by the natural rhythms surrounding her. Her setting reminded her of Danyl. The newly borne leaves reflected the green of his eyes and the warm, earthy tones mirrored his unassuming nature. He shunned the titles of his highborn status yet took on the responsibilities demanded of him with true devotion. What of her station in life? Who was she? Ramira closed her eyes and slowly drifted off to sleep, the nagging questions drowned out by the silver river flowing beside her.

Nyk and his men gave the Khadrys' realm a wide berth but he knew they watched nonetheless. The forest elves had been nervous of late and Nyk refused to provoke any kind of confrontation by riding too closely to their land. The woods began to thin out, the terrain changing to broken ground dotted with boulders, thorny shrubs and gangly trees. He scanned the area to their west and north and saw the faint division between healthy land and the unmistakable reddish brown of the Broken Plains.

"We're too far north," his captain reminded him. Nyk nodded but his gaze never wavered from the far-off plains. The mountains separating the desert from their present position were a combination of flattened plateaus and sharp, spiky peaks. The horizontal then vertical sequence began somewhere up in the far north and continued down, out of their sight, to the sea in the south. There were gaps in the foothills close to Kepracarn where the Herkahs could slip unseen to their enemies, including passes west of the Khadry country. Nyk wiped away the perspiration on his face, a look of disgust for the reddish dirt managing to cling to his skin even from this distance. Khadry, Herkahs and no communication with Cooper: were they all somehow connected or pure coincidence? Nyk hated this part of the land. It offered no cover and what did exist here reminded him of death. The soil was the color of dried blood and the trees and brush were almost skeletal, appearing tortured by the elements. The hues that did exist seemed pale and sickly; the land never bloomed, not even in the spring.

"Nyk." His captain brought him back to the problems at hand, motioning toward the north.

Six riders sat atop coal black steeds outlined by crystal blue skies. It was difficult to distinguish horse from rider and even harder to accept that they actually existed at all. Heat rippling up from the rocks made the lower halves of the horses waver; a breeze pulled at their manes and the riders' clothing.

"I never thought I'd live to see the day…" muttered Nyk in fearful fascination as he beheld the most dreaded of all the races. The elusive and deadly nomads had had no contact with the elves for so long no one left alive could remember such an encounter. Their skill with weapons and their penchant for living in the harsh desert had evoked a host of myths and legends. These continued to grow, even to this day, especially in light of their fierce skirmishes with men. Nyk knew Cooper and his ilk usually instigated the conflicts but what eluded him was the answer to why the King would pursue the nomads.

"They appear to be mildly interested in us…what are the chances of having a little chat with them?" asked the captain.

Nyk stared at the Herkahs, their mystique holding him captive. Rumor had it that they were brutal killers who drank the blood of their enemies, the latter Nyk found rather farfetched but something many believed. The prince slowly exhaled, gripping his reins more tightly as his father's orders to find and communicate with the nomads echoed in his mind. Nyk was on the cusp of fulfilling that obligation, but would the Herkahs receive the elves?

"There's only one way to find out."

He was about to kick the sides of his horse when the Herkahs, as one, turned their attention from the elves to something to the patrols' left. Nyk and the others followed their line of focus. They detected nothing at first then were taken aback as the earth began to shake and tremble. A deep fissure split the land apart, widening with every second. A noxious, sooty mist issued forth from the crack, spreading outward over the jagged lip and onto the plains. The nervous horses tugged on their reins as the nightmare took on another threat: the Herkahs suddenly sprang into action, riding toward them upon steeds whose hooves barely seemed to touch the ground. Confusion momentarily set in as Nyk's mind went blank. What to do? Were the nomads attacking them, too? His blood ran cold as an unearthly sound rose from within the fissure, one forged of hissing, snarling and wailing. He slowly turned his head, peeking apprehensively over his shoulder at the things surging out of the enlarging fracture in the ground.

Man-like in shape but spindly and twisted in form, their claw-like limbs bristled with razor sharp talons, their faces featureless except for fangs gnashing at the air. Ghastly shrieks and screams preceded them as they raced in their direction. Flight was no longer an option so the elves drew out their swords to fight the abominations bearing down on them. The Herkahs closed the distance with incredible speed, but whether they were in league with these monsters or coming to the elves aid was something Nyk and his men had no time to determine. The demon-like things launched themselves upon the elves with a hateful glee, slashing and tearing at the elves and their horses with a vengeance. Wherever their swords cut into the things a noxious black liquid oozed out, burning wherever it splattered. The horses panicked, trying to buck off both rider and attacker as the things dug into their flesh with their claws. Nyk was thrown to the ground, the impact knocking the wind out of him. He tried to get up but the unmistakable pain in his side and difficulty in breathing stole his strength. He stared at the carnage occurring all around and realized that of twelve men only three were still atop their horses. His eyes glazed over with agony as he struggled to stand and come to the aid of the nearest elf fighting against two demons. One of the misshapen things lunged at him and hooked the prince along his side and back. The immediate, searing pain from the wounds was so intense he momentarily forgot about his bruised ribs. Nyk's teeth clamped together as he brought his sword down upon the monster, the disgust for the still-twitching thing etched on his face. He could hear his men screaming for help, the sounds of their flesh being torn from their bodies making him cringe with revulsion. The effort of facing the loathsome creature took its toll on him as he swayed unsteadily on his feet. The wounds burned as if someone was jamming torches into his body and, as the world spun crazily around him, he fell to the ground in a heap. Flashes of black hurtled past him, the hooves so close he thought one would surely cut him into pieces as the nomads systematically destroyed the demons. Their faces were apathetic yet the savage glitter in their eyes made even the seasoned elf cringe.

He gritted his teeth to endure the stabbing pain in his side then attempted to roll away to avoid being set upon by a pair of demons. A powerful set of legs draped in black blocked his escape. A Herkah towered over his prone form and he silently accepted his fate as everything around him began to blur. The Herkah pulled out a pair of wicked-looking knives, quickly dispatching the monsters blinded by bloodlust to destroy him. The other Herkahs were inflicting the same damage, for the howls of the demons changed from hatred to pain and anger. They fled back to their foul fissure, those slain by the nomads reduced to viscous black pools bubbling on the plains.

Nyk watched as the apparent leader of the Herkahs nodded toward the two surviving elves, and to his utter horror witnessed their execution. He stared in complete shock as the nomads stabbed all of the dead men; the elves' dead faces twisted with agony and terror. His strength and stamina gone, he could only glare at the leader hovering over him with his knife poised over his throat. He stared unafraid into the black, merciless orbs peering intently at him from within the face covering. Nyk opened his mouth to speak but nothing came out except a wheezing sound. The prince began to lose consciousness and knew his mortality was about to seep out of his throat and stain the soil. Time ticked by and still the Herkah had not yet dispatched him...what was he waiting for? He was completely at the Herkah's mercy yet the blade did not slice into his throat. The eternal wait began to abrade his nerves as much as the searing aching of his body, yet death continued to hang motionless over him. A few moments later white-hot flashes of pain rushed through his mind and body as darkness descended down into the center of his being.

-3-

Danyl studied the map spread out over Karolauren's massive desk, his finger tracing the route he had taken to the Broken Plains then back to Bystyn again. He estimated where the cave was located by where he and his rescuer had ended up, following the edges of the plains to the fringes of the Khadry's domain. Elven patrols had detected Herkahs west and north of the forest elves' lands and to the south of Kepracarn. Cooper, ever the opportunist, might have rankled the desert dwellers by finding something of value on or near their lands. Such an intrusion might be the reason why they were so uncharacteristically visible of late, but it did not explain why they were seen so far north of Kepracarn. He absently drummed his fingers on the map; his eyes focused on the printed parchment. He looked up as the door opened and greeted the historian, an ancient collection of brittle bones and unruly white hair seemingly lost within his black robes.

"What are you doing?" he asked in a voice as clear as his bright blue eyes.

"I might have known when I started but not anymore...Karol...what do you know about the Herkahs?"

"Not very much. Why?" He picked a book off a pile teetering on the edge of collapse.

"I'm not sure...it just seems rather odd that they would venture so far from the desert."

"They've been coming and going for generations; people are now paying attention to them," was Karolauren's crisp reply.

"Or perhaps they want or need to be seen. Do you think they have anything to do with Cooper's silence?"

Karolauren shrugged his bony shoulders, cocking his head at the prince who immediately vacated the historian's chair. He leafed through his book then peered over it at the prince who sat patiently waiting for Karolauren to answer his question.

"Herkahs live near the eastern edge of the Great White Desert," he began. "They have been there for a very long time, despise man; they are expert horsemen, unparalleled marksmen and have not had any contact with elves for hundreds of years. They leave virtually no evidence of their passing but if you happen to meet up with one, chances are you'll never even know, unless, of course, you are the subject of their interest. That would negate meeting one because you'd probably be dead."

"I already knew those things, Karol."

"Then you are also aware they have no written language, passing their knowledge on orally from one generation to the next?" Danyl nodded. "Did you also know they banish their annoying children when they ask too many questions?"

"Your subtlety never ceases to amaze me, Karol. I will leave you alone." Danyl left with an armful of information, the wry smile on his face eliciting a chuckle out of the historian who resumed his reading.

Danyl returned to his room where he intended to study the books he had borrowed, but he soon became distracted by his thoughts of Ramira. The mystery surrounding her only intensified, for if she had been his rescuer, what had she been doing in such a dangerous place? Obviously, he was thankful she was there; he certainly would not have survived had he been alone. She had faced the dangers they had encountered with great courage and kept him alive during their short journey together, if she was the one who saved him.

He tried to concentrate on the papers scattered on his desk but the faint recollections persisted. He wanted to believe Ramira was his link to those terrible days, and the only thing keeping him from confronting her was the promise he made to Sophie. He would leave his queries for another day and allow Ramira the chance to become accustomed to her new life in Bystyn. The prince sighed heavily and began to sort through the pages before him, even though his interest in her never completely disappeared from his mind. He forced himself to pay attention to the task at hand, hoping it would distract him from his personal plight.

The Herkahs had always mesmerized him. He had often wondered what an encounter with one of the elusive desert dwellers would be like. Their harsh environment demanded they be resilient or perish: it was as simple as that. Karolauren was correct in saying the elves, even with their keen hearing and sight, would never notice a Herkah standing a few yards away. Hiding in the forest was easy, concealing yourself in a sea of shifting sand was much more of a challenge. Their horsemanship was legendary, as were their abilities with a variety of weapons although they had no interest in bows and arrows. They were, in essence, warriors rarely seen at close quarters.

"'Like ghosts at midnight beneath moonless night skies, with blades forged of silver and death in their eyes,'" he whispered as he stared at what was believed to be the heart of their realm. The words he spoke came from an ancient account with the mysterious nomads hundred years earlier. A patrol had ventured too far onto the Broken Plains in the northern section and chanced upon a group of Herkahs. Although there was no confrontation, the elves were close enough to see the nomads' faces. One of the scouts had been struck by the fearsome power the nomads exuded, shivering with awe and respect despite the blazing sun overhead. The Herkahs had scrutinized the elves then simply turned and ridden away. The prince gazed out the balcony window into the darkness, his imagination conjuring up the nomads' departure. Long-legged stallions, muscles rippling beneath their black hide carrying their masters back to the desert...the Herkahs leaning across their great necks until they nearly become one creature. The sun glints off the daggers shoved in their belts, but even these imposing weapons pale besides the dangerous glittering in their eyes. Elusive. Deadly. Legendary.

He shook his head then rubbed his eyes, wondering when he would lose this childish intrigue. He thought about his brother and how he envied him. He would have done just about anything to trade places with Nyk.

Nyk slowly emerged from oblivion. The first thing he discerned was the throbbing in his head. It took on a louder and more persistent tempo the closer to consciousness he came. He opened up his senses and probed the darkness around him. The sounds of muffled voices and neighing filtered into his ears; a dry heat touched his overheated skin. He gingerly rolled onto his side, breathing sharply through clenched teeth, his wounds burning as if he had rolled onto an open fire. He gasped and gagged, waiting for the wave of nausea to pass, the noises he made extending beyond his confines. He heard silvery jingling sounds then sensed someone crouching down beside him, but when he tried to open his eyes the queasiness returned.

"Lie still," a gentle voice quietly commanded him. "You will undo the sutures if you move around." She helped him sit up, letting him drink some water before easing him back down.

"I'm still alive," he managed to say, surprised that the Herkah blade did not slice into his throat. His men! They had butchered his men! The woman managed to calm him down enough to explain what had happened.

"Just barely," the woman affirmed, pulling back the blanket to check on the ugly gashes crisscrossing his side and back. "You and your men were attacked by Kreetch, demons in your language, and were poisoned when they clawed you. You would have become like them had we not interfered."

"They...you killed my men but not me...why?" he demanded.

"Your men had no protection against their abominable blackness: we saved their souls from a fate worse than death by slaying them."

"Why let me live?"

"Rest now." The spice-infused compress she placed across his forehead helped ease his unsettled stomach, its cool touch relieving the throbbing in his head. Helpless to do anything else, he drifted off to sleep.

He awoke hours later, chilly air seeping into his shelter. His body was incredibly sore, the fiery sensation still clinging to his flesh, but the nausea had gone away leaving him feeling very hungry. He opened his eyes, allowing them a few moments to get accustomed to the near darkness before looking around the room. No, not a room...a tent. A pole supported a dark canopy overhead, the night winds stirring the material, making them ripple ever so slightly. He turned his head to the side and saw large pillows, a few small wooden boxes and other items within the deeper shadows he could not quite identify. The memory of the battle and the ensuing slaughter of his men flooded back, and the thought of those same killers now tending to him filled him with a simmering anger. Then he remembered her words. Nyk would never have believed such abominations existed in the land had he not seen them with his own eyes. Their mindless ferocity had no equal, yet the Herkahs fought them with an unalarmed attitude. The Kreetch feared and loathed the nomads, scattering before their blades, their howls of hatred the only defiance they could muster. The elves were not the recipients of such unwilling respect and were therefore slaughtered. Nyk shivered at the thought of those demons running rampant throughout the land, leaving him feeling cold inside. He had to return to Bystyn as soon as possible. He groped for his clothes in the dimness, trying to ignore his aching body as his fingers found everything but his garments.

"You are in no condition to travel, elven prince," the woman firmly reminded him.

"I must tell my people about those things."

"In due time," she replied. "The Kreetch are limited to the plain for now."

"You seem to know quite a bit about them," he said, barely hiding the suspicion in his voice.

"We know enough."

"And you know who I am."

"Yes, we do. I am Zada of the Herkahs."

Nyk stared at her indistinct shape for a long time, the discomfort of his wounds, swirling emotions and horrible memories gradually abating as the realization of where he was set in. He abandoned the search for his clothes, his gaze never leaving the woman lost in the shadows of the tent. I am Zada of the Herkahs, her voice echoed in his mind. She leaned forward, the lamplight illuminating her elegantly refined bone structure framed by thick, brown hair. Her slender arms were graced with dozens of finely crafted silver bracelets, the dainty tinkling sounds repeating as she shifted her legs.

Wisdom emanated from her dark eyes and patience marked her calm demeanor. The prince lowered his gaze then his head in deference to the stately woman sitting across from him.

"Tell me about those evil things," he asked after a long silence.

"Kreetch are the lowest form of demons," she explained in quiet tones. "They possess no intelligence, existing only to destroy anything composed of flesh and blood. The poison running through their bodies is steeped in an ancient evil, one that corrupts the spirit then transforms it into one of the demons. There is no antidote."

"Why did you not kill me as well?" he asked, his fingers gingerly touching his wounds.

"That would incite a war with your people, wouldn't it?"

"Who would know?"

"We would. Now please rest and we'll speak later." She rose to her feet in one fluid motion, the soft light visible through the tent flap making him squint. How long had he been here? Exactly where was he: on the desert or somewhere along the Broken Plain?

Nyk could not sleep. Demons? It had been a long time since anything forged of darkness walked the land. He would not have believed Zada had he not seen them for himself. Nyk was a soldier, fighting things of flesh and blood that succumbed to blade or arrow, but only the Herkah knives killed the Kreetch. Was there something special about the blades? Did the nomads know exactly where to strike the demons in order to slay them? Did he believe Zada when she told him the Herkahs saved his companions' souls by shedding their blood? The vivid memory of the Kreetch's ferocity and mindless need to rip and slaughter gave credence to her statement but did nothing to assuage the guilt he felt. He dropped his head into his hands lamenting the high cost of accomplishing his mission. He struggled to his feet, careful not to break the stitches, and took a few steps forward. The effort made him perspire, the sweat trickling over his wounds making them itch and burn. He gritted his teeth, his sharp breathing aggravating his bruised ribs, the biting pain bringing tears to his eyes. Nyk swayed unsteadily, grabbing the pole for support as he painstakingly inched back to the blankets. He eased himself down, feeling the sutures stretch to their limit, and hoped he hadn't ripped any of them open.

He lay still, concentrating on the sounds outside the tent: a horse nickered; a spoon clanked against the side of a pot and a bird screeched far off in the distance. The noises drifted into the tent along with a dry heat and the aroma of marinated meat. A simple life for a complicated people…or were they? The Herkahs had incited fear in the Kreetch and with good reason. The desert dwellers had systematically slain his men yet tended to him as if he belonged to the tribe. Zada was right about one thing: if they had murdered him the elves would seek retribution. *That can't be the only reason I was spared…I was poisoned just like my men and am now a liability*. Nyk began to tire, his eyelids drooping no matter how hard he tried to remain awake. His mind wanted to continue analyzing these strange circumstances but his body demanded rest. He finally acquiesced and drifted off to sleep.

Bright sunlight filtered through the open tent flap, blinding the elf even though his eyes were still shut. He had been in the semi-darkness for nearly a week. He propped himself up on his elbow and watched Zada carry a tray of food to him. The murkiness within the tent gave her an almost ethereal appearance. He studied her velvety features in the lamplight as she gracefully hunkered down beside him and removed the towel over his food. She heaped vegetables and marinated meat onto the flat bread, expertly rolling it up and handing it to him. He finished it before she had time to make another one.

"Eat, elf prince. You will need every ounce of energy."

"For what?"

"To return to your people," she said, offering him a third helping.

"I was sent to meet with you, Zada," he stated, taking the food. "I am asking for you to come back to Bystyn with me."

"That can be arranged."

"The sooner the better."

"Then it is up to you to regain your strength and hasten the process."

Zada rose to her feet in one smooth motion and left Nyk alone. He was actually going to bring one of the nomads back to Bystyn with him. Was it supposed to have been this easy? He looked at the wrap in his hands, first nibbling then attacking it. He would most certainly "hasten the process."

The days began to lengthen as late spring claimed the land. Leaves covered branches and flowers sprouted everywhere as the earth reveled beneath the warm sunshine. The smell of freshly turned sod lifted into the air as farmers prepared the fertile land for sowing; heavily muscled plow horses strained to pull the blades through the ground. Everything was as it should be, yet the elven king sensed the barely perceptible ripples of conflict at the edge of his kingdom.

Alyxandyr rubbed his temple, tossing the latest report onto his carved wooden desk. The tall, lanky man standing beside him focused his gray eyes on the map hanging behind the King, his steely features holding his emotions in check. Mason, the King's first advisor, glanced briefly at the report then returned his attention to the chart.

"How can Nyk and his men have simply vanished?" asked the King. "Not one body, no signs of a struggle…nothing."

"Taken by Herkahs?" inquired Mason, his deep voice like rumbling thunder.

"Or Khadry. We know what the Khadry might do to them, but the Herkahs? That is another issue."

Alyxandyr stared at his lifelong friend. They had met at Terracine, the great learning hall in the far northwest corner of the land, as children, educated by the Masters of Knowledge. Mason's brother, Cooper, already had his sights set on ruling Kepracarn and was elated when Mason voluntarily left, leaving him free reign over the city. Alyxandyr and Mason went to Terracine as boys, emerging as learned and highly skilled young men. Their friendship was firmly cemented in the ideals, beliefs and goals they shared, the very things Mason and Cooper disagreed on. Alyxandyr asked Mason to come to Bystyn with him, and with Sophie in tow started his new life in the elven city. When Alyxandyr was crowned king, many were suspicious of Mason's influence over him, never forgetting his roots in Kepracarn. This intensified when Alyxandyr announced Mason would be his confidant. It had taken years for Mason and Sophie to gain the confidence of the elves: Mason with his unwavering loyalty to the King and Sophie with her steady yet unobtrusive commitment to the city. There were a few who still grumbled about Mason's background, their discontent mired in their inability to prove themselves worthy of obtaining such a high status. In any case, he felt satisfied and very fortunate they were both in his city.

"So much unconnected activity all within the span of about a month…" the King thought out loud.

"And still no word from Kepracarn," Mason quietly reminded him. "The scouts report no movement of any kind: not on the grounds nor the surrounding villages. If they plan to eat this winter they should at the very least be tending to their fields."

"You think something happened over the course of the winter, don't you?"

"Yes, but not pertaining to the possibility of Cooper's capitulation. Besides, who else could stir the Herkahs into action quicker than Cooper?"

"Why would he consistently poke a stick into that hornet's nest?" asked Alyxandyr, completely at a loss for an answer as to why anyone would want to harass the nomads.

"They have something he wants," stated Mason, a distracted expression in his gray eyes. "Rumor has it that an ancient city abounding with treasure lies on or near the Herkah lands. As a child I heard some of the tales and dismissed them as just that—tales. Cooper became obsessed with finding the fortune. Apparently it is real enough for him to accost the desert dwellers."

"Do you think the nomads are protecting this supposed city?" asked Alyxandyr, intrigued by the story.

"I believe they are simply safeguarding their home, Alyx."

"So many questions could be answered if we could speak to just one Herkah," said the King, leaning back in his chair.

"Perhaps. The difficulty lies in locating one."

"What of that supposed city, Mason?" Alyxandyr asked after a while.

"That city remains a mystery to this day. It was destroyed long ago, so it is difficult to ascertain what it may or may not hold. In any event, if my brother thinks there is something to dig up from within its ancient foundations, I must believe his objective is not without merit."

"You expect there is something beneath those sands?"

"Something, yes. The problem is the Herkahs do not want Cooper to retrieve it."

"Can you blame them?"

"I think they don't want anyone to take whatever lies beneath the desert, be it gold, jewels, or something else."

"Cooper's situation indicates a problem I don't think we want to get involved in, but I'm sure eventually we will." The King knew all too well what affected Cooper and his city eventually worked its way to Bystyn; man's scheming ways had a habit of rebounding on them. He vividly remembered early on in his reign when Cooper decided to harass a city far to the south of Kepracarn. Cooper's dogged pursuit for tribute ended when a group from that city sneaked onto Cooper's lands and burned all of his crops. The King came to Bystyn seeking food and fortunately for him, the elves had enough to share during that mild winter. There were other such incidents over the years but the thought of having to contend with the Herkahs was another matter: Alyxandyr had no intention of confronting the nomads.

"The messengers should be arriving soon, Alyx," said Mason. "I'll attend to them and send the reports up to you." The King did not acknowledge him. He stared past the walls toward the west, hands clasped behind his rigid back. *Where are you, Nyk?*

Sophie had been busy baking and cooking for the spring celebration. She took inventory of the platters full of food and jars of refreshments, worrying she had forgotten something.

People had streamed into the city to be with friends and family, to catch up on the news or just to escape the four walls that had imprisoned them for so many months. Traditions such as setting up food and drink in front of homes and exchanging little trinkets crafted during the dark and endless hours of winter kept the elves connected with each other. The land had not always been bountiful and the elves had depended on each other for survival, facing starvation on more than one occasion. The gifts harkened back to those times, promising no one would ever be deprived of sustenance again.

Ramira reached out and helped herself to a little cake before Sophie could turn around, but the guilty look on her face did not fool Sophie for a moment.

"You keep eating those things and the only man who'll have you is the baker. Don't bother speaking—you'll only choke."

"You don't miss much, do you?" Ramira was finally able to say, after swallowing the treat.

"Not when your cheeks are the envy of every chipmunk in the land!"

Danyl entered the kitchen just as Sophie disappeared into the pantry, his finger up against his lips before shoving two cakes into his mouth. Sophie reemerged from the pantry and looked down at the plate, bursting out in laughter as both raised a finger to implicate the other. She shook her head then reached into the larder for another plate of cakes.

"I always leave a few for the mice," she said, smiling at the two of them, "or I would have none for my guests." She headed out the front door, quietly chuckling to herself as she greeted a passerby.

Ramira busied herself with the food, the prince studying her as he leaned against the counter with crossed arms. Her long hair was bound in a single thick braid and fell to the small of her back. It swung gracefully back and forth as she moved about, the simple leather tie binding it somehow inappropriate. The plain tunic and trousers she wore over her supple frame accentuated her beauty even if they were a size too big for her. Her fluid movements brought her closer to the back door; her quick, lateral glances making him grin.

"Are you done staring?" she asked in a slightly annoyed tone of voice, inching ever closer to the door.

"Almost." He approached her, gently turning her around until she faced him. He watched her search his face, momentarily hesitating where his injuries had been, until her amethyst eyes shifted and looked into his emerald ones. The room began to dissolve around them, taking with it all the sounds and smells. She stared deeply into the green pools, for although she could not identify what lay within their verdant depths she sensed its presence. She pulled away from him and the unfamiliar sensation.

"You seem to be rather interested in how my face healed." His need to know what happened pushed aside the strange feeling that passed between them. For now, anyway.

"I heard you recently suffered some bad luck," she replied, trying to avoid the subject she knew he was alluding to. Perhaps she should have been more reserved with her contact with the elf. The budding familiarity between them was becoming more difficult to ignore.

"My brother recently disappeared in the area near where my misfortune occurred. I thought you might know something since you traveled here from that part of the land."

"I'm sorry but I don't," she said rather unconvincingly.

"Ramira, I..."

Danyl was about to pursue the matter when he heard Sophie and her guests entering the house. He decided to continue this topic another time when there would be no interruptions. Ramira straightened her tunic then repositioned the plates for the fourth time, her attention focused on anything but the elf. He noticed the slight flushing in her cheeks as he lifted her chin, the determined expression on his face making her flinch just a little. He offered her a slight nod then headed out the back door.

She slowly exhaled but the tightness in her chest would not go away. His convictions had given him the strength to survive and were now on display once more: he suspected her and for good reason. Sophie surely must have noticed the dirt and pouch, and she had told her from which direction she had traveled. The woman's loyalty to him had undoubtedly prompted her to reveal this information, hoping to ease his confusion. She brought her fingers up, massaging the tense muscles in her arms until the memory of that odd feeling resurfaced. Her hands immediately dropped to her sides.

She tried to shake those thoughts from her head but her guilt would not relinquish them. She needed a distraction, finding it on the front step where Anci chatted with a few neighbors. They politely motioned over to her then resumed their conversation, occasionally glancing her way. Ramira intrigued them for they often asked Anci and Sophie about her. They graciously declined to discuss their guest with anyone, which only increased the neighbors' nosiness. Ramira caught Anci looking over at a young elf sitting a few houses down and the shy gaze he shot back at her. Their admiration, it seemed, was mutual and it wouldn't be long before he came to the house to court the young girl. A subtle smile crossed her face as she imagined Sophie scrutinizing Anci's nervous suitor.

She left the house to find a place where she could be alone with her thoughts for a while. She went down the avenue toward the gate, one of only a few that were leaving instead of coming into the city, and headed for the river. She was halfway there when the sound of hooves caught her attention. She turned to watch a group of riders advancing toward the city and wondered if they bore any news concerning the prince. She hoped they did for the family's sake.

She continued on and soon found herself beneath the bright green canopy of trees hugging the river. She picked her way over the exposed roots and small gaps in the ground until she reached an isolated area next to the river. She removed her short boots, rolled up her trouser legs and let her feet feel the softness of the grass growing along the banks. She sat back, staring up into the branches, watching the birds and squirrels flit and scurry, her mind wrestling with the information that Danyl wanted to know. She could help Danyl but not his brother, a sad reality that made her frown. She had grown fond of her new life, the quiet yet busy days and nights giving her a purpose. Wouldn't her preferred anonymity change once it was known she saved the prince's life? Would he agree to keep that information quiet? She thought of her own murky past, the longing to know tempered by the dread of finding out. Who exactly was she, and why did her memory refuse to open up? She closed her eyes, willing everything from her mind, hoping it would fill with something, anything, from her past. She could not go any further back than the cave. She began to slouch, pressing her lips together as her head bowed down. She rolled over and leaned toward the water, her fingers absently drawing circles in the silvery blue liquid that undulated by when an image slowly formed in its shallow depths.

Stars glittered overhead in an indigo sky; a chill breeze blew across her body. She shivered as she stared at a dark line of low-lying hills that shifted and changed with every breath of wind. Silent whispers pulsed from those mounds as they sought to seduce her with soundless promises floating in her direction. She thought she saw the knolls waver then reform into faint human forms. She watched in fascination, as they appeared to drift slowly toward her. They were familiar yet completely unknown at the same time, a feeling that did not change the closer they came. She was unafraid of them, their assuring undertones beguiling her until she fell under their enchanting spell. She exhaled like an expectant lover, opening her mind to receive it but another presence insistently begged for her attention. Ramira tried to look beyond this intruder whose closeness began to fragment and shred the scene…

She bolted upright blinking several times, the bright light briefly blinding her. She had somehow become accustomed to the vision's darkness and, as she looked at the gooseflesh on her skin, the cold as well. She scanned the area for whoever had broken the connection but found herself alone. She splashed some water on her face, slipped her boots back on and headed back to the city, still reeling from the experience. She emerged from the trees, surprised at the long shadows stretching to the east. The vision faded away with each step toward the city, her composure nearly recovered as she walked beneath the gate. She could not, however, shake the inexplicable feeling it left with her. She heard people speaking and laughing but their voices were nothing more than distant echoes She stumbled on the uneven cobblestones and would have fallen had an elf not grabbed her arm. She smiled weakly in appreciation, ignoring his raised brow as she gathered her senses together. Ramira finally reached the comfort of the kitchen, the peculiar vision now a distant memory.

She fixed a plate of food and ate it on the terrace, the sounds from the street more muffled now that the leaves had sprouted. Ramira stared out into the garden, its rebirth a joy to behold. The bright spring blooms along the fence gave way to the herbs and other perennials, the little vegetable patch along the shed already germinating. She finished her meal and went inside, poured a glass of wine then took it back out onto the patio to watch the sun set.

"Ramira," Sophie walked out onto the patio smoothing down her fine dress, "Anci and I will be dining at the castle this evening."

"You look lovely, Sophie. Enjoy your dinner."

"Thank you. I'll bring a few sweets home for you."

Ramira smiled and leaned back into the chair, the women's voices ending as the front door shut. She looked up at the trellis laden with climbing roses and imagined their sweet fragrance washing over her during the hot summer months. That is, if she were still here then.

Things change quickly, she thought as she clung to the present with a renewed appreciation for the good fortune she now enjoyed. The day would come when she would remember her past, yet she doubted it could be more pleasant than her present life, a life she would not easily relinquish.

Sophie joined Danyl on the balcony after the meal, the two of them staring silently over the castle gardens. The long-dead Queen had created a refuge where one could read, think, converse and court. Fountains and benches were neatly tucked beneath roses, wisteria, and other climbing plants; there were rows of finely manicured hedges and flagstone paths weaving throughout the garden. The Queen had especially loved the white roses growing in the far corner. She had often sat there during the early evening hours when the breeze lifted their delightful aroma up toward the star-encrusted heavens.

Danyl's mother had died a year after his sister Alyssa had been born, the sickness spreading throughout the city, claiming many lives. It had been a terribly cold and damp winter with few escaping the chill that invaded virtually everyone. Many to this day still thought about that awful time, for everyone had lost friends and family. Danyl's father had been devastated by her death and even now longed for her sage advice just as he rued the loss of all those who had succumbed to the epidemic. Danyl and his siblings were very young then, but they remembered her nonetheless. Sophie was determined they should never forget and helped rear the royal children, forming the strongest bond with Danyl.

"There is beauty here even in the dead of winter," Sophie said in soft tones.

"She is always here," he replied tenderly.

"You have something else on your mind though, don't you? Ramira, perhaps?"

"Yes."

"Did you speak to her about the plains?"

"I started to but between her being evasive and your untimely return, I didn't get very far. She did, however, give me the impression she was hiding something."

"Perhaps tonight might be a good time to continue that conversation," she suggested then sipped from her glass. She disliked the idea of prodding the girl into disclosing something she obviously did not want to divulge, but he did have the right to know. Besides, Danyl would honor the privacy she seemed to seek. He offered her a slight smile then slipped away into the darkness. The Queen had imparted a lot to her children and Sophie fervently hoped she had been successful in perpetuating those attributes. She had help, of course: Karolauren, Mason and Alyxandyr had taught them with both their strengths and weaknesses. All of them firmly believed you must teach with failure as well as victory. The latter could not be appreciated without first being exposed to the former. Danyl was about to learn a valuable lesson. Ramira would require not tact but honesty in his search for the truth. If he failed then Ramira, Sophie was sure, would be on her way, but if he succeeded, then a close friendship would surely be born. Sophie sighed and rejoined her dinner companions, Danyl and his endeavor never far from her mind.

Ramira began to nod off beneath the trellis and decided to head upstairs. She rose and stretched, jumping as Danyl materialized out of the darkness. The light from the kitchen illuminated his set jaw and the resolute look in his eyes. He was going to pursue their earlier discussion and there was nothing she could do to stop it.

"I hope I didn't startle you," he apologized.

"I was just heading to bed," she muttered, her mind racing to find a plausible excuse.

"Perhaps you'd like to join me for a glass of wine before you do?" He promptly retrieved a glass and bottle before she could so much as protest.

"You should be with your guests, not wasting your time here," she stated lamely, the words as ineffectual in her ears as she was sure they were to his. He couldn't help but grin. She knew she was trapped and her desperate attempt to evade the inevitable was funny indeed. He wondered what tactics she would use to wiggle her way out of this predicament.

"Most of them have already retired," he replied, the sudden light in her eyes steeped in the hope that Sophie and Anci would soon be home. He decided to let her believe the women would return soon even though they would not be back for at least another hour.

"You've had a long day so shouldn't you…"

"I am not tired, Ramira, but I am in need of some information which, I believe, you may possess."

There was no point in trying to sidestep it any longer. She motioned him into the kitchen then described what had happened from the moment she pulled him from his imminent death to how she came to be in Bystyn. A dark, unapproving look crossed his features when she recounted her conversation with Lance but he remained silent until she was through. He studied her face while she spoke and although his scrutiny made her uncomfortable, she did not waver from her story.

"I owe you a great debt," he began after quite time then raised his hand to silence her protests. "It's obvious you do not want anything, including recognition, for saving my life. I will respect that for as long as I can but one day it may be necessary to reveal what you have done, do you understand?"

"Yes." She sighed slightly, relieved he now knew the truth.

"Now," he said gently, the urge to reproach her for keeping the information having passed, "what were you doing in the cave?"

"I don't know. I woke up when the storm hit and that was the first recollection I had."

"Are you a Herkah?" The quizzical expression on her face answered that question. "Not elf, not man…then what?"

"Just lost, I guess." Her words were tinged with sadness and a small amount of fear like those of a child who cannot find its mother.

"We all become 'lost' at some point in our lives, but there are always those who help us find our way…like you aiding me in my hour of need. If you had not been 'lost,' then I would now be dead."

Danyl read her face and saw no deception within it. He wanted to continue questioning her but not at the expense of stirring up her private torment. He cringed at the thought of facing Sophie if he managed to irk Ramira enough that she would simply disappear into the night. Sophie had taken to this woman from the onset and he found he, too, was somehow mesmerized by her uniqueness. The elf was not one to surrender to beauty; he needed more than an attractive façade to make him take notice of a woman. He disliked the phony attempts at seduction that were so prevalent in the court, finding Ramira's restrained demeanor refreshing. He reached over and cupped her chin in his hand, raising it until her amethyst eyes met his. Her skin was warm and soft to the touch, a faint blush rose into her cheeks.

"You did peek!" He smiled as she averted her eyes, her cheeks darkening with the memory.

"I tried not to," she quietly confessed, rising from the table, attempting to busy herself to escape his good-natured comment. She heard him approach and a moment later felt his arms encircling her from behind, the contact easing her embarrassment until she sighed inwardly with contentment. That peculiar sensation began to arise again, originating from a place deep within them. It was faint, rising upward with an ethereal quality not unlike smoke curling up from a fire. The impression was both deeply sensuous and frightening at the same time.

"You should be upset with me for keeping what I knew hidden," she said, placing her hands over his, reluctantly extricating herself from his embrace. He initially resisted until her growing uneasiness warned him to let her go.

"That would not be beneficial to either one of us." The brief, inexplicable flare in the core of his being left him feeling confused and exhilarated. He noted the same emotions on Ramira's face as she, too fought to make sense of them.

"I'm sorry, Danyl. Why is it so important that I tell you about that night?"

"My brother and his patrol were sent back to the plains to try and contact the Herkahs. We haven't heard from them in quite some time and are getting worried. I was wondering if you might be able to tell me something, anything that might help."

"I wish I could, Danyl, but I know nothing more than what I have already told you."

"Ramira, did you see anyone else during the time we were together?"

Ramira thought back, remembering she had spent most of her time caring for him and not looking around for anyone else. If there had been others, they certainly had taken little interest in the ragtag pair scrambling to safety. If anyone had been searching for her, they must have passed each other by without noticing. She shook her head.

"Why did you risk your life for me?" he asked.

"Your cry for help told me that you refused to give up even in such a desolate and dangerous place," she said. "I guess I needed that kind of strength to pull me back to reality just as you needed to be hauled back from the brink of death."

Danyl stared into her eyes, the fear from that experience clearly reflected within their depths. It had been a difficult decision, one that would have been even worse for her had she chosen to ignore his cries and remain in the shelter of the cave. She could have left him to fend for himself once the wolves came but again she endangered her life to defend him. The need to protect, it seemed, had been deeply ingrained in her even if she could not recall her past. Danyl reached out and touched her cheek, the innocent contact stirring that odd sensation back into life. He could sense its unfamiliarity bewildering them both and decided to leave well enough alone for the time being.

"I should go," he stated bluntly and disappeared out into the night.

She watched him leave, standing in the middle of the kitchen for a long time as she tried to make sense of what had just occurred. The attraction, if it could be called that, must not be allowed to grow. He was a prince and she an unknown outsider with an unrevealed past, its truth a possible poison to him. The only way to make sure it would not progress was to avoid any contact with him unless absolutely necessary. She felt better after having confessed her part in his rescue but not about her decision to dodge him. *I cannot allow that particular sensation to reoccur.* Ramira inhaled deeply and went upstairs to bed.

She managed to be absent for most of the day and well into the evening for nearly a week until Sophie had had enough. She kept an unhappy Ramira busy with chores around the house. She noted her tense reaction every time the bell sounded, relief flooding her features when she spotted a neighbor or other acquaintance. Ramira's distancing began the day after the conversation she had with Danyl. The few times he had paid them a visit, she always feigned an errand or a task. Sophie had seen his reaction, the quiet disappointment in his demeanor speaking volumes about his feelings. She knew the prince well and had seen a variety of emotions cross his handsome features but never one steeped with such an inner struggle. Sophie watched Ramira work in the garden from the kitchen doorway, her far-off gaze staring well beyond the weeds poking up through the soil. A sad but knowing smile touched Sophie's lips as she realized Ramira avoided the elf because she had feelings for him. Sophie slowly shook her head, wanting nothing more than to go up to Ramira and tell her it was perfectly acceptable to be with Danyl. The young woman's private apprehensions, however, would continue to keep her at bay. She had to deal with them on her own terms, but Sophie wondered how much might be lost before that conclusion was reached.

"Mind your own business, woman," Sophie chided herself. "You've already stuck your nose in too far."

Nyk grew stronger every day. He could no longer abide lying still within the tent for that purposeless state of being was beginning to drive him crazy. His wounds smarted if he moved too quickly, but he managed to rise and dress without too much difficulty. He slipped through the flap of the tent and squinted into the late afternoon sun. When his eyes had adapted to the light he realized he was somewhere on the edge of the Great White Desert. The dunes rolled away toward the horizon like waves on a silver ocean, the shimmering sands both harsh and beautiful at the same time. Heat pulsated from the crests of the dunes and enveloped him even in the shade of the tent. He glanced eastward at the long line of mountains running from north to south. The rocky barrier appeared less imposing from this side, or did the desolate Broken Plains give them that impression? The Herkah camp undulated upon the desert like a black dune. He guessed there were nearly a hundred dark tents and maybe twice as many nomads. Many Herkahs were tending to their magnificent horses while others approached the camp from several directions. The prince watched as a black-garbed man advanced toward him, his cat-like movements closing the distance in moments. The Herkah stopped in front of him, and as Nyk looked into his eyes, he knew this was the Herkah that had almost slit his throat.

"I am Allad," the man said, removing his face cover. Allad's hawkish features, browned by the sun, were as keen and sharp as his blades. "You are most welcome in our tribe."

"Thank you," replied Nyk, not sure how he should react. Allad had come within inches of killing him immediately after the elf had watched the nomad slay his men. He was successful in the assignment his father had given to him...a small consolation given the sacrifices that were made.

"You'll need to change clothes, young elf, for the nights here get very cold and the days will burn the flesh right off of your bones. Zada has set aside some things for you in the tent."

Nyk nodded. The sun was still hot enough even in the late afternoon to make him perspire, the sweat trickling down and irritating his wounds. Allad motioned toward the shady spot in front of the tent, inviting him to sit cross-legged upon a red woven rug and share in some refreshments. The prince noted the Herkahs glancing at him every now and then, their curiosity as great as his own. Nyk noticed the nomads did not burden themselves with useless luxuries but what they did own would have made any king envious. The thick rug on which they sat was plush and comfortable, the stylized horses and rolling dunes standing out starkly on the rich red background. The plates and cups were forged from a light and sturdy metal, their etched borders composed of intertwined cords and knots. The pillows were soft and the embroidery silken to the touch, and the blankets light yet warm. Everything was easily transportable; an absolute must for their nomadic way of life.

Zada's melodic tinkling caught his attention. He accepted a plate of food from her, the meat marinated in unknown spices making his mouth water and his stomach gurgle. She handed him a flattened piece of bread and a mug of strong tea then prepared the same for Allad and herself.

"When may I leave?" he asked after swallowing a mouthful of food, the tender morsels nearly melting in his mouth.

"In a few days," replied Allad. "First you must heal more."

"I feel fine," lied Nyk, knowing just a few minutes on a horse would open up more than one of the stitches on his body.

"There are some injuries you do not want to aggravate," Zada reminded him.

"Zada, why has no one from Kepracarn been heard from yet?" he asked, hoping they would be able to supply an answer, news of their bitter confrontations running rampant through his mind.

"You think we destroyed them all, don't you?" Allad half teased the elf, grinning as the prince sat up straight and opened his mouth to speak. "No, we don't know what they are doing but we prefer the conflict over this peculiar silence. It is better to confront your enemies and know where they are rather than guess at their absence. Especially Cooper."

"You think they are regrouping and attempting some other plan?"

"Kepracarn is shrouded in utter stillness...no one goes in or out, young prince," Zada informed him.

"What could have happened?" he asked, watching the Herkahs exchange a secretive glance. "You know, don't you? Does it have something to do with those Kreetch?"

"Partly," she replied. "There are other...things at work that go beyond the Kreetch, Nyk, things that have yet to materialize. "

"I mean no disrespect but your words explain nothing. I must inform my people of what has transpired here yet, except for the Kreetch, I know nothing." He glanced from one to the other, his set expression demanding some sort of an explanation.

"There are three levels of demons," Zada began after a long pause. "Each is bound to an ancient evil for a particular purpose: the Kreetch, the Radir and the Vox. You have already encountered the first group, and though the Kreetch are bothersome, they usually mean nothing by themselves. The Radir are just as ferocious as their brethren are, but they have a viable intelligence. This ancient evil uses them to 'see' what is going on in the land and if they are spotted, then we become nervous. Their arrival indicates the evil is gaining strength and intends to infiltrate the land once more."

"What 'evil'? You mean it has surfaced before?" asked Nyk, his brow furrowed in concentration.

"Yes, elven prince. You see, it seeks a specific power called the 'Source.' If the evil senses this magic, it will send the Radir out to find it."

"How is it that you know so much about this evil and its ilk?"

"We have been living with it for nearly a thousand years and are as familiar with it as your people are with what exists where you live. We don't know, for example, how this evil originated or what this source of power looks like. Legend states if the evil succeeds in acquiring the Source, all life will be extinguished. The land will become so desolate the Broken Plains will appear like a lush garden in comparison."

Nyks mind wrestled with the information. He placed little confidence in the mysterious arts although he knew they had at one time dwelled within his own people. The Herkahs had no reason to lie to him. If the Kreetch were a harbinger of this evil then the elves could conceivably be forced to confront the demons on their own lands. He needed more information.

"I know what the Kreetch look like but what about the Radir?" he asked, wondering what misshapen form they would have.

"Therein lies the problem," Allad said, holding his mug in both hands. "They steal and eat the souls of others, existing within their bodies while living amongst the possessed person's family and friends. The Kreetch blindly attack from without and the Radir poison from within."

"So they could be just about anyone," Nyk said. "Is there no way to identify them at all?"

"Sometimes, young prince, the Radir act contrary to their host," Zada explained. "But unless you have the right weapons to defeat it, you will become its next victim."

"And the Vox?" he inquired with a shiver.

"Ah...the Vox." She exhaled sharply before continuing. "Their place in the scheme of things should be left for another day as should the evil."

"You think this evil is near, don't you?" Nyk asked.

"We aren't sure, elven prince, but I would be surprised if it wasn't trying to get back into the land."

"You keep saying 'getting back into the land'...where does it originate from?"

Zada's brown eyes gazed through Nyk and out onto the desert, remaining unmoving even when he shifted in his seat. The elf glanced over at Allad, the Herkah's intense focus on Zada hinting at a coiled snake ready to strike. The prince swallowed several times ignoring the dryness in his throat as the motionless drama persisted. Allad began to lean closer and closer to her, his eyes never leaving her perspiring face. Nyk could have sworn the Herkah floated toward the woman, the dry heat wavering behind Allad distorting his form. Then, without any forewarning, Allad barked out her name.

"Zada!"

Nyk nearly jumped out of his skin, his racing heart prompting him to breathe again. His wide eyes watched Allad catch Zada as she slumped forward, cradling her in his arms as she sluggishly regained her composure. The Vox clearly concerned Zada and Allad, a fact that gave him a sickening feeling in the pit of his stomach. What sort of monsters were they that frightened the mighty Herkahs? He hoped he would never find out. The elf needed to pass on what he knew, even if it was all just conjecture at this point. He tried to ignore the healing claw marks but the itching and burning increased with every passing second. He would have to tolerate them and get back to Bystyn as soon as possible.

A Herkah signaled for Allad who, after casting one more look at Zada, walked over to him. Zada invited Nyk to join her, leading the elf to the crest of a nearby dune. The sand shifted beneath his feet, the white grains changing color as the sun began to set. It glittered with shades of red, then lavender and finally silver.

"It's actually quite dazzling to behold," he murmured to himself.

"And extremely dangerous. The wind is changing direction…a storm is brewing out there." She pointed toward the heart of the desert. "It will follow the air currents from the west striking here sometime late tomorrow morning. We will leave at dawn and head north along the mountains to escape it."

"What lies out in the desert and how do you manage to survive there, Zada?"

"The power to test your soul," she replied, subconsciously fingering her bracelets.

"I don't understand."

"The challenge to endure in any place whether desert or mountain is to know your limitations, young prince. The desert is vast and uncompromising place. You are tricked into believing the arid land is nothing more than endless sand and burning sun when, in fact, it is a far more complex than that. There are places where water flows close enough to the surface, allowing broad-leaved trees and waxy bushes to grow. These places, oases, permit us to exist. They can disappear very quickly, too. A single storm can devastate them in an instant."

"Have you ever gone to one of these sites only to find it gone when you arrived there?"

"Indeed we have, Nyk, and yes," she anticipated his next question, "the hardships we endured on the way to the next oasis were severe indeed."

The elf scooped up a handful of sand letting the grains flow through his fingers. They were still warm to the touch, as yet unaffected by the cold breeze beginning to blow over the dunes. He had been with the Herkahs long enough to dispel the myths surrounding them and to gain a growing respect for them as a people. He brushed away the last of the sand then looked over at Zada. She had remained quiescent, rising now that he was paying attention.

"Follow the same path back to the camp or the sand will devour you."

Nyk sat down on the dune, his arms resting on top of his knees as he stared out into the night. Where the sun had set fire to the sands earlier, the moon and stars now flooded them with an unearthly shade of silver that sparkled like diamonds. The cold air began to flow over the dunes until it touched his skin and made him shiver. The elf rose to his feet and turned only to find an older woman a few feet away. She wore a simple brown dress, her mahogany features radiating compassion as she offered him a slight smile in greeting.

"Good evening, Grandmother," he said in respectful tones.

You have come a long way...that is a good sign.

"What do you mean, Grandmother?" Nyks brow furrowed for he had clearly heard her speak yet her lips never moved.

It means all is not lost.

"What hasn't been lost?" He felt the hair on his arms begin to stand on end.

Hope.

"I don't understand..." he began, but the small brown woman lifted her hand to turn aside any more questions.

Hope will light the way even during your darkest hours, child. Take care not to let the foul winds that are blowing extinguish the flame burning brightly in your breast. Look closely upon the Children of the Sands...gaze past their black concealment and see the light blazing in their hearts.

Nyk was about to question her further but she disappeared like a mist chased away by the morning sun. Had he seen a ghost? Her words still echoed within his mind and her aura of kindness clung to his body like a warm blanket on a cold winter's night. He inhaled very deeply then headed back to the camp where he kept the encounter with the woman to himself. Her unspoken words, though, haunted him.

The small band of Herkahs rode northwest toward the camp, their last perimeter check just completed. They had left at dawn and would meet up with their tribe before the sun disappeared beneath the horizon. They crested a dune when two unmoving blotches of black appeared up ahead. Haban, the leader of the party, reined in his horse and scrutinized the silhouettes, the others forming a protective circle around him facing outward. The steeds pranced nervously, causing the tassels on their black blankets and along their bridles to tremble and jerk. Satisfied the two shapes were the only oddities, Haban and another Herkah approached them their eyes narrowing with alarm as they recognized what they were. Haban dismounted cautiously, advancing upon the dead horse and rider, drawing his blades out from their sheaths as he squatted down between them. The Herkah had stabbed the horse in the neck then ended his own life, the dried blood on their bodies indicating this had occurred many hours ago. Haban nodded to his comrade, the two of them proceeding to bury their blades into the hearts of the dead nomad and horse.

"This does not bode well, Haban," stated his companion, his eyes scrutinizing every square inch of the dune while nervously fingering the small dagger hanging from his neck.

"No, it does not," Haban replied quietly. The sun slipped halfway down the sky, flooding the dunes with vivid reds and oranges, making the scene even more grotesque. Shivers of alarm ran up and down their spines as they hurriedly buried the dead. The remaining Herkahs joined them, their shared silence during the uneasy task hastening the process. Haban offered a quick prayer for their souls from atop their fidgety horses, then the party galloped back to camp. They arrived just as the sun slipped below the horizon, Haban heading straight for Zada's tent where he passed on the news. Zada's lips clamped tightly and her skin grew paler with every word he spoke, her hand reaching over to take Allad's. Haban left the subdued couple alone.

"They are here."

"It is time to leave, Zada. Tomorrow morning."

Nyk kept out of Zada's way as she packed away everything but their bedrolls, surprised at how few boxes held the contents of the tent. Her tight features and rapid movements alarmed him; Allad's brisk orders from somewhere outside only confirmed his concern. He quickly sidestepped the Herkah as she brushed past him without seeing him to retrieve a pouch hanging on the pole. He finally could not stand the tense silence any longer.

"What's going on?"

"We'll be leaving at daybreak."

"I can see that, but why?"

"Because of the storm and…"

"And what?"

"Vox. I'd prefer you not asking any questions about them right now."

"Why did you let me live yet take the lives of my men?" asked the prince after a while.

"Because the poison did not affect you the same way it did them."

"That is a very vague answer, Zada."

"Allad noted a certain…strength running through you and decided to take a chance by letting you live. If we conclude you have been influenced or show signs of being tainted at any point in the future we will kill you."

"Then you are taking a grave risk by keeping me in your tent."

"On the contrary, young prince. Allad and I are your worst adversaries if you have been poisoned by the Kreetch."

Nyk locked eyes with her and realized that for all of her gentleness and apparent fragility she was still a Herkah. Generations of the nomads had fought the demons and the bodies the abominations occupied meant nothing to the Herkahs. Their only choice was to eliminate the threat regardless of whose face they wore or risk the same fate. The nomads would not hesitate to slay him despite the resulting strife that would occur with the elves. The spread of the Kreetch to Bystyn through Nyk was totally unacceptable to the Herkahs. It was not a pleasant situation but if they did not protect the rest of the unsuspecting races, and themselves, then who would? The elf marveled at their resolve, but he did not envy their position in the scheme of things.

"I am both terrified and grateful at the same time," he stated, suddenly aware of his mortality and the delicate balance upon which it hung.

"You should be," she replied in tones devoid of arrogance or danger but resonant with a certainty that made him drop his gaze.

Nyk absently touched his wounds, remembering the great care with which Zada had tended to him. He found it difficult to imagine her wielding a dagger against his neck, unlike the very real image of Allad out on the plains. *Look closely upon the Children of the Sands*…the ghost had told him. The Herkahs were as fierce and unforgiving as the demons and therefore they, and through them the other races, survived. He had no idea what this "strength" was, but it was evident it had only momentarily saved him. Allad would not hesitate to carry out his dark deed if Nyk showed any signs of turning into a demon, a sobering truth indeed.

"Rest, Nyk, for tomorrow will be a long day."

The prince was awakened the next morning as the Herkahs hastily broke camp. He helped as best as he could, the uneasy feeling in the pit of his stomach growing the closer the ominous wall of sand gyrated toward them. It was still recognizable even in the semi-darkness; a vast blackness bent on devouring the world was heading straight for them. The elf glanced over at the Herkahs who silently packed their belongings without ever looking at the monster. The nearer it came the faster they worked, and less than fifteen minutes later, they were all mounted up and ready to ride. The elf tucked the flaps of his head covering more tightly into the folds as the wind began to whip them against his face. A deep rumbling sound reverberated in the distance, increasing as the sandstorm grew in height and breadth.

"Stay beside me, Nyk, and do not tarry," Allad commanded as he stared past the elf at the sandstorm, his demeanor dark and forbidding.

They started out at a brisk pace heading north in the direction of the mountains separating the desert from the Broken Plains. Nyk could feel the leading edge of the storm push against his left side, forcing them all to ride at a slight angle. He sniffed the air, grimacing with disgust at the foul odor drawing near, the rank smell reminiscent of rotting corpses left too long in the sun. The blasting air began to drive into them from a more northerly route, pounding into them from the front. Nyk began to believe the massive sandstorm was shifting direction and one look at Allad confirmed his worst thoughts. The Herkah's grim facial cast made the elf breathe sharply and grip his reins more tautly. The hard ground allowed the horses to run at full speed but even at this distance the violent funnel pummeled sand into their eyes. It seemed as if it intended to smother them all. They pulled up their face coverings to minimize the effects, squinting as they fled the gigantic mass of swirling sand gaining ground on them. They followed the undulating foothills of the mountains, Nyk's anxiety intensifying as their escape route became blurred and lost within the whirling sand and debris. The wind became so loud he could no longer hear anything, and it took a great deal of effort to keep his horse from bolting. It strained at the bit, ears laid back and snorting nervously. Trapped between the annihilating storm and the rock, they kept riding on as panic began to build in Nyk's stomach. He had no choice but to place his trust in the Herkahs' ability to survive, keeping pace with Allad as they continued on. The lead group rounded a bend up ahead, but when Nyk and the others reached that spot, the riders had disappeared. Allad edged his horse into Nyk's mount, pushing him into a deep crack within the rocks.

"Keep your head down and do not stop!" Allad shouted as they sped up the rocky slope and into the darkness.

Visions of striking a low hanging ledge or vanishing with his mount into a chasm filled Nyk's mind as the darkness swallowed them up. He instinctively dropped low over the horse's neck, breathing hard as the oppressive confines of the mountain replaced the wide expanse of the desert. The elf swallowed hard, clinging tightly to his horse as they sped into the crevasse. He jolted upright as a tremendous roar followed them into the stony darkness; the storm, deprived of its victims, lashed out at the mountain with a fury that almost seemed surreal. He swore he heard it shriek, the piercing sound sending shivers up and down his spine. Sweat poured down his body and into his wounds, but he was so engrossed in the dangers at hand he never noticed the pain. They proceeded on into the bowels of the mountain, the Herkahs forward progress never wavering, He could discern the outlines of numerous tunnels branching in different directions by the torchlight, but the nomads moved ahead without hesitation. The elf could still hear the angry howling behind him, a sound echoing with ferocity as it streamed into the tunnel with them. The sound took on an almost human tone and he could feel the hair stand up all over his body as he fought the temptation to dismount and cower in the gloom. The well-trained Herkah steed kept pace with the others and would have ignored his command: he had no choice but to hang on and pray that he might live to see another day. The air became heavy and, save for the hooves striking the rocky ground and the creaking of leather, all other sounds faded away. When all of the Herkahs were finally within the safety of the mountain's protection, they slowed their pace and stopped. Allad rode down the line checking to make sure everyone was accounted for.

Nyk stayed behind Allad and Zada, often looking back but seeing nothing more than an occasional torch and vague silhouettes. He recoiled from the outcroppings appearing out of nowhere then silently chastised himself for dodging something that really wasn't there at all. Time seemed to stand still, becoming disproportionate and vague, the lack of any landmarks making the elf feel disorientated. For a few brief moments Nyk believed he was in a procession of the dead as they made their way into the underworld. He half expected the searing heat of hell to rise toward them then witness the great flames shoot upward to burn them all. He shook his head to dislodge the disturbing images, collecting his thoughts to keep himself from panicking. They stopped for a while, resting their horses and making sure everyone was still in line and, except for a whispered word here and there, remained silent.

If there was something skulking about in the darkness he preferred knowing about it ahead of time. He approached Allad to find out.

"Do we remain quiet for a specific reason?" he asked in hushed tones.

"The mountain can be quite unstable."

Allad's succinct reply left Nyk feeling even more anxious than before. The elf glanced up, the thought of tons of rocks and stones collapsing down on top of them making him yearn for the grasslands even more. He banished the question "has it ever happened before?" from his mind. The time for resting was over. They remounted their horses and resumed their trek through the mountain. Nyk strained his eyes searching for that pinpoint of light indicating their journey through this gloomy and dangerous place was over but all he saw was endless blackness. The torch held by the lead rider began to flicker, prompting the Herkah to light another before it went out. The thought of being in total darkness within this oppressive place made Nyk shudder. He was used to a wide expanse covered in green, not this inky vault threatening to crush him to dust. His keen hearing picked up sounds reverberating faintly through the vast network of tunnels. He heard crackling and skittering noises as bits of the mountain broke loose and slid off somewhere in the blackness. Wind rushed through the passageways off to his right, moaning weakly like some injured animal. He thought he detected the sound of water rippling in the distance and visualized an icy black river carving its way through the mountain. If a creature managed to exist within this sterile, empty environment, he was positive he did not want meet up with it. The bowels of the mountain may have been desolate but they were certainly not devoid of activity.

The elf did not lose his claustrophobic apprehension within the stony tomb as the mighty weight pressed down on him. The nomads were cautious yet showed no fear or confusion as they wound their way through the silent labyrinth. It suddenly dawned on Nyk he had learned more about the land and its people in the past week than he had in all the years prior to that. He grinned wryly. The elves would be astonished when they saw the dreaded nomads, and he could well imagine the city erupting in shock at their arrival. He assumed Zada and Allad would accompany him to Bystyn while the nomads camped beyond the Broken Plains but not too close to the Khadry. The forest elves would certainly take note of the Herkahs but rein in their aggressive nature to avoid any conflicts with the nomads. Nyk brought his horse alongside Allad and leaned over toward him.

"How long before we are through the tunnel?"

"It will be well after dawn," Allad whispered. Dawn. It would take an entire day to ride through the mountain. He sighed with resignation, resuming his place in line, Allad's shadowy form his only link to the direction they were traveling. He had plenty of time to think but every time he began to focus on his thoughts his dismal surroundings seemed to consume them. He gave up trying, deciding it was easier to concentrate on nothing.

The darkness and rhythmic swaying began to lull him to sleep and soon his chin rested against his chest. He dreamt of cloudless blue skies and squinting up at the brilliant sunshine. He closed his eyes against the glare, smiling as the warmth penetrated into his very core. What was that? A cloud obscured the sun then spread outward to encompass the whole sky, a chill suddenly replacing the heat. He watched with horror as the wall of sand devoured everything in its path, grinding up trees and buildings as if they were made of paper. He turned to run but his feet were stuck in the ground, holding him in place as the monster bore down on him. He opened his mouth to yell but the storm filled it with sand, his upraised arms a futile last gesture…

He awoke with a start, sweat streaming down his face as he gulped in huge draughts of stale air. He was still within the mountain but something was very wrong. There were no torches, no fellow riders anywhere; even his horse was missing. Nyk blinked several times attempting to squeeze the sleep from his eyes yet they beheld the same thing every time: he was very much alone. How could he possibly have managed to veer away from the line? He couldn't have been asleep for too long. Completely blind, he groped all around to find a wall but found only emptiness. His breathing increased, the sharp intakes spreading the stitches and aggravating his ribs. Hysteria began to build in his stomach, extending up into his chest until it reached his throat. Nyk shouted at the top of his lungs then fell to the ground seconds later as something came crashing into his head.

Ramira sat beneath the shade of a maple tree, wiping the sweat from her face, watching Ida approach carrying a pitcher of cool water. She had spent quite a bit of time here, the couple's warmth making all the work worthwhile. She had managed to chop and stack enough wood for a week but there were some tasks requiring the help of others. She had attempted to tackle them on her own, the efforts leaving her bruised and frustrated. Jack tried to assist her but his gnarled hands weren't strong enough to hold anything for any period of time. It was disconcerting for them both but neither one complained.

She heard the horses before they rounded the lower part of the orchard, catching sight of Danyl, Lance and two other elves. She returned their greeting, remaining seated as they approached and dismounted in front of the house. The couple welcomed them, and after a brief conversation, they began to work on the projects she could not handle. She finished weeding the garden, her gaze subtly traveling over to Danyl now and then. The elves repaired a section of fence, straightened out the sagging shed and replaced the posts holding up the porch roof. Ramira wandered over to the stables, the unenviable chore the last on her list. The earthy odor of manure clung to her skin and clothes, the flies indiscriminately landing on and biting anything reeking of muck. Ramira glanced sideways at Danyl as he used his tunic to wipe away the perspiration running down his face. She could not help but admire his lean yet strong upper body, smiling despite herself until he looked over at her. She immediately turned her head hoping he hadn't seen her stare but she knew better. Danyl did not miss very much. She felt the flush rise up in her cheeks and increased her exertions, trusting they would distract her from her thoughts. The hours passed and Ida had to force them to stop and eat. She ushered them to the garden behind the house where a cool breeze stirred the clematis growing on the arbor. Ramira had washed up as best as she could, sitting slightly apart from the others. She claimed she didn't want to ruin anyone's appetite. Her companions' wrinkled noses relaxed as she sat downwind from them, taking their playful jabs good-naturedly. Danyl smiled but the short-lived flicker in his eyes was anything but amiable. Her attempts at avoiding him chafed at his normally easygoing nature, turning his disappointment into frustration and, to some degree, anger.

She finished eating and, beginning to wilt under Danyl's quiet ire, headed over to gather up a pile of kindling. She looked up and felt her stomach tighten as Danyl purposefully strode over toward her. She outwardly pretended as if nothing was wrong as she picked up the larger twigs and placed them in the wheelbarrow. Inwardly, however, was a different story, and it took a great deal of effort to still her trembling hands.

"You've been scarce," he said in a voice devoid of accusations.

"Sophie has been keeping my days full," she replied without looking at him.

"She has a knack for doing that," he agreed, then gently took her by the arm and sat her down across from him on the soft grass. "Although it can't all fall onto her shoulders, now can it?"

"No," she quietly admitted. "It can't."

"Then perhaps you would be so kind as to explain it to me?"

What could she say? That she had reveled in the embrace and found herself attracted to him? That she believed she had no right to harbor such feelings for someone of his stature? That her unknown past could bring shame, or worse, upon all whom she touched? He needn't be friendly with her simply because she had saved his life. He would not think that at all and would be upset if she spoke those words to him. He deserved better. She pushed aside a soggy strand of hair, flinching with discomfort as she bumped her finger. She turned her hand over and saw the splinter buried deep beneath the skin. The elf took her hand, trying to work out the sliver from her stiff forefinger with the tip of his knife.

"Let it relax, Ramira."

"I still feel a little guilty for keeping the rescue from you."

His attention remained on the task at hand even though her feeble explanation should have garnered a skeptical expression at the very least. He dug out the piece of wood from her finger, the tangle of emotions stealing her voice.

"Perhaps...but I think there is something else, isn't there? That sensation maybe?" He watched her squirm, his words urging her down a path she didn't want to walk on.

"That could have been rooted in a lot of things, Danyl," she stated a bit too harshly.

"Tell me."

"I'm very confused about what happened that night, Danyl, and frankly speaking, it scared me."

"So you figured that by running away from me you wouldn't have to confront those feelings?"

"Perhaps," she admitted as she stared at the ground.

"Perhaps it's something more than that," he mused. "Maybe there is something more between us than either one of us is willing to admit."

"No," she shook her head, "there can't be."

"Why not?" he asked, his eyes narrowing at her emphatic reply.

"You are a prince and I am...I don't know what I am..." Her voice trailed off into silence.

"I see," he said quietly. "You don't think you're good enough for me. What you fail to see is there are more important qualities to a person than their position in life. My feelings for you are real, Ramira...but I won't force them on you. I apologize if my bluntness disturbs you, but I have to let you know where I stand on the matter." The prince stood up, gazed down at her for a moment then rejoined his men. She stared after him for a few moments then continued her task, his honest words making her feel foolish.

She maintained a discreet distance from the elves although she could sense Danyl glancing over at her every now and then. Danyl didn't care about her past or that she wasn't highborn, it mattered only how he felt about her. She thought back to those days in the cave when he was simply "Danyl," a person in dire need of help. She had no right to change her perspective of him once she found out his status. She applied her rules onto Danyl then expected him to comply with them. She had no right to do so and now faced not only his disappointment but also her own as well. She sighed heavily; she glimpsed Danyl working by the barn then hung her head in embarrassment. The afternoon slipped away, the shadows lengthening across the land. Ramira waited for the elves ride out of sight and only then did she gather her things to leave. Ida fretted about her taking so long. She missed the opportunity to have a horse carry the basket and would now have to lug the heavy item herself. Ramira smiled at her, heaving the load over her shoulders.

"It's not that heavy, Ida."

"Then why are you straining?"

"I'm…I'll be fine," she stated, struggling to lean forward to give Ida a kiss on the cheek. She walked down the front steps, the straps pressing her flesh flat against her bones. Ramira could barely maintain her balance. The basket threatened to topple her backward, forcing her to lean forward and drive the bands even deeper into her shoulders. It didn't take long for blood to seep out of the raw abrasions and stain her tunic. Ramira broke through the trees and stopped in her tracks, chagrined as she spotted Danyl. He stood with crossed arms in front of his horse, disbelief flooding his face as he spotted the red blotches on her tunic. He grabbed her burden, placing it on the animal then flung her on the saddle before she could protest.

"You have got to be the most stubborn person I know! Honestly, Ramira, ask someone for a little help every once in a while."

They rode in silence for a while, Ramira's discomfort stilling her tongue, Danyl enjoying the fact that she couldn't run and hide from him. She began to relax although she did not lean back fearing that the peculiar sensation would arise once more. Besides, the sweat and pungency she had acquired while cleaning out the stables lingered on her clothes and body. She wrinkled her nose and wondered how he was able to tolerate her stench.

"I stink," she said apologetically.

"Yes, you do," he agreed and began to laugh, the joyful sound quickly spreading to her own throat.

"That would be your repayment for lurking behind the apple trees," she said in a playfully vindicated tone.

"Elves don't 'lurk,'" stated Danyl with mock indignation.

"What do they do then?"

"They carefully conceal themselves so they can set themselves upon smelly, obstinate women."

"Lurk," she corrected.

Danyl smiled; she could call it anything she wanted to. Her dour demeanor melted away, taking with it her rigidity and silence. He slid his arm around her waist, subtly leaning forward until he could see her face. She turned and looked at him, the tentative acceptance in her eyes and her hand resting on his forearm a promising beginning. He wished the ride to the city took hours instead of minutes, the gray walls looming larger and larger with every beat of his heart. They passed beneath the gate, the understated contentment radiating from their faces drawing more than one look from the passersby. They were in front of Sophie's house before either one was ready to end the contact.

"Thank you for the ride."

"My pleasure. Why don't you let me carry that in for you?"

"Because it's not as burdensome anymore." She offered him a shy smile then disappeared around the corner of the house. Danyl patted the horse's neck, heading up the avenue no longer feeling tired.

"Nyk? Come on, son, wake up."

Allad gently shook the elf, ignoring the bruise visible even in the faint torchlight. Nyk began to slowly return to consciousness, suddenly bolting upright as he remembered what had happened. He grabbed the front of Allad's tunic, the fistful of cloth anchoring him to the present. The prince glanced around and saw Zada and the others staring down at him, the snorting horses and occasional coughing easing his panic. He gradually loosened his grip, his breathing returning to normal as Allad helped him to his feet.

"What…?"

"You dozed off then fell from your horse," Zada explained to him. "You were fumbling around, still in a daze and began to yell. Allad was forced to…"

"I apologize for the blow to your head, Nyk, but your screaming could have been disastrous."

The elf reached up and carefully touched his hot cheek, flinching as his gloved fingers probed the sore area. He nodded in understanding, embarrassment flooding his face. He should have been more alert and not allowed himself to drift off thereby placing all of them in danger. He mounted his horse and waited for his companions, the tight line along his jaw and clenched fists noticed by Zada and Allad.

"The mountain seduced you, Nyk. That has befallen all of us." Zada patted his arm, her confession only slightly alleviating his lapse in judgement.

They moved on again, the elf determined not to fall under any more spells, traveling through the near darkness in silence. The hours they had spent within the mountain seemed like days or years and Nyk was sure they would never reach the other side. A rumble then the sound of something large, loosened and bouncing until it splashed into a body of water, met their ears. Nyk tensed up immediately, relaxing only when he heard Allad's voice up ahead.

"The lake…good; we are almost on the other side."

Nyk squinted into the darkness to his right. A bizarre forest of twisted fingers of rock hung from the ceiling and reached upward from the ground. Some appeared dull while others shimmered with luminous hues. The pale blue, pink and green shades gleamed wetly in the torchlight. The elf strained to see into the gloom beyond them and caught the briefest of flickers of light far below him. It was the torchlight reflecting off the inky and oily surface of the water. Ripples spread out from the center of the lake, the black bands expanding silently outward. Nyk rubbed the back of his perspiring neck hoping the mountain and not something living within those dark waters caused the ruffling. A chill rose up from that depth, compelling him to ride nearer to the uneven wall to his left.

The Herkahs finally emerged from the darkness of the caves into the early morning light. They shielded their eyes until they became accustomed to the brightness and Nyk heard more than one sigh of relief from his comrades. The warm sun chased away the shadows of the trek through the mountain but for a moment the elf remembered the dream that nearly brought the rocks down upon them. He glanced over at Zada, her smile confirming they were indeed safe. The nomads urged their mounts on even though they were tired from their all-night journey. None of them wanted to be on the Broken Plains after dark. They headed northeast, angling toward the edge of the forest, hoping to reach it by noon and rest beneath their cooling branches. The prince analyzed what had so far transpired, shivering at most of the memories even though the day was becoming quite warm. He looked over at Zada, her ashen face and unfocused eyes staring into a place he instinctively knew he did not want to see.

The Herkahs were now far from their homes, heading for Bystyn and the shock and confusion that would undoubtedly await them there. He had more than fulfilled his father's order by contacting and bringing back the elusive desert dwellers. He grinned despite himself, thinking how his brothers could not possibly surpass this assignment. They reached the edge of the forest, carefully concealing themselves as best as they could within the trees and brush. The nomads were not used to the closeness of the trees and bushes nor the unyielding ground beneath their feet. They were too tired to really notice the difference, preferring to rest instead. Guards were posted and the Herkahs attended to their horses in utter silence, a feat that never failed to amaze the elf.

"How far to your home?" asked Zada in hushed tones, the color slowly seeping back into her face.

"About a week," he said, scanning the area south and east of where they stood. "If we travel a bit farther south we'll run into patrols from my city…it might be prudent to be seen by them and minimize the…" He wanted to say their dumbfounded and frightened expressions but no amount of advanced notice of their coming could avert that.

"The what?" she asked.

"The commotion our approach will make." He could picture the open-mouthed stares and hear the sharply inhaled breaths as the Herkahs advanced upon the plain. Many would rub their eyes to make the nightmare go away while others would usher their children indoors. The elves normally welcomed anyone seeking shelter but those who came were anything but typical travelers.

"We must have quite the reputation in your city." She spoke without malice.

"Yes, well, it's amazing how the lack of knowledge coupled with an intense imagination can turn an ordinary person into something completely different."

"How *are* we perceived within your city?" she asked, curious to know what sort of welcome she could expect.

"Dangerous, brutal…perfect killing machines," he stated in embarrassed tones. He had witnessed those very things firsthand.

"That we are, young prince, that and more," she added cryptically.

"Zada, tell me about the storm. It was sent, wasn't it?"

"Yes, Nyk, it was. Evidently, the evil has managed to gain enough power to exist in the land once more."

"What do we do now?"

"Whatever we can," she replied, and closed her eyes.

Nyk stared hard at her, for those three little words did not fill him with comfort. The nomads were visibly uneasy with the events that had just transpired but, by the same token, were undaunted with what they would have to do down the road. If these great warriors fretted over the demons they had fought over the years, how would the elves react? Had Cooper encountered them on his forays onto Herkah lands? Had the demons infiltrated Kepracarn and killed everyone within its walls, leaving the fields and countryside abandoned? He picked up a water skin and took a long drink from it, wiping away the rivulets running down his chin with his sleeve. He ripped off a piece of his tunic, saturating it with water then placing it on his cheek. The bruise had spread upward giving him a partial black eye but it hadn't impaired his vision. He dabbed at it a few times then lay back on the grass, the dappled sunlight playing on his face and soothing him to sleep.

They moved on a few hours later, Nyk leading the procession, mindful of the forest at this juncture since they were now in Khadry territory. They made camp after dark, posting sentries along the perimeter as they spent one of many unsettled nights on their journey east. Nyk knew the Khadry watched them; he could sense their movements within the trees and picture their astonishment. Various farmers and travelers spotted them, the former running into their homes, the latter sprinting into Khadry land. They preferred facing the wrath of the forest elves rather than spending another second on the plains with the Herkahs. They scattered like rabbits darting away from an approaching fox, seeking their burrows where the hunter could not get to them. Allad shook his head and Zada raised a brow in amusement, neither one glancing over at Nyk. The elf pushed back the hair from his face and rubbed the back of his neck, the effort not easing a single muscle.

They made good time over the course of the week, covering more distance than Nyk had anticipated. A patrol spotted them three days out from the city, their dumbfounded expressions humorous, eliciting several chuckles throughout the tribe. One of the riders managed to regain his composure and immediately peeled away from the group, speeding back to Bystyn as fast as his horse could gallop.

"Here we go," Nyk said to no one in particular as he kicked his horse and rode forward, hands up and palms facing the patrol.

They waited until he was within shouting distance before ordering him to stop. The prince heeded their command and removed his head covering. The elves stared hard at him, unsure of whether they were seeing a ghost or if this were some sort of trap. They fingered their weapons with one hand, tightly clenching the reins with the other while waiting for the Herkah to make the next move.

"It's Nyk," he shouted.

The leader of the patrol urged his mount a little closer. He scrutinized the Herkah, noting the wild hair and swarthy face marred by an ugly bruise extending past his eye. The elf glanced over at the other Herkahs then back to Nyk again.

"Drand! It's me…Nyk!"

"Nyk? Is it really you?"

They rode forward in unison, Nyk with a sense of urgency and Drand filled with disbelief and apprehension. The prince had been gone a long time, and although no one doubted he'd return, none would have thought he'd come back with all of these Herkahs.

They dismounted and embraced the patrols' wary eyes, never leaving the line of black-garbed riders. Nyk hastily scribbled a message to his father, dispatching an elf who hastened to catch up with the first rider.

"It's good to see you…unharmed, my lord," the captain stated as he looked at the bruise. "We thought, well, we didn't know what to think."

"How are things in the city?" asked Nyk, eager to hear any news.

"There is nothing out of the ordinary happening there." He glanced over at the Herkahs then added, "Not yet, anyway. There is still no news from Kepracarn, but your return will thrill the entire city."

The prince nodded but said nothing. He had been absent for many weeks and was puzzled that the only news to be had was of the tribe following him. He recalled what he had been through…like the Kreetch, the news about demons, the insidious evil prowling the desert, and the killer storm that had nearly destroyed them. Zada had been right about the evil being restricted to the desert area, a momentary bit of good fortune. She had told him the elves needn't worry at this point, for the darkness was unable to penetrate beyond the mountains. What would happen when it had the power to sustain itself beyond the range? The Herkahs had some sort of skill when fighting the Kreetch, the ability the well-trained elves apparently did not possess. What was that capability and would the nomads be able to teach the elves if the demons skittered to their gates? He looked over at Zada and saw that same wan and unfocused appearance. Who exactly was she? She and Allad were indistinguishable from the other Herkahs yet an underlying sense of deep reverence for them was prevalent amongst the nomads. The couple led the tribe without any visible trappings of power. They wore no crowns nor carried scepters and no one bowed down to them, either. Nyk watched as perspiration began to appear on her forehead, the concern in Allad's expression growing with every passing moment. The Herkah narrowed his eyes, calling out in his tongue, pulling her back from wherever she had gone. Where did that inner sight keep taking her?

"My lord." The captain interrupted his thoughts. "How will you explain the Herkahs to our people, not to mention anyone else who happens upon Bystyn?"

"I'm not quite sure yet." Nyk assumed after the initial shock wore off the elves would demand an explanation, but what could he tell them? That there were demons loose in the desert and the Herkahs sought sanctuary with the elves? Many believed the nomads were demons and to see nearly two hundred appear at their gates would surely overwhelm them. Would the nervous elven guards accidentally initiate an incident that might become very ugly very quickly? Allad informed his people that under no condition were they to unsheathe their weapons against any elf, an order Nyk would give to his people as well. But what if the myths were too deeply ingrained? He exhaled slowly and prayed everything would somehow fall into place before they reached the city.

They rode on for a while longer, setting up camp as the sun began to dip below the horizon. Drand sent the remainder of the patrol off, staying with the tribe and keeping close to Nyk. The captain watched the prince interact with the nomads as if he had been with them forever. The Herkah garb seemed to better suit the prince than did the green and brown elven attire. His mannerisms, too, represented more tribe characteristics rather than elven ones. Nyk waved him over to eat, sitting down cross-legged in front of the fire in one easy motion as the captain joined him. The prince handed him a plate of food, the aroma of spices tantalizing yet foreign to him, but Nyk ate without really noticing them. Drand remained respectful of his hosts, keeping his emotions in check, still stunned and, to some degree, frightened by their presence. He consumed his meal in silence, every bite tastier than the previous one.

"More, Drand?" Zada held up a large spoonful of marinated meat and vegetables, smiling as he stuck his plate out to her.

"Thank you, Zada. It's delicious." The captain finished his second helping then stood to help with guard duty.

"That won't be necessary, Drand," Nyk said.

Drand shrugged and retrieved his bedroll, placing it on the ground next to the prince. Nyk grinned for the captain was bound and determined to safeguard him regardless of the highly skilled Herkahs surrounding them. The captain was quiet for so long Nyk thought he had fallen asleep when Drand's voice broke the silence.

"My lord?"

"Yes, Drand?"

"You've done well."

Nyk interlaced his fingers behind his head and stared up at the stars and quarter moon. Crickets chirped and a gentle breeze played with an unruly lock of his hair, perfect rewards for surviving the trek through the mountain. He had accomplished his goal but to what end remained to be seen. The news he was bringing back was troubling to say the least. He fell asleep slowly, the smell of grass and dirt the last thing he remembered.

The King glanced over at Nyk's chair, then took a sip from his glass. Had his son somehow survived? he thought for the thousandth time. If so, why hadn't there been any news? He looked over at his remaining children, grateful he had them here. He watched his daughter Alyssa roll her blue eyes with disapproval as the serving girl made an insignificant error while holding a tray of food. Everything had to be just right for his daughter, but he could not grasp why she fretted over such little things. She straightened out an errant curl, her impeccably coifed auburn hair held in place with bejeweled hairpins. The King sighed for the only thing more annoying than her pursuit of perfection was her attempts at finding suitable mates for her brothers. The King had lost count of how many arguments he had to end because Alyssa would not relent to her brothers.

She ran the daily functions of the castle with an iron will, and few living within its gray walls outranked her. She gave Mason and Karolauren a wide berth: the former too serious for her, the latter too cantankerous. The King admired his daughter. Although she could be difficult and demanding, she ran the household well, keeping everything in perfect order. Danyl, he noted, was rather subdued this evening while Styph, the crown prince, playfully engaged the historian in conversation. He met Mason's gray eyes and the first advisor knew the King pined for his son. They were doing everything they could to find him, all to no avail.

Alyxandyr's eyes strayed to the door where a dirty and exhausted guard demanded to see him. He exchanged tense words with the guard at the door then came forward as the King nodded to him. The guard bowed and handed him a letter that the King opened and read then reread it again to make sure he had not misinterpreted anything. He slowly looked up, the incredulity firmly etched on his face as the words in the message began to register. He suddenly shot upright, grabbing the startled guard by the front of his tunic, and dragged him to the far corner of the room.

"Where did you get this?" demanded the King.

"The prince handed it to me two days ago, my lord."

"Is it true? Are there Herkahs with him?"

"Yes, my lord, nearly two hundred." The King released him, scanning the message once more.

"Go clean up and rest, son. You have done well."

The guard nodded and left as the King dropped into a chair by the hearth. His friends and family gathered around him, eager to hear the news contained within the letter. The King remained motionless for a long time, the note clenched in his hand.

"What does the message say?" everyone asked, almost in unison

"It says Nyk is on his way home," the King replied, the relief in his voice shared by the others.

"What else does it say, Alyx?" Mason inquired in his deep voice.

"That he is not alone." He handed the piece of paper to Mason, whose usually veiled thoughts and emotions crowded onto his gaunt face.

"Two days, Alyx? Two years wouldn't be enough to prepare the city!"

"For what?" demanded Styph.

"What is said here is not to leave this room tonight, understood? Nyk is scheduled to arrive in two days time and is accompanied by nearly two hundred Herkahs."

They looked at him unblinkingly, his words so incomprehensible he might just as well have spoken in a different tongue. Two hundred Herkahs were coming to Bystyn? Evidently, Nyk had succeeded in his task, but why bring them all here? What would prompt the nomads to travel all this way? How in the four corners of the land were they to explain their black-garbed guests to the elves? Styph let out a long breath of air, one that he had been holding for quite some time, then poured a glass of wine.

"He couldn't have brought back one or two," muttered the crown prince, sipping from his goblet. "What are we going to do with two hundred Herkahs?"

"Well," began the King, as he took the letter back from Mason. "For one thing, we are not going to turn them away."

"What if they are using Nyk to get into the city?" asked Alyssa, the idea of so many black-garbed killers on elven lands making her shiver.

"The scout who brought the message spoke with Nyk and indicated he never noticed anything out of the ordinary. Well, save for the Herkahs themselves. He said Nyk was dressed like the nomads and seemed rather relaxed, never giving any sign of danger. "

"Why would they all leave the desert and come here?" asked the princess.

"Why indeed," agreed Mason, although he surmised their departure had been out of necessity rather than a visit to satisfy their curiosity.

"The question is, what do we do with them once they have arrived?" stated the King.

"Learn from them," Karolauren said, his bright blue eyes sparkling with delight at the prospect of being able to spend time questioning the Herkahs. Such an opportunity, he knew, was rarer than a thunderstorm in the middle of winter. He was already thinking about what he would ask them and only half listening to the conversation around him.

"First we have to come up with a plan to limit the chaos out in the streets," the King reminded them. "Then we have to decide where they can make camp and steel ourselves for the news of whatever brought them all to our door."

They worked well into the night, catching a few hours sleep as dawn painted the sky in pastel shades. Danyl would inform the elves living within the city; Styph would meet with the guards and patrols, and the King and Mason would meet with the lords. It was made very clear to everyone that no conflicts would be tolerated, the King vowing to severely punish anyone, regardless of station, himself.

The news traveled through the city like wildfire, its embers igniting imaginations even before the body of the blaze burned through. The elves congregated on stoops, in shops and on the street talking about the mythic nomads converging on their city. They kept glancing nervously toward the gate as if the Herkahs were about to enter, holding their breaths whenever a group of riders emerged from the shadowy portal. Sophie navigated her way through the crowds, nodding politely as people addressed her but refusing to stop and add her opinions. She had seen the nomads before when she was a child living in Kepracarn. They did not frighten her then nor did they now, a fact she was unwilling to share with her friends and neighbors. Not yet, anyway. She snaked her way past the last throng in front of her home and escaped with her bags into the house.

"What's all the excitement about?" asked Ramira. She had been watching the commotion from the front window and, other than fingers pointing toward the main gate and dismayed faces, could not figure out what was happening.

"The elves are concerned about Herkahs coming to the city."

"Herkahs? Coming to Bystyn?" Ramira's eyes went wide with excitement.

"You haven't heard?" Sophie clicked her tongue at the elves' shortsightedness, a slight smile of appreciation for the nomads on her face.

"You don't seem to afraid of them," remarked Ramira.

"Well, I'm not."

"Why do the elves fear the Herkahs?"

"Their reputation, fueled by rumor and imagination, have turned them into things they are not."

"You sound very sure of yourself."

"When I lived in Kepracarn I would go out riding alone, Ramira. The nomads would occasionally roam the edges of Cooper's land immediately following one of my brother's raids, but they never accosted me. They had every right to, you know, for the terrible things he used to try to do to them, but chose not to. Afraid of them? Hardly. I will welcome them into my home."

Sophie studied Ramira as the young woman leaned back in the rocking chair and placed her hands behind her head. She stared up at the rafters with an introspective look on her face, her feet casually moving the chair to and fro. There was a glimmer of hope in her eyes, hope of possibly encountering her kin. There is nothing wrong with having Herkahs as your kinfolk.

Ramira found sleep difficult that night and not just because of the expected arrival of the Herkahs. She tossed and turned as vicious nightmares tormented her, leaving her drenched in sweat and overly anxious. Her dreams revolved around voiceless phantoms pointing their fingers at her in an accusatory manner as if she were the bane of the land. She finally managed to shut them out, but their wordless insinuations continued to echo within her mind. She rose well before dawn, ate a few bites of food and headed down the avenue, the cool air re-energizing her still hot skin. There were quite a few elves out on the plains, their curiosity concerning the nomads exceeding their fear. Was that the reason she now ventured forth? She had told Danyl "no" when he had asked her if she was a Herkah, but could they indeed be her kin?

Daylight began to warm the land, the soft morning rays chasing away the shadows lurking amid the stones and brush. She heard the sounds of hooves behind her, the hollow echoing marking their course through the tunnel-like gate. She turned and spotted Danyl, who motioned his men on before riding over to where she stood.

"Are you all right?" he asked, stopping in front of her and dismounting, his hand reaching up to touch her warm cheek.

"I had a sleepless night."

"Anything I can do to help?" The sun had yet to flush the phantoms from her features, leaving her face pale and drawn.

"No, nothing. Your men are waiting for you." His knotted brows and the concern in his gaze embarrassed her. He had more important things to do than worry about her. He stared at her for one more moment, silently vowing to speak with her later.

Ramira decided coming onto the plains wasn't a good idea after all and turned to go home. There were an increased numbers of guards patrolling the streets and stationed along the parapet: the King was determined no incidents were going to take place. She shrugged and walked up the path alongside the house, joining Sophie and Anci sipping their tea on the terrace. Ramira poured herself a mug and sat down beside them.

Sophie noticed not just her fatigue but the restlessness in her behavior. Ramira lifted her cup to her lips, the slight trembling in her hand prompting her to steady the mug with her other hand. She blinked several times then rubbed at her eyes and the back of her neck, staring off into space.

"They must be close by," Sophie said. "I saw Danyl leave a little while ago."

"I passed him on my way back into the city. I needed some air."

Danyl and his men rode west, locating the undulating black line near mid-morning. The prince urged his mount into a full gallop, his face tense with excitement. He had been waiting for this moment all of his life and he couldn't get to the meeting point fast enough. A thrill ran up and down his spine as three of the black-garbed riders made their way toward them. The rest of the Herkahs waited off in the distance. The prince held his breath as the trio approached, their fluid movements and elegant carriage remarkable to behold. The horses' long manes and tails shimmered and fluttered like black silk threads; their glossy black bodies were adorned with tasseled bridles and blankets. The Herkahs slowed their steeds, trotting toward Danyl, who shrugged off the elves forming a protective circle around him. The Herkahs wore loose fitting attire concealing everything except for their eyes. There was something frightening about a person who exposed the most vulnerable part of their body. For all of Danyl's respect and admiration for the Herkahs, even he shivered as they halted before him. One of the horsemen pulled back the face covering and it took Danyl several long moments to realize it was Nyk. The younger prince stared at his brother's deeply tanned face, the black clothing and the ease with which he interacted with the nomads. Nyk offered his brother a lopsided grin, effectively breaking the spell Danyl had been under. They dismounted and heartily embraced each other, Nyk ruffling Danyl's hair then slapping him on the shoulder. Danyl's complete attention was riveted on the Herkahs who now joined them.

"Danyl, this is Zada and her mate Allad."

Danyl stuck out his hand after wiping the perspiration on his trousers, his eyes sparkling with animation at the couple before him. Allad's hawkish features and piercing black eyes commanded Danyl's respect, the nomad firmly gripping his hand as if he held a sword. Zada studied the prince with soft brown eyes that were equally as intense as those of her mate. The subtle tinkling her bracelets made as she lifted her hand to Danyl elicited a smile, the dainty sound so contradictory with their perceived myth.

"It is an honor to meet you both."

"You and your brother share a great many good qualities," remarked Zada. "Your father must be very proud."

"Thank you, Zada." They jumped back on their horses, the princes keeping the Herkah pair between them while Danyl's men rode along behind. The guards paid extra attention, fearful the Herkahs would suddenly strike out and kill the princes. Allad informed Danyl the Herkahs would remain camped outside the city but he and Zada would accept the invitation to stay in the castle. They had much to discuss and both races wanted to learn more about the other.

Nyk sighed as they wound their way past the last line of trees and espied the city. It had been a long two months and the sight of his home sent a wave of relief over him. Allad motioned for the Herkahs to set up camp, Danyl ordering the elves to stay with them. The guards hesitated and exchanged wary glances, unsure if they were more afraid of leaving the princes or of being left in the midst of the nomads. They weren't given a choice and watched their charges continue on to the city. They rode up to the mighty edifice, straining their necks as they gaped up at the ancient elven stronghold. He could see many heads sprouting up along the walls, hair and clothing draping over the gray stone as they glimpsed the nomads. The elves whispered to one another, a sound normally too faint to hear from so far up but not when dozens of voices spoke at once. Nyk looked up and scanned the rampart, first confused then disturbed by the odd expressions gawking back at him. The expected reaction was more subdued than he had anticipated, although he hadn't foreseen the wariness directed at him. The murmuring accompanied them under the gate and up the avenue, passed on by the bystanders staring with disbelief at the fabled desert dwellers. The couple had completely removed their head covers, Allad's black hair and Zada's shoulder length tresses stirring in the breeze a less imposing sight to the elves. The Herkahs busily absorbed the sights, smells and sounds of the city, nodding approvingly at what they beheld. Zada smiled at a little girl holding a pale pink rose then leaned from her saddle as the girl rushed forward to hand it to her. The nomad inhaled the scent then tucked it into a fold in her tunic. Zada hesitated when they reached the main intersection, the sensation precipitating the indecision gone before she could identify what had sparked it, attributing it to the unfamiliarity of her surroundings.

"She's a lovely woman," observed Sophie as she stood on the front steps with Anci and Ramira.

"One head, two eyes, the correct number of arms and legs."

Ramira's sarcastic reply made her smile, for some of the elves had exaggerated the Herkahs appearance to the point of ridiculousness.

"It shouldn't take the elves too long to see that the Herkahs are composed of flesh and blood," Anci stated, her eyes wide with wonder.

Ramira watched them go by, disappointed that her vivid cast did not match the swarthy nomads. Perhaps they knew of her people. She sighed, her attention wandering over to Danyl. He was at ease with his guests, pointing to the layout of the city as they wound their way to the castle. The elves, she noted, huddled amongst each other once the riders passed by, talking but not daring to point at the nomads. There would be plenty of conversations and opinions as the days wore on. Ramira retreated into the house after the trio progressed beyond her line of sight, her list of chores awaiting her.

The King greeted Zada and Allad as they dismounted in front of the main entrance under the sharp eyes of his guard. The Herkah pair followed Alyxandyr to a room at the end of the corridor where they could refresh themselves before the prepared meal. They dined then listened to Nyk as he recounted what had transpired since he left the city weeks earlier. He spoke of the meeting with the Herkahs, his time amongst them and the horrifying fight with the Kreetch. More than one elf recoiled when Nyk described his men's terrible fate. The elves noticed although the Herkahs were regretful about having to slay Nyk's men, they showed no guilt for their actions. They understood and accepted their lot in life and would make no excuses for carrying out that unenviable duty.

The elves and nomads studied each other without appearing disrespectful: the curiosity was mutual. Alyxandyr had always been fascinated by the nomads but accepted the fact that he would die before ever meeting one of the elusive desert dwellers. Deep down inside he held them in the highest esteem and his children, except for Alyssa, seemed to share that intrigue. Finished with his report, Nyk glanced over at Zada, who began to tell them of the demons.

Zada described the first two levels of demons then took a deep breath and began to speak of the Vox. Nyk listened intently, narrowing his eyes as the words he had been waiting to hear for a long time filled the air.

"Vox are almost as dangerous and frightening as the evil itself," she began. "They were at one time Herkahs, taken by the evil and twisted until they became an almost direct extension of the evil. The Herkahs know how to prevent themselves from becoming a Vox but are on rare occasions caught off guard and taken by the evil. Once the evil manages to acquire one, he treats them with the utmost care because they are so difficult to replace. It will only dispatch them with the most urgent of tasks, and anyone getting into a Vox' way will meet an end no one living can describe."

"How do you protect yourselves from becoming one of these Vox?" asked Danyl, the information Zada gave them keeping the room completely silent.

"Every Herkah has a small dagger dipped in my blood; they will use it to end their life if confronted by a Vox."

"Your blood is an anathema to them?" Mason's deep voice rose from beside the King.

"Evidently." She then added, "That was something we found out rather accidentally. We were missing one of our tribe who happened to return a few days later, apparently well, but there was something odd about him. Allad had taken one of my knives from me when it nicked my hand. When the Vox saw the blood it flinched involuntarily, inspiring Allad to instinctively slash at it. We were stunned as we watched it writhe in pain then die because the wound Allad had inflicted was hardly fatal and could not have caused the agony."

"Is there magic flowing through your veins?" Karolauren stopped writing long enough to ask his question, his messy script an enigma to them all.

"There is something distasteful but what that is I do not know. I wield no arts, historian, but the elves do, which is why we have undertaken this journey."

"What do you mean, Zada?"

"We have fought the Kreetch and the Radir, King Alyxandyr, and shortly before we left we found one of our tribe with his coated knife thrust deep into his chest. The Vox are seeking new recruits and that means the evil is active in the land once more. It searches for the source of power that would allow it to annihilate every living thing in this land."

"Where is this Source and what does it look like?" asked Alyxandyr.

"We don't know the answer to either question; all we know is it is somewhere in the land and the evil has ventured forth to find it."

"Does the evil know what its appearance is?" inquired Styph, the strangeness of their predicament growing with every passing moment.

"No, I don't believe so, or it would already have possession of it."

"You seem to know quite a bit about this evil and its ilk," stated Mason. "Why?"

"The evil, first advisor, originates from the desert and our histories, what little remains of them, tell us it destroyed a city on the edge of the desert about a thousand years ago. We do not know why. The evil has been silent for almost a thousand years even though we have battled its minions over that same expanse of time."

"Kepracarn is silent." The King looked her in the eye. "Could the evil and its subordinates have caused them harm…or worse?"

Zada shrugged, the reasons for Cooper's silence a mystery to her.

They stared at her, her words materializing before them, hovering with the promise of horror and death. The Herkahs had come to Bystyn to offer the elves their swords and to ask the elves to use their magic against the demons. The darkness beginning to swell in the west was going to sweep across the land, and weapons of steel would not be sufficient enough to fight it. The elves' powerful might, long dormant, had to be awakened. They glanced at each other wanting to disbelieve the Herkah yet knowing the nomads would not proceed to Bystyn without a valid reason.

"How much time do you suppose we have before this evil comes to our gates?" asked Styph.

"It will grow in strength but will not venture from the desert until it is time to take possession of what it so desperately covets."

"What if we go to the desert—find and destroy it before it has a chance to become a threat?" suggested the King.

"We barely escaped from the sandstorm, Father," Nyk reminded him. "It apparently can defend itself from such an assault."

The long afternoon shadows chased the light from the city, the darkness sweeping through from east to west. Those gathered within the chamber remained silent, each lost in the words spoken by Nyk and Zada. Alyxandyr gazed down upon his clasped hands, the unbidden vision of a bloodstained sword tightly clenched in them surfacing in his mind. Styph stared out the long window striving to imagine the abominations growing steadily in the west. Karolauren shuffled through his notes, his furrowed white brows forming one continuous line across his forehead. Danyl absently scratched at his arm, his attention repeatedly drawn to the Herkahs seated diagonally across from him.

Zada met his gaze, grinning slightly as she beheld the innocence radiating from his face, his inquisitiveness reminiscent of a little boy peeking around his mother's apron. There was something else, too, but she could not quite pinpoint what that was.

"It is getting late and you have had a long journey," stated Alyxandyr. "We should adjourn and meet again tomorrow."

Danyl headed for Sophie's house, the words sending chills through him despite the warm and comfortable summer evening. He increased his pace, relying on his feet to help him escape their dire significance…for a little while, anyway. Sophie and Anci were out visiting but Ramira sat at the kitchen table reading from one of Anci's books. The shadows obscured him as he watched her labor over the elven script, smiling as she followed each symbol with her index finger. One in particular was difficult for her to decipher, her forefinger remaining poised underneath it for quite some time. He silently slipped up behind her, her concentration so intense she didn't even notice him enter the kitchen. He leaned over her shoulder mere inches from her head and read the word that puzzled her.

"'Shast' means to 'explain something that has no physical substance.'"

"Sweet mercy, Danyl!" she cried out, startled by his appearance, her hand placed flat against her wildly beating heart.

"I didn't mean to intrude or scare you."

She looked up at him, the anxiety making his features appear tense and tired. She poured them both a glass of wine, patiently waiting for him to tell her what was on his mind or to simply sit in silence. After some time he shifted and straddled the bench, studying her face by the flickering lamplight while running his fingers along her soft cheek. Something deep down inside of him came to life, gently urging him to trust this woman, and so he revealed what he had learned at the meeting. He watched her reaction, inwardly pleased that, although the words alarmed her, there was no sign of panic in her eyes.

"What will you do now?" she asked after a few moments.

"We don't know, Ramira."

"And your magic?"

"It slumbers somewhere within these lands," he replied, rubbing at the tension throbbing in his temples. "The first king and his people were all imbued with this power. The farther they ventured from their land of birth, however, the more the magic began to coalesce into only a few individuals. The king retained all of the power by the time they reached the future site of Bystyn, and upon his death it no longer dwelled within any elf. It did surface a few times when we battled other races wielding their own particular arts, but other than that it has been silent."

"When was the last time it was used?" she asked.

"A few hundred years ago Queen Sathra battled the witch Envia from the city of Daimoryia in the east. Envia had almost decimated the dwarf city by the time Queen Sathra and the elven army arrived, yet still had enough magic left to nearly destroy the Queen. Sathra ended up dying from the potent wickedness Envia had exposed her to, but not before defeating the witch. Since then the magic has been silent."

"Perhaps the other power roused it from wherever it went, and maybe that's how it will awaken this time."

"Maybe, but from what Zada said, this evil makes the other confrontations seem insignificant. I remember reading about how potent our power was, but I'm not sure if it is strong enough to defeat this enemy, especially if it manages to acquire this Source."

"Do the Herkahs have any magic?"

"Zada says no but I have a feeling there is something they are not telling us. Nyk told me about this unfocused look in her eyes, one so intense that Allad became very concerned for her."

"An inner eye?"

"Possibly," he replied. "She also mentioned the evil covets Vox, meaning Herkahs taken, then transformed into annihilators that even the evil is wary of."

"You don't believe they are responsible for this evil, do you?"

"No, but they are somehow linked with it."

Ramira looked into his eyes and saw a great deal of concern but not any criticism for the Herkahs. The nomads were as vulnerable to the evil as the elves, but at least the desert dwellers were willing to face it with the Bystynians. She took a sip from her glass and closed her eyes, the ruby colored liquid warming her stomach. Danyl toyed with his glass, his fingers absently turning the stem, his head supported by his other hand. There were dark circles under his eyes and his normally tanned face had lost some of its color. His hand reached behind his neck, rubbing at the tension that had been building up for several days. Ramira got up and sat behind him, leaning into his back, her arms wrapped protectively around his shoulders. He took her hands into his and pressed them against his chest, welcoming the rare contact she offered him.

"You need to rest."

She led him to her room, made him lie down and took off his short boots, the prince fast asleep before she had the second one off his foot. There were many serious tasks he and the others had to contend with and sleep, she surmised, would become a luxury. The moment took her back to the cave months ago after she had pulled him out of death's grasp. She had urged him to sleep then, too, watching over him as she wrestled with her own confusion. Ramira somehow knew she would always watch over him and that was just fine with her. She smiled at him, pushed aside an unruly section of hair then left, closing the door softly behind her.

-4-

Gard had watched the nomads pass by his forest, his bright gray eyes squinting as if he were seeing things. They were heading for Bystyn, the reasons prompting the nomads into making such a journey possibly tied to the oddities occurring in his own land. Game had disappeared from the far western fringes of the forest and the trees and brush there appeared singed and dying. Guards patrolling that area went out but never came back and no trace of their bodies were ever found. Some unknown force kept pushing them farther east until they were driven into the hollows, the unmarked boundary between the forest elves' land and that of the Bystynian elves. The tribe's exodus from the desert did not bode well; their willingness to trek to Bystyn only underscored the unsettling feelings steadily growing in his chest. He exhaled slowly, contemplating his options while scanning the hastily erected camp within the hollows. Makeshift lean-tos and unpacked parcels reminded him of how often they had to flee on a moment's notice. The forest elves' nervous reactions increased every time whatever spooked them into flight skulked from the west, the foul winds preceding the panic the only warning they had. Gard knew the Khadry would end up at the gates of Bystyn before the summer reached its zenith if this retreat continued. He was their leader, a descendant of royalty and unafraid to face any obstacle, but there was nothing he could do to stop what hunted them. He stuck his hands in his pockets, resting one foot on a decaying tree trunk, his other firmly planted on the moss-covered ground. He glanced to his right toward their abandoned lands then to his left where he knew the city stood. A young woman approached him, her strained features adding years to her face as she held out a water skin to him. He reached out and cupped her chin but barely received a wan smile in return. His people were tired of running from something they could not see. Gard didn't like his options. The split between the Khadry and city elves had been bitter and final centuries ago. Bloody skirmishes had erupted over the years, further cementing the mistrust, but that had to change if he were to keep his people safe. The Khadry were a fiercely proud band, but the whispered fears that arose from the strange happenings within their lands gave them only one logical solution. Gard pushed a section of his wild black hair from his forehead, revealing a small mark branded into his skin: a lightening bolt zigzagging through an oak branch. The nomads leaving their lands was a bad omen and if the Herkahs were afraid then so should he. He respected their ability to survive their harsh desert climate and the irksome Kepracarnians seemingly existing solely to bother the nomads. Gard could not imagine what the black ones possessed that would so motivate Cooper to instigate those endless attacks. Had Cooper finally driven them off the desert? Gard didn't think so, but that did not explain the Herkahs' mass departure. He had to find out what was happening and to do so meant going to Bystyn. He chose five companions and rode south and east toward the main road. With any luck they would at the least meet up with an elven patrol and be able to send word to Bystyn requesting a meeting between the elves.

Danyl, Allad, Lance and Ramira reined in their horses beneath a copse of trees and dismounted, stretching their legs and drinking some water as they scanned the area. The patrol they were a part of had left Bystyn to conduct a widespread search just short of the borders. The principal route passing from west to east and back again was little more than a well-worn dirt road with a few old inns and an occasional farm as its only landmarks. Allad, dressed in elven garb, was growing used to the greenery. He commented on more than one occasion about the vast tracts of farmlands that were already bountiful with produce. He told the elves about roots, berries and wild growing vegetables the nomads gathered during the course of the seasons. The precious spices they used were located at only one oasis and the journey to that life-saving place was hazardous even for the hardy tribe. Danyl asked what perils lay concealed within the sands and raised a brow when Allad explained them to him.

"The dunes are not stable, and if you are not careful the sands will suck both horse and rider down so quickly the deed is done before you even realize what is happening. Sand scorpions and snakes are rare but lethal, and the storms that crop up unexpectedly change the shape of the entire desert. We only travel at night in order to use the stars to guide us; to try during the burning heat of day is sheer folly."

"And I thought nothing could survive in the desert," stated the prince with a newfound respect for the Herkahs' ability to persevere. Zada's earlier words about the oases echoed in his mind, too, yet her words were more mystical than Allad's.

"Quite the contrary, Danyl, for although the sands may seem barren, there are areas where things grow, and where there is vegetation, there is life. The scorpions and snakes thrive around the oasis and, ironically, it is there where the greatest danger lies."

"An oasis must be a welcome sight even if there are perils along its perimeter," said Ramira.

"Indeed it is, Ramira, but when you are thirsty or in need of sustenance, the danger is worth the risk."

Lance looked up at the sky toward the northwest and caught Danyl's attention. A long, low line of clouds hugged the horizon. Sheets of rain pouring out from their fat, gray underbellies could be seen even from this distance; lightning streaked randomly throughout them. The leading edge of the wind stirred their hair and tugged at their clothes. Danyl urged them onto their horses, leading them to an inn a couple of miles farther south. They arrived just as the sun relinquished the afternoon to a driving thunderstorm. Two of the guards saw to the horses while the rest entered the inn and made themselves comfortable at a corner table. They could see the innkeeper mentally counting his profits as he approached the table and gave them a hearty welcome. They ordered bowls of stew and mugs of ale, which the innkeeper promptly brought. He placed the bowls in front of his guests, the strange elf's expressionless and cold features compelling the innkeeper to stretch out his arms to serve him. Allad's scars and dark, remorseless gaze clearly stated he did not tolerate such open scrutiny. The innkeeper dropped his gaze and busied himself elsewhere very quickly.

"Is it always this quiet in these parts?" asked Allad, aware of the innkeeper's eyes studying them from across the room.

"There should be more movement along this road but word of the Herkahs on elven lands might have dampened a host of travel plans." Danyl quickly added, "No offense meant."

"None taken."

"It hasn't dampened the innkeeper's mood," remarked Lance.

"We're probably one of the few customers he has gotten in a while," replied the prince, as the innkeeper brought them bread and refilled their glasses. He couldn't scurry away fast enough when he was through.

"We'll undoubtedly make up the difference when we pay for this," stated the captain, cutting the bread into slabs. The captain glanced at the innkeeper, who immediately amended his assessment of the most hard-hearted of those sitting at the table. He absently scratched his left palm while re-estimating the cost of the meals he had served them. A few less pieces of silver wouldn't hurt him any, he abruptly decided.

"Captain Lance's unspoken convictions may leave us with a couple of extra coins jingling in our pouches," Allad stated wryly, chuckling softly. Danyl was about to speak when the door opened, and to his amazement, a half dozen elves dressed in brown walked in from the rain. Danyl's men immediately drew their swords and surrounded the prince, a confused Allad and Ramira following suit. The prince's eyes met a pair of bright gray ones radiating distrust and bitterness. They gathered in information as they studied each member of the group sitting at their table. The innkeeper dropped a glass and backed up against the wall, looking as if his worst nightmare had come to life. Ramira was aware of the tension in the air, every nerve in her body becoming tauter as the seconds ticked by. They were elves like the ones she was with yet the smoldering energy passing between them indicated their dislike for each other. She watched one of the elves stride forward, his upturned hands facing outward to show he was not armed. Danyl gave a quick order, the sounds of swords scraping their scabbards relieving some of the tension in the room. The prince met the other elf in the middle of the room, the unabashed scrutinizing of each other lasting for several long minutes.

"I am Gard, leader of the Khadry. You are Prince Danyl."

"Yes," replied the prince, wondering what the forest elf wanted. He watched the emotions ripple across Gard's weathered features, indecision and displeasure lingering the longest. Danyl invited Gard to join him at a table away from the others, a sudden sinking feeling growing in the pit of his stomach. Both sets of elves watched intently, their hands still on their swords as their leaders moved away from their protection.

"You travel with a Herkah and an outsider," remarked Gard, his eyes looking from Allad to Ramira.

"I don't think my choice of companions is what brought you here," Danyl crisply replied.

"Actually, it is. You see, we observed the nomads heading to your city."

"I'm sure they avoided trespassing upon your lands."

"That they did, but such a trek for those people is highly unusual, don't you think?" Gard was trying to elicit information from Danyl and the prince was beginning to tire of the game.

"What do you want, Gard?"

Gard studied Danyl in silence, attempting to gauge his character and trustworthiness. He had to make a choice whether or not to unburden his problems onto the elf across the table from him for his people's sake. Danyl's patience was wearing thin but the city elf waited for Gard to continue speaking.

"Some strange things have been happening in the forest, and after watching the black-garbed riders heading for your city, I surmised they might be related."

When Danyl asked what these peculiarities were Gard told him.

"What do you want from us?" Zada's words sounded even more sinister now, for the Khadry were experiencing the first ill effects of the evil.

"We are slowly being pushed into the eastern half of the forest and do not expect to be left alone there either, city elf. I want you to know we are there in case there are any unexpected encounters." Danyl understood what Gard was saying and nodded, a brilliant flash of lightning and an immediate rumble of thunder punctuating the dire circumstances of which Gard spoke.

"There is an evil entity that has awakened in the west." Danyl gave him a quick yet ominous review of the situation. "And it threatens all of us, as you can well see for yourself. You and your kin will find sanctuary within the gray walls of Bystyn. That I promise you."

Gard nodded once and stood up, hesitating for a moment before sticking his hand out to the prince. Danyl took it and the two of them shook to the temporary truce that would last at least until the current dilemma had been resolved. The two elves returned to their respective tables, the innkeeper closing his eyes and sliding down with relief into a chair, fervently praying the storm would quickly abate. Profits or not, he wanted his inn to empty out.

Danyl ate his meal, ignoring the others as they engaged in small talk, all the while burning to know what had been discussed. His counterpart grabbed a goblet and sat by himself in front of the fireplace, mulling over what Danyl had revealed. Gard had much to think about, not the least of which was the day they were to face Bystyn's walls. His meeting with the city elf went better than he had anticipated. Gard believed the ill tidings sweeping across the land had already prepared the Bystynian elves for any possibility, including the Khadrys presence. What would transpire once the Khadry knocked on Bystyn's gate was another matter, one he would have to confront in the not-too-distant future, of that he was quite sure. He just hoped Danyl would keep his word.

The storm intensified then drifted away only to be replaced by another one. Thunderstorms this time of year followed each other in succession across the land. The fields depended upon them, and individuals like the innkeeper made most of their wealth when many sought shelter in his inn. This host, however, prayed for them to stop so the two enemies sitting in his dining hall could leave. When Danyl had eaten his fill, he joined the Khadry, much to the consternation of both sides.

"The Herkahs were forced out of their lands for the same reason you now face," said Danyl to Gard, the latter narrowing his eyes at the information the prince shared with him.

"I thought as much," he stated, glancing over at Allad. "It's a bad sign when the nomads are flushed out of the desert, for they do not easily abandon the white sands. Don't tell me Cooper has gotten the upper hand on them?"

"No. We haven't heard a word from him nor have the Herkahs, for that matter."

"We have not spotted any of his raiders…I mean, patrols, either," confessed Gard. The thought of Cooper being quiet and leaving the desert dwellers alone was yet another piece of the puzzle.

"By the way," added Danyl, "I would avoid any sort of confrontation with whatever is lurking in your forest, because as skilled as you are, what hunts you will not be felled by your blades."

"Why are you telling me all of this?" The suspicion was clear in his voice and in his glittering gray eyes. The few words he and Danyl had spoken were more than had been exchanged over the past several generations.

"I don't know, but the problem that may be growing in the west is better met with friend than with foe."

"Are you asking me for help, city elf?" Gard stared hard at Danyl.

"I am saying that you will not be turned away if and when you come to our gates."

"What would your king say to such an unabashed invitation?"

There was a hint of sarcasm in Gard's voice as the remnants of the bitterness between the two elves surfaced but Danyl ignored it. There was no logical reason for him to argue with the Khadry about the deep-seated animosity lingering between them, for he was sure his distrust was as noticeable as Gard's. There was too much at stake here to resort to petty emotions. The King had witnessed the arrival of an entire tribe of Herkahs: would another unexpected group make any difference?

"He would say you are welcome." Danyl left, the Khadry watching him as he walked back to the table.

The weather refused to break as the afternoon turned into evening, and it soon became clear they would have to spend the night. The innkeeper assigned the elves rooms at opposite ends of the building, just in case their reprieve was short lived. The city elves made their way upstairs after dinner, nodding to the guard posted in the hallway outside their rooms. The watch was scheduled to change twice more during the night.

Allad and Danyl sat in front of the fire, the elf telling the nomad about the conversations with the Khadry. Ramira sat in front of the window staring out into the stormy night, the tempest reminding her of the cliffs far to the west by the Broken Plains. She glanced over at Danyl, the friendship developing between him and the Herkah quickly taking root. She liked and respected the nomads; there were no flowery pretenses to their ways. They preferred to remain alone without disturbing anyone but by the same token if they were harassed, the repercussions were swift and deadly. She was relieved they had befriended the elves.

She yawned and stretched then lay down upon the bed, her eyes closing as she listened to the exchange between the elf and the Herkah. Their words soon became indistinguishable then muffled until she heard nothing more. There were no dreams that night and she gladly accepted the rare and peaceful slumber. She awoke briefly during the night and realized she was not alone. Danyl slept beside her but instead of rising and moving away, she placed her hand over his as it lay by his side. His fingers caressed hers, her head rolling against his shoulder as sleep whisked her away.

They rose to a milky dawn and went downstairs to eat. The innkeeper gave both parties heaping plates of food and pots of tea hoping they would fill their bellies and leave. The rains had been relentless, leaving puddles of mud the size of small ponds everywhere.

"I don't think I'll be riding behind anyone," muttered Allad as he surveyed the slushy earth.

Both groups of elves congregated under the porch in front of the inn as they waited for a chance to depart. Danyl walked over to Gard and handed him a letter.

"If you need to get to Bystyn, deliver this to the first patrol you see and it will grant you safe passage into the city. Word will already be spread that you are not to be harmed."

Gard took the message, the resigned expression on his face tinged with bitterness. The Khadry knew time was against them. Allad joined Danyl on the porch as Gard mounted his horse and sped off toward the dark green line of trees off to the north. They stood there for a while before they, too, resumed their journey home.

"The evil is tainting their homes." Allad reined his horse closer to the prince's. "The Kreetch have been busy." Allad absently tugged on his ear thinking how unfortunate and unprepared the Khadry were to be plagued by those nasty fiends. The evil was forcing them into the forest and Kreetch hated being in enclosed places.

"Why? What are they hoping to accomplish?"

"The evil must eat, and the souls of the good are just as easily digestible as those of the bad."

"Can those spirits ever be set free, Allad? I mean, after they have been 'eaten'? Are they still alive while being inhabited by those...things?" Danyl nearly whispered the words, the mere thought of those things inside him making him swallow hard.

"The hosts are, in fact, alive, but it is more merciful to kill them rather than to try and revitalize them. They are never the same afterward, especially if the evil survives. Defeating the evil, young prince, would break the connection, but in the meantime it will consume so many more."

Danyl contemplated on the legendary Herkahs' encamped outside the gates, the Khadry who had asked for help and an ancient evil intent on destroying them all. All of this was precipitated by the emergence of a source of dark power the evil coveted to obliterate all living things from the land. Flesh and blood alone would be unable to fend it off, but the elven magic remained dormant. He glanced over at Ramira, who offered him a slight smile, one that he couldn't help but return. The news they were bringing back only heightened the fact that what was developing in the west was moving toward them at a steady pace.

A vast hall chronicling the lives of the elven rulers stood adjacent to the castle garden. A series of floor to ceiling windows ran the length of the wall; the plants, trees and shrubs were visible beyond the thick panes. The elves sought to bring in the peaceful outdoors, filling the wall space between the windows with well-manicured birches and flowering bushes. Careful pruning kept the ancient birches as supple and delicate as saplings as they guarded the treasures beneath the cathedral ceiling. Mahogany pedestals held a variety of ancient artifacts once owned by the great kings and queens of the past. Weapons, jewelry, and personal items lay upon beds of velvet as if awaiting their long dead masters to pick them up and use them once more. A narrow and thick woven red rug ran the length of the chamber and led to the altars. None of the shrines was larger or more ornate than any other, including the one belonging to the first king of Bystyn. A large tapestry hung on the wall at the end of the hall depicting the elves crossing the land on their way to the future site of Bystyn. The tapestry had been woven by Annal, the first king's queen with great skill and infinite patience, the endeavor needing years to complete.

The foreground consisted of a small knoll covered in sparse brush, the background a line of majestic peaks and a dense forest line located at their feet. A string of shorter mountains tapered off to the left of the picture, the land at their bases lush and plentiful. Danyl knew that land all too well and how very different it was today. The Broken Plains had undergone a cataclysmic change since the elves passed by it a thousand years ago. He shivered slightly then concentrated on the piece; his eyes focused on the elf standing apart from the rest of the travelers who milled around campfires to the right. The image of the dead king looked squarely up at the knoll and right into Danyl's eyes no matter from which direction the prince stood. Alyxandyr's stare was so intense it made the hair on his arms stand up.

The table beneath the tapestry held the King's sword and Annal's silver circlet: simple items for such esteemed people. Their foresight and courage brought the elves untold leagues to their present location where they had thrived ever since. Alyxandyr had never fully revealed the reasoning behind the trek east, but faded references mentioned strife within the elven community he had abandoned. The split between the Bystynian elves and the Khadry could have been rooted in the same conflict then accentuated by the King's decision to alter the method of ruling. He had opted for a monarchy, foregoing the council that had governed the other society. He wondered not for the first time if their kin still lived somewhere far in the west and how different they would now be from them.

He cocked his head to the side remembering what Zada had told him about the evil. The time frame would have put the elves in the area at about that time: Alyxandyr and his people had crossed the Broken Plains just before they were razed. The King had sent back a patrol a year after establishing the city so he was aware of the devastation yet chose to write very little about that in the historical records. A peculiarity considering Alyxandyr kept meticulous records. The prince glanced back to the King and stared so long and hard at him that the branches and brush in the foreground began to fill up his vision. An unseen wind stirred them to life and blew a strand of his hair across his forehead. He heard insects and felt the floor beneath his feet become soft and yielding as the smell of earth drifted up into his nose.

"What are you looking at?"

"A true mystery," stated Karolauren, chuckling at the startled prince.

"Do you know?" he asked, throwing the bemused historian a dark look.

"I've scoured every written word but he never mentions a thing."

"So you think there is something there, too, don't you?"

"Absolutely, now I have some work for you to do if you can spare a few moments," the historian said, then turned and left the hall. Danyl stared at the scene for a few moments more then followed him to the expansive library around the corner from the hall.

Karolauren handed Danyl a list when an attendant arrived and informed him he had a visitor. The prince smiled as Ramira walked in, her jaw dropping as she took in the cases and shelves filled with maps, books and other documents. Danyl introduced her to Karolauren, who nodded then pointed at the inventory in his grasp.

"What a pleasant surprise," said Danyl as he approached her.

"Sophie asked me to give this to you." She passed him a letter, her eyes still scanning the marvels all around her. Danyl unsealed it and stared at the blank sheet of paper, grinning at Sophie's ingenuity. He folded the note and put it into his pocket, making a mental note to thank the meddling woman the next time he visited her.

"Why don't you stay for a while?"

"I'd get in the way," she replied.

"Unlikely, for Karol despises idle hands." He grinned as the historian threw him a crusty look.

"I'll show you around." He motioned for her to follow him, proceeding to give her a quick tour of the maze of information that seemed to go on forever. He pointed out the different sections where everything from birth and death records, yearly harvest tallies and the chronology of the city had been stored. She accompanied him into the far corner of the room where a set of massive oak doors bound with iron hinges and handles stood. He opened the doors with ease, grabbing a couple of lamps before inviting her inside. She walked into the center of the chamber and gasped. It was hard to believe that flesh and blood hands had created the priceless artifacts occupying the shelves. There were busts of people; small jars carved out of pink stone and burnished shields bearing family crests. Chests of oak, maple and cherry wood sporting fine brass hardware gleaming brightly even in the lamplight were stacked along one wall; a folding screen in need of repair leaned against the opposing wall. She spotted an item partially concealed within its bed of velvet and set far from the edge of the counter it sat upon.

She picked up and examined the small perfume bottle fabricated out of pale blue glass, its delicately carved stopper formed into an undulating point. She held it up to the light and swirled its contents then deftly plucked the top free just as the historian walked into the room. The strangled cry of panic stuck in his ancient throat matched the alarm on his face, but she never noticed him. She was overwhelmed with the fragrance emanating from the bottle, the intoxicating combination of spices, incense and essences of exotic flowers taking her far away from the library. She imagined herself along the banks of a far off river beneath a full moon that bathed everything in a silver hue. She could hear a waterfall from somewhere nearby and feel the gentle caress of a satin-soft evening breeze. Anticipation and seduction floated in the air, prompting her to shiver with pleasure as she dabbed a drop behind her ears, closing her eyes and smiling as it warmed her skin. One word came unbidden to her mind: Nephret.

"You could have broken that!" The agitated historian sputtered his disapproval, the string of old elvish words bringing her back to the present.

"It's a perfume bottle...just a slight twist with the stopper." She demonstrated it for him. "I'm sorry...here." She handed it to him, the relief on his face replaced with displeasure. He took the bottle from her, unsure if he should be angry or thank her.

"That girl is your responsibility, boy!" He shot the prince a look of warning then huffed back toward his book-strewn desk.

Danyl shrugged his shoulders when a little stone box situated near the perfume bottle caught his attention. The prince had spent countless hours within this chamber handling every item more times than he could remember but never that particular box. His curiosity got the best of him. He opened the lid and lifted out a delicate bracelet, its clasp broken but still intact, as he held it up for Ramira to see. The little blue beads caught the light and for a brief moment Danyl thought the color deepened until they resembled sapphires.

"Very lovely," she said, taking it from him. The beads felt warm even though they had been within the confines of a stone box in a cool room for a long time. He returned it to the box and slipped it into his pocket, determined to get a better view of the item in the daylight.

The historian was absent when they emerged from the rear of the library, giving Danyl a few moments to examine the piece of jewelry. It was not elven, for the blue glass was foreign and the method used to string the beads along a fine filament of gold was unknown to their craftsmen.

"You seem rather fascinated with that," remarked Ramira as she watched his intent features flow from one emotion to the next. He squinted one moment while trying to bend the end back into shape then grimaced in exasperation the next when the delicate piece took on the consistency of iron. It was not going to comply with his wishes.

"I was just wondering whose skilled hands made it and why it was in one of the first king's boxes."

"Perhaps someone placed it in there to keep it from being lost or further ruined," she suggested.

"Maybe." He searched for a piece of cloth and carefully wrapped the bracelet before placing it in his pocket. *I'll fix you yet!* he thought.

"The historian will undoubtedly be angry," she playfully warned him.

"He won't know, will he?"

"It would be my duty to report any kind of thievery, wouldn't it?" She grinned at him, eliciting a playful pout before he returned his attention to the list. During the ensuing silence her thoughts drifted to the forest elves. Pride, not arrogance marked their demeanor, yet it was their bitterness toward the Bystynians that had impacted her the most. The forest and city elves belonged to the same group once and, in essence, still did. What kind of mistrust had arisen between them to warrant such a reaction?

"How did your father take the news concerning the Khadry?" she asked, unwilling to wallow in the silence any longer.

"He was mildly astonished, but I think recent events told him that was inevitable. If they do end up within the city, the shock the elves received by the Herkahs' presence would surely blunt the commotion the forest elves would bring."

"What will happen if all three peoples were to end up in the city for the winter?"

That thought had not occurred to the prince, since he believed any confrontation from the west would happen prior to the long, cold season. Distrust of each other, limited food supplies and a host of other problems could arise and send the city into chaos. If the conflict were to transpire in the spring while the groups were at odds with each other, the evil would already have won.

"I hadn't thought of that, but it is something we will have to address if need be."

"Well," she stood and faced him, "I must leave. Sophie told me to return before noon so I can take some things to Jack and Ida."

"I'd like to go with you, if you don't mind. I think I've had enough of these walls for a while."

"What about your list?"

"What list?" he asked innocently, sliding the piece of paper in amongst the pile on Karolauren's desk.

Danyl, Ramira and the ever-present Lance rode to the house beneath a brilliant blue sky, the warm sun chasing away the shadows and doubts. Allad spotted them as they passed under the gates and accepted the prince's invitation to join them. They chatted amiably as they rode toward the orchards, avoiding any discussion concerning what lurked in the west. They rounded the lower section of the trees and spotted the house, the couple sitting in the shade of the porch. Jack and Ida eyed the Herkah as they dismounted in front of their home, unsure as to what to expect.

"It's a pleasure to meet you," Allad stated earnestly while extending his hand to first Ida then Jack. Their eyes were wide with astonishment and just a little fear as they hesitantly accepted the nomad's handshake. Allad's friendly grip eased their apprehensions and the couple visibly relaxed before the contact was broken. Ida offered them refreshments and they sat together for a bit, the old couple studying the nomad, the countless stories about the dreaded desert dwellers becoming fainter as the minutes ticked by.

Danyl noticed the barn doors sagging and the ramp leading in had begun to splinter. Much to the dismay of Jack and Ida, their guests headed over to repair them. Ramira and Ida watched as the nomad and the young elves removed their tunics, noting the myriad of scars running all along Allad's back and chest. He had seen, and survived, many battles. The marks marring his lean yet muscular body were a testament to that fact. When and if it came time to fight, it was clear he would not back away from the conflict.

"Kreetch, Danyl," explained Allad, as he saw the prince glancing at his scars. "They tend to leave a lasting impression, don't they?"

"I didn't mean to stare, Allad," said Danyl, but his curiosity got the better of him.

"Allad…when the demons attacked Nyk and his men, you dispatched them to keep their souls from being taken yet you are not affected?"

"The Kreetch despise us more than anything else and find us 'distasteful.' They can and have killed Herkahs, but we are somehow immune to their poison."

"But the Vox…" began the prince.

"The Radir, on the other hand, have the ability to inflict their venom into us, and the Vox are a demon unto themselves. They exist independently of the evil, choosing to tie themselves to it in order to further their own agenda. They can just as easily survive without the evil, understand?"

"So any other creature slashed by Kreetch are not immune to them?" asked Lance.

"None that we know of, Captain." He grunted with effort as the weight of the unhinged doors taxed their strength.

"Is there a way to tell if someone hasn't been overcome by their poison?" asked Danyl, as he removed the metal mounts from the door.

"Don't know," replied the nomad. "If there is, we haven't been able to determine that yet."

"Then why was Nyk spared?" asked Danyl, needing to know the answer.

"Your brother, young elf, wasn't killed because without him we wouldn't be here."

"That was quite a risk. What would happen if he showed any signs of being possessed, Allad?" If Nyk were tainted by the evil, the last place he should be was in the castle where he could wreak havoc, possibly poisoning others with the evil's dark intentions.

"There is a strength that runs through his veins, Danyl, one that would cease to flow if our worst fears came to light." The Herkah spoke diplomatically yet the look in his eyes clearly indicated Nyk's blood would be spilled if there were any doubts.

"You would slay my brother and jeopardize a confrontation with the elves?"

"Son, I would execute anyone if it meant deterring the evil. May I suggest you speak with Nyk...he of all people should at least understand, even if he doesn't agree with our reasoning."

"I think I will, Allad, even though I do not gainsay what you have told me."

"Good, now, let's get to work on these doors."

They worked on through the afternoon repairing more than the doors and the ramp while Ramira helped Ida in the house. She stared out the kitchen window at the elves and the nomad laboring on, a wry smile touching her lips for titles and stations in life meant nothing if you removed yourself from life. Was she separating herself from life because she feared what her past might hold and how it might affect those she cared about? The Herkahs accepted their lot in life even if it meant killing good men defiled by the evil. That did not make them corrupt but pragmatic and, to some extent, honest. The elves, too, lived straightforward lives. Their existence, like the Herkahs, demanded they remain a cohesive unit. Her past was a distant haze, one where bits of memory invaded her dreams. The sun warmed her back, chasing away the nagging doubts preying on her mind. Her gaze strayed over to Danyl guided by the courage dawning in her heart. It would be an easy thing to reach her hand out to him. She glanced down at her hands. There was dirt encrusted under her nails and her palms were slightly rough. She pressed her lips together. There were plenty of splinters and blisters. She crossed her arms over her chest ignoring the emotion that had briefly flared within her. Ramira heard Ida clear her throat and turned around to see the petite woman holding a tray of glasses and a pitcher of tea. She carried the refreshments over to the laborers, carefully masking the thoughts that were too slow to settle in her mind. She placed the tray on a weathered oak table and filled the glasses.

"You do good work," she stated, handing them each a tumbler of cool tea.

"It'll do for now. This whole side is going to need replacing next spring," said Lance.

She refilled their empty glasses, watching the shirtless elves and Herkah discuss the restorations. Danyl and Lance stood on either side of Allad, hands on their hips except when they pointed to the barn. Danyl moved a step closer to the Herkah, his face filled with a quiet admiration. The stoic Lance, too, subtly looked at the nomad with regard. It was hard not to feel that way about the nomad.

Ramira went back into the house to help Ida pack up the items to take to Sophie, like jars of jams, dried spring herbs, and some embroidered cloth. By the time the women had filled the baskets, the others had washed and joined them, their work done for the day. Jack placed a small bundle into Ramira's hand and watched as she unfolded the cloth, smiling at the silver hair clip he had crafted. She held it up and saw a tiny engraved songbird nestled within the boughs of a blooming apple tree. He must have spent hours polishing it, for it shone and sparkled like the joy emanating from her eyes as she kissed him on the cheek in gratitude. They mounted their horses and looked down on the couple.

"We can't thank you enough for your help, especially you, Allad," the old man said.

"I have thoroughly enjoyed the afternoon, Jack, and I hope I will be invited back."

"Wait! I almost forgot!" Ida disappeared into the house then came back out carrying a sack, which she handed to Danyl. He lifted it to his nose and inhaled the scent of the spicy sweets, making his mouth water.

"Those won't make it past the orchards," Jack teased, as the prince plucked out four of the little treats and tossed one to each of his companions.

"Thank you," he said around a mouthful of cake then turned and rode back to the city as the long shadows of late afternoon stretched across the plains.

They entered the city as the sun began to sink, feeling tired yet content at the same time. Allad watched the vermilion orb float over the land then sighed heavily as the gate blocked out the image. They had accomplished much during the day and now the prince and Allad would need to attend to their own duties. Danyl glanced at the expressions on the elves' faces, noting the variety of responses the nomad elicited as they rode by. Their eyes reflected everything from uncertainty to a lingering fear, but the one thing they all shared was respect for the Herkah. It was difficult not to admire him. Allad and his people chipped away at the myths surrounding them in indirect ways, helping where they could, remaining at arm's length where they could not. Their constant presence with the princes also eased some of their apprehensions for if the family trusted them, then so should they. The prince studied the nomads' profile, noticing the proud bearing of his head and the fierce determination in the set of his jaw. The wisdom shining from his black eyes did not come from reading tomes in a comfortable library but from the harsh realities that made up his world. The burning sun, vicious sandstorms and confrontations with the demons were forces he and his people resisted on a daily basis. Nyk had had a brief taste of those conditions and barely survived. Were the elves beginning to realize the nomads' dark demeanor was rooted in their harsh setting? He certainly hoped so. They stopped in front of Sophie's house where Ramira dismounted, grabbed her baskets and wished them a good evening. She expertly caught the cake Danyl tossed to her without dropping a crumb, finishing the treat before she walked the few paces to the front steps. Danyl stared after her for a few seconds before Allad interrupted his thoughts.

"She reminds me of a koro flower."

"What is that?" asked the prince.

"It's a snow-white flower composed of layers upon layers of petals the size of a plate with a scent you would give an entire kingdom for," began Allad. "It's also highly poisonous. Nestled amongst those velvety petals is a single thorn and more than one has pricked their nose on it as they inhaled its perfume."

"Are you saying she is venomous, Allad?" asked Danyl, who failed to see Lance's interest in the conversation.

"I'm simply advising you to find the whereabouts of that thorn, young prince."

Allad had noted the attraction between Danyl and Ramira. She was physically beautiful and her intentions, those he could identify, were honorable yet there was something about her that disturbed him. Her movements were fluid like those of someone who had practiced them so often they were deeply ingrained and carried out without a thought. A subtle and barely perceptible air of danger clung to her: one she subconsciously struggled to contain. She was not an elf nor did she belong to the tribe; Kepracarn was not home, either, which did not leave too many other choices. For the time being she was an enigma to him and, from what he had seen, to herself, as well.

A cloud drifted across the full moon, momentarily concealing its silver light. A hunched figure dragging his withered leg clung to his crooked staff as he made his way beneath the arched entrance. Torches flickering in brackets along the walls cast distorted shadows upon the thick gray stones, their flames discharging bits of smoke. The old man's eyes were focused on the ground, carefully avoiding anything that might trip him. He passed by the guards who looked him over but did not stop him. One of the sentries, however, did call out to him.

"Do you need help, old man?"

"No," he replied, his voice raspy and breathless.

The guard nodded, watching the ancient being shuffle into the city.

The old man turned left, crossing in front of the silent anvils then right into the dim alley between the blacksmith shop and the stables. He halted in the gloom and slowly turned around. Satisfied he hadn't been followed, the old man leaned the staff against the wall and stood erect, the sound of bones cracking and popping echoing hollowly in the side street. He began to tremble then convulse, his ragged cloak swelling as if a mini tempest were raging within it. Then the old man dropped to the ground with a soft thud, leaving behind a hazy figure of a man. He peered into the narrow space between the two buildings then down at the corpse. He opted to toss the rod next to the remains instead. He straightened out his clothing, checking to make sure no one had heard him before vanishing into the night.

Bathed and fed, Danyl retreated to his room and poured himself a glass of wine then sat in front of the fire to catch up on the day's events. A bit of cloth lying on his desk caught his eye; he ignored the messages, concentrating instead on the bracelet. He held it up to the light and for a brief moment thought he saw something swirling within the beads. He rubbed at his eyes then looked again but the results were the same. He used the tip of his knife to try and isolate one of the beads when his hand accidentally slipped, breaking one of them. Before he could curse his awkwardness, a strange thing happened…

He was no longer in his chambers but walking down a side street beneath a full moon, a cool breeze stirring the pure white sand on which he stepped. Thick walls painted silver with the moonlight flanked him while the scent of spices and simmering meat tantalized him from a nearby open window…

The image lasted for no more than a few seconds but he could not figure out why it had appeared to him in the first place. The details had been so sharp his senses had been roused in response to what he had experienced. No. That was impossible. He was just tired, that's all. He looked down and saw the remnants of the bead, the tip of his knife tapping closer and closer to the bracelet. Karolauren wouldn't notice two missing beads, now would he? Danyl shattered another blue sphere.

A small, skinny man with a shaven head and piercing black eyes sat cross-legged across from him. His mahogany-colored skin was clad in a crisp white kilt on which a pile of scrolls rested. He wore an earring in one ear and a broad necklace studded with blue, white and green stones. They were in a courtyard, the sound of splashing water from somewhere behind him and tall, wide leaves hanging from slim trunks provided shelter from the unbearable heat. The man sat as if waiting for him to speak…

Danyl snapped back to his room and put the bracelet down, the visions as alarming as they were exciting. A part of him wanted to keep on breaking the tiny blue globes for the remarkable scenes completely fascinated him. Something stayed his hand, however, as if warning him that all of the images would not be quite so innocent. One more couldn't hurt, could it? Danyl picked up the knife and, after hesitating for a second, brought the point down.

He was leaning on a boulder for support, his legs burning with exertion while gulping in air to fill his heaving lungs. Perspiration poured down his face and into his eyes, forcing him to lift his hands to wipe it away every few seconds while the sun's merciless rays baked the back of his head. Everything became blurry, the dizziness and nausea dropping him to his knees as he sought any amount of remaining strength to get back onto his feet and on his way…

The room slowly materialized around him but that offered no measure of comfort. Whatever he had experienced had felt so incredibly real his own legs, lungs and stomach still reeled with the aftereffects of the vision. What were these beads? If he didn't know better he would say they were almost like repositories for memories, but such a thing could not exist. He quickly wrapped the bracelet in its cloth and placed it in his drawer then refilled his goblet and walked out onto the balcony. He was shocked to see the sun's first rays staining the sky and realized that what he thought had taken only a few moments had actually taken all night. The bracelet beckoned to him from its hiding place, but Danyl had had enough of it and ignored its tempting summons.

Ramira lay wide-awake. Her nightmares crouched on the edge of sleep waiting for her to close her eyes so they could further torment her. She shook her head and got out of bed, denying them the chance to pounce, and was about to go downstairs when she sensed something lurking just beyond the edges of her senses. She grabbed her knives and cautiously moved out into the hallway but heard nothing except Sophie's soft snoring. She could not shake the feeling that someone was inside the house. She slipped downstairs, checking every corner of the house, but found nothing then eased her way onto the terrace and stopped as every hair on her head stood on end. The eerie sensation washed over her and seemed to be everywhere yet nowhere at the same time. It seemed to probe her with cold, dank fingers and was unapologetic for the intrusion, with few parts escaping its contemptuous transgressions. She felt overwhelmed until it suddenly vanished with such abruptness she sank onto her heels as if it had taken her strength with it. The unnerving dreams invading her tired mind were understandable but now she was imaging things while awake. The echoes of that strange sensation lingered on effectively suppressing her desire to go back to bed. She walked into the kitchen, lighting the fire and putting the kettle on the hook just as Sophie came down the stairs. She saw the fatigue in Ramira's face and vowed to do something about her sleeplessness.

"Ramira, why don't you let me brew you some tea to help you sleep?"

"That would be the same thing as throwing me into a pit of snakes and slamming the door closed. No, Sophie, I'd rather be able to waken and escape."

"What kinds of nightmares haunt you?" asked Sophie, as she studied Ramira's withdrawn features. Sophie grimaced inwardly for she knew Ramira was somehow protecting her from their horror by veiling it.

"The kind which torment more with what they aren't saying as much as with what they are." She gave Sophie an "I don't want to discuss it any further" look.

"Why the knives?" she asked, the wicked looking blades stark against the smooth tabletop.

"I thought I heard something downstairs but I was mistaken." She filled two mugs with tea and handed Sophie one. "Apparently, my nighttime delusions are spilling over into the day. Don't worry, Sophie: I won't mistake you or Anci for an intruder."

"I wasn't even thinking that, girl, but I am worried about you," she stated, and touched Ramira's cheek.

Sophie sipped her tea, her mind on Ramira's nightmares and the inky black knives that lay upon the table. She had never seen anything like them before. She squinted and was barely able to make out some mysterious symbols engraved on them but was unable make out what those characters were. The craftsmanship was extraordinary but the daggers did not appear to be for everyday use, leaving Sophie to wonder how Ramira had acquired such enigmatic items. Ramira finished her tea and picked up the daggers, stowing them within her tunic. She offered Sophie a tired smile before heading out into the early morning.

Zada strolled through the fragrant garden, opening her mind to the peace that thrived within it. She smiled because there was much laughter and love floating amid the flowers just as there were tears and sorrow clinging to the leaves. She saw the faint shadows of children hiding around the shrubbery and the silhouettes of lovers holding hands while opening their hearts to one another as they walked upon the flagstones. She felt a sensation touch her, gently propelling her to a corner of the garden where a rosebush with radiant white flowers had been planted. She sat upon the pink granite bench beside it and waited. Soon the ethereal figure of a woman approached her, seating herself on the other end of the bench. She was exceedingly lovely, the kindness radiating from her glowing form made the Herkah's head bow in reverence. Zada's inner sight held no specific powers but it did allow her to sense things from a place she could only go to one time.

There are those of us who have planted the seeds that will hopefully become fruitful when the time comes. We can no longer nurture them like the living. Your presence tells us that so far we have not failed. The road is fraught with the dangers of indecision and doubt, and that is when we will truly see if we have been successful. Remember: things are not always what they seem to be, Zada.

"Who needs to be guided, lady?"

They must make their decisions on their own, Zada, but they must do so armed with as much information as possible.

"What can I do to help?"

You are already helping...

Zada opened her eyes and found herself alone on the bench. She knew whomever the woman was she exuded a sense of power, the kind that caused the sun to shine and the birds to sing. It gave her an immense feeling of comfort to know that those who had passed on long ago continued to watch over those that now lived. The hopes and dreams they had instilled in their scions would survive, but it was now up to the living to carry out that legacy.

The Herkah rose from the stone bench and turned to look up at the façade of the castle, the seat of the elven power. It had managed to exist for a thousand years yet it, like everyone else, was now in jeopardy. She was the leader of the tribe and had gone through extensive and sometimes painful training in order to determine if she was truly worthy of the role, and prevailed through it all. She learned the lore and exercised her mind until it was receptive to what others abhorred and strengthened her body through the art of combat. It was only then that she could walk to the center of the desert to meet her final challenge. There she was tested: every shred of heart, mind and body strained until they were nearly torn asunder by what she had to face in order to become the leader. The scars from the Horii were covered by the silver bracelets, but that could not stop the memory of them burrowing into her skin, their touch setting all of her on fire. She pushed the bracelets back, gazing down at the numerous small slashes crossing her wrists, and remembered what the Horii had done.

She had voluntarily placed her arms out to them, invoking their presence with a series of chants. She had watched with a mixture of dread and horror as the tiny snake-like creatures thrust their black bodies upon her skin. Their razor-sharp teeth sliced their way through flesh and bone as they tunneled deep within her all the way to her soul. They had prodded and cut their way through until they had become one with her spirit where they saw all of her strengths and weaknesses. The pain and agony their presence created were unimaginably intense, but she had been able to release the suffering without so much as a scream. Any thoughts of inadequacy would have been disastrous, and the anguish she had experienced would have paled beside what the Horii would have done to her had she proven unworthy.

She had endured the rite, passed their unyielding scrutiny of her before they slipped back into the sands of the Great White Desert. A harsh and cruel death would come to the imposter, the unprepared, or unsuited, for they simply never returned. The leader was not privy to the origin of the tribe, something she had never been able to understand but had to accept in order to fulfill her duties to the tribe. The Horii had deemed her deserving; her people believed in her and now they had befriended the elves. All would need to depend on her to expose her mind to what they would need to defeat. She, like all the others, could not afford to fail: failure meant a fate worse than death. She exhaled slowly, her eyes returning to the bench beneath the roses. The dead woman seemed to know more about their predicament than she did and expected the living to prevail using more than sword and bow. Those who walked beneath the sun would also need to wield their deep-set convictions and beliefs if they wanted a chance to succeed.

"Zada?" The King quietly called her name. "May I join you?"

"The garden is yours, you needn't ask me for permission."

"The garden might be mine, but the solace you seek within belongs to you," he stated, offering her his arm. She took it, the two of them walking through the garden for a while, the King telling her about his people while Zada listened and learned about the elves. Alyxandyr's voice was filled with passion for his home yet there was a faint hint of sadness in it, too.

"What was your queen's name, Alyxandyr?" she asked, respectfully, waiting for him to answer. She could see just the thought of his queen's name brought back a host of memories.

"Anjya," he replied as if from a distance. "It means 'summer's day' in the old elvish tongue. Strangely enough, she died on a midwinter night." Zada did not wish to further pain him, offering him her quiet presence while the memories flooded back into his heart and mind.

They walked in silence for a little while longer, each lost in thoughts that the garden seemed to evoke. Zada somehow knew the shade by the roses had been Anjya, the dead queen as concerned for her family and friends in death as she had been in life. The fact that the dead were disquieted only added to her anxiety. The evil was sending ripples of horror across the land and apparently the departed were not immune to his foulness. Zada glanced over at the King, noting the lines of worry already adding years to his face. The garden eased some of those furrows but it could not alleviate the danger growing in the west. They left the solitude of the garden, returning to the castle and the unending tasks awaiting them. The memories of the dead would have to wait for a spell or there would be none to remember them.

The blacksmith walked up the steps to his shop and went inside. He took off his tunic, hanging it on the hook while staring out the window. His gaze fell on an odd heap in the alley. He squinted his eyes then gasped, racing out the door as fast as his legs could go. He squatted down next to the corpse and gently pulled the tattered material away from the face.

"Sweet mercy!" he breathed, the old man's open eyes wide with fright.

He tenderly picked the dead man up, his light frame barely making the blacksmith's enormous muscles ripple. He carried the wretched burden out onto the main street, immediately getting the attention of several guards on their way to the gate. They ran over to him.

"What happened, Cryst?"

"I found him in the side street."

"That's the old man who passed me last night. He didn't appear well then and it doesn't surprise me that he passed away."

"He looks terrified," said Cryst, placing the old man down.

"You'd have the same look on your face if you died alone in an alley."

"I'll make a note of this in my report; in the meantime we'll make sure he is taken care of, Cryst."

The blacksmith nodded and headed back to his shop, the old man never far from his thoughts.

On a dreary and dismal evening two weeks later, the Khadry sent Danyl's letter back to Bystyn. The prince, Allad and a few others rode out to meet them. The rain soaked through their cloaks before they reached the intersection in the city, the wind picking up once they left the protection of the high walls. Danyl's dampened spirit was not caused by the weather but rather by the implications of the Khadrys' arrival. The evil had forced them out of their home and that meant the search for the Source was steadily moving east. The power it sought was not in or near the desert, and it suspected it had to somehow make its way to this part of the land. Why not? Everyone else had and it was quite possible it could have been inadvertently picked up, the bearer unaware of its significance. For some strange reason he chuckled over this last thought, for if the Source was some sort of talisman then who wouldn't pick up a lost sword or charm or whatever else that was desirable? Was it nothing more than a fine mist carried away by the wind?

Danyl's blood suddenly ran cold for if the evil was edging eastwards then its minions would certainly be in the forefront of its search. He shuddered as he remembered Allad and Nyk speaking of the Kreetchs' mindless rage and destruction, the only redeeming factors being that the Herkahs were capable of at least fighting these demons.

"There." Lance interrupted his thoughts, pointing to a line of drenched figures waiting for them to approach. They stopped and stood slightly apart from the Khadry, Allad determining if they were demons or not. He nodded then Danyl urged his mount forward and closed the distance between them.

"We meet again under difficult circumstances," Gard greeted the prince, the harshness in his voice directed more at what forced them to Bystyn as opposed to the city elves. Gard glanced south noting the Herkah tents that had sprouted up like black mushrooms before turning his attention back to the prince. The road ahead was more threatening than he had first thought, for the nomads were indeed camping outside the city far from their lands. He wondered who else would seek refuge from the ill wind blowing from the west.

"You are welcome here. What provisions do you need?"

"None, for now. We will be satisfied if we can set up our camp along the edge of the woods on the western side of the walls," stated Gard. The edge of the forest was close enough to the city in case they needed quick access to it, yet far enough away from any confrontations with either the elves or the nomads. Gards demeanor matched the friendless night as he surveyed the area around him.

"Agreed, but I must ask you to come with me for a while to pass on whatever information you have concerning this situation."

Gard assigned duties to his men then joined Danyl for the ride back to the city. Gard glanced around at the impressive fortification but said nothing for although its size and defenses awed him, he was used to the confined openness of the forest. The trees and the canopies were his walls and ceilings and that suited him just fine. The rain forced most of the Bystynian elves to remain indoors but that did not keep the news of the latest visitors from spreading. Faces peered from behind windows, the reception the Herkahs had received warm compared to the severe stares being thrown at the Khadry. Gard did not care what they thought for he had no intention of continuing this alliance with the city elves once this matter was put to rest. If the evil hadn't threatened him and his people, he would not have cared what it did to any of the others in the land. He glanced from left to right as they wound their way up the main avenue absorbing the details of the city. Even he had to admit that the Bystynians had planned the layout very well and had properly maintained it over the centuries. The castle became visible from behind the trees in the park and he could make out the extra guards standing upon the balconies and surrounding the first advisor. The Khadry and Mason locked eyes long before the group halted at the gate, each studying the other with an intensity that was palpable. Gard understood the no-nonsense look in Mason's steely gaze for he, too, wore the same expression. Gard was well aware of Mason's fierce loyalty and staunch support of the elven king but that did not diminish the fact that he was Cooper's brother. To Gard, anyone hailing from Kepracarn was suspect. He had to be careful not to let his suspicion show or allow his feelings to jeopardize this truce.

They dismounted in front of the castle, Danyl urging him to change into some dry clothes before meeting with the king. At first Gard declined the offer, wanting to finish the business at hand as quickly as possible, but he realized the extra few minutes it took to dry off wouldn't really matter. He disliked the soggy clothes clinging to him like a dead man's hands and the additional time would allow him to collect his thoughts. An attendant showed him to a spare room while Danyl waited for him in the hallway. The prince knew his father, brothers, Mason, and Karolauren as well as Zada and Allad would be waiting for them as he led Gard to the main study. The sounds of thunder reverberated across the city, the ominous booms shaking even the mighty gray walls. Introductions were made then those gathered within the chamber waited while Gard filled them in on what had compelled the Khadry to the city gates.

"Danyl, I'm sure, informed you of our previous meeting. The reason for our presence is although we have not noticed any of those demons, there has been something even more sinister happening in the forest. Foul and baneful winds have been blowing ever deeper into our home, leaving the trees and brush singed and withered. A few of my people have been 'touched' by this loathsome thing and the results have been particularly gruesome. Their bodies are found contorted and burned, the agony and shock on their faces hideous to look upon. Whether our coming here only delays the inevitable or not I cannot say, but I will not run and hide, losing more of my people along the way."

"How far into the forest is this wind blowing, Gard?" The King studied the elf noting how tired and frustrated he was, the need to appeal to the city elves not an easy choice to have made.

"It has reached the hollows," he replied, as Karolauren's brows shot skyward. The hollows were halfway through the forest and well past Khadry territory.

"What do the patrols say of the borders south and west?" the King addressed Nyk.

"Most towns and villages have been abandoned and there is still no sign of anyone in Kepracarn. As to the condition of the land, it's hard to say, for that area was never really fertile to begin with."

"Cooper has still not been heard from?" Gard asked, the look of surprise on his face turning into trepidation even though the Khadry despised him and his people. There were rare encounters along the far western edge of the forest but the Kepracarnians learned quickly that it behooved them to avoid the Khadry. Those from Cooper's patrols who foolishly ventured into the woods never saw the light of day again. The distance and lack of fortunes prompted Cooper to avoid the forest and its denizens. Gard, however, preferred to deal with his pesky enemy as opposed to being in the dark about his absence. He could see the same opinion etched on the faces of those gathered in the room.

"No, Gard, and neither have the emissaries I sent to him." The thunderstorm intensified, making it difficult to hear or speak, so the King ended the meeting, promising to hold another one within the next few days. Danyl escorted Gard back out the gates then stopped at the house on the corner for a chance to escape the disconcerting news even if it was only for a little while.

He was drenched and Sophie fussed over him until he dried off and changed, sitting him down in front of the fire with a steaming cup of tea. She noticed his strained features and, as much as she wanted to know what caused the tension, understood that he came here to escape it. Ramira joined them and Sophie smiled, for her appearance seemed to lift some of the worry from his face. Anci lost all interest in her lessons, suggesting they play cards, and as the evening progressed, some of the pressure melted off Danyl's shoulders. The storm lasted for several hours and the prince and Ramira exchanged more than one glance as the memories of the Broken Plains surfaced in their minds. Unlike that time, however, they were safe within the confines of the city and amongst friends. Or were they? Anci yawned and bid them a good night as she headed for bed.

"She cheats as badly as you do," Sophie teased him.

"Me? Cheat? How dare you, woman!" he cried in mock indignation.

"I dare," she emphatically stated, bringing her hands to her hips. "You had more cards lying at your feet than Alyssa has attendants!"

"They slipped out of my hands!" He playfully defended himself, winking at Ramira, who rose and placed another log on the fire before refilling the kettle with water.

"Yes, I'm sure they did," she patronized him with a laugh then wished them a pleasant night.

Ramira cleared off the table, washing the few dishes that remained from the evening. She stared out the window at the rain falling from the inky darkness above, dreading the demons awaiting her upstairs. A few moments later Danyl's reflection filled the window as he came up behind her and encircled her with his arms. His need to momentarily escape his nightmares were as great as her own, and she accepted the embrace. They remained that way for several long minutes, and then she slowly turned and faced him. That peculiar sensation began to arise again, sending ripples of energy from one to the other. The elf slowly closed the distance between them until his lips brushed against hers, the tender kiss filled with emotions neither had ever encountered. It lasted for only a few seconds but that was long enough for them to realize it was futile to fight what strained to be free. Something deep inside both of them responded, but it was more than just their physical nearness that stimulated it. Whatever it was it seemed to shelter them from their own particular demons, allowing the bond to grow unchallenged between them. He rested his face against her neck and smiled with pleasure. He could detect the perfume she had applied in Karolauren's library, its subtle fragrance eliciting a number of thoughts and desires. The latter compelled him to break away for neither of them was prepared to deal with that aspect of their gradually growing relationship.

"It's getting late and I had best be going before someone misinterprets my absence." His fingers lingered on her warm cheek, and his body was reluctant to pull away from hers. He could have stayed this way forever. He kissed the tip of her nose then disappeared into the soggy night, the memory of her touch and perfume accompanying him home.

Ramira stood rooted in place for a while, finding herself completely calm for the very first time. It was as if he had created a barrier around her, protecting her from the nightmares that usually began to prowl at the edges of her mind before she even closed her eyes. She finally blew out the lamps and went upstairs, falling into a deep and restful sleep moments after her head lay on the pillow.

Danyl entered his home and was handed a note by one of the stewards. He nodded to the attendant then walked up the wide staircase to the second floor to his father's rooms, where a guard opened the door for him. The King was sitting at his desk, his fingers against his lips as his son walked in and sat down across from him. Danyl noted how tired his father looked and realized that he probably stayed up well into the night contemplating how to deal with their current dilemma. The King looked into his son's face then exhaled heavily.

"I need you to ride to Evan's Peak, Danyl," began the King. "I think it would be a wise decision for Seven to know what is happening in these parts."

"Have you sent a messenger on ahead already?" asked Danyl, the thought of seeing the dwarves a bright spot even if it was to deliver bad news.

"No. I want this information to come from this house personally. I have offered Allad the opportunity to accompany you and he has accepted. Seems as though he has heard of dwarves and would like to broaden his knowledge concerning this part of the land."

"I can think of no better traveling companion." The nomad would be welcome considering his ability to discern and kill any demons that might have slipped beyond Bystyn. Besides, he greatly admired the hawkish man and wished to further his friendship with him.

"Explain to Seven that it would be wise for him to join us for a while because I would rather have the dwarves here and not be needed rather than have them come too late when they are."

"You anticipate a conflict, don't you, Father?" asked Danyl in tense tones.

"Yes, son, I do. Everything we have so far learned points in that direction and I for one do not intend to sit idly by thinking that it won't. Zada and even Gard are under the same impression because they would not be outside our gates if they thought otherwise."

"When do I leave?"

"Tomorrow morning. Everything has already been prepared for the journey, but do not tarry once you have arrived, Danyl, understand?" The King knew all too well how easy it was to lose oneself within the charming and entertaining hall of the dwarf king where food and drink flowed as freely as the stories and dancing. The carousing usually lasted two days, the recovery period three days after that. Alyxandyr grinned ever so slightly, his son nodding his head in response to his father's unspoken memories. The prince had experienced more than one banquet at Evan's Peak.

"Understood, Father." Danyl embraced him and returned to his own rooms, the journey east already settling into his mind. They would be gone for at least three weeks. With any luck, they would meet up with no one or nothing more sinister than the few roving bands of thieves that inhabited the no-man's land between Bystyn and Evan's Peak. He undressed and slipped into bed thinking that perhaps Ramira would make the trip with him. She could also see the land east of Bystyn and maybe they could further their slowly evolving relationship along the way. He doubted his father would care and Sophie would surely set her free for a while. The problem was convincing Ramira to go; she would undoubtedly feel obligated to stay and not shirk her duties.

"I just won't give you a chance to say 'no,'" he whispered.

-5-

The riders stopped in front of Sophie's home, their horses laden with blankets, provisions and extra weapons for the long journey. Danyl dismounted and walked around to the back of the house already looking forward to the reunion with the dwarves, whom he hadn't seen in a couple of years. He greeted Sophie as he walked in the door but declined the mug of tea she held up to him.

"Can you spare Ramira for a while? We are heading out to see the dwarves," he explained.

"I don't see why not." She noted the restrained excitement on his face then watched it change into something else as Ramira walked into the kitchen. Tenderness and desire filled his eyes for a fleeting moment but he quickly subdued them. "You are up early," she stated, as she took the cup intended for the elf, her eyes narrowing as she began to surmise something was afoot.

"We are on our way to pay Seven a visit and I was wondering if you would like to go with me."

Sophie nodded, but her expression was one of concern, for she knew Danyl was going to the dwarf king to ask for help. That meant things had changed dramatically over the past few days. She began to collect supplies for Ramira but Danyl stopped her.

"Who's Seven? Where are we going?" she asked even when Danyl brought his hand up to still her questions.

"We have enough, Sophie. She needs to bring a few changes of clothes and whatever personal items she'll need. I'll explain along the way."

"Send Seven and Clare our love," Sophie said, as they walked out the door, her mind reeling with many memories of the dwarves. She wanted to go and visit with them but knew Seven and his people were going to grace the city in the near future.

Ramira was ready in no time at all and they were off before the sun lifted its sleepy head over the horizon. They headed east, swinging around the orchards and past Jack and Ida's home heading toward the swiftly flowing

Ahltyn River. They forded it at its lowest point but even there lifted their legs and supplies to keep them from getting wet. They reached the lush meadows on the other side before midmorning, where they stopped and rested. Ramira sat down beside Danyl, questioning him about the dwarves.

"Who is Seven?" she asked as she accepted a slice of bread.

"Seven is the dwarf king living in the foothills of those mountains." He indicated the low line of purplish stains in the east with the tip of his knife. "He and his kin have been our friends and allies for a very long time and what affects one eventually concerns the other."

"What's he like?

"Seven is…well…he must be seen and heard to be appreciated," replied the elf with a lopsided grin and a twinkle in his eyes.

"You're going to ask for his help, aren't you?" she asked quietly, noting the instantaneous disappearance of mirth. She immediately regretted that question, but it was too late to take it back now.

"Yes. Things have progressed far enough to warrant such a request," he responded in a subdued tone of voice.

She didn't need to ask what he was alluding to and nibbled on her food in silence. They resumed their trek east, making camp just before dark. The guards placed along the camp perimeter melted into the shadows, their presence offering them some measure of reassurance.

The evening was chilly so they clustered around the fire while they ate and chatted amongst themselves. The broad canopy of oak, maple and pine trees blocked out most of the stars but here and there one managed to peek through. It glittered in harmony with the sounds of the insects chirping and rasping all around them. Night birds flitted overhead, occasionally calling out to their mates while small animals moved furtively about in the underbrush.

"How will the dwarves react when they see who rides by your side?" asked Allad. He had heard of dwarves but had never seen one.

"Seven will study you from the top of your head to the tips of your toes, maybe poke at you to make sure you are real then offer you some of his homemade poison. His queen, Clare, will undoubtedly reprimand him for being rude then attempt to remove that burning liquid from the table with very limited success!" replied the elf with a laugh.

"There is great love and admiration in your eyes when you speak of them," Allad stated, watching Danyl's face light up as he spoke of the dwarves.

"They are indeed some of the best people in the land, Allad, and I would without hesitation lay my life down for them."

"Your words convey more than you know," said the Herkah, as he smiled at the prince's enthusiasm.

"And you, Ramira? Have you ever met a dwarf?" asked the nomad.

"I don't believe so, Allad," she replied quietly as she enjoyed the lighthearted attitude Danyl sported for his friends. It was beginning to infect her, too. The joy the dwarves derived out of life had taken root in the elves as well. Queen Clare, it seemed, had her hands full with Seven.

"I must warn you that Seven is quite outspoken and boisterous, but his antics and words are meant to entertain and not to offend. And you, Ramira, will be scrutinized as well for Seven…just be prepared," he stated. Ramira knew what he meant and stared into her nearly empty mug.

"We should get some sleep," suggested the nomad as he walked over to his blanket and rolled himself up into it. He was asleep within moments yet Danyl and Ramira knew his senses were as keen now as they had been when he was awake.

She lay down a few feet away from him and pulled the blanket up over her shoulders, trying to envision what the dwarves, especially Seven, looked like. She failed to get a physical impression but the one thing that stood out was he must be a bundle of energy that never tired of doing anything. Somehow that was a comforting image and she fell asleep, the smile on her face lasting well beyond the setting of the moon.

Their routine never varied during the week it took to reach the mountains and, fortunately for them, the weather remained fair. There were easily crossed rivers and streams in this part of the land presenting them with a continuous supply of fresh water. The broad canopy of leaves shaded them from the summer sun beating down from a cloudless blue sky as they traveled on. They met few travelers in these parts because other than a few isolated villages, those that did inhabit the area were outlaws. The thieves preyed on wealthy travelers choosing to keep their distance from patrols and well-armed groups of riders. The prince knew a vast network of tunnels in the mountains to the north was their main outpost. The base's exact location was unknown, for the land around it cleverly concealed the entrances to it. The area they now traveled in was basically a no-man's land. If thieves accosted them in these parts, they would be too far from both Bystyn and Evan's Peak for any assistance. Danyl was looking forward to the protection of the dwarf lands and knew they would be at the border of Seven's realm by late morning on the following day. The reunion would be brief before he placed their dilemma firmly in the king's lap.

"I'm worried I am beginning to like the proximity of the trees too much," Allad said as he sat down beside the prince just beyond the firelight. They had stopped for the night after having endured an unbearably hot day, and all those who sat beneath the cool confines of the trees were soaked with sweat and covered with dust.

"A big change from the vastness of the desert, I'll wager."

"Somewhat. I just think of them as big brown and green dunes that can be walked through instead of over," he said, evoking a quiet laugh from the elf.

"I wish our predicament was as easy to deal with."

"Sometimes things that appear daunting only seem to be because we make them so," Allad said as he glanced over at Ramira. "She furrows her brow too much."

Danyl nodded and told him about her inability to remember her past but left out the part she had had in his rescue. Allad knew there was further truth to the story but did not pursue it. Ramira was beautiful yet peculiar at the same time; he was unable to determine what race she belonged to, leaving the impression she had been created rather than being born. There were elements about her that had not yet surfaced and these characteristics might offer an insight as to her origin. Allad got to his feet and left the prince to his musings as he walked over to his blankets and lay down to rest. Ramira and her blankets had moved closer and closer to Danyl's every night until she slept a scant few inches from him. He smiled to himself. She was overcoming her own doubts and worries and that, he was sure, would only bode well for her, and them, in the future. He felt her hand on his shoulder, the subtle touch as important to him as it was to her, and turned around to face her.

"You'll not find a more comfortable bed than in Seven's house," he whispered to her.

"It isn't so bad out here," she replied in hushed tones, the natural tranquillity flowing from the ground to the sky one of the reasons, she believed, the nightmares had not returned since they left the city.

"The dwarves will spoil you even if we only stay for a few days, and I know you won't speak those words on our return home."

"Perhaps," she answered with a little laugh. He smiled then pushed aside a strand of her hair. Her presence seemed to ease the burden he carried, leaving him feeling grateful for the unintentional gift she gave him. He rolled onto his side and fell fast asleep, Ramira's hand resting on his shoulder.

The sounds of shouting and metal striking metal woke them several hours later. As one, they rolled free from their blankets with swords drawn prepared to confront their attackers who clashed with the sentries just outside the firelight. Danyl signaled for Ramira to stay put as he and the others disappeared into the darkness. The clamor increased immediately as the elves found and repelled their attackers while Ramira kept scanning the area around her for any unfriendly intruders. She didn't have long to wait. Two burly men dressed in mended homespun clothing emerged from the shadows with swords drawn and sneering expressions on their dirty faces. They pulled back their lips and she winced with disgust as the few teeth left in their mouths reminded her of ears of corn after insects had had their fill. They approached, mocking her as she pulled out her blades.

"What are you going to do with those, wench?" growled one of the men.

"Come closer and find out."

"I say we just tie her up and take her along before her friends come back…those who are left, anyway," suggested the other thief, leering.

Ramira waited for them to come within a few feet of her then pounced on one, cutting him down with one motion. A strangled cry of pain and surprise escaped his lips then he fell in a silent heap at her feet, his throat neatly sliced just under his jaw. The other man unsheathed his sword, perhaps hoping that the length of his blade would keep hers at bay. The sounds outside the circle of light lessened, replaced by their loudly pounding hearts. Ramira noted the perspiration trickling down his forehead, but she remained as cool and steady as ever. A sense of preparedness surged through her, her body relaxing and assuming a fighter's stance. She twirled her blades then gripped the black hafts, her eyes never leaving the rugged man clutching his weapon with both hands.

The thief glared back at her then furtively glanced toward the remaining clanging of metal and occasional shouting. The conflict was almost over. Was she worth the risk? He moved his foot and tightened his grip on his hilt, his eyes watchful of the woman who stared at him from a few yards away. To Ramira's relief, she identified several of the voices and knew her companions, not her adversary's, had survived.

"What are you going to do, master thief?" she asked, offering him a chance to retreat.

"I'm going to kill you," he hissed, his sword hacking and slicing as he lunged forward.

Danyl and Lance, followed closely by Allad, rushed toward the horses, the first things that the thieves would try to seize. The thieves learned in a hurry that elven mounts answered only to their masters and the harder the outlaws pulled on their reins the more dangerous they became. One man lay on the ground with half of his skull crushed while another released the bridle of the horse he held, ducking behind a tree to avoid a similar fate. Danyl barked out a sharp order to the horses then raised his sword to deflect an attack from the side as the thieves began their charge. The horses, freed by the intruders, galloped away from the fighting, leaving their riders to defend them. The darkness concealed the fighters' identities, making the possibility of killing one their own a deadly reality. The elves forced the unwilling riffraff out from beneath the obscuring canopy of branches and onto the plains where the moon gave a feeble yet welcome light. Danyl could hear Allad sparring within the woods, his foes resistant to exposing themselves out in the open. He heard an abrupt scream from the general vicinity of the camp and hoped Ramira's throat was not its source, cursing himself for leaving her alone. Her predicament prodded him to finish the business at hand and soon his opponent lay dead. He sprinted back to the camp, Lance felling an outlaw along the way, also expecting to find her crumpled on the ground. The sick feeling that began in his stomach reached upward and gripped his heart, for losing her would be disastrous to him. He broke through the trees and brush, skidding to a halt as he espied a figure squatting beside a body just beyond the firelight. Lance and Allad flanked him, their swords drawn in readiness.

"Stand up slowly and turn around." Danyl's tight voice gripped the area like some giant's hand, unafraid to crush the life out of anyone or anything threatening those he loved. The figure rose obediently, turning as it reached up to pull the hood back from its head where it had fallen while leaning over the corpse. Another body lay several paces away, his eyes staring unseeingly at the embers of the fire, his final bleeding continuing to stain his tunic. The elves and the Herkah breathed a sigh of relief as they beheld Ramira's features, but that release was short lived. The expression on her face was hard and menacing, her knives still dripping blood. Lance narrowed his eyes and Allad contemplated the skill necessary to overcome two men of larger stature and experience. All Danyl could do was stare at her for several long seconds before finding his tongue.

"Are you hurt?" The shock at her unemotional demeanor continued to rattle him, for it was a direct contrast to the caring beauty he had come to know.

"No," she replied, the darkness beginning to ebb from her features. The return of the rest of the group, most suffering nothing more than a few minor cuts, broke the hold the scene had on them. They packed up their belongings and broke camp even though sunrise was still a couple of hours away. They knew those thieves who had managed to escape would return with more of their companions; the outcome of that confrontation, they were sure, would not end as favorably as this one. They rode out onto the plains, more than one pair of eyes glancing at the woman riding in their midst.

Smoke curled up over the treetops about a mile away and Danyl knew they were close to Evan's Peak. A valley opened up in front of them as they passed through the last line of trees, and cradled in an immense crevasse along the mountainside was the city. Its stone buildings, constructed of the surrounding rocks, were nearly indistinguishable from the mountain. Only the open windows gave any indication that they were homes. Gardens seemed to pour down the undulating slopes as the plants clung to the soil; the bright red and deep blue blossoms were visible even from this distance. A deep and wide river, fed by the melting snows to the north, ran along the base of the mountain in front of the city. It swung farther south and branched out into dozens of tributaries stretching out onto the farmlands. There were caves and recesses within the split where the dwarves could seek refuge if the river could not hold back any attackers. It was also where they stored their goods and supplies. A group of dwarves rode toward them but as soon as they recognized the new arrivals, one of them peeled away and sped back to the city. Before the elves covered half the distance to the river, dwarves poured over the two bridges to welcome them.

Allad and Ramira peered from face to face, for the dwarves' enthusiasm at their arrival was almost overwhelming as they shouted greetings and questions. They guided them over the bridge and over to a weathered dwarf with crossed arms and a glowering expression. He shot one look at Ramira, then the Herkah, then focused on Danyl's sheepish countenance. The prince dismounted and walked up to the dwarf, bowing deeply from several steps away.

"Lord King Seven…" he began, but the dwarf rushed forward and picked the elf up, hugging him as if he were a long lost son. The prince heartily returned the embrace, ignoring the auburn braid dancing maniacally along the king's broad back. The dwarves clapped and began to sing, knowing there would be a feast tonight to welcome the elves and their fellow travelers. When the joyous mayhem finally calmed down, Seven invited the riders to join him in his home where his queen, Clare, had already prepared food and refreshments for them. Clare's moss green eyes gazed kindly from her demure face, her light brown braid snaking around her neck, resting on her chest.

"It's good to see you again, boy," Seven boomed as he slapped the elf on the back. "Who'd you bring? Other than the usual dour Lance, I mean." The captain nodded respectfully unmoved by Seven's jab.

"This is Allad of the Herkahs." Danyl introduced him to the nomad who offered him his hand. The King took it after studying the nomad for several long moments. He stared at Allad who had exchanged his Herkah garb for elven clothes, and although the garments fit, they seemed slightly out of place on his body. Black, thought Seven, would have suited the nomad the best.

"Hmm. Not at all what I expected," he stated without any disrespect in his tones.

"It is an honor to meet you, King Seven," Allad said, his piercing black eyes glittering with admiration.

"Please, just call me Seven." He was already scrutinizing the slightly apprehensive woman at the prince's side.

"And Ramira."

"Neither are you," he said, a broad grin spreading across his face. Clare clicked her tongue at him, but she could not stop him from staring at the woman who stood just behind the prince. Seven had tried to imagine what sort of woman he would eventually choose and theorized she would be quite different in every aspect. The creature standing before him was beyond anything he could have imagined.

"I am Clare and you are all most welcome here. If you need anything, ask me, not him," she added, breaking the King's musings with a playful nudge to his side. She noted the torn garments and patches of blood but before she could voice her concerns, the elf presented her with an answer.

"We had a little run-in with some of your neighbors."

"They love your horses, boy. Can't say that I blame them," stated Seven with respect for the steeds. "Are you all accounted for?"

"We were fortunate," replied the elf, glancing at Ramira, who was busy absorbing everything around her.

"Good, now come inside and refresh yourselves," commanded the Queen, as she led them into their home.

The riders washed away the dirt they had accumulated before being ushered into the hall where food and drink covered a long wooden table. Ramira and the nomad craned their necks as they took in the room, feeling lost beneath the ceiling that was actually part of the mountain. Three huge fireplaces lined three of the walls while the fourth disappeared down a long hallway leading to the sleeping quarters. Huge beams led up to the ceiling; the spaces between them occupied by a variety of objects. One section held musical instruments including drums, flutes and stringed devices while another held a rack of spears. The area behind Seven's chair was reserved for a large cask of ale that rested upon a V-shaped cradle. One of the dwarves was busily filling tankards that another dwarf placed on the table. Covering the smooth, hand-hewn stone floors were thick, brightly colored woolen rugs. Blankets and small pillows covered the chairs surrounding the massive wooden table. The table itself was laden with so much food the visitors thought it would surely collapse with the weight. Bowls of fresh fruit, platters of meat and piles of bread and cheese were everywhere. They suddenly realized how hungry they really were. Although they did not go without food during their journey, their meals during the trek had become rather mundane. They had eaten dried meats and slowly hardening bread for nearly a week and looked forward to the sumptuous meal before them. The food stilled their tongues as they ate heartily while listening to Seven and his stories.

"No offense meant to your traveling companions, Danyl, but before you fill my ears with bad news, tell me something good. How is everyone? Is that old bundle of sticks still skittering around the castle? I'd ask about Alyssa and her tricks to find a mate for you but somehow I doubt she'd pick Ramira…no insult meant, girl."

"Seven," Clare growled at him.

"What? I just meant that whomever Alyssa chose, Danyl did not care for and…"

"No offense taken, Seven," Ramira interjected, saving him from a certain tongue lashing by the Queen. More than one voice snickered at Seven, who decided, for the time being anyway, to sit quietly and listen while the elf filled him in on the goings on within the castle.

"Karolauren is as lively and cantankerous as ever and no, Alyssa had no hand in Ramira," replied the prince, who then started to relate the health and gossip of the castle.

"Let the boy eat, Seven! Honestly, Danyl, I don't know where he stores his manners sometimes!" interrupted Clare, as she nodded for another plate of steaming slabs of bread.

"I doubt he would keep them on the table or he would have eaten them long ago," muttered the prince good-naturedly as he sneaked a glance at the king.

"Insulting me in my own house will be countered with being forced to listen to more of my stories," said a smug Seven.

"Sweet mercy, not that!" Clare cried in mock horror, making everyone, including Lance, laugh.

They finished their meal listening to Seven bring them up-to-date on what had transpired at Evan's Peak over the past couple of years. Things had been relatively quiet but those gathered knew their visitors were about to change all of that.

Danyl finished eating first and gave them a brief summary of the past few months. He told them why he had come and he watched their faces cloud over with worry; although the evil had not yet directly affected them, it would eventually alight on their doorstep as well. Seven's personality took on a whole new demeanor and those who had never before met him now understood why he was king. A cold, calculating intelligence shone from within his dark eyes, replacing the merriment that marked their meeting. He scrutinized Allad as the prince recounted what the Herkahs had said to him, the nomad remaining at ease beneath the King's stare. Seven found it a bit peculiar that Danyl made no mention of what Ramira had to do with it all but said nothing. He would eventually reveal that to him as well. When the prince was through, the room remained silent for a long time.

"If you are asking for our support, you know you have that," Seven finally said to him. "But it sounds as though that will only delay, not avert, the problem. Do you have any idea when you expect that dark troop to knock on your door?"

"We really do not know, Seven," confessed the prince. "But we must assume that it will."

"The convergence of the different races upon your city is a hopeful sign, Danyl," added Clare.

"In that we are somewhat heartened," replied the elf. "I fear my father secretly cringes at that notion, for if the evil does battle in front of Bystyn, then many will die and he will feel responsible for their deaths."

"Alyxandyr did not instigate any of this so he shouldn't feel that way," stated the dwarf king, his mind already sorting through the information Danyl had given him.

Seven's eyes glanced at a silent Ramira who sat looking down at her clasped hands while listening to what had been said by those gathered around the table. He could tell she had already heard this news, yet she seemed almost undaunted by it and that somehow intrigued him. She was unafraid of things that should frighten her. The Herkah, too, sat with a determined nonchalance, but then again he and his people had fought these demons before and knew what to expect. How would everyone else react if they were forced to fight those creatures? Seven noted the wearied expressions on his guests' faces and decided they needed to relax for a spell.

"You've had a long journey. Go and rest for a while and I will speak with my kin. We'll meet again later on."

The Queen led them down the hall and opened the door for each of her guests. Clare raised a brow at Ramira as they neared her room, but the prince subtly shook his head. The Queen shrugged her shoulders and led him to the next chamber, a bit wiser about their relationship. She did not know Ramira, but Danyl was not one fooled by mere beauty. He must have seen or sensed something in the girl to be drawn toward her.

Ramira entered the room, shutting the door and immediately heading for the bath. She stripped off her clothes and sighed as she eased her road-weary body into the steaming tub. The hot water soaked away the stiffness of spending too many days upon horseback and too many nights upon the ground. The bath, coupled with the bed, would be a welcome treat. Danyl was right: she would recant her words.

She found the dwarves to be a delight, their effervescence contagious and their love of life a true joy to behold. She surmised when they gathered together this evening there would be little, if any, discussions about the evil. She looked forward to such a night, for hearing the dwarves sing and laugh would chase away the impending shadows from the west. For a few hours, anyway. The water began to cool so she rose and dried herself off before slipping into a set of fresh clothes. Clean and fed, she felt her eyelids droop and decided to lie down for a few moments before heading out to the hall...

She awoke and smiled as Danyl gazed down upon her then glanced past him to the window where the setting sun stained the sky. She had slept much longer than she had anticipated but felt refreshed and ready to undertake anything. She reached over and laced her fingers with his, welcoming his kiss.

"Clare wasn't sure if she should put us in the same room." He smiled as a slight blush blossomed on her cheeks beneath his fingers. "Dinner and entertainment are minutes away and I thought you'd honor me by allowing me to escort you to the hall."

"It is you who would honor me, Danyl." She stood up and combed out her hair, but when she attempted to braid it he put his hands up and stopped her.

She left it loose and took his arm, the pair making their way to the hall under the watchful eyes of those already gathered there. Seven could barely contain his delight and Allad's black eyes absorbed the couple as they sat at the table across from him.

The dwarves began to celebrate old friendships and new ones as music filled the air and food overflowed on plates. Their vim and vigor took the breath away from those that watched and participated. Laughter and song were side dishes from which all took huge helpings.

Danyl saw the glow on Ramira's face and wondered how much more vitality lay hidden within her being. Full of life and unafraid to take on opportunities when they appeared, she represented quite the enigma, one he sought to understand.

"Whatever you do, Ramira, do not drink from the goatskin he will surely pass to you later on," warned Danyl, even though his eyes sparkled with joy.

"What's in it?" she asked.

"I don't think even Seven knows, but it will remove all the air from your lungs and leave you with a terrible headache in the morning."

"Sounds as though you are speaking from experience," she teased, then laughed as he rolled his eyes.

They ate until they thought their stomachs would burst then the dwarves mercifully removed the food and concentrated on the merriment. A group of musicians set up in the middle of the hall, their stringed instruments, low toned drums and high pitched flutes making even the normally reticent Lance tap his fingers to the beat. It wasn't long before Seven grabbed Ramira's hands and dragged her to an open space in the hall. Clare nearly fell off of her chair as Ramira tried to keep time with him, but the King only managed to confuse her. He finally gave up and hauled her over his shoulder, performing the dance while Ramira held on for dear life. He brought her back to the elf who helped a dizzy Ramira find her seat before seeking out his next victim. Allad immediately held up his hands in playful warning for Seven's glance had firmly landed on him. The King shrugged his shoulders, grabbing Clare instead, and the pair danced in perfect unison across the floor.

"Danyl, I think I need some fresh air," she whispered into his ear. "Please stay…I'll be back in a few minutes, but first tell me which door leads outside." He pointed to a door in the far corner. She slipped outside and walked down near the river, the night air steadying her head and her stomach. She had eaten too much, was very tired, and her head still reeled from being spun about by the dwarf king. She inhaled deeply and closed her eyes; grateful Danyl had revealed yet another wonder in the land.

"Are you feeling ill?" a voice spoke from the darkness behind her: it was Clare.

"No, just very warm. The King gave me quite a ride."

"Seven never tires...I should know." She laughed then her attitude became more serious as she studied Ramira by the light of the full moon. She was fascinating, and although she had known the prince since he was a child and somehow surmised he would find a woman completely different from any other, she had never envisioned someone like Ramira. Seven, of course, was thrilled. He thought he'd die before Danyl chose his mate and initially Clare had hushed him, telling him to mind his own business and behave. But he was right. Whether these two recognized it or not, there was something between them, and Clare hoped they would be better because of it.

"It is beautiful here," Ramira said as the cool breeze touched her skin. The full moon ignited the river until it shone liked molten silver and the sounds of crickets and birds instilled a sense of calmness into her being. The energy the dwarves possessed came from the land and it seemed as if the land thrived off the dwarves as well.

"It is home and we like it," agreed Clare. "What's your home like?"

"I'm not sure," replied Ramira quietly. "I can't remember and I don't know why."

"An injury, perhaps?"

"Maybe."

"I didn't mean to temper your enthusiasm," Clare apologized as she heard the sadness in Ramira's voice.

"You haven't, Clare. Besides, I've found more happiness in Bystyn and here to last a lifetime."

"And in Danyl?"

"I don't know what I'll find there."

"Perhaps you'll find what you're missing." The dwarf queen left her alone.

Ramira heard the muffled merriment as the evening breeze carried it from the mountain to where she stood. Was Clare right? Would she find what she was missing in Danyl? She inhaled deeply several more times, letting the cool night air wash over and through her as she stared at the fireflies that flew all around her. They were oblivious to the worries of the world, leaving that dubious chore to those without wings. Danyl was right about this place; it seemed like an isle of paradise in a sea of uncertainty.

Ramira stayed for a little while longer then made her way back into the hall, giving the elf a slight touch of reassurance on his shoulder as she sat down beside him. Seven had resumed his seat and engaged the Herkah in conversation, asking him questions concerning his people, answers Allad was more than willing to give. The two of them began to form a friendship, one that was based on respect and admiration, Danyl subtly nodding at the progress they were making. For all of their differences, the nomad and the dwarf were so very much alike and were discovering that fact with every passing second.

The hall began to empty out as the night progressed until only a handful of people were left; among them Danyl, Ramira, Allad, and the King and Queen. Although it was quite late, those gathered ignored their fatigue and continued to laugh and talk as if it was still early evening.

"Everything was absolutely delicious and delightful," Ramira said as she leaned back into her chair, too full and content to move.

"You caught us off guard so we had to throw all of this together at the last minute." Seven grinned. "Here, try this." He handed her a skin with a spout on it. Both Danyl and Clare lifted a brow in warning but Seven filled their glasses with a small amount of the clear liquid and handed one to everyone at the table. They sipped it, and just as Danyl had described, it took their breath away.

"Good, yes?" laughed Seven, then handed the skin to one of the dwarves as Clare poked him in the ribs.

"Peppermint…" The first sip made her shudder, her face scrunching up as the potent liquid assaulted her mouth and tongue. Ramira smiled after a few minutes, the refreshing aftertaste almost worth the fire it caused as it went down her throat.

"I think there is some of that in there, too," replied Seven.

"I told you the ingredients were a mystery even to him." Danyl teased them both.

"Allad?" The King turned his attention to the nomad, his anticipatory expression eliciting a muffled chuckle from more than one person.

"Refreshing…crisp…not too bad, Seven," replied the Herkah as he held out his glass for more, which thrilled Seven to no end.

"You just made a lifelong friend," muttered Danyl good-naturedly as he sipped from his glass.

"I think we should let them get some rest, Seven." Clare's suggestion was more of an order; the King would keep them up until daybreak. "Escape while you can," she pleasantly told them. They rose hesitantly, not quite wanting to let the evening end, bidding the couple a good night before heading down the hallway to their rooms. Allad nodded to them then entered his chamber, leaving the elf and Ramira alone in front of her door.

"Thank you for inviting me along," she said. "Even under these dire circumstances."

"I figured you'd enjoy it here," he replied, then touched her cheek before disappearing to his own room, the feelings growing within him becoming too powerful for him to control. She watched him for a second then went inside, undressed and slipped into bed, falling asleep almost immediately.

Danyl did the same, but he remained awake for a while, his mind alive with a host of thoughts. They swirled around inside his head, demanding his attention. The demons menaced while the absent Kepracarnians stared hollowly from within shadowy recesses, taunting him with the unknown. The elven magic, too, flitted somewhere just outside of his sight and hearing, daring him to discover its secret: a secret that could help them beat the unseen evil. It took quite some doing but he finally quelled their incessant demands for attention and drifted off to sleep.

He strode through an endless stone corridor where heavy oak doors appeared to his left and right, but when he tried to open them, he found them firmly locked. He looked ahead and realized he would walk forever, so he turned around to go back the way he had come when he realized that that distance was equal to what lay behind him. Was he lost in a maze that was nothing more than a straight line? That was not possible. He cocked his head and listened but heard nothing more than the far-off drip dripping of water. He was underground and therefore there must be a staircase leading back up so, should he continue on or turn back to find it? Was he turning back when he stopped or heading forward? This unknown place confused him, warping his sense of direction, but by that time he had turned around so many times he had lost his bearing altogether, if indeed he had them to begin with. He tried the doors again but they would not yield, and no reference point appeared in this strange hall for him to follow. Frustrated but unafraid, he chose one direction, for he would eventually reach the end of the corridor since everything had a beginning and an end. The question was, which destination would he reach and what would he find? If he came to the end then it was all over, and if he arrived back at the beginning he would be right back where he started. Simple, but that did not explain why he was within this labyrinth to begin with.

He headed in a direction, trying the doors as he passed, straining his senses for any sound, but no clues existed in this place. It slowly dawned on him his senses had no place within these vaulted walls and that he would have to rely on something else that could penetrate the semi-darkness around him. What that could be was a mystery. The stone corridor irked him with its secretiveness, and that only increased his determination to find his way out of the maze consisting of a straight line.

Danyl awoke, the labyrinth still fresh in his mind, as he swung his legs over the side of the bed, stretching and yawning while trying to make sense of the dream. The oak doors had no keyholes yet he had been unable to push them open. What secrets did they hold that he was not privy to? He shook his head hoping to dislodge the dream as he walked to the hall where food and drink had magically appeared on the table. He was still full from the previous evening but did help himself to a mug of tea, which he carried out onto the wide stone steps leading down from the city. He smiled as he watched the dwarves already involved in their daily chores, their enthusiasm now focused on the work at hand. He looked over his shoulder and nodded a greeting to Allad, who also carried nothing more than a cup of tea.

"It is good to share the land with such people," he remarked, scanning the scene around him. "It makes fighting the evil so much more important."

"Yes, I agree, Allad."

So many good people and so many of them will die; Allad kept his thoughts to himself, although one look at the trepidation on the elf's face told him he thought the same thing. They had been gone from Bystyn for more than a week now and by the time they returned nearly three would have passed. What, if anything, was happening not just there but everywhere else? Had the evil pinpointed the Source yet? Hopefully not. Of all the trials and anguish they were going to endure, it was the inability of the evil to find the Source that gave them any measure of hope.

"Danyl…the elven magic…how is it used?"

"Well." The question took him off guard for a moment until the elf remembered Karolauren's teachings. "It somehow manifests itself into a suitable bearer and he or she wields it…or so we think."

"Would not such a powerful transformation be too devastating to someone composed of just flesh and blood? Would this transfer not destroy the bearer?"

Danyl never thought of it quite in that way, for the original elves had each carried a part of the magic with them until it all flowed into the first king. Allad had a point, though. The shock of such a sudden transfer might be too much. Other than it manifesting itself into a talisman, how else would the power arise? He was about to respond when Ramira joined them, sipping from her mug in the glorious morning.

"You look well rested," Danyl said to her.

"It was that clear liquid, I think," she said and chuckled. "No headache, though."

"You didn't have enough."

"Yes, I did," she corrected him.

"Seven!" Danyl loudly greeted the obviously ailing king as he shuffled over to them, his hand rubbing his aching head. He threw the elf a sour look as the prince made as much commotion as possible.

"Clare 'suggested' I give you a tour." The others laughed for they knew it was Clare's way of teaching him a lesson when it came to overindulging. The King had had more than his share of food and drink last night and the cask that rested behind his chair had coughed up the last of its ale when they had gone to bed. The King motioned toward the stables, accepting the cup Danyl thrust at him and swallowing the strong liquid in one gulp, then finished what was left in Ramira's mug. By the time the horses were brought around he seemed to have regained some of his old spark.

Lance held the reins as the riders mounted the animals, following Seven as he headed out over the main bridge, then turning left toward the farmlands. The area stretched south and east, its flat terrain and numerous streams ending in the far distance. Once clear of the mountains they could see a blurry line of trees far to the east and behind them a low, rolling series of hills. The day was warm and sunny with few clouds to mar the beautiful blue sky or the great birds of prey floating upon the winds. Danyl glanced westward contemplating what might be occurring in Bystyn, his features reflecting the slight anxiety touching his mind. He felt a gentle touch on his arm and looked over to find Ramira giving him a little smile of encouragement and subtly nodded in reply. Seven held up his hand and they reined in their mounts, stopping on the plains a few miles from the end of the range.

"More of our land is in the north and ends where that river flows," he explained, as he pointed to a silver ribbon running up from the south. It was one of the last tributaries of the Ahltyn River and seemed to disappear as it wound its way to the northeast. A section of the river meandered north, hugging the base of the mountains as it flowed. Seven told them the river was deep everywhere and the loop that ran north provided the dwarves with a natural line of defense. It was incredibly swift and wild and efficiently cut off any attempt at an attack from that direction.

"I didn't realize that the river ran so far east." Ramira shaded her eyes in order to follow its meandering form.

"It ends not too far from here," added Danyl. "Right along the border of the wild people living within the outskirts of the trees you can barely see."

"That bothersome ilk likes to raid us on occasion, and we will have to keep an eye out for them," said Seven, the dark undertones in his voice not lost on his companions.

"With any luck we won't run into any," said Lance, as he carefully scanned the area with his keen eyes.

The five rode for about an hour, swinging up alongside the mountain when a group of riders appeared off in the distance. Seven spat on the ground and watched as the horses headed straight in their direction. They somehow doubted they charged at them to exchange pleasantries.

"Barbarians." He spat on the ground again and gauged the distance back to the city then realized they were going to have to fight. "Seems like we'll get a bit of exercise this morning."

He withdrew his sword and waited, knowing full well Clare was going to give him an earful about riding so far without the proper guards in attendance. In truth he worried more about that than the unruly group racing toward them.

Ramira couldn't help but smirk, for the King apparently enjoyed these confrontations. He calmly sat on his horse checking the edge on his blade, looking up at the riders every once in a while. This time, however, he recognized who led the barbarians toward them. He shot a glance over at Ramira as if he were worried for her safety, but one look at the intensity her face radiated and his concern disappeared.

"Rock lords," he quickly explained. "We should have gone back."

As the distance between them diminished, they could see the tall and highly muscular men with short-cropped hair barreling on at a full gallop. Their bare chests were marked with swirling black emblems, their upper arms bearing bands of gold. Animal hides used as blankets flapped around their legs as they sped on and, as one, drew weapons that glinted menacingly in the morning sun. Their features seemed to stretch wide across their faces and appeared almost deranged as they prepared to fight.

They nearly crashed into the small party, their fierce eyes glancing at Ramira many times as their swords clashed. They quickly managed to isolate her, much to the dismay of her companions, but the rock lord that had forced her off her horse was about to receive the surprise of his life, as were the others. He smiled, already anticipating having his way with her, when she unsheathed her knives and assumed a combative stance. He laughed at her then withdrew his own short swords more to mock her than to actually fight, but Ramira had other ideas. The lord feinted to her right, yet she did not move, then he slashed a little closer from the other direction with the same results. Danyl and the others tried to make their way over to her but the other rock lords kept them at bay. She was on her own for a little while. Danyl and the others were about to witness how she had defeated the two outlaws the previous night.

The lord was no longer amused and charged at her, swinging his blades up from underneath, but she deftly sidestepped him, blocking his strikes with her black blades. He growled at her then proceeded to push her back. His knives moved so quickly they were hard to distinguish from one another, but Ramira's blades warded them off with ease. She was much smaller than the brawny lord was, but the expert training she had apparently received allowed her to keep pace with his attacks. The lord rushed forward trying to crush her with his strength, grinning as she tripped over a rock and fell flat on her back. He pounced on her, slashing into her midsection, but she rolled to the side and managed to get up on her feet before he regained his balance. He tired of the game and he hated her for making him look ineffectual in front of not only his men but his enemies as well. He attacked her with a renewed fury. Ramira knew death would come to one of them and she vowed it wouldn't be her. She braced herself and waited for the lord to come to her, and she did not have long to wait. He lunged at her with all his might, slicing and cutting her flesh as he bore down on her. She evaded his assault but began to tire and knew that if she did not act now it would be over. She pretended to twist to one side, and as he fell for the ploy, she rotated the other way, where her knives found his throat. Surprise, shock and anger were the last emotions on his face as he grabbed at his windpipe then dropped to his knees, falling forward into a lifeless heap. Her head snapped up as one of the rock lords lifted his sword over the back of Lance's head. She let fly one of the blades, watching as it buried itself up to the haft in his chest. The captain nodded his thanks then turned to take on a new opponent.

Her weapons and technique awed Allad, for they were very similar to his, as he dispatched two of the rock lords and severely wounded two more. A quick glance to see how his comrades fared told him that they, too, had noted her fighting capabilities. They could hear hooves in the distance and knew help was on the way, but the lords pressed on, determined to fight until the last possible moment before being forced away. Ramira was about to be challenged by another lord when he and his men decided they had had enough and rode away, leaving their dead but taking their horses with them.

"Any serious injuries?" bellowed the King as he watched the rock lords disappearing behind clouds of dust their horses kicked up.

"Nothing a suture or two won't fix," replied Danyl, as he spread the rips in his tunic to estimate the depth of several cuts he had received.

The prince glanced over at her, noting the same dark look upon her face he had seen after the battle with the outlaws. This side of her personality confused more than alarmed him, but did nothing to dampen his feelings toward her.

"Ramira?" he asked as he went over to her, admiration for her capabilities shining clearly from his eyes.

"The same," she replied quietly. Her eyes stared at the blades as if she couldn't believe how well she had handled them, then down at the lifeless man at her feet.

Allad stared at her, his thoughts hidden as he renewed his perceptions of this odd woman. She bore elements of Herkah training and mannerisms yet had fought more like an assassin rather than a fighter. *Your traits are slowly coming to the surface, Ramira.*

The tour was over and they rode back to the city, word of their confrontation already in Clare's ears as they entered the hall.

"Honestly, Seven, you should have known better than to ride so close to their lands," she chastised him. "You are all lucky it was a small party of rock lords or you'd be dead or taken prisoner!"

"Well we aren't," he grumbled, although he was inwardly quite pleased with himself. "You and Allad were quite impressive, Ramira."

"I'm curious to know what master taught you how to use those knives...may I see them?" Allad held out his hands. Ramira unsheathed them and handed them over, wincing as Clare began to sew her cuts. He marveled at the craftsmanship and the fact that there wasn't one nick or scratch on them. He stared at the jet-black surface but was unable to determine what metal it had been forged from nor could he decipher the picture-like images etched into the blades. The images seemed to move and shift as he held them up and slowly turned them around in the light. They felt heavy in his hands, giving him an eerie sensation they didn't want him to touch them. This perception sent a shiver up his spine, urging him to give them back while something warned him never to touch them again.

"I'm not sure but I am grateful to whomever trained me."

"So you should be," added Seven. He had watched both Allad and Ramira wield their weapons with an almost refined cunning. Each precise stroke not only blocked their opponent but also had dictated how the lords would fight. In the end, the expert swordsmen fought like novices by comparison.

"What of the rock lords, Seven? Are they always so aggressive?" asked Allad.

"Ah, skirmishes between us are normal. They are an ill-natured, ill-tempered bunch whose only pleasure in life comes from fighting. The lord Ramira killed was Dross, and I'm sure his father will be beside himself when he finds out a woman got him." Seven chuckled as he imagined the old man spitting and foaming at the mouth at the indignity of a woman besting any lord, especially his son.

"Will they retaliate?"

"Absolutely, Allad. I can't wait, either."

Clare suggested they clean up and rest for a while, stating the medicines she gave them would make them sleepy. They agreed and returned to their rooms, already becoming drowsy as they lay down upon their beds.

Ramira closed her eyes but sleep would not come so easily. Her mind concentrated on the moves and techniques she used during the conflict. She forcefully slowed down her movements until they moved a mere fraction of a second at a time.

He reached around her, grabbing her wrists, but she knew she was not being attacked. A pair of large hands attached to deeply tanned and muscular arms guided her. The hands turned her wrists, the fingers pushing and twisting her hands to increase her flexibility and hold on the wooden knives she practiced with. She focused on the images of the snakes tattooed between the finger and thumbs on both hands and swore the creatures moved. Their exposed fangs dripped venom and their hooded heads undulated back and forth. She felt a tall and powerful presence behind her, watching as his hands conducted her arms so she could cross the blades under and over her arms without slashing herself. The movement was awkward and slow at first then, as her timing and confidence increased, the blades whirled and bisected each other at an amazing speed. She was shocked at her ability, and her momentary hesitation was enough to break the rhythm, causing her to lose control of the knives. She managed to cut herself; one incision drew blood on her upper right shoulder while the other sliced away a few layers of skin on her left thigh. She felt the presence move away from her as if the lesson was over.

Ramira bolted upright and ran over to the lamp on the table, pulling her tunic down over her shoulder where she spotted the faintest of scars. She excitedly checked her thigh and saw another faded mark. She acquired the scars during her unknown past by someone with tattooed hands that had taken a great deal of time to train her. For what exact purpose she might never know, yet the training had served her well. She silently thanked the unseen man and lay back down on the bed. Her fingers absently traced the long-ago-acquired scar on her shoulder as if it would reveal more of her past life. It didn't, but that did not discourage her from trying to remember more. How many other unforeseen circumstances would release another of her memories? The probability of that occurring both frightened and thrilled her as she slowly closed her eyes and drifted off to sleep.

Zada walked onto the balcony and looked up at the moon, its silver face calmly gazing down upon her while stars glittered overhead. The night was warm and she inhaled the fragrances lifting upward from the dark garden below, the redolence washing over her in delightful waves. She sighed, closed her eyes and relaxed her mind, opening herself up to the unseen realm. There was nothing for a long time and just as she was about to close off that part of her, she sensed a far off stirring. She tried to focus on it but it remained elusive, evading her attempts but never quite disappearing either as if it found her interesting. The standoff continued for some time, but the effort drained the Herkah's energy, forcing her to break the contact. She turned to return to the room when Bystyn disappeared...

She found herself in the middle of the desert standing upon the crumbling platform where she had endured the Horii. The broken columns that stood on each corner of the square dais rose to their full height, the spectacular images carved into them alive with color. Brilliant banners attached up above snapped in the wind, their elongated forms ending in silk tassels. Clay bowls filled with incense, fresh fruit, flowers and precious spices lined the areas between the columns and in the center stood an elegant basin filled with water. This is what it had originally looked like all those years ago. It had been a place of offering to who or what she could not guess. She felt the sun beating down on her and the dry breeze drifting across the endless white sands but nothing else. Then she noticed the changes around her, subtle at first like the wind becoming colder and the darkening sky. The ground began to rumble, becoming louder and more violent until one by one the clay bowls exploded, sending their contents in every direction. Fear began to gnaw at her but until the vision passed she could do nothing but endure what was happening.

The columns began to crack and topple with all but one falling into the sands. The last one fell across the middle of the dais, shattering the basin and fracturing the platform as the now black sky erupted in vivid flashes of lightning and bone-shattering thunder. Zada wanted to scream but the angry sand swirled and filled her nose and mouth until she thought she would suffocate before the trance was over. The wind tore at her garments and pummeled her with sand, the grains biting into her flesh like a thousand fire ants. The shrieking sound increased, forcing her to cover her ears and block out the maniacal sound. She begged for the vision to be over then, mercifully, it was...

Zada gulped in huge draughts of air as she picked herself off of the balcony floor. She had had potent visions before but never one so real, never one that tried to kill her. She tried to fathom why she had been shown its destruction. The storm that had destroyed the platform was eerily reminiscent of the one that had driven them off the desert and to the elven city. Had she glimpsed their future? Would the same tempest bear down on Bystyn? The Horii still existed beneath the dais, continuing to choose the leaders of the tribe as they had for a thousand years. They were able to withstand the assault then, but if the evil acquired the Source, would they still survive? Did that far-off stirring have anything to do with her vision or was its presence merely coincidental? The sensation she had felt prior to the vision did not feel evil yet the image went from serene to violent to the point of nearly killing her. If it were a message from whatever had chosen her to lead her people, it was a frightening one at that. She shivered, suddenly feeling the need for Allad's arms around her. Regardless of what prompted the image, she was sure it was an omen.

The time for merriment and exploration was over. The dwarves, elves, and Allad gathered in the main room to make plans against the evil. Ramira stayed for a while then left, heading out into the sunshine and fresh air, following the edge of the mountain as it wound its way northward. It ran in a relatively straight line for miles until it curved westward, running past Bystyn and over to the Broken Plains. The sheer vastness of the range nearly overwhelmed her. She imagined the mountains had been thrust up from the earth to keep mere mortals from finding out what dwelled on the other side...or was it the other way around? She shivered and decided to concentrate on more pleasant things, glancing instead up the side of Evan's Peak softened by the sun's warm rays. Faces peered down at her from rectangular windows carved out of the mountain. The dwarves had hollowed out the outer section of the mountain where a network of tunnels connected the various homes and halls. The openings along the highest points were for the sentries who could see for many miles in three directions. There were observation posts on the other side of the mountain, too, in case the rock lords and their bad intentions planned to visit.

She found a shady spot beneath a cluster of oak trees near the river and sat down, removing her boots to dip her feet in the cool water. She moved too quickly, wincing with pain and fearing she had torn one of the stitches. She lifted her tunic, moved the bandage and sighed with relief. She would have hated to have to endure another round with the needle and thread. She lay back, placing her arms under her head, and gazed up through the green canopy overhead. She caught sight of a squirrel that seemed to be studying her with its unblinking eyes, its tail flicking back and forth. It scrambled over to another branch, evicting a bird that scolded it from its new perch. The scene made her laugh quietly even after the bird flew away and the squirrel had clambered over to an adjoining tree and out of sight. She felt truly relaxed and leaned over to splash some water on her face, the cool moisture dripping down her neck as she gazed off into the distance. Somewhere out there was the key to her past and she hoped it was not as awful as her nightmares indicated. There had to have been an equal measure of good in her life since even the worst person had a modicum of decency somewhere in their make-up.

She looked down at her folded hands, which had given her a glimpse into her past. They had not forgotten how to wield the knives nor had her body forgotten the stances and reflexes the faceless man had taught her. What other incident would arise that would further prod her memory out of the darkness? She dabbed at her cuts and hoped it wouldn't take another injury to find out. She watched as a figure approached. Danyl made his way toward her and that meant the meeting was over.

He greeted her with a smile and sat down on the grass beside her, pulling off his boots and placing his feet into the refreshing water. He leaned back on his elbows, staring pensively ahead, occasionally knotting his brows.

"We'll be leaving tomorrow," he began, the need to leave and return home versus the desire to stay amongst friends pulling against each other in his heart. His father's words of not tarrying reminded him of all they still had to face.

"I'm going to miss this place," she stated as she reached over and slipped her hand into his. He appreciated her gentle touch then repositioned himself so she could lean up against his chest. The two of them sat in silence for a while, each lost in their own thoughts, neither one noticing the sun's descent in the west. They were content just to share the physical contact, a connection allowing the strength of one to flow into the other without either one realizing it.

"Clare and a handful of dwarves will accompany us back to Bystyn," he stated after a long silence, his fingers absently twirling a silken strand of her hair. "Seven and the rest will follow in a few days. He wants to make sure there are enough people left to confront the rock lords when they come back to seek retribution for their slain kin."

"Perhaps I should just have injured him."

"That would not have been an option, Ramira, and you know it," he chastised. Dross wanted nothing less than for her blood to stain his sword.

"I know, Danyl, but I did not come here with the intent of making the dwarves' situation worse."

"It already was, besides, you did Seven and the others a great favor by getting rid of him. The others will come once or twice to show the dwarves they aren't afraid but that will pass."

"Why do they fight them?" she asked.

"The rock lords take great pleasure in combat."

"That's it?"

"Well, that and the spoils they acquire after they have bested their foe."

"What do their homes look like?" she asked out of interest. A people who lived to kill brought to mind a very Spartan existence with few liberties.

"They live in mud brick houses nearly indistinguishable from their surroundings filled with the fruits of their plundering. I've heard their homes are an odd collection of things taken from a variety of people including furniture, fabrics and wares. They prefer the metals—the gold, silver, and bronze items, some of which they melt down and fashion into really marvelous pieces of jewelry. They don't have too much use for the gems, though: they pry them off and toss them into the waterways surrounding their land. The gemstones occasionally wash up along the riverbanks where the dwarves put them to good use. Their hospitality leaves a lot to be desired as you may have deduced for yourself."

She nodded then changed the subject, for she had learned enough about the rock lords for one day.

"Why is the city called Evan's Peak, Danyl?" She had been curious about the name from the moment she had heard it. She could feel him take a long, deep breath before speaking, and then listened to him explain the origin of the city's name.

"Evan was a great warrior who lived a long time ago, even before the elves established Bystyn. He found out that Earl, his king and closest friend, was secretly making deals with their enemies, the treachery resulting in the deaths of many good people. It fell to Evan, the highest-ranking warrior, to rectify the dilemma. He tried to reason with the King and nearly lost his life for doing so, leaving him no option but to slay Earl and the few who followed him. The deed was for the greater good of the dwarves, but Evan could never come to grips with what he deemed to be an equal breach of faith. The dwarves wanted him to rule but Evan abhorred that thought, for the blood of his lifelong friend had stained more than just his hands. His guilt first destroyed his confidence then his heart until one day he climbed to the top of that mountain," he pointed to the peak directly over the main entrance, "and jumped to his death."

"How very sad," she said softly, almost reverently as the pain and misery that must have infused itself into Evan reached out to her even after all those centuries.

"And 'Bystyn' means 'dawn' in the elven tongue; the spot it would be built on was first seen by the rays of the morning light," he said, anticipating her next question. She lowered her head and thought about both cities, their names reflecting the hopes of their respective people. Evan killed his own king in order for the dwarves to survive; Alyxandyr's folk followed him into unknown lands to start anew. Perhaps the bad things that happened in the past served to further cement the determination for the future, the lessons they provided an effectual deterrent against repeating the same mistakes.

"Thank you for bringing me along."

"I'm glad you came," he replied, hugging her tenderly. He caressed her neck with the side of his face, the softness of her skin and the lingering perfume arousing his senses.

"I wish I could take you to a place as special as this."

"You can." He felt her shift in his arms and regretted those two little words the moment they left his lips. She was readying to bolt from him and all he could do was reluctantly move his arms back. To his surprise, she twisted around to face him, awkwardly bracing herself to keep her weight off of him. He held his breath ignoring the sinking feeling in his stomach while her beautiful amethyst eyes studied his features.

"I can't take you to a place I've never been to," she quietly admitted.

"I didn't mean…" She silenced him with a kiss.

"Yes, you did," she whispered, relaxing her body until it rested against his.

"Yes, I did." He held her tightly, grateful he wasn't watching her retreat back to the hall.

He felt a slight chill in the air and realized they had been sitting under the oaks for quite some time. He nudged her and the two of them walked back to the main entrance hand in hand. They entered the hall, passing by the table piled high with food and drink. Two dwarves struggled with a cask of ale, the unwieldy barrel stubbornly refusing to roll in the right direction.

"Don't let Seven see you!" Danyl good-naturedly teased them then went over to help. Ramira laughed at the trio as they finally managed to gain control over the keg and lift it up onto the cradle behind the King's seat. Danyl winked at the red-faced dwarves then offered his arm to Ramira. Together they trod down the hall and to their respective rooms.

They freshened up and joined their companions for the evening meal, a sumptuous feast where everything from roast duck to fresh berries in cream-filled bowls on the table. They were so full afterward that even Seven was unable to leave the table to dance. They decided to sit and listen to the musicians playing while enjoying their last night together. At least until all the dwarves could converge upon Bystyn and spread their mirth there.

"I hope your brief stay here was satisfactory," Seven said to them as he lit up his pipe, the smell of the tobacco filling the room with a woodsy aroma.

"Your kindness and hospitality could not have been better, thank you," replied Ramira.

"Indeed it has, Seven," Allad said as he patted his protruding midsection. "Zada will undoubtedly repay your kindness, but I doubt she'll so much as throw me a crumb until I lose this!" They laughed. All of them would carry the dwarves' generosity back to Bystyn with them.

Seven insisted they drink to the coming trek and glasses sprouted up in front of all who sat at the table, glasses that were soon filled with Seven's elixir. Clare said nothing; the only thing worse than waking up with a headache from the liquid was to ride while its aftereffects still coursed through the veins. She knew the elves would be careful and watched as Danyl warned both Allad and Ramira to restrain from overindulging, or the ride back would be most unpleasant.

"When you come back to visit, we'll show you what a real dwarf banquet is like," chuckled the King.

"What do you call what we've been eating over the past few days?" asked Allad, who rubbed his stomach.

"Those weren't proper meals, my friend. No, hardly worthy of guests at all!" cracked Seven.

"Seven firmly believes that a 'meal' should consist of at least a dozen courses, a minimum of three casks of ale, and should last no less than two days and nights." Danyl laughed at Allad's and Ramira's disbelief.

"Followed by several skins of my potion since it does help settle your stomach, you know," added Seven, who proudly wore a huge smirk across his seasoned face.

"It's true," Clare stated then shrugged her shoulders. She could tell by their expressions they were trying to imagine such an evening but were having little success. They eventually gave up and silently swore to satisfy their curiosity when all of this was over.

The night went by more hastily than they wished, but they needed to get some rest before the long journey home. They dispersed to their rooms, Danyl bidding Ramira a good night then going to his room. Sleep would not come for a long time. His mind was preoccupied with what might transpire over the next few weeks and also with the woman slumbering on the other side of the wall. He could still feel her body against his and smell her perfume. It would have been a simple thing to abandon his bed for hers, but he ignored that temptation and forced himself to sleep.

Seven and Clare remained in the hall after everyone had gone off to bed. They sat quietly for a while, Seven brooding over his nearly empty tankard while Clare stared off into the shadows.

"It's going to get mighty ugly, Clare." The King's voice broke the silence.

"I know, Seven," she softly agreed. The Queen knew there was a good chance some of those with whom they had dined wouldn't have an opportunity to visit in the future. It was a sobering fact yet one that had to be acknowledged. The dwarves, like the elves, firmly believed everyone had a part in the greater scheme of things, no matter how insignificant a life appeared to be. They need not be strong enough to wield a sword, for example, but might be in a position to offer a word of encouragement to help the person that can. Individuals composed the fabric of life whether they were good, bad, or indifferent and right now that textile was fraying at the edges. She slipped her hand into Seven's, clasping it to reassure both of them, then led him to their chambers.

They gathered their things the next morning and made their way to the bridge where their horses awaited them. The mounts were eager to return home even though their riders wished they could tarry for one more day. They bade each other farewell and mounted up, following the winding path back into the forest overlooking the river then turned around one last time. The elves looked down upon the valley and stared at the faces looking back at them. The thought of leaving this wonderful place weighed as heavily on their minds as the reason why they needed to get back home to their friends and families. Seven would leave for Bystyn soon but at least they had Clare and a few dwarves to make the trip back less mundane. Clare blew Seven a kiss while the others waved then they turned as one, leaving Evan's Peak behind.

Seven remained rooted in place for a long time watching his companion and friends disappear into the woods. He had learned much in the past few days about events that loomed upon the horizon. Herkahs riding with elves as if they had been allies for years had dined at his table while he had danced with the mysterious woman who would be the prince's mate. The King had believed he would die of old age before either event could occur and that thought elicited a chuckle. Well, he had a host of things to do before he, too, headed west, and he forced himself to return to the hall to attend to them.

The third night out, Ramira's eyes snapped open as faint sounds reached her ears. She turned to glance at Danyl but the elf was fast asleep, as were the other members of the party. Their keen hearing would certainly have noticed the far-off noises, which led her to believe she had imagined them. The night breeze stirred the leaves, and other than the chirping insects and soft warbling of a night bird, all was still. The sensation, however, would not go away. She slipped from her blankets and disappeared into the darkness, emerging from the woods to stand at the edges of the plain. Stars and a quarter moon illuminated the land as she scrutinized the shadows for the source of her confusion. She strained her senses, trying to pinpoint what had awakened her, but there was nothing out there. She sighed and was about to return to her bedroll when the wind touched her skin, carrying with it the sounds of creaking leather and muffled hooves. Somewhere far out on the plains a group of riders was passing by completely unaware of the party sleeping at the edge of the forest behind her. Were they friend or foe? Should she awaken the others or wait until the morning to tell them about the strangers? She heard footsteps behind her, their deliberate strides announcing their owner so she would not be startled.

"Vagabonds," stated Lance quietly. "They travel along these plains in search of people to steal from."

"I thought I was hearing things."

"You fought well against the rock lords. I am indebted to you once again."

Ramira could barely make out his features but the tone of his voice had softened, taking on a host of emotions she did not expect. The captain was not a conversationalist nor did he allow his feelings to show, yet there had to be another side to him. Lance had focused all his energies into safeguarding Danyl, heedless of his own wants and desires. He had voluntarily forsaken his personal life to serve the prince without any regard as to what he might never experience. That dedication was both noble and poignant.

"You would have done the same, Lance," she said, as pity for him touched her heart.

"Nonetheless I am grateful that you fight on our side."

"Lance?" She called out his name in a tentative voice, unsure how he would react to her question.

"Yes?"

"How were you...how are captains chosen to protect members of the royal family?"

"Those who guard the family have none of their own, Ramira," he began in a mild voice. "We are given the chance to learn everything our charges do and are, in a way, absorbed into the family. We understand our primary goal is to keep our charges safe, even at the expense of our own lives, and this responsibility begins at a very young age."

"You grew up with Danyl, then."

"Yes."

"What would happen if you were to..." She could not finish her sentence, but Lance completed it for her in a most unexpected way.

"If I were to die then I would, of course, be replaced by one of the other members of his personal guard."

His response was so matter-of-fact all she could do was stare at him for several long moments before the captain did the unexpected: he smiled. Even in the darkness she could see the grin just as he could discern the disbelief on her features. Ramira did not think such a serious topic warranted that kind of response but could not find her tongue in order to say so. Lance, however, did.

"It is a privilege to serve the family, Ramira, and an even greater honor to die for them. I consider myself fortunate to be in this position, and although you apparently think otherwise, I am not deprived of anything."

Lance turned and left, leaving her standing alone, her embarrassment cloaked by the night. He had answered her unspoken question, an inquiry she had no right to ask in the first place and in a way she had not anticipated. As she headed back to her blankets, she vowed to refrain from pursuing such questions in the future. She rolled over on her side and studied Danyl's profile as he slept on his back, and she could easily understand how Lance could dedicate his life to this elf. Her last thoughts as she drifted off to sleep were of how she was beginning to do the same thing.

The message arrived while they were eating breakfast. Alyxandyr glanced over and smiled at Zada and that was all she needed. She sprang to her feet and accompanied the King as they made their way out the main entrance and onto the broad balcony that fronted the second floor of the castle. They smiled as the party made its way up the main avenue, the elves as happy to see the dwarves as the dwarves had been to see Danyl and the others.

Alyxandyr waved to them as they neared the front of the building then all went downstairs to greet their friends and family, hugging them with warmth and friendship. They were allowed to clean up then gathered in the King's private rooms where everybody was brought up to date on what had and had not happened over the past three weeks. The Khadry had remained inconspicuous, preferring to keep to the edge of the forest while the Herkahs were interacting with the elves on a more frequent basis. Danyl nodded for there would come a day when one would have to fight beside the other and it was better to do so on friendly terms. Allad whispered a few words into Zada's ear, words that made her raise her brows in surprise. Danyl knew what he had conveyed to her then looked into the Herkah's eyes, as did Ramira, who stirred uncomfortably in her seat.

"We had a little skirmish with the rock lords, Father," he began as he rubbed at the wounds along his side.

"No one was severely hurt or killed, were they?" asked the King.

"They suffered both of those fates," replied Clare. "It seems as though Ramira was able to slay one of the high lord's sons." Ramira looked at the floor, the unwelcome attention making her fidgety.

"Really? You must be either very lucky or highly skilled," stated the King, studying her more closely.

"Highly skilled would better approximate her talents," explained Allad.

"Well." Danyl tried to change the subject. "I'm starved. Did you leave us any breakfast?"

Ramira was very aware of the stares and although invited to stay and eat with them, she chose to decline and left. She headed down the hall but Danyl caught up to her just as she reached the door to leave the castle and pulled her out of earshot. More than one pair of eyes observed the tenderness flowing back and forth between them.

"He had to be told."

"I understand."

"Sophie will be glad to see you again. I'm sure she's saved up plenty of chores for you to do."

"She'll have to wait until after I've bathed and slept for a few hours."

"I'll look in on you later," he promised then walked her to the door under the scrutiny of the attendants. The gossip, he knew, was already beginning and he would have to deal with Alyssa before the day was over.

"Later" ended up being several days. Between catching up on his duties and helping Clare prepare for the dwarves arrival, Danyl's days were extremely busy. Alyssa was already asking questions and her prying was beginning to grate on his nerves until he point-blank told her to mind her own business. This did not sit well with the princess, who was now determined to find the answers he would not give her. She decided to visit Sophie's house. Ramira was absent.

"You're all alone this afternoon, Sophie," Alyssa smoothly asked.

"Yes. Tea?"

"No, thank you, Sophie. I just stopped by to say hello and to invite you to dinner tonight."

"Anci and I are honored…"

"And you'll bring Ramira as well, won't you?"

Sophie smiled pleasantly at Alyssa, inwardly marveling at the young woman's undaunted determination. She was setting in motion a situation that would undoubtedly backfire on her. She never learned her lesson.

"I'm sure Ramira will gladly accept your request to dinner."

"Good. I'll see you all later on."

Sophie watched the princess go out the door and down the steps. Her entourage quickly swallowed her up in a flurry of silks and jewelry. Alyssa held her head erect and her shoulders back, greeting the elves with a regal nod. The princess' concern for her family, friends and people were genuine but her meddling in her brothers' affairs was truly annoying. If nothing else, this would prove to be an interesting evening.

It was already dusk by the time an exhausted Ramira entered the kitchen, both surprised and relieved Sophie and Anci were dressed to attend some function at the castle. All she wanted was a bite of food, a long bath and sleep, but the expression on their faces told her otherwise.

"We…all three of us will be dining with the King tonight," Sophie said, as she smoothed a wrinkle on her dress and waited for Ramira's refusal. Too tired to argue and knowing she wouldn't win anyway, Ramira bathed and started slipping into the dress Sophie held out for her. "Princess Alyssa expects us within the hour."

"Sophie…no," she moaned.

"Yes. Just go and let Alyssa take a look at you." She was about to pull the gown up over Ramira's waist when she saw the scars. "What are these?"

"A token from my visit to the dwarves. We had a little conflict with people Seven called 'rock lords' and, well, now I have these to remind me."

Sophie eyed her for a few seconds then buttoned the back of the dress.

"As I was saying, you'll get to see Danyl and Clare and meet Zada, so it won't be such a bad evening after all. Let me look at you," she said and made Ramira turn around. Pleased with the deep lavender gown, she made a few minor adjustments then ushered her out the door.

The evening breeze chased away the heat of the day as the carriage brought them up the avenue to the castle, but it could not scatter the unease she felt. Ramira would rather face the rock lords than endure the princess' scrutiny. Alyssa's resolve knew no bounds and she would apparently face any consequence to satisfy her nosiness. Danyl would be furious, a fact that Alyssa was willing to accept. Ramira hadn't planned on being attracted to the prince, but try as she might, she was unable to escape the bond forming between them. She gazed up at the gray stones forming the castle's façade and the lights seeping out of the windows as the carriage stopped. She took a deep breath, accepted Sophie's little smile of encouragement then left the carriage and headed for the entrance to the castle.

They were escorted to the dining hall where most of the guests, including Gard, were already gathered and deep in conversation. The prince was puzzled yet pleased as Ramira entered the room, her simple gown and single braid only enhancing her beauty. His reaction did not go unnoticed by those present, as he rose and introduced her to Zada and Nyk.

"I am honored to meet you." Ramira offered the nomad, then Nyk, respectful nods.

Zada wanted to discuss many things with her but the King entered the room with Alyssa on his arm. The princess glanced at Ramira then over to Danyl, who immediately understood what was going on. The brief look he threw his sister promised he would deal with her later. He couldn't help but smirk because as much as Alyssa wanted to corner Ramira, the King and Zada managed to inadvertently intervene. Danyl whispered into Styph's ear, his older brother grinning then agreeing as he anticipated thwarting his sister's plans. When the dinner bell rang, the younger prince escorted Ramira to the seat beside him while Styph sat next to his fuming sister.

The King watched the conflict between his children and indicated they cease their foolishness. Fully grown or not, they knew they would hear from him when the night ended. Alyxandyr understood all too well his sons would never concede to Alyssa's prying and gave her a look that would have stopped an army. She held herself erect for a moment then wilted under his glare, leaving the princes victorious for at least this night. The elven king wondered what relationship was brewing between his son and the woman beside him and vowed to speak with Danyl about it later on. Sophie and Zada exchanged glances and it took all of their will power not to laugh as Danyl raised his goblet and saluted his sister. The princess acknowledged him with narrowed eyes.

Dinner was pleasant for everyone but Alyssa, although her outward demeanor could not have been more gracious. Her brothers had momentarily denied her the chance to speak with Ramira, but the night wasn't over yet and she was determined to get at least one opportunity to question her.

They retired to the balcony where lamps gave off a soft and cozy light, the fragrant oil meshing perfectly with the scents floating upward from the garden. They sat together realizing good had come from the darkness slowly rolling east, because the friendships and alliances forming would sustain them in the end.

Gard had been fairly silent through most of dinner, but he was beginning to relax as the evening wore on, appreciating the fact that he was being treated like everyone else. The bitterness handed down through the generations was no different than drinking from an empty cup, and he began to wonder why he still held onto that vessel. The Bystynian elves had absolutely no intention of taking away what the Khadry had built over the years; therefore there was no need to feel threatened or to hate. Indeed, none of the races gathered in the comfortable darkness had their sights set on anything but surviving, giving up much to unite with one another. The Herkahs had, for the time being, lost their home as had his own people. The dwarf queen was a reminder that her folk would also abandon their city in order to go to Bystyn and stand beside those already gathered here. Gard's eyes strayed to a quiet Ramira, who watched and listened from her seat beside the prince. The moon and duskiness only enhanced her beauty, giving her a nearly ethereal quality. It was easy to see why Danyl found her so alluring, but Gard knew enough about the prince to deduce he was not a slave to beauty. Gard remembered the fairness and respect the prince had bestowed upon him when he had confronted him at the inn weeks ago.

The nomads, although quite fierce and proud, also radiated those same characteristics. He glanced over at Zada, whose soft voice and tinkling bracelets brought a certain calm over their gathering, her elegance and grace disguising her brutal capabilities. He wondered what expressions would drift across her tanned features as she wielded her knives. Allad's features, he was sure, would be devoid of anything but a glacial resolve as he smote his enemy. He was renown for his notable skills, proficiencies that pulsated even here where no real threat existed. The Khadry had seen the Herkahs from a distance and now stood beside them sharing drink and conversation, yet they remained as enigmatic as ever. The one thing he did know was that he did not want to be their foe.

"I would like to propose a toast to those gathered here." The King raised his glass. "May we face the future side by side and let the faith and honor that has grown between us continue into that future." They clinked their glasses then sat down in chairs or leaned up against the balustrade.

"I understand you have developed a deep admiration for the dwarves, Ramira." The King smiled as her face lit up with the memories of her time at Evan's Peak.

"A most delightful people," she began, as she offered a beaming Clare a little nod. "I hope that I am invited back."

"You most certainly are welcome any time…there will always be a bed open to you."

"When Seven comes here, you know he will be laden with his poison, Father," smirked Styph.

"Yes, I know. Thank goodness Clare will also be here to temper his enthusiasm in making us drink it."

"I will have to bring our version of that drink," Allad stated with a knowing little smile. "I believe he will find it equally refreshing."

"Yours is as potent as his?" asked Mason, who leaned up against the rail, his sister and niece sitting on the bench beside him.

"Let's just say the glass from which it is sipped is only this high," he replied as his thumb and index finger indicated about an inch.

"Seven will call a vessel that small a waste of clay," laughed Danyl.

"How are your mementos, Ramira? All healed?" asked Clare.

"Yes, and I must say your stitching will leave virtually no scars." She remembered her dream and the faint marks left on her body along with the ghostly perception of the man who had taught her to wield the knives. The fight was on the mind of Zada, too, for she had been studying her for most of the evening ever since Allad had recounted the battle.

"I hear you are most adept at handling knives, Ramira. Allad tells me he was most impressed."

"I was fortunate to have been able to defeat the rock lord, Zada. It could have easily gone the other way," she humbly replied.

"Perhaps, but I think Captain Lance would beg to differ considering he is alive today because of the blade you flung at the lord who was about to decapitate him," she said. Ramira, thought Zada, might not be such an enigma after all. It was just a matter of certain situations, dire or otherwise, that would prompt her to revert to things she had learned in her past. The skirmish on the plain, for example, awoke her skill and training with her knives. Perhaps a certain food or something as simple as stroking a cat would elicit some other response. People lose their memories but their bodies never forget.

"I was thinking when Seven arrives we might have a little festival," began the King. "Nothing too elaborate, just some food and drink and maybe a few contests out on the plain in front of the city. It might help relieve some of the nervousness and strain of the past few weeks."

"I agree," Zada and Clare said simultaneously.

"Alyssa." The King looked over at his daughter. "You will make the arrangements." And you will then be much too busy to stick your nose in affairs that do not concern you. His sons grinned broadly, enjoying Alyssa's defeat.

"Well." Danyl offered Ramira his arm. "Care to stretch your legs with a walk in the garden?" She smiled and the pair disappeared down the staircase and into the night. Alyxandyr watched the darkness swallow them up then returned his attention to his guests.

They strolled away from the balcony until they reached the far corner where a stone bench stood in front of a fountain. Its carved fish spouted water from their open mouths while ivy completely hid the gray stones where they clung. A circle of shrubs with tiny wax-like leaves provided plenty of privacy. Pale yellow hooded flowers exuding a soft fragrance clustered at the base of the fountain adding to the serenity.

"Your sister has quite the stubborn streak."

"Alyssa means well but her methods are truly annoying," he said. "When our mother died, she took on many of her responsibilities, but she didn't have that fluid way our mother had of getting things done and therefore comes across as being impatient. Besides, she has this strange notion that my brothers and I are incapable of finding a suitable companion while she ignores the stirrings in her own heart."

"That is sad, Danyl."

"It doesn't have to be," he softly replied, then lifted her chin and kissed her lips.

He straddled the bench and pulled her up against his chest. That peculiar sensation slowly began to vibrate deep within them again. He noticed the scent of the perfume and wondered if she had somehow managed to place another drop on her neck. He asked her but she said she hadn't touched the bottle since that day.

"When will the dwarves arrive?"

"I'm guessing tomorrow." The thought of the exuberance they were going to bring elicited a quiet, little laugh.

"What's so amusing?"

"Seven loves tormenting Karolauren, and I do believe the historian revels in getting back at the King. You'll see what I mean within the next few days. Come." He began leading her away from the corner. "I want to show you something."

They walked along the flagstone path to the opposite corner where a magnificent rosebush bloomed, its snow-white flowers radiant even in the darkness. Ramira crouched down and lifted one of the fragrant blooms to her nose, inhaling its enchanting aroma.

"My mother planted this when she wed my father, a sort of token of their love and new life together. She has been gone many years yet it flourishes as if she still tended to it."

Ramira closed her eyes; her fingers lingering upon the velvety petals, the touch invoking an image behind her eyelids.

She was a little girl sitting on a lap, the woman holding her rocking and humming in her ear. The room in which she sat was small and sparse, lit by a single lamp on the table before her. The arms holding her were warm with love and every once in a while she felt a kiss on the top of her head, which made her squirm deeper into the embrace. She was getting sleepy.

I want to be big, she told the woman.

You will be someday, she replied.

Tomorrow?

Maybe…or the next day.

Will I still fit in your lap?

You will always fit into my lap, my sweet…

"Ramira? Are you all right?"

"What?"

"It's almost as if you went somewhere else for a moment."

"I guess I did," she replied, the memory increasing the yearning for the woman who had so loved her. She smiled at him and told him what she had seen.

"Not everything in your past life has been unpleasant, has it?"

"Nor much in my present one, either," she said, caressing his cheek. "It has been a long day, Danyl, and I need to rest."

He wanted to escort her home but she refused, reminding him he still had guests. She thanked her hostess and bid them all a good night. Ramira walked down the avenue nearing the intersection when the world around her changed for a split second in time. The shops and homes became hulking shadows, the yellow globs of light shining from within their windows reminding her of wolves' eyes. She thought she heard low growling sounds issuing forth from the grotesque shapes, the noises so real her skin began to crawl in response. Her hands instinctively reached for the knives, but they lay upon her dresser in the house. She blinked and Bystyn returned, but she could not shake the uneasiness coursing through her mind and body. She took a deep breath and crossed the street in front of her home, her eyes scanning the gloominess around her. She entered the house and froze, scanned the darkness then bolted up the stairs and into her room where she retrieved her knives and searched the house. She found nothing and began to wonder if she were imagining things. She exhaled and poured herself a glass of wine, careful not to spill any on her dress, taking it with her upstairs to bed.

Ramira and Anci were carrying their packages home when a group of riders came down the avenue. They could see Clare among the nomads and princes as they got closer: Seven was close by and they were riding out to meet him. The riders stopped in front of them and Danyl held out his hand encouraging her to join him, his bright green eyes sparkling invitingly. Styph was already helping Anci up into his saddle, their parcels ending up in the arms of a guard while Ramira jumped up behind Danyl. She looked up at the walls and smiled for many had gathered upon them to watch the dwarves arrive. They trotted beneath the gates and out onto the plain where she saw the Herkahs advancing toward the walls, waiting to see the dwarves. Groups of elves had joined them, talking and pointing as if they had been friends for years.

Ramira could hear them long before they broke through the orchard, and when she turned to look over at Clare, she saw pride and love radiating from her face. The dwarves sang in their own tongue, the cheerful rhythm and booming chorus energizing all who waited. She peeked over Danyl's shoulder, the prince giving her a quick sideways glance, his free hand flat against hers as they held onto him. The first wagons entered into view, the King riding beside the one laden with casks of ale.

"Very protective, isn't he?" chuckled Ramira.

"An army couldn't pry that cart from his fingers!" Clare said, shaking her head back and forth.

The bulk of the band passed beyond the orchards, the sun glinting off weapons hauled in three of the wagons. Ramira felt Danyl tense momentarily as he fought the apprehension attempting to extinguish his enthusiasm. She patted his hand, pulling him back from the dark brink he was about to step into. The Queen suddenly kicked the sides of her horse and raced forward to meet her folk, the elves not too far behind. Styph reined in his mount, jumping off before it came to a complete stop, and was immediately picked up by the King. The crown prince stood at least a head higher than Seven did, but that did not stop the dwarf from hoisting him way up in the air. Danyl and Ramira grinned at them before dismounting and walking forward the rest of the way.

Seven came prepared for there were many wagons filled with provisions and the one cart sagging with the weight of ale barrels. Ramira laughed because the King had brought the most essential of supplies and was determined, she was sure, to bring them home empty. She kept off to one side allowing the princes and the others the chance to be around Seven, content to be a part of the celebration. A loud cheer erupted from those gathered on the parapet as they passed beneath the gate, the dwarves raising their hands in greeting while eyeing the black tents with curiosity. They made their way up the avenue waving at the elves lining the street, catching the flowers tossed their way. Ramira peeled away from the group as they passed Sophie's house. She joined the woman on the front steps, watching Danyl crane his neck to look for her before smiling at him from the house. He shook his head ever so slightly then winked at her before being swallowed up in the crowd following them to the castle.

Ramira glanced over at Sophie, the adoration for the dwarves visible on her features. The dwarves' awareness of their own mortality urged them to enjoy what time they had with each other, an idea the elves heartily embraced. From what Ramira had seen so far, some of that exuberance was already rubbing off on the Herkahs, especially Allad, who had taken to the dwarf king almost immediately. Sophie tapped Ramira on the arm, her gaze never leaving the vanishing figures heading up the avenue.

"You had better grab a few hours sleep because it's going to be a long and raucous night," Sophie told her, then went into the house. Ramira followed her a few moments later.

Ramira smiled pleasantly at the animated dwarf king as she walked into the main reception hall, watching as Sophie braced herself for the bear hug. Seven picked her up in one arm and Anci in the other, heartily embracing them as if they were no heavier than a pair of dolls. It took some doing but Sophie was finally able to disentangle herself while maintaining a measure of self-respect as she straightened out her dress and took her seat near the fireplace. It was the perfect time to exchange stories and further cement their friendships.

"I still think Styph and I bested you," laughed Danyl, his brother in crime nearly spitting his wine across the room.

"Yes, that incident nearly caused a war between the dwarves and the elves," Seven scowled good-naturedly. "It seems when those two were no higher than my knees, they decided they were going to go bear hunting. The little imps went into the woods, mistook me for one and each let an arrow fly! I came out of the brush with an arrow embedded in each cheek, feeling no pain because all I wanted to do was get my hands on their little necks. When their father finally finished laughing," he threw the amused elven king a playful look, "he managed to discipline them. I still have marks…"

"No, Seven!" Clare stopped him before he could show everyone the scars. She glanced over at Allad, who approached the King with a glass bottle filled with an amber liquid.

"Do you remember when I proposed you try our version of your concoction?" he asked as he poured a small amount into a glass. Seven swirled the contents under his nose but before Allad could tell him to sip it, he drank it down in one gulp. Zada placed her hand over her mouth as the dwarf king began to sweat almost immediately, the tears running down his cheeks indistinguishable from the perspiration. He opened his mouth but the fire burning in his throat incinerated any words he endeavored to speak. After a few very long moments he wiped his face and nodded his head in approval.

"You and I are going to become good friends, Allad," he finally managed to say in a raspy voice. The nomad smiled and slapped the dwarf on the back in agreement.

"It isn't enough that Seven has tainted the elves," Clare quipped. "He won't be happy unless he does the same to the Herkahs."

"The Herkahs are not innocent bystanders, Clare," said Zada, watching Seven shudder after drinking another glass of Allad's potion.

Zada felt her inner sight stir urging her to rise and head out onto the balcony, an ever-vigilant Allad trailing but not crowding her. She stood with her hands on the balustrade, closed her eyes and opened her mind.

There was a rustling sensation, then whispers, nervous and frightened. She turned and faced west, feeling the foul wind as it curled and twisted around everything in its path, searching for the power. Everything it touched wilted and died, unable to survive the horror and hatred it was composed of. She gripped the banister more tightly for even at this distance the evil was almost overwhelming. She gasped as she recognized the solid shadows lurking within its fetid haze: Radir. Zada knew that the Vox would not be far behind and time was growing short, and she withdrew her inner sight for fear of being "seen."

Allad caught her as she fell, grateful they were alone as she returned to her surroundings, the look in her eyes one of fear. He instinctively knew she had bad news. He saw a figure emerge onto the balcony, watching as Ramira came and knelt down beside them as if summoned by some unheard call. Her eyes were wide, staring at the prone woman with awe then bewilderment. She reached out and touched Zada's shoulder before Allad could block her and was immediately immersed in the aftereffects of her vision. Ramira's face blanched, the strangled cry in her throat impeding her breathing as she endured the snippets of Zada's inner sight. Then, the unexpected happened: the nomad's sight flared up again.

They stood hand in hand upon a sliver of rock reaching high into the cloudless orange sky. They dared to look down at a thread-like river meandering its way through barren canyons and broken ground. Its silver waters turned crimson, as did the mist slowly wending its way up the sides of the bedrock. A loathsome wind preceded it, swirling around them and threatening to push them off their small platform and down into the blood-red haze. Zada tightened her grip but Ramira began to move toward the edge, heeding the voice that had suddenly erupted from within the fog. Ramira's expression began to change from horror to ecstasy, spurred on by the sensual murmurs rising upward. The Herkah grabbed her with both hands, silently screaming for her to stop, but Ramira moved closer to the brink. Bits of stone and dirt gave way beneath her feet as she reached out to touch the mist.

Allad forcibly yanked Ramira away from Zada, the brief contact making him suck in his breath through clenched teeth. She sat against the wall breathing heavily, her eyes never leaving Zada. Allad helped the wobbly woman to a nearby bench, holding her as she fought off the dizziness and nausea.

"Help...Ramira..."

Allad hesitated then walked over to Ramira. He towered over her, his face pulsating with anger and his rigid body far more terrifying than anything she had ever seen. She pushed herself against the wall, struggling to contain the whimper trying to escape from her throat. She trembled more from his wrath than from the vision she had shared with Zada. Pity for the frightened woman chased away the rage and released his locked limbs, allowing him to kneel beside her.

"Foolish girl," he muttered.

"I'm sorry, Allad...I didn't mean to..."

"Of course you didn't, but don't ever do that again!"

"Leave us," said Zada, placing her hand reassuringly on his arm.

Allad paused then went inside, closing the door after him and persuading the others that everything was fine. Danyl glanced over to the balcony then back to the Herkah, who positioned himself close to it, the dark look on his face never fading. Seven and Alyxandyr exchanged perplexed looks while Gard kept his thoughts to himself.

"Come and sit, Ramira." Zada held her hand out to her.

"No..." she replied in a raspy voice.

"The trance is over ...there will be no more images." They sat side by side, silent for a long time as the Herkah scrutinized Ramira's profile. Others had touched Zada while her inner sight controlled her but they had recoiled from the power, not been absorbed into her mystic state.

"Where were we?" Ramira finally asked.

"A place between the land of the living and the dead." Zada watched her stiffen, the idea that such a region could exist sending terror into her heart.

"I…I wanted to jump, Zada. What would have happened if I…"

"You'd be dead. That fate would have befallen me, too, which is why Allad is at my side when the visions come. He is my link to the present. The images usually play themselves out before it gets to that point, but this one was different. You obeyed its call." *And that concerns me a great deal.*

"I didn't want to, Zada."

"I know, child. Are you feeling better now?"

"Yes," Ramira lied. The seductive whispers began to fade away although they never truly left, adhering to the vestiges of her nightmares.

Their friends became silent as the ashen-faced women entered the room. Danyl started forward but Allad held him back as Zada and Ramira seated themselves in front of the fire. The nomad took a deep breath and told them what she had seen, keeping the conversation she had with Ramira to herself.

"Zada," asked the elven king with a hint of trepidation in his voice. "Did your vision tell you if the evil has found the Source?"

"I doubt that very much."

"First Kreetch then Radir…how soon will the Vox come?" asked Styph.

Zada shrugged because although the demons were heading eastward, the Source was still out of the evil's grasp. The downside was the farther east the evil had to search, the closer he came to the city, bringing with him his minions. Zada knew the days of merriment were gone and there would be no festival on the plains. She suggested they hold the celebration in the city, and after hesitating for a moment, the elven king agreed. It would be better than nothing.

"It begins," stated a solemn Alyxandyr.

-6-

Ramira approached the orchards a few days later, the brilliant blue sky and hot sun not quite bright enough to chase away the chill of the shared vision. She shifted the heavy basket and realized how quiet it had become. Nothing moved, crawled, or chirped anywhere. Even the breeze had ceased to blow over the grasses. She strained to hear any sound, but the only thing she heard was the beating of her heart. It reminded her of the sensation she had when she chased the phantom intruder in Sophie's house. Ramira peered into the bushes and along the tree trunks. Shadows moving within the semi-darkness took on a spooky cast as clouds floated in front of the sun. A cool breeze began to steal the warmth from her body. She reached down toward her knives, the cold feel of their hilts reassuring to the touch.

Zada lifted her cup to her lips but never drank from it, the sudden and overpowering second sight freezing her into place. The danger was so near that she was unable to prepare herself for the thrust into the black void. Allad warned everyone back, then stationed himself near Zada as he kept watch with the others.

The darkness turned gray but she could make out the image of a house by the orchard, a figure standing nearby: Ramira. She stood there with her hands hovering over her knives, her eyes scanning her surroundings. There was something indeed wrong and Zada knew it originated in the house, the very place Ramira was heading. Ramira advanced a few paces, hesitated then moved forward once more. She slipped the straps off her shoulders, the heavily laden basket falling to the ground, spilling its contents over the grass.

Ramira disappeared from her inner sight, replaced by a black haze she could not penetrate. Zada didn't need to "see" to know what skulked within the mist. The Kreetch's foul presence invaded her mind, forcing her to bear witness to their vileness. Zada shuddered with disgust at the smell of blood and the feel of tattered flesh the demons were feasting on. They fought amongst each other for the prime body parts then tore apart and ate their mortally wounded kin. Their gnarling and high-pitched screeches wrenched her nerves until she thought she would scream. And Ramira headed straight for them.

"No...don't..." Zada could barely breathe the words. The tension pressed down upon them like the oppressive air right before a severe thunderstorm.

Ramira let the basket fall, ignoring the thump it made as it hit the ground. The specters she had chased in her home were here and their presence ignited something within her. It responded to the menace, forcing every thought and emotion from her until all that mattered was eradicating the threat lurking inside. She moved forward with purpose, fearless in her intent, eager for the encounter. Her foot reached the first step. Claws instantly scrabbled across the wooden floor, responding to the intruder irrational enough to confront them. Ramira tiptoed up the stairs, her muscles tensing as the things scratching and skittering came to a halt. The wind stopped blowing. Her heartbeat and breathing increased. Perspiration began to trickle down her face. Her eyes narrowed at the high-pitched whining inside the house. She clenched then relaxed the grip on her knives. She stared at the door for a second, then pushed the handle down and went inside.

Zada snapped out of her trance, her face bloodless and hands shaking with fear. She spoke to Allad in their native tongue, her mate's features taking on a dangerous cast. She gazed at Danyl, the sadness and fright etched on her countenance stealing his breath from his lungs.

"Where is she?"

"Come with me," Allad commanded, then nodded to Lance and Nyk. He would need their brawn to keep Danyl from interfering with what was taking place on the plain.

They mounted their horses, Allad calling for two more elven guards to join them before speeding from the city. He signaled for more Herkahs as they passed under the gates and within moments four more horses joined the group racing for Jack and Ida's house. They were riding so swiftly that speech was impossible, but the look on the Herkahs' faces indicated it was bad news indeed. The horses raced across the plain, ears back and tails horizontal to the ground, and still their riders urged them on faster. The fruit trees loomed up ahead then the chimney poked over their tops. They hastened past the basket and its contents and finally arrived at the house.

A terrible silence met them. They dismounted and it took all of Lance's and the elves' power to keep Danyl away from the house as he called out her name over and over again.

"Do not, I repeat, do not under any circumstances go near that house. If you approach it we will be forced to kill you, understand?" Nyk understood perfectly because he had seen this before. There were Kreetch inside and the Herkahs were the only ones prepared to confront them. Nyk shifted over to stand beside his brother, motioning Lance to the other side with a jerk of his head.

Ramira stood in front of the closed door, searching for the demons, her hands firmly grasping her knives. A movement to her right and scrambling sounds near the kitchen caught her attention. Shadowy forms darted around the main room, vying for the best spot to attack her from. She counted at least four of the things, each with teeth and claws capable of shredding her flesh. Nothing moved for several long minutes, the creatures choosing to watch her in the semi-darkness. Suddenly one of the demons launched itself from across the room, its hideous, twisted black body intent upon ripping her to pieces. Her hands came up, the knives blurs of motion as she slashed across the fiend's midsection. It shrieked in pain once then dropped lifeless to the floor, its foul and slippery blood spreading outward from its mortal wound.

She turned as two others attacked her from opposite sides, their assault more difficult to defend as they closed the distance. They rotated to the side as they catapulted by tearing their claws along her side and shoulder. She inhaled sharply through clenched teeth as the burning pain coursed through her body. The blood seeping from her wounds excited the Kreetch, anticipating her death and gorging on her meat. One of the Kreetch miscalculated its pounce to her back, paying for the mistake with its life. Another tried to rake its claws across her chest but it, too, was a second too slow to escape her blades. That left one more and she hoped it would show itself soon because the poison was beginning to steal her strength away. She became weak and sick to her stomach, the perspiration running down her face stinging her eyes. Her loose tunic was so shredded it fell off on its own accord, baring her bloodstained undershirt. *Where are you!*

It crept out from the kitchen, its head covered in blood and pieces of flesh hanging from its jaws. Ramira hated it even more for what it had done to the old couple. It emitted a low growling sound, its mangy hackles lifting upward as it stalked into the main room. She raised the blades, its hunger for her death the only reason for its existence. It lunged at her, forcing her to spiral to the side and slip on the blood-soaked floor. She dropped to the floorboards with a thud, rolling away just as the demon launched itself on top of her. The demon raked her in the same gash made by one of its wicked brethren, the pain so intense she screamed in agony. The Kreetch jumped up and down, maniacally howling with delight at the anguish it had caused. She surged forward, her rage energizing her drained body, and cut the unprepared Kreetch in half. She gasped for air, fighting the fire claiming her mind and body, staggering as she searched for more demons. There were none. Bleeding and in pain, she went into the kitchen where the bloody remains of the gentle couple lay.

She had one more task to fulfill, and crouching between them, she stabbed them with her daggers. She would not let the demons use these bodies. She stared at the corpses for several long moments, the thought of being bereft of their compassion gripping her heart. They had done nothing to deserve such savagery. Their tragic deaths summoned the grief within her soul as tears and silent sobs wracked her pain-filled body. She forced her leaden feet toward the front of the house, each step a monumental challenge. Her burning muscles and ragged breathing made the short trek to the front door seem an eternity, but she had to get away from the horror behind her.

The sun beat down on those waiting to see what or who might come out of the house. The Herkahs did not move their eyes steadfastly converged on the door. They heard the sounds of footsteps then swords being withdrawn from their scabbards. Lance tightened his grip on Danyl, the knots on the prince's shoulders growing beneath his hand with every passing second. The latch clicked and the door opened sluggishly, the shade beneath the porch obscuring the figure emerging from the house. For a moment they could see nothing then a bloodied Ramira shuffled out and down the stairs. She staggered into the sunlight, her head down and bloodshot eyes framed by deep purple stains, unable to catch her breath. He glanced at her wounds and cringed at the blood flowing freely from within the rents in her garment.

"Ramira!" His voice sliced through the utter stillness, startling his companions but not Ramira.

Allad swallowed hard, the duty at hand the hardest he had ever to perform. He grasped his daggers with sweaty palms, his determination undaunted.

Nyk exhaled slowly, the dying screams of another necessary slaughter echoing in his mind. He remembered the sorrow and anger he felt and wished Allad had left Danyl behind. It wasn't fair to his younger brother, whose affection for Ramira would not die with her. Pity began to seep into his heart, but it would not deter Allad from his obligation.

Ramira could barely remain erect, the blistering heat robbing the rest of her strength. She struggled to make sense of the dark smudges, and for a brief moment she was able to identify Allad. Her constricted throat imprisoned her cry for help and soon her mind forgot how to ask for it. Allad became a blur again and she swayed unsteadily on her feet, the last of her stamina washed away by the perspiration pouring out of her skin. The sweat ran down her neck and chest, following the curves of her arms to her hands. The blades slid from her nerveless fingers and buried themselves to the hafts in the hard ground at her feet.

The nomad stepped forward fully expecting the demon-possessed woman to strike, but she did nothing. The Herkah moved toward her, his blades glinting in the light heedless of the prince's cries behind him. He hesitated, the poison not provoking the usual reaction. Was this some sort of trick? Had the evil contrived a new way of ensnaring Herkahs?

He narrowed his gaze at the rivulet of sweat trickling from the corner of her unresponsive eye then realized it was a tear. Ramira had been defiled but she wasn't a demon. Not yet, anyway. Allad squeezed the hilts, uncomfortable with the decision before him, one he had mere seconds to make. She began to collapse and he instinctively lunged forward to the sound of Danyl's outcry. The only thing anyone saw was the flash of Allad's knives as she fell into his arms as limp as a rag doll. No one moved or even breathed for many long moments, rooted in place by the scene before them. Ramira's head lay on his shoulder; her body sagged against his, and Allad's knives were nowhere to be seen. Allad had fulfilled his somber obligation. The stillness was finally broken when the Herkah shouted at one of the other nomads, who hastened to retrieve a blanket. Allad wrapped it around her, a raging Danyl breaking free of the arms holding him. He hurled himself at the Herkah but Lance tackled the prince just before he pounced on him.

"She has been corrupted by the demons, elf prince. Her tears make me believe she might be able to beat the poison, but if she cannot then I will bury my blades into her flesh. Until we are sure of what may or may not thrive within her, she will remain under Herkah guard, understood?" He mounted his horse, took the unconscious woman in his arms and headed back to the city. Danyl rode alongside Allad, his attention riveted on the lifeless form cradled within the nomad's arms. He tried not to think of what would happen if the Herkah judged her to be a demon. The ride back to the city took forever.

Allad continued to hold her as he raced into the castle and toward a room in the back with barred windows. He wanted her to be well contained in case his judgment turned out to be wrong and she needed to be slain. Zada waited for him, her eyes still wide with the memory of what she had seen as he gently placed Ramira's body on the bed and began to undress her. Zada immediately stopped him. Some of the blood had dried the shreds of cloth into her wounds and it would take a steady hand to loosen them without further injuring her. His hands shook with a myriad of emotions and he therefore relinquished the task but refused to leave. Zada positioned herself between those in the chamber and Ramira to offer her some measure of modesty. She washed away the blood and sweat then frowned with concern at the wounds inflicted by the Kreetch. She was going to need a lot more help, and called for the healer and Clare.

They worked on her for a long time, yet Ramira never moved or even flinched. She seemed dead to them, or worse. She began to sweat more profusely as the poison coursed through her body, its heat burning her from the inside out. Zada ordered towels soaked in cold water to help relieve the fire but Ramira worsened with each passing hour. She had perspired through two sets of linens and they had forced as much water down her throat as she could take without choking her. Nothing seemed to help. Three Herkahs stationed themselves at her bedside, their attentive stares never leaving the recumbent woman.

"Are there no medicines she could take?" asked Danyl.

"No, son, there aren't. She is either strong enough to live or she will die," replied Zada, unwilling to tell him the truth.

"So she'll just die of thirst?"

"That is not what is happening, Danyl." She placed her hand on his chest and looked him straight in the eye. "For some reason the demons venom did not take her right away, but it is in her body and she is connected to them."

"What does that mean?" he demanded, a spark of anger in his eyes and a painful lump of dread in his throat.

"It means the toxin is a thread to the evil and through it could manipulate her to do its deeds."

"What can be done?"

"The link to us must be stronger."

The elf squinted at her as suspicion began to set in. Her wounds were not life threatening but he had heard enough about the demons to know Allad had taken an enormous chance in bringing her back to the city. The Herkah had been trained to kill those who housed the abominations yet something had stayed his hand. He was eternally grateful for who or whatever had done so, but he knew she was still vulnerable to the nomad's blades. How could they possibly form some sort of connection if she were barely conscious? He gazed helplessly down at her pale and sweat-soaked face, strands of hair darkened by the perspiration sticking to her skin. He reached over to push them away, feeling her clammy flesh beneath his touch. He wondered what else lay in store for her. He looked over at the Herkah couple who kept their lips sealed, not volunteering the answers he so desperately sought.

She felt suspended, floating in the blackness and enduring the agony of every fiber of her being until all she wanted was to die. She was without direction and all she had known was far beyond her reach. She was so very alone, so very scared. She hated this stifling silence and strained to hear a sound, any sound that could offer her a way out of this hell. All she heard, however, were insidious whispers arising from somewhere far below. They were identical to the ones from her visions beseeching her to join them, but this time she could not simply wake up and ignore them. The fire burned into her being, the suffering so intense it began to sear away all she had been and knew. Her mind and body were drifting away from each other; forever lost in an endless sea of black, tormented by the things existing just beyond her reach.

"How is she?" Allad asked Zada.

"I will be surprised if she lives through the night."

He had recounted what he had transpired outside Jack and Ida's home then confessed his uncertainty about bringing Ramira back to the city. His judgment could very well have placed them all in great danger, if not now then perhaps later on. He sincerely hoped his instincts had not failed him. Her road, if she even survived, would be arduous to say the least.

"Did you tell him about the convulsions and the slow suffocation?"

"No, Allad," she said, and squeezed her eyes shut. She reopened them then looked over at Danyl, who sat by Ramira's side holding her hand, his face deeply etched with worry. He was willing to do anything to help her but there was nothing anyone could do. Mercy at the hand of a blade was the best thing. She sighed and accepted Allad's arms around her, his nearness her only comfort.

The spasms began late that night, the ragged breathing shortly thereafter. Low moaning slipped from between her cracked lips; her furrowed brows nearly disappeared into her saturated hairline. Her body jerked violently, reopening wounds that were more than willing to release more blood. Ramira's twisted dressing gown became a hindrance and had to be cut away. Clare, Zada and the healer failed to restrain her and called for more help. Allad and Clare grappled with her legs while Danyl straddled her, pinning down her arms as Zada and the healer tried to work on her injuries. It became senseless to sew the wounds again as long as she was in the throes of the venom. Danyl was at his wit's end, as he could do nothing but watch her breathing coming in sharp gasps and raspy exhalations. She had saved his life all those months ago, her presence touching his spirit like no other, and he was damned if he would let her die. What could he do? How could he help her? How was he supposed to initiate that "connection" of which Zada spoke? He looked upon her contorted features, the pain and agony transforming her beautiful face into something pitiful to look upon. It was then that peculiar sensation began to swirl deep within him. It grew in intensity, snaking upward from deep within as if it sought to be freed of its flesh and blood prison. He could not stop it nor could he control the force surging upward, enveloping him from within in a shimmering shade of green. It scorched him, threatening to burn him to ash then abruptly dissipated, leaving him in a vast blackness as cold and forlorn as a tomb. The change was so sudden it took several moments for him to adjust to this desolate and frightful place. He finally understood and took a deep breath before thrusting himself through the corridor connecting him to her…

He entered a cold darkness that reminded him of the family crypt deep within the bowels of the castle. He was hurtling downward in an endless spiral, past cobweb-like things and far away shrieks of glee. This place reeked of death and suffering, the unseen things waiting in the blackness for the chance to snatch him to their foul lairs. He wouldn't stay long enough to allow that to happen, but he wasn't leaving without Ramira. He called her name over and over again but received no response. How far had she traveled in this black morass?

Then amid the disgusting odors swarming around him he detected one offering him some hope: perfume. It was faint but present nonetheless. He was close, reaching out in every direction for her, but his hands found nothing more than the gummy air that surrounded him. She had to be near! Those things shrieking all around him could not possibly have taken her! Panic began to set in, sending his arms wildly about, yet they still came up empty. Finally after what seemed like hours, his hand brushed against hers and he closed his fingers around it, stopping the downward motion. The screams and howls intensified, the hateful sounds becoming angry and demented as he pulled away their prize. The struggle back to the world of the living was fierce and he wondered if he had passed the point of no return. The exertion upon his will began to take its toll. He refused to yield and accept defeat even as he sensed the flailing claws of the deprived reach up to yank them back. From somewhere deep inside he found the strength and courage to go on, and he slowly pulled her out of that frightful chasm…

Weak with his exertions, Danyl slowly opened his eyes and gazed down upon Ramira then over at Zada who stood by the bed. He was exhausted, the effort sapping him of every ounce of strength. The look of astonishment on her face was the last thing he remembered as he slipped into a deep sleep, his arms placed protectively over Ramira.

Zada stood as if rooted in place not so much because of what he had accomplished but what that incredible feat had revealed about him. She glanced over at Ramira, who breathed much more easily and whose convulsions had been reduced to mere twitches. Zada's incredulity was based on the elf's eyes…eyes that burned brighter than the purest of emeralds without a hint of their whites showing. The prince housed his people's legacy and used it to steal Ramira back from the evil. He had bested the evil because the elven power he unwittingly housed chose this particular time to reveal itself. The Herkah slumped down into a nearby chair, her gaze never wavering from the sleeping elf, her mind racing with the implications of his act.

"Why now?" she whispered.

Cooper loathed the things that had taken everything belonging to him and hated himself even more for being outsmarted. The stranger that had come to him about buried treasure in the desert had played his part well; he had come across as a stupid man with great expectations. Cooper smugly thought he could easily cheat him then effortlessly cast the stranger aside or kill him. This one, however, should have set off every alarm in his mind, but the idea that the hated Herkahs guarded so much gold was enough to convince him. Instead of sitting on a pile of treasure, he found himself a prisoner in his own city, confined to his rooms. He spat on the floor for the thousandth time, the act having long ago become redundant.

His people lived on stale bread and stagnant water, walking skeletons with sunken eyes and no hope. He didn't care that they lacked hope; he wanted them fed so they could serve him, a little detail allowing him to rule all these years. And Antama! She could not wait to ally herself with that hulking monstrosity! He had allowed her to amuse him for many years and this is how she repaid him. She had spent countless hours reading every book, studying every map she could find and listened in on all of his decisions. She was smart and he had allowed her to get even more resourceful, a mistake he swore he would not repeat. That is if he got out of this situation. He vowed the first time he got his hands around her neck he'd choke the life out of her. He grinned as he imagined his hands pressing down on her throat, her brown arms reaching up to stop him.

The door swung open and one of the Herkah things summoned him to his own throne room, an act still making him simmer even after nearly a year. He absently scratched the back of his neck as they took him down the long hallway. The neglect of the past year could be seen everywhere, from the debris and dust strewn about to the huge spider webs draped in every corner. The grime coating the windows blocked out the world and filled the castle with a grayish light. Cooper had forgotten what color the sky was or how soft grass felt beneath his feet. There was a disagreeably damp feel to the air upon which the fetid odors floated. Cooper firmly believed they could clean for months and never remove that awful stench. The streets reeked of the same foul odor, for it often drifted up to his windows, seeping in whether they were open or closed. The demons opened the door at the end of the corridor. Chained at the ankles, he stood before the master devil: Mahn. Cooper looked up at the black-clad man-shape reaching nearly nine feet in height, but the animosity and pride surging in his body kept him from groveling at his feet. Mahn sensed that and it gave him a strange sort of satisfaction.

"You will go to Bystyn." Mahn's voice boomed and reverberated throughout the room, scattering the Kreetch and other vile minions that had taken up residence in his expansive mansion.

"What for?" Cooper replied, his tongue still filled with arrogance.

"You will soften them for me."

"I'll do nothing for you..." he began then felt the giant's hand as it reached into his body and pulled at every vital organ its fingers found. The world began to turn black and Cooper's face turned purple with agony. Every vein and tendon stood so far out from his face and neck they threatened to burst through his skin, his eyes watering until he thought he would go blind.

"You will go," Mahn repeated, relinquishing his hold on the King, who dropped to the floor and threw up.

Cooper could barely breathe as he tried to gulp in enough air to fill his lungs, his innards throbbing from the evil's assault. He loathed everything in the land as he rested on all fours staring down at his vomit, swearing he would seek revenge on everyone even if it killed him. Nobody was going to do this to him and get away with it. The Vox yanked him to his feet and hauled the unsteady King out of the throne room. He could feel eyes staring into his back even after the doors closed behind him.

Cooper stared at the Vox as he rode behind them. They gave him the creeps, their presence making his skin crawl. He hadn't quite figured them out yet; although they looked like the desert insects, they acted very strangely. They ignored insults, for one. He had once tried to see how far he could antagonize them before they reacted, receiving only a hiss when he kicked an empty bottle into one of their legs. He knew they were kept at bay simply because Mahn needed him for some plan, or they would have tortured him long ago. Funny, he thought as he left Kepracarn, they listen to him yet they have their own way, almost as if they just tolerated Mahn. He began to plan his escape, not an easy task considering he'd be watched all the way to Bystyn.

He could head south, the secluded villages providing ample places to hide in. When things quieted down he could ransack his city or the elven one, take what was left and start over again. His number one priority was to get away from these things so that he had a chance to survive. The only thing Mahn was going to give him was a slow and agonizing death, something he was already receiving in his city. He intended to survive and continue to indulge himself in any and every earthly delight. He grinned, then leered as he thought about the elf princess. Now there was an enjoyment well worth seeking out. She would be about the right age by now. And feisty. Come to think of it, there wasn't much that the pointy-eared ones had that he didn't want, like fertile plains, plenty of riches and lots of beautiful women. All he had to do was defeat them, the Vox and that devil, and all of those things could be his to do with as he pleased without putting up that ridiculous front called "tact."

He sighed. His anger sustained his determination to run and hide until the perfect opportunity arose. The prospect of scrounging around like an animal did not appeal to him and neither did his only other option: begging the elves for help. They had never trusted him and, he freely admitted, had every right not to. Undermining the elves was his second favorite pastime. This, however, was different. If he could get them to listen to him, they might grant him asylum. It certainly would be easier to work his plans from within their walls than from outside.

He watched the Vox as they continued to lead him along his lands just south of the Broken Plains. He didn't think the Herkahs could become more menacing but here he was riding with things making the nomads look like children. The desert insects were brutal in battle but they fought with emotions. The Vox didn't fight to kill but to feed off the energies of the living souls. No one could stand up to one of the Vox and survive. This sobering thought brought him back to his only route to staying alive, barring any miracles occurring between here and Bystyn.

What did Mahn expect him to do in the city? "Soften them up"? Was he supposed to instill a sense of hopelessness into them by revealing how all-powerful Mahn was? Despair was a wonderful weapon, one he had used on many occasions. The elves, however, were more resilient and resourceful than any group and would not fall for that ploy. If, however, the right ingredients were to present themselves and chaos could somehow be stirred up then…well, that tactic might work. What didn't "work" was his abrupt release—a freedom, he surmised, that wasn't quite as free as he was led to believe.

A sharp hiss invaded his thoughts, the Vox' face inches from his, inducing him to recoil away from it. He sneered at the demon but obeyed its order to dismount. The Vox stared dispassionately down at him then left him standing alone at the edge of his lands. Amazement, relief and confusion roiled through his tall frame as their retreating backs diminished in the distance. The King inhaled deeply several times, the smell of green grass and clean air cleansing the stench that had infused itself into him for so long. Every time he exhaled he purged more and more of those foul odors from his body until he felt refreshed for the first time in a year. He was finally ready.

"I guess I will pay you, dear brother and sister, a visit, for we have much catching up to do."

He rode for many miles, the sun beginning to slip beneath the horizon behind him when he spotted a suitable place to spend the night. He dismounted and peered at his horse knowing the beast had ceased being a mere animal quite some time ago. The evil had turned it into one of those repulsive things. He rued that transformation because he used to dote on that horse like some overwhelmed lover, allowing no one but himself to groom and feed it. He ignored it now, letting it graze as it chose without even bothering to remove the saddle and bridle. He knew it would remain where it stood, watching over him with its vacant eyes. He ate a cold meal then rolled himself into his blankets. Although the ground was hard and the night chilly, he was somewhat free and that was enough for him. For now, anyway.

Zada placed a cool cloth on Ramira's forehead then lifted the covers, careful not to disturb the sleeping elf, to check on the wounds they had re-sewn. She clucked her tongue for even all of Clare's skill could not keep these scars from turning ugly, especially after Ramira had ripped them open during her convulsions. That she lived was amazing enough, but what had the poison done to her? And why did she enter that house with such conviction? Zada had watched the confrontation with her inner sight and shuddered at the ferocity with which she had destroyed the Kreetch, a viciousness even the Herkahs could not match. Her expertise with the knives had stunned Zada, too, for none but the nomads wielded them in that manner. Where had the girl learned that? Zada picked up Ramira's knives and studied them under the light. The metal—if that's what they were cast from—was unfamiliar as were the strange symbols that appeared and disappeared all along the blades. The vague outline of a hawk-like bird came into view then withdrew…or did it metamorphose…into something akin to a feather. The figures surfaced on the entire exterior of the daggers and the more she turned the knives the more images emerged. She was almost tempted to say they were ceremonial in nature, but what would Ramira be doing with such knives? Zada's inner sight turned on but rather than showing her a vision, it warned her to put the blades down. She put them away then looked up as Allad silently entered the room, drawing strength from his hands as they rested on her shoulders.

"What did Danyl do?" he asked her quietly, wanting an answer but somehow afraid of what she would tell him.

"He plucked her from the jaws of hell."

"But how? How can he simply delve into and through her into that vast darkness?"

Zada's mind flashed back to the moment when he "returned" from within Ramira. His face had been flushed and covered in sweat, his intensely glowing eyes frightening her with their significance. The elven power, awakened by the desperate act of the unaware prince, flourished in the land once more. She would keep this information to herself for the time being. Danyl would need time to adjust to the magic and the tremendous responsibility it represented; wielding it unprepared would be catastrophic.

Danyl opened his eyes and immediately checked on Ramira even though every fiber of his being ached. Satisfied she was doing well, he rose from the bed to stretch his sore muscles as he gazed over at the ever-vigilant Zada. She smiled, then offered him a "she's going to be fine" look. He rubbed at his tired eyes, his stomach growling in protest for having been neglected so long. The faint light filtering through the drapes announced a new day.

"Why don't you go and clean up? Eat something, Danyl, I'll watch over her and let you know if anything happens."

He caressed Ramira's cheek then withdrew from this room to go to his own, where he bathed and changed into a fresh set of clothes. He headed downstairs to the kitchen and fixed a plate of food, taking it out into the garden, where he ate without tasting a single bite. He stared off into the distance unaware of a figure approaching him.

"How is she?" asked a concerned Seven, sitting down beside the prince.

"Resting," he replied. "Why would she deliberately go into that house, Seven?"

"She sensed danger and wanted to protect the couple inside, I assume. Zada 'saw' what happened, Danyl, perhaps you should ask her. Either that or wait until Ramira is able to tell you," he suggested.

Danyl nodded. First he would speak to the Herkah then, when Ramira was strong enough, he would talk to her. He accepted the glass Seven offered him then shuddered as the clear liquid burned his throat, the spirit harsh yet soothing as it began to relax him. He breathed deeply then looked over at his friend who was almost like a father to him. The dwarf king had held him in his arms when he was an infant, reprimanded him when he was a young boy and watched him grow into a man. The love in the King's eyes never faltered for one instant; instead, it grew whether they were together or apart. Seven's big hand reached up and touched the elf's cheek, a simple gesture of encouragement the prince greatly appreciated.

"That was very underhanded of you," Danyl said, as he lifted the empty glass.

"Yes it was, but don't tell Clare," he begged, as he rose and left Danyl alone with his thoughts.

The elf did not stay much longer, his concern for Ramira urging him to return to her room. He watched Allad place the sleeping woman back on a freshly changed bed, her body discreetly covered in a sheet. Zada had bathed her as best as she could, brushing out her hair and re-braiding it. The spasms had left her body drenched in perspiration and her hair knotted and wild. Danyl pulled back the blanket by her side and grimaced; the edges of the wounds were bright red and hot to the touch.

"Infection?" he asked, his face lined with worry.

"No," she replied, dabbing at the jagged lines with a thick spicy mixture. "Her body is expelling the last of the poison…in a day or two this will look normal."

"Zada, how many people have survived the Kreetch?"

"Just Allad, Nyk and a couple of others. Some of them were beyond my talents and had to be…" She didn't have to finish for the prince understood all too clearly.

"The marks across his body…" he muttered aloud, remembering the day at Jack and Ida's when Allad helped them repair the barn.

"Yes, Danyl. She will, unfortunately, bear the same reminders. Does it trouble you to behold her scarred body?"

"What bothers me is how she will feel every time she sees them."

"Allad's scars constantly remind him of his own mortality. They heighten his awareness and need to fight the demons to spare others their ultimate horror."

"What will it make her?" he asked as he took her limp hand into his.

"Time will tell," was her cryptic reply. The voracity with which Ramira had sought out then executed the Kreetch told her the woman feared very little in life. If she didn't know better, Zada would have sworn Herkah blood ran through her veins.

The brothers sat atop their horses, and along with Gard, Allad and Seven, watched their men practice side by side. They instilled the need for cooperation into them, a necessary component if they were to be successful in battling the army the evil was going to send. The men exchanged techniques and methods; the result was a more competent fighting unit. Almost all of those upon the plain were veterans of many skirmishes but nothing they had faced heretofore could match what awaited them.

Autumn was still over a month away but the elves already began to stock up on supplies. The extra mouths and the uncertainty of what to expect in the future prompted them to err on the side of caution. The dwarves had brought many items with them and the highly skilled Khadry hunted in the surrounding woods for meat that was dried and stored away. The city had nearly twice as many people living in or around it than before and the last thing they needed was for hunger to create dissent amongst the citizens. Seven glanced over at Danyl, his features more relaxed now that Ramira was out of bed and recovering from her encounter with the Kreetch. She was regaining her strength and both Zada and the prince made sure she remained in the castle under their watchful eyes. It had been nearly two weeks since the incident, and although Zada hadn't sensed any others, that didn't mean they weren't about. The Khadry and most of the dwarves had elected to remain on the plains surrounding the city until the weather changed for the worse or they were set upon by the evil. The Herkahs divided themselves up, staying with the others for their protection in case any demons attacked. They had no idea how the Kreetch that slaughtered the couple were able to approach undetected, compelling Zada to be more vigilant with her inner sight. She kept herself in a semi-trance, hovering at the edge of that nebulous darkness marking neither the world of the living or the dead. There was a great deal of disquiet emanating from that in-between world and the noise issuing forth almost overwhelmed her. The souls begging for release from the evil sensed her and clamored for attention, filling her mind with a cacophony of rustlings. She learned to ignore the whispers, concentrating instead on the feelings of dread preceding the arrival of the demons. The strain forced her to close that "door" and rest every once in a while, leaving them all vulnerable, but she was, after all, only human and could only endure so much. They tried to address practically every possibility they might encounter, fully aware the unforeseen events could leave them very defenseless. They would have to cope with those unexpected situations when they arose.

Ramira arose from the bed, slipping on her robe before heading out the door and into the kitchen. Her hunger would not wait until morning and she was not about to wake anyone up to take care of such a simple need. After a few wrong turns within the quiet hallways, she finally found the door to the kitchen. She opened the cupboard with one hand while gingerly touching her side with the other, scanning the shelves for a snack when she heard the voices. She turned around thinking someone had walked in, but the large room was empty save for her. Then the room itself dissolved into darkness.

Her bare feet recoiled with each step as they moved over the frigid stone floor. The walls were perfectly set and aligned but unadorned and almost menacing in appearance. Torches were jammed into brackets along the corridor, but the magnitude of the hall made their light appear feeble and dim. She passed many other corridors, their shadowy fronts the only evidence of their existence. She ignored them, her objective up ahead of her. The farther she moved into the stone void the stronger the herbs and aromas wafting toward her became. Their redolence clung to her as she moved through the faint haze, her purpose now close at hand. She stopped before a monumental set of doors, the iron rings used to open and close them big enough to fit her body through, and listened. From within came the sound of a woman chanting words in a language she could not understand, but the eerie tones made the hair on her body stand up.

She opened the huge doors with surprising ease and saw a thin woman clad in a red material that floated about with the slightest of movements. Her eyes were as pale as her skin and glittered with fear and loathing. They darted from Ramira to a pair of black knives carefully arranged upon an altar of gold situated in the center of the vast chamber. The woman hurriedly began to pour a mixture over the altar, her hands shaking with impatience while keeping an eye on Ramira. Ramira watched the viscous liquid flow down the narrow channels of the altar toward the knives, channels filled with the same symbols as on the blades. The closer the liquid oozed to the knives the more it began to hiss and boil until steam rose from the altar. Ramira ignored the red woman's unintelligible mantra, her attention riveted on the coagulated mixture seeping along the channels.

Her fingers twitched involuntarily at her sides, the sudden desire to lunge forward and grab the weapons before the fluid compound reached them unbearable. Ramira gave in and plucked them from the sacrificial stone just as the solution was about to envelop them. The woman shrieked with fury, continuing to fume and scream as Ramira headed for the door. She turned as the red woman ran after her, lifting the daggers the other so coveted and bringing both blades down into the shrieking and seething woman. Ramira felt no remorse watching the red woman fall into a heap at her feet. She stared with contempt at the dying figure then felt a low and ominous vibration begin from even deeper within this stone enclosure. A foul and frigid wind flowed from beneath the altar and spread outward and hid her feet. It gradually increased, obscuring her ankles then her knees. She shivered and gagged, bolting from this forbidding place and heading back the way she had come. The torches went out one by one, leaving Ramira in total darkness. She did not waver or give in to the disorientating effect, maintaining her flight out from this unsettling place…

Ramira snapped out of the vision grasping the counter for support, her cold feet aching at having to endure the icy floor. Thoughts of food no longer interested her as she hurried back to her room where she massaged the life back into her feet in front of the fire. She thought about the deadly encounter within the stone chamber and wondered what she had interrupted. Her strides to the vaulted room had been purposeful…as if she knew what was happening and had to stop it. But why? Who was that woman and why did she feel no regret in slaying her? What had she attempted to do to the knives? Ramira retrieved the blades and held them up to the light, their feel as familiar as they were foreign. The knives were a perfect extension of her fighting capabilities, the results at Evan's Peak and at the house by the orchard a testament to that fact.

"Well," she whispered to the daggers. "At least I know how you came into my possession."

Ramira lay back down upon her bed but did not fall asleep. She thought about the snippets of her past and what their implications were for her future. There were both good and bad people in her life and each in their own way was influencing the decisions she now made. One person had taught her how to fight and the gentlewoman love and kindness. The red woman, however, puzzled her. Their shared hatred flowed freely between them, and Ramira could not shake the feeling the red woman had been preparing the knives for her demise. She rolled over and grimaced as the blanket and nightgown constrained her side. She tugged on them until the pressure eased and fell into a fitful sleep.

Cooper woke up, his cramped muscles and filthy body putting him into a dark mood. He pulled out his provision pouch and glared inside then flipped the cover back over and tossed it aside. He had spent nearly two weeks on the road and hadn't gotten one break or idea and was sick of eating dried food and sleeping on the hard ground. Completely frustrated, he stomped over to the stream and stuck his entire head in the cool water, holding it there for several seconds before lifting it out. Rivulets of water ran down his chest and back as he sat there with his arms resting on his knees, his eyes focused on his as yet unseen destination.

"Face it, Coop," he said to himself, his voice suddenly calm. "You are going to your death and there's nothing you can do about it."

He watched the day unfold, the dark line of clouds indicating a lot of rain, yet he remained rooted in place as if the only sure thing in his life was the grass beneath him. He knew he was not the one who had unleashed Mahn upon the land. He also understood there was nothing he could have done to stop what had happened to his city. As to his forced trek to the elves? He was Mahn's pawn just like the elves were going to be. Then again, maybe not. Why couldn't the evil do to them what he had done to him? Why did he need his bizarre army to attack them? Why did he send Cooper east when he knew that he of all people would be least welcome in Bystyn? What was there that prevented Mahn from just taking it?

Mahn radiated power. The only race he knew of that had any form of magic was the elves. Did their power protect them and prevent him from swooping down like some bird of prey and taking the city? Yet he was amassing an army, taking it to Bystyn…going with his black arts to confront their might? No, he would already have done so. He has power but won't…or can't use it? The "won't" would be easy enough to figure out but the "can't"? He had been debating these thoughts ever since leaving Kepracarn yet the answers eluded him no matter how hard he tried to find them. Cooper knew he was not stupid so why couldn't he figure this out?

He finally got up and collected his things, absently kicking at the ashes of his campfire to make sure it was out. Instead of mounting his demon steed, he stared at the pile of gray, his mind trying to tell him something. Fire. Sticks and twigs are ignited producing flames that heat and warm. He cocked his head and a slow smile spread across his features as the answer gradually manifested itself into his mind. Magic. An unearthly element ignited by the wielder and used to destroy. Mahn had the power but he did not have the device necessary to make it work! He was like a fully prepared fire without the flint essential to create the flames. He slapped his thigh as he burst out laughing, the tears rolling down his cheeks as he imagined the mighty Mahn searching his pockets for some flint. He roared so hard the demon-possessed thing stared at him and that only made him laugh even harder.

When he finally calmed down, he hopped on the beast's back and proceeded on, the revelation giving him a sense of satisfaction and a whole new outlook. Cooper wondered if he was supposed to figure that out then pass it on to the elves. Perhaps if they concentrated on searching for this thing, they would forego any battle plans and let their guard down, allowing the black army to sweep over them. An elf with his guard down in these perilous times was a fool, and although he had called them many things that word never passed his lips. He wondered what this thing was that Mahn searched for and if he could possibly find it first. He could use it to get back his city or anything else he fancied. He would be near Bystyn soon, and once he had assessed the goings-on, he could further his own plans. That thought eased some of his discomforts and gave him some measure of hope as he rode on.

Danyl worked at his desk and reached into the top drawer where he found the bracelet. He had forgotten about it and now, as it dangled from his index finger in the late afternoon light, he decided to pay Zada a visit. It was time to find out what this little trinket was all about, and who better to tell him than the nomad. He found her resting in her room and wanted to leave her alone, but she insisted he join her.

"What brings you?" she asked, handing him a glass of wine.

"This," he replied, as he pulled the bracelet out of his pocket and handed it to her.

She lifted it up to the light, the delicate deep blue beads glowing as she spun it around. Danyl recounted how he had discovered it in Karolauren's chambers and breaking a bead transported him elsewhere, where he experienced everything within the vision. She stared at him in disbelief while he spoke, for she had never heard of anything such as this before.

"How is that possible?"

"I don't know, Zada, that's why I brought it to you. Shall I?"

She took a deep breath and nodded, watching as the point of his knife crushed the bead. Nothing happened. Danyl looked at the remnants of glass, his puzzlement clearly etched on his face. He waited a few moments then crunched another one with the same results.

"I swear that what I told you was the truth," he stammered.

"Then if the images did not appear here before us, where then did they materialize?"

"Perhaps those were…well…empty," he suggested, and was about to try a third time when she placed her graceful hand over his.

"Don't," she stated, as she looked into his eyes the memory of the night he pulled Ramira back from the brink of the abyss still fresh in her mind. She took the piece of jewelry from him and placed it in her pocket, intending to give it back to the historian.

"Zada," he asked, the hesitation in his voice rooted in the uncertainties and oddities of the past few months. "Will Ramira fully recover?" The thought of her having a relapse, possibly even succumbing to the effects of the evil weighing heavily on his mind.

"She seems to be doing well, Danyl, but we may never know what the poison has done to her. Listen, to this day I am still very watchful over Allad and, as much as I love him, would not hesitate to deny the evil a chance to use him for his foul purposes."

"Are you saying that I would be forced to do the same?" he asked, the repulsion he felt at having to slay Ramira clearly showing on his face.

"If you love her, then, yes," was her honest reply.

"That is a heavy burden."

"Indeed it is, young prince, and it does not get lighter with time."

"I still don't like the idea of her returning to Sophie's house."

Ramira had left earlier in the day and no amount of cajoling could get her to stay. What would happen if the poison did necessitate her demise? Was he to assign a guard to be with her every hour of the day or would the Herkahs take over such a duty?

"If Ramira believed she was a threat to Sophie and Anci she would never have gone, Danyl."

"Allad isn't convinced he isn't a threat or you wouldn't have told me about killing him."

"That is true, Danyl, but…" She couldn't finish, for how would she be able to tell him the elven might had done more than help him yank her back from those horrible depths? The magic, she was sure, would have negated the poison running rampant through her system or she would already be dead. Allad did not have that luxury. Zada dropped her gaze as she tried to hide her thoughts from him.

"But what?"

"I'm convinced she is no danger to anyone."

"What if she is?" he quietly asked her.

They locked eyes, hers showing him nothing but the awful truth of the situation. He did not doubt she would kill Allad, but was he strong enough to do the same to Ramira? He nodded then rose, for he needed some time alone to think about what she had said. She took the bracelet back out after he had gone and dangled it from her fingers, the tiny beads seducing her in ways she had never been before. They appeared innocent enough and it was clear whoever made them had an incredible talent and a mountain of patience to thread the minute holes with the single filament of gold. Such an endeavor required a sharp eye and steady hand.

She tried to imagine what kind of woman had worn such an ornament, deciding she was not overly ostentatious or vain. The bracelet's delicate pattern marked a simple woman who appreciated fine workmanship combined with a refined elegance. She bit her lip, the desire to break a bead contrary to what she had just told the elf, but the bracelet haunted her. She gave in to the urge, breaking the one nearest the twisted clasp.

She found herself in a small, thick stoned home lit only by a single lamp set upon a table and a fire burning in the hearth. A pot hung from an iron arm inside it, the aroma of spiced stew filling the room. She heard someone enter and turned around, coming face to face with a stocky woman, her graying hair pulled back in a bun. Her simple tunic was well worn but clean and the surprise on her face melted away as she waved to a cushioned bench. Zada was speechless. Danyl had not mentioned just how real the images were.

"Good evening, good woman," she greeted, then apologized. "I did not mean to startle you."

"That's all right, child. I see you too have found the bracelet."

"Ah…yes. Do you know who it belongs to?"

"Yes, it was a very special gift."

Zada could see lines of worry on her brown features, and although she paid attention to her guest, the woman seemed overly guarded.

"Are you expecting someone?" asked Zada.

"Hopefully not," she replied. "But I think you had better leave or the moment will pass and you will be forced to stay. This is not your place, child." She rose to her feet, holding out her hand, and when Zada took it, she felt the warmth pulse past the work-hardened palm and fingers as the woman began to fade away into mist…

Zada stared into the empty air that wasn't empty moments ago, saddened by this woman's disappearance but knowing she had turned to dust centuries ago. Zada realized the visions were more defined because of her inner sight, and therefore more dangerous. The woman warned her not to stay too long or she would not be able to return: but from where? Where had the trinket taken her? She sensed no power from it yet it exuded a kind of connection…a link to the past where everyday activities and people made up the future. The beads were telling a story but not from beginning to end. The story wasn't due to a clear-cut series of events as much as a haphazard collection of circumstances that was more important than the logical progression of outcomes. The unforeseen was more potent than the expected, a lesson they had best take to heart.

Danyl's description of the little brown man told her the wearer was being educated and the house he passed may well have belonged to the woman she "visited." This last image, however, troubled her. The bracelet seemed innocent enough, but it had the power to imprison her in a different time, one that made the brown woman quite nervous. What had she been afraid of? And where had those two images gone after Danyl had broken the beads? Were they indeed "empty" as he had suggested? She sighed heavily as she stared at the delicate item suspended from her finger.

"Tiny bits of glass revealing for only a brief period of time their extraordinary secrets..." she murmured almost reverently to herself.

Ramira left the castle bound for Sophie's house, much to the consternation of those she was sure watched her leave. She wanted her own bed and the less hectic pace the house offered even if she spent most of her time doing chores and running errands. Danyl had been the most vocal of all, but she assured him she would not to depart from the city without at least one guard. She walked into the kitchen, her eyes lighting up, the aroma of freshly baked cakes greeting her before Sophie's arms wrapped around her.

"Sweet mercy, girl, it is good to have you back!" said the woman as she touched her cheek.

"It felt strange not being given a long list of things to do," she chuckled.

"You weren't exactly in any condition to do them or I would have handed you one. Here." She handed Ramira a plate of still steaming treats. "You're too skinny."

Ramira took a couple and realized she had lost quite a bit of weight since the battle with the Kreetch. She had been unconscious, then unable to eat much of anything for nearly a week, and even now ate only a few bites at a time. She suddenly felt tired. The short walk from the castle to the house drained her energy. She went upstairs to lie down for a while, listening to Sophie bustle about in the kitchen as she fell asleep.

She opened her eyes and swung her legs over the side of the bed, the dingy gray light indicating it was either early evening or the weather was changing. When she approached the window and pulled back the curtain, she knew it was the former. She patted her itchy side, careful not to scratch and further aggravate the wounds as she headed downstairs to the kitchen. It was very quiet and she assumed Sophie and Anci had gone out for a while, leaving her alone with the plate of treats.

...She stood in darkness, the insidious whispers brushing against her skin, making her shudder and telling her that death would come to those around her. They promised to fulfill their evil intentions and gleefully hissed their delight in carrying out their cursed vows...

Dazed by the sudden appearance of the malicious vision, she grabbed the back of the chair and steadied herself from the appalling onslaught, only to be accosted again a few seconds later.

...She stood beneath a searing sun, its rays threatening to burn strips of flesh off her body as things bumped against her legs. She looked down and gaped in horror as the faces on the rotting corpses stared up at her. Their accusing eyes were recognizable even though they were contorted and swollen with every possible affliction. Skeletal hands reached up toward her, their fingers flexing and gripping at her until she thought she would go mad...

She collapsed onto her knees, the jarring effect sending waves of pain and nausea through her, her eyes wide with fright and horror. She wanted to scream, wail at the awful vision, but her throat would not release a single sound. She managed to rise onto the bench where she dropped her face into her hands, the unanticipated and incredibly life-like scene slowly dissipating from her sight. People she knew and those she had never seen before had glared at her with an accusation so horrible she could barely contain her sanity.

When her hands finally stopped shaking, she poured herself a cup of strong tea and walked out onto the terrace on wobbly legs. She sat down beneath the roses but even their soothing fragrance could not fully erase her nightmare. It took all of her will to still her trembling, both within and without, when Sophie and Anci trod onto the terrace. The shadows hid the dread on her face, her voice remained strangled in her throat while Anci spoke of the day's events. Anci's light tones helped chase the darkness away, the joy of her innocence a balm to her tortured soul.

"You're rather quiet," Sophie said after a while, as she tried to peer into her face.

"It's been a long few weeks," she managed to say, as she stared into the night, the sound of insects and birds all around her. There was a slight chill in the air not just from the changing seasons but from a more perverse reason steeped in death. It might have been a mistake to leave the protection of the castle. If the images were going to come to pass, the last place she wanted to be is where they could fulfill their awful threat. Wouldn't being in this house...no, this city, bring the same fate? She shivered as she contemplated that terrible possibility.

Cooper glanced at the farmer hauling a wagonload of vegetables off to his right. The weathered elf stared at the King not quite believing what his eyes beheld. His grip on the reins loosened so much that they dropped to the floorboards between his feet. He scrambled to retrieve them before the horses decided to adopt their own pace. He collected them then slapped the horses' backs, heading toward a patrol to the northeast of their position.

"That's it," muttered the King under his breath, the forced smile never leaving his face. "Go fetch the boys for me, you mindless idiot." He slowed his mount down then brought it to a standstill, watching the farmer frantically waving at the scouts. The guards raced over to the elf, listening as the animated homesteader pointed over at the King. The farmer watched the patrol ride away, remaining standing to get the best view of what was about to transpire.

Cooper waited patiently as the elven patrol approached him, narrowing his eyes as he detected Herkahs, dwarves, and forest elves riding with them. He raised a brow as the information sank into his mind, for it seemed as if Bystyn had been very busy of late. He silently congratulated the elven king for such a remarkable feat then wondered what other surprises awaited him. Alyxandyr had overcome fear and bitterness to win the support of the nomads and Khadry, and the dwarves, well, they had been allies for a long time. The elves were also preparing for a long war, for wagonloads of goods poured in from the east and he could see soldiers practicing along the western plains. No, the elves were no fools, and neither was he.

"King Cooper?" was Nyk's astonished yet suspicious demand. What in the four corners of the land was going on? Cooper rides in all by himself after nearly a year's absence? Nyk sensed a trap and treated the situation exactly in that manner. He glanced over at Allad, who shook his head: Cooper was not demon infested.

"Yes, good day to you, too, Prince Nyk," replied the King with his usual arrogance. He nodded ever so slightly at Allad, who openly stared at him. This nomad unnerved him, for Allad exuded a power and tenacity that knew no bounds: he would slay a king as quickly as a thief and regret neither death. If Allad was here then Zada would be here as well. Now there were a couple of Herkahs Mahn would love to have in his stable! Nyk's voice interrupted his musings.

"What brings you to Bystyn?" he inquired, not bothering to hide his skepticism.

"I bear a message for you."

"From whom?" Nyk probed, the hint of sarcasm in his voice eliciting a slight smile from the King. Nyk couldn't help but notice how similar in appearance Cooper and Mason were but how vastly different in their dispositions and goals.

Cooper ignored the question for the time being, intent on the demon steed's destruction. He gathered up his courage and locked eyes with Allad then hinted at the mount. He needed to get rid of the beast, not to protect those who crowded in and around the city, but to further his own ambitions.

Allad stared at the animal, its docile appearance deceiving but not as deceptive as the reason behind Cooper's betrayal of it. Allad had no choice in the matter because even if the demon's death was for the king's benefit only, it still had to be slain. He caught Nyk's eye and indicated the horse.

"Dismount," Nyk ordered. The King got down off the horse and unwillingly backed away from it. The animal thing sensed something wasn't quite right but its reaction was too slow. Allad pounced into the saddle, bringing his blades up under its great neck then rolled away effortlessly as it fell in a shrieking heap. Everyone, even Cooper, shuddered with revulsion. Allad's black eyes ensnared Cooper's, demanding to know if there was anything else that he should be telling them. Cooper kept his composure even though his skin crawled beneath the nomad's intense gaze and shook his head. After a few long moments the Herkah released the King.

Nyk sent a messenger to the city, keeping Cooper where he stood, the foreboding his presence elicited sharp in his mind. He had ridden all this way on the demon steed, exposing its true identity at the gates of the city, but was this solely his choice or the orders of whatever sent the King east? He knew Cooper would sacrifice anything or anyone to further his own cause, but he trifled with something well beyond his capabilities. They waited for nearly an hour, Cooper never once complaining or even speaking, until the guard returned and whispered into the prince's ear. Nyk glared down at him for a moment longer then ordered them to move toward the gate, the King walking in the middle of the well-armed and watchful group.

Alyxandyr stood staring out the window in his rooms, hands clasped behind his back as he contemplated their present situation. He was looking for a common thread that bound them all together because finding it meant being able to trace it back to the truth. This was a difficult task for the variety of individuals currently involved in this dilemma had no known bonds. The only clear fact was that the races were gathering at his doorstep where the evil intended to annihilate them. He could not shake the feeling that this evil had a personal quarrel with the elves. What that could be he could not even guess. Nothing in the elven archives ever mentioned anything remotely linked to the evil. He was at a loss to understand why that thought persisted in his mind. Cooper would be here shortly and the other leaders already waited for him in the main hall, as curious about what he had to say as Alyxandyr was. The elven king questioned Cooper's reliability yet he was bound to say something that would shed some light on this matter. The evil had sent him and would therefore be under his control, but Cooper still retained his own identity and would not capitulate to it quite so easily. They would have to listen carefully to what he said and make their own assumptions. He breathed in deeply one more time then joined the other leaders.

Cooper felt their glares impale him the moment his heavily armed guard escorted him into the chamber. There were no false pretenses heaped upon him, only unbridled looks of contempt and suspicion. Cooper offered them a brief courtly bow and was not surprised when those around the round oak table barely returned the courtesy. It took all of his willpower not to smirk at the cold deference paid to him by the Herkahs. It's good to be king, he crowed silently. Alyxandyr waved to a chair and they all sat down, their stares firmly fixed on Cooper.

"What is happening in your city, Cooper?" demanded Alyxandyr.

"That's a long and complicated story…"

"Condense it for us." Mason's deep voice reached out and into his brother's heart, his animosity making it skip a beat.

"About a year ago a stranger came to Kepracarn," began the King, steadying himself with a deep breath and grasping the edges of the table. "He told me that there was treasure buried on the desert insec…" Careful, Cooper, he reminded himself as Allad's eyes glinted dangerously across the table from him. "On the Herkahs' lands. He had a map but no diggers and offered a percentage of the gold in exchange for manpower. I agreed and sent out an expedition with him."

"Why not kill the man, take the map and unearth the riches yourself?" asked Mason.

"That thought might have crossed my mind, but this was no ordinary man, *brother*." Cooper suppressed the derisive grin pulling on his mouth as Mason cringed at the mere mention of such a connection. "The stranger did not have the diagram with him, claiming he had stashed it near the dig site. I agreed to accompany him, finalizing my scheme on the way to the location. Fifty men came with me and never returned to the city." Genuine fear and hatred began to filter into his voice as he continued speak.

"We dug for days, carting away loads of sand, and never found a single thing. I was beginning to tire of this fool's errand until we uncovered a flat rock placed over a hole in the ground. The excitement rippling through the camp was short-lived, for when my men pried it open…"

Cooper closed his eyes and watched as the scene replayed itself behind his lids. Sweat glistened off the workers straining to hoist the cap off the opening. The stranger seemed to stand a little taller and the hands resting on his hips looked larger and stronger than Cooper remembered. The men groaned in unison, their musclebound bodies inched the cover to the side until the opening was completely exposed. The stranger stepped to the edge and stared down into the blackness then spoke in a tongue completely foreign to Cooper. At first nothing happened then the King had heard screams and shrieks rising up from the depths. Soon a noxious mist curled up from within the darkness, spreading over the lip of the opening and staining the white sand all around it. Cooper backed away from the menacing fog, seeking an explanation from the stranger who welcomed its embrace. The rangy man with the weathered features began to alter right before his eyes, growing in height and girth until he towered over him. His once tattered and dusty cape had been replaced with a coal-black cloak that billowed behind him like an ominous cloud promising severe weather.

The haze infused itself into his men, their cries and howls cherished by the monster standing in the middle of the upheaval. The King watched helplessly as gangly things with matted black hair scampered out of the cavity and immediately set themselves upon his men. They ripped them apart, gorging on their flesh and each other if one got too close. Cooper had dropped to his knees, cowering as the madness persisted all around him. It intensified as the fiend strode toward him, his massive legs pushing aside everything in their path.

"Rise!" it bellowed down at him.

Cooper could not speak let alone force his rubbery legs to support him. He remained on his knees, swaying with disbelief at what was occurring around him. A black-gloved hand shot out from within the immense cape, grabbing him by the throat and yanking him unceremoniously to his feet. Tears of pain and panic blurred his sight then ran down his cheeks. Their expulsion allowed him to see once again, and what he saw sent bile up into his mouth. Antama, his companion for decades, stood unmolested in the center of the horror, her flawless features radiating sheer contempt for him. Confusion and chaos filled his mind, for she had never indicated any unhappiness in her life with him. She had access to everything, including his decision-making. It had, evidently, not been enough for her. She wanted to be queen, and allied herself to this demon to fulfill her will. She lifted her arms out to her sides and permitted the red mist swirling at her feet to flow up her body. It crawled upward with tiny talons that sliced into her flesh until her blood was indistinguishable from the haze. Antama shuddered, the expression on her face more akin to ecstasy rather than agony. The fog finally enveloped her then immediately retreated into her body. She wavered once then stood perfectly still, her eyes entirely bright red…

He opened his eyes and stared at his clasped hands, telling his peers what had transpired in a voice devoid of emotion. The leaders remained shocked and silent throughout his account and for many long minutes when he was finished.

"Your greed set the evil free!" Mason was aghast.

"I wouldn't have complied had I known what he was! Give me a little credit…" Cooper rose from his chair, pointing at Mason with one hand while the other curled up into a fist. Mason pushed his seat back, more than willing to converge on his brother.

"Stop it! Both of you!" demanded Alyxandyr.

"King Cooper." Zada's clear voice cut through the tension. "Please proceed with your report."

"I was brought back to the city," he stated after a short time. "Mahn had taken over it while I was at the site and kept me prisoner in one of my rooms. The only contact I had was with the Vox and, on occasion, with Mahn. He didn't kill anymore of my people but he should have. They became like rats scrounging or fighting for bits and pieces of food, living in filth and despair. This went on until he decided the time was right for me to come here."

Some of his equals exchanged wary glances while others stared off into the distance trying to picture the horror he had described. He met the gazes of all who looked upon him except for Zada's. Hers was steady and direct, lacking any animosity but radiating danger nonetheless.

Unlike the nomads who killed only those men straying onto their lands to commit some misdeed, Cooper purposefully hunted them. His one and only desire was to kill them…well, for pleasure. His victories were rare and cost him many men, but that didn't matter for the surge of power and excitement those scarce conquests gave him made it all worthwhile. The nomads had every right to slay him where he sat—he certainly would have if their roles had been reversed—but they remained calm and non-threatening.

"Why do you think this Mahn forced you to our gates?" asked the elven king after a long pause.

"My guess would be to help precipitate your downfall."

"And how would you fulfill such an obligation?" Mason's deep voice reached across to his brother like a vise grip, its touch squeezing his innards as effectively as Mahn had. Cooper would never admit it, but he was even more afraid of Mason than Allad. "I don't know."

Mason, however, did know, for his brother was filled with craftiness, intelligence, and the patience to wield it in the most unassuming of ways. His methods had allowed him to remain king and alive for all of these years. Mahn had sensed these things inside of him and knew such duplicity could work in his favor without the need for Cooper to become a demon. Cooper's danger lay in the fact he could create havoc, doubt and distrust amongst the fragile alliance now guarding the city. It was imperative the King be isolated and his communication restricted to a chosen few who would not heed his snake-like words, and he whispered as much into Alyxandyr's ear. The King agreed and ordered Cooper to wait outside the chamber while those within listened to what Mason had suggested. It was decided he would be secured in the room Ramira had recovered in and the Herkahs would watch over him. They escorted him to the room and locked the door behind him.

Ramira dunked the washcloth into the water and wrung it out before replacing it across her face, blocking out the early evening light. The house was hers until later on, and she took advantage of the quiet, indulging in a hot bath. She heard someone enter the house through the partially open door and looked up to see Danyl standing in the doorway. She pressed her body against the side, arms and hands resting on the edge as he moved toward her and sat on the chair beside the bathtub. That peculiar sensation flared to life once again, the fire burning away their inhibitions and even the world beyond the room. The elf closed the remaining distance between them until mere inches separated their faces

His fingers gently traced her features, his eyes studying and remembering every detail. He leaned forward and kissed her, his hands caressing her wet arms and back. Her limbs snaked up his forearms, the pair rising to their feet as one never breaking their embrace. He lifted her out of the tub and wrapped a towel around her, removing his sodden tunic and dropping it on the back of the chair. He scooped her up in his arms and carried her up to her room, pulling back the covers before tenderly placing her on the bed. He lay down alongside her and kicked off his short boots, withdrawing the corner of the towel tucked into a fold. He gazed into her eyes, the passion reflected within them matching his own. Danyl removed the rest of his clothing and joined her beneath the covers.

Sophie walked into the kitchen and put away the leftover food from the dinner she had attended. She glanced into the bathing chamber, wrinkling her forehead as she approached the tub. She reached into the cold water and yanked out the plug, blowing out the lamp next to the half full glass of wine. She picked up the tunic carelessly tossed on the back of the chair and stared at it for a moment. Her gaze traveled to the ceiling then back to the garment. She slowly exhaled and headed upstairs, softly knocking on Ramira's door. Sophie pushed down on the handle and cautiously entered the room, her eyes quickly adjusting to the moonlight flowing in through the balcony window. She gazed down at the bed and pressed her lips together.

Danyl slept behind Ramira, his arms protectively encircling her slumbering form, their hands clasped at her side. The couple dozed peacefully beneath rumpled blankets, their content faces framed by nearly dry hair. Sophie looked away and retrieved his trousers, hanging them and his shirt over the armchair. She left the room and stepped out into the hallway, glancing back once before closing the door.

He emitted a low hiss of satisfaction as the Source's approximate location appeared before him. He had been searching for it for a long time and it now lay within his grasp. He could not go and take it but he could make it leave…force it to expose itself then reach out and grab it. His dead eyes gazed down into the narrow and winding streets, the grimy walls and channels filled with muck and alive with rodents. It was a most welcome sight, one he planned to heap upon the rest of the land once he had the power.

He drew great satisfaction from the skeletal forms scurrying through the city. Their starving forms were barely able to remain erect as they used their precious strength to wrest a morsel of food from someone even weaker than they were. Perhaps he would let a few mortals remain alive so their last instincts for survival could amuse him. He could throw a few crumbs between two of them and watch. Maybe not, he sneered at the wretched things below him. He would be lord and master of everything soon enough, then he could decide what their insignificant fates would be. He turned as the doors behind him opened, admitting one of the Vox. The Herkah shell inhabited by a most fearsome demon even caused him to pause in admiration. It bore a message.

"Cooper has entered the city and the beast, as expected, has been slain." Its sound more of a choked wheezing than a true voice due, he was sure, to the still-living Herkah struggling within its violent internal embrace.

"How long before these creatures are ready?" He indicated the contemptible figures below the window.

"They can be ready within days."

"Good. Have the three been dispatched?"

"Gone since this morning," it breathed heavily. The sound was very deceiving, for the Vox could run and fight for days without tiring.

Mahn nodded and the Vox slipped away, leaving the evil to contemplate his plans once more. If the Source abandoned the city soon then his armies would be at the gates of the city within two weeks: if it did not, then the snows would hamper but not stop his advance. If the Source managed to slip through his fingers for a few days or weeks then that suited him just as well. His legions would weaken whatever defenses the elves and their useless allies constructed until he wouldn't need the power to bring down those gray walls. He had sensed the elven magic beginning to awaken, but there was no one within the city capable of wielding it. The White Witch had bestowed the sight upon the nomad, a burden he planned to exploit to the fullest. He anticipated tormenting her and the White Witch. He could not wait to exterminate her followers: without them she would fade into obscurity, a forgotten symbol wasting away into oblivion. No, not killed but absorbed into his dark realm—an even worse fate.

He began to roar with anticipation, imagining the souls he would feast on. The most gratifying ones would be the shrieking and screaming mortals running over each other to get away from him. His hatred and bitterness radiated outward and spread down the side of the building and into the street. It not only drove the pitiful humans into their homes or any other place to escape its horror but scattered his minions as well.

Zada gasped for air as Mahn's twisted jubilation traveled to her sensitive sight. Her hands clutched at her throat, the rancid odors trying to drown her, stealing her breath even from this distance. Clare rushed over to her, grabbing her just as she began to topple forward, then met Alyxandyr's eyes as she held the woman in her arms. There was no need to speak, for they could well decipher the nomad's reaction. Alyxandyr turned around, clasping his hands in the small of his back as he stared out the window into the rainy afternoon. They were all so different yet the one thing binding them together was the need to persevere against things they could not understand. They were offering their faith and lives and the King had nothing to give them back except a place to die. That concept made his blood run cold. His sons came and stood beside him, their hands on his shoulders. The evil grew in power every day, his plans for the mortals well underway. Mahn and his slaves were coming to Bystyn and there was nothing they could do to stop him. The elven king looked down at the dwarf queen, who still held the Herkah in her arms, then glanced over at the Khadry. They were all bound to one another, regardless of their beliefs, and were determined to offer up their lives for one purpose. Alyxandyr thought about the thread and realized it was hope.

Burdened with packages, Ramira entered the kitchen and stopped in her tracks. She could not believe her eyes, as the most powerful leaders in the land crowded around Sophie's table enjoying platters of food and a variety of beverages. Seven, Clare, Alyxandyr, Zada, Allad, Danyl and Styph greeted her then resumed their feast. Sophie took the supplies and Anci shoved a bowl and spoon into her hands before she could utter a single word.

"You'll trip over that if you don't close it," chuckled Seven, his chin pointing to her jaw.

"They've already opened every drawer and cupboard looking for food, girl, and they'll look in there for more, too," joked Sophie.

"What...?" she managed as Sophie gave her a healthy serving of stew then sat her down between the elven king and Danyl. The space was barely wide enough for her slim frame but none other was available. She began to eat, lightly pressing herself into Danyl, who softly nudged her shoulder.

Seven finished first and produced a bottle of his clear poison. Not to be outdone, Allad deposited his version of the drink on top of the table, much to the delight of the dwarf but not of Clare or Zada. They initially gave their respective mates a look of warning then thought better of it; nights like these would be few and far between in the coming weeks. Ramira subtly glanced from one to the other. Seven was his usual animated self; Allad was remarkably handsome as he smiled and laughed next to the dwarf king and an impish air surrounded Styph, who smirked at his brother across the table. Alyxandyr participated in the fun but his tense body felt like a brick wall against her side. She hesitantly placed her hand on his brawny arm to get his attention and held her breath as his commanding gaze landed on her. He seemed to grow in stature without ever moving a muscle.

"Yes?" The King's voice was both gentle and direct.

"Could you please pass the..." What had she wanted? She glanced down at her bowl then over to her glass. Yes, that was it. "The wine?" Ramira watched the elven king fill her glass and thanked him.

She noticed shadows crossing the terrace, the ever-vigilant guards keeping their distance while protecting their charges. The peril emanating from the west hovered outside the kitchen and only the good-fellowship shared here kept it at bay. For the time being, anyway. Danyl reached for her hand under the table and gently squeezed it. She shifted her focus to the prince, the love they had shared shining from his eyes. Ramira desperately tried to restrain the blush creeping up onto her cheeks. Relief came in the form of a glass Alyxandyr handed to her and she hastily downed Seven's concoction. She shivered as it burned everything on its way to her stomach and ceded to the flush.

"Easy, child!" Clare called over to her.

"You know what happens if you drink those too quickly?" Seven said with a wink.

"You wake up with a head that won't fit through the door and you end up drinking everyone else's tea?"

"No…" Seven pointed a finger at a smirking Danyl.

"You get lectured by Clare while holding a cold cloth to your forehead?" Styph offered an amused Clare with a stately nod of his head.

"No!"

"Your tongue becomes so loose it falls out of your mouth and trips you." The dwarf queen jabbed his side for extra emphasis.

The dwarf king pretended to glower, brightening immediately as Allad poured him a glass of Herkah liquor. He slapped Seven on the back, the dwarf nearly panicking as the liquid threatened to spill over the rim.

Zada studied Danyl and Ramira, noting the understated changes in their behavior toward one another. His gaze lingered on her face, his body responding as she leaned closer against him. She smiled then frowned slightly as she remembered what the elf bore and how he had unknowingly used it to snatch Ramira out of the evil's grasp. The power elevated him beyond the mortals gathered here, including the woman he had chosen to be his companion. She tuned out the stories and laughter as an interesting thought presented itself to her. The foreign magic that had been brandished deep within Ramira should have somehow affected her. She showed no outward signs that it had or of any delayed aftereffects from the Kreetch's poison.

She carefully focused her inner eye on the couple and took a sharp breath at what she saw. A faint, greenish haze rolled along Danyl's body much like the lazy mists after a cool summer rain. It diminished when the contact between the two of them was broken, reemerging when they touched once more. The longest of the tendrils swirling around him wavered, becoming more brilliant with every passing second. It swayed in warning over his head like some cobra readying to strike, hypnotizing Zada with its deadly dance. She attempted to move beyond the boundaries of her sight toward it until her inner eye abruptly ended the trance.

The conversations sounded loud in her ears and the smell of food and tobacco smoke overwhelmed her nose. Perspiration trickled down the side of her face as she dared to look at the prince who sipped unaware from his goblet. Zada kept her cold hands in her lap, her awe much more difficult to conceal.

Allad tapped her arm, interrupting her deliberations: it was time to go. It had been a long and delightful evening, but their drooping eyes and stifled yawns urged them to seek their beds. They shuffled still laughing toward the front door, leaving Danyl and Ramira alone for a few moments. He wrapped his arms around her, kissing her lightly on the lips then, gently caressed her flushed cheeks.

"I don't suppose I could convince you to return to the castle with me," he whispered to her.

"The temptation is there," she shyly replied. "But I have to stay and help Sophie clean up."

"Eventually that will change, Ramira. You know that, don't you?"

"Yes," she sighed, touching his face. He nodded then joined the group walking back to the castle amid the guards.

"You were rather surprised to see them all in here," Sophie said, as she cleared the table of the glasses and empty plates of food. Anci shuffled sleepily up to her room, the two women smiling and shaking their heads at the exhausted girl.

"So much power in such a little room…"

"They always end up here when they visit; it's just that this time there were more to share in the friendship."

"Sophie?"

"Yes?"

"You aren't angry with me about the other night, are you?" Ramira and Danyl had awoken and found his clothes neatly folded on the chair beside the bed. Sophie had not mentioned a word about what had transpired, but it was her house and she had a right to speak her mind.

Sophie thought back to the few precious years she had spent with Anci's father. She had first seen Tabryn, the King's quiet cousin, in the garden where he spent a great deal of time reading beneath a bower heavy with white clematis. He had invited her to sit with him, telling her about the city she had recently begun to call home, a ritual that lasted for most of the summer. She remembered his kindness and attentiveness, and the pure joy he elicited from her soul. He died after being thrown from a horse shortly before their daughter was born, and she missed him dearly to this very day.

"No, child," Sophie said softly, cupping Ramira's chin in her hand. She untied her apron and went to bed, pausing at her door as the memories persisted.

Ramira sat down in front of the hearth, the unmistakable stirrings in her mind telling her she would not sleep well that night. The dark and foreboding dreams hovered at the edge of her consciousness, promising to assail her the moment she closed her eyes. She began to rock back and forth in the chair, the motion offering her a measure of comfort as she focused on the woman from her childhood. She imagined the arms enfolding her and the unmistakable kiss on the top of her head, the far-off humming echoing within her mind. The memory numbed her fears, replacing them with a sense of security that only true devotion could instill. Love from this woman flooded into her being, allowing Ramira to fall asleep without dread.

Autumn slipped into the land as the nights became a little cooler and the first faint hints of color touched the leaves. This time of year was usually the elves' favorite. They labored in the fields, filling their larders with canned vegetables and fruits, and gathered nuts and roots from the forests. The elves stocked up on meat and fish; the smokehouses were busy day and night. The Herkahs offered up their spices; the Khadry hunted deer and the dwarves brought in wagonloads of wood. The city had doubled in size and everyone had an obligation to perform, for there would be many more mouths to feed this winter.

The highlight of the season was the harvest festival held just before the first frost. Carts of food and drink would sprout up on the plains, available to the throngs who watched the competitions of strength and speed, participated in games, or enjoyed the entertainment. The celebration lasted for several days, after which many would leave the city and return to their outlying homes for the long winter. The King could not chance holding the ritual on the plains, opting to have it in the city instead. It was better than nothing and would alleviate some of the tension and anxiety building in the city.

He watched as the festival unfolded where the two main avenues intersected. He could see groups of singers and musicians milling about the partially filled square and the bright awnings covering stands of food and drink. He was pleased to see black and brown garb mixed in with the green. It seemed even the Herkahs and the Khadry were looking forward to being distracted from the terrors prowling along the plains. It was still early, though; perhaps the streets would fill up as the day wore on. He turned away, reentering his chambers and the matters at hand.

More than one patrol had reported seeing Mahn's army already on the plains far to the west, and its size grew with every account. The evil had grown enough in power to mobilize his legions and begin the trek east, and it wouldn't be long before it landed in front of the gates. Zada had sensed Mahn concentrating his search in the surrounding area, the Source's nearness both alarming and relieving at the same time. He returned his attention to the map strewn across his desk and the reports streaming in from all parts of his lands. He read one then made a short notation on the map in conjunction with the information from the patrol in that area. He repeated this several times, noting a pattern developing before his very eyes. There was little movement from the northeast and south, with the bulk of Mahn and his army flowing toward Bystyn from the west. They did not seem to be in any hurry, a fact opening up a few possibilities to explain why. The most important reason was he did not have the Source. What were the chances of finding it and using it against Mahn? If nothing else, they could conceal it, hoping it would forever be lost.

That was a foolish notion because power, especially the evil kind like the Source, would never allow itself to remain absent, and there would always be someone to find it. There would always be someone it would find and corrupt, he corrected himself. The Source was a powerful form of magic and could not be destroyed, wielded, or hidden: so what were they to do with it if they happened to find it? The King leaned back in his chair, interlacing his fingers behind his head as his eyes scanned the map. He...they...were missing something, overlooking a clue that could help them.

"Where are you?" he asked the Source in quiet tones.

Ramira sat next to Sophie on the front stoop as they took in a more restrained version of the autumn celebration. The number of people milling about grew steadily in the early afternoon hours. Groups of Herkahs mingled with dwarves and elves and even a few Khadry walked among the crowds. A pair of desert dwellers had set up a stand off to the right and people wanting to buy their meats and sweets mobbed it. The elves had developed a taste for nomad food and one of the Herkahs made several trips back out to the camp to restock her supplies. The singers, musicians, and dancers lifted the folk out of their anxious moods. The dancers wore brightly colored costumes, whirling and twirling to the beat of the drums' and the flutes' cheerful notes. Many sang along or simply clapped, a few even dancing to the catchy tunes. The food carts became focal points where many gathered to chat, and Sophie was certain their present problems were more prevalent than any other topic. Well, at least they were sharing them with each other rather than brooding over them in private.

She glanced over at Ramira and frowned. The dark circles under her eyes had become more prominent. She had appeared tired and drawn of late and Sophie knew her bad dreams were robbing her of more than just sleep. Could the aftereffects of the poison be to blame for that? It would break her heart if one of the Herkahs had to…she couldn't finish her thought. The overall pain her death would cause would be too much to bear. Sophie reached over and gently squeezed Ramira's hand and was rewarded with a tired smile. With any luck, all of this would soon be over and they could return to their normal lives without the fear of demons lurking outside the gates or within their minds.

Ramira appreciated the touch more than Sophie could know because the nightmares were taking over her daylight hours as well. Although she still sensed a presence in the house, she had ceased searching for it for fear of frightening the women. The knives never left her side, providing the only comfort to her as she strained to survive through the day. Danyl's visits were brief and rare; he was heavily involved in the planning that seemed to occur day and night as more and more information poured into the castle. His closeness offered her a measure of quiet, but she could not shadow him during these dismal times so she suffered them alone. The claw marks had healed but the ugly scars still bothered her, especially when she sensed the phantoms about. Cool cloths were unable to quell the subtle burning they emitted, forcing her to endure their discomfort until her hallucinatory feelings subsided. Ramira assumed Allad and Nyk experienced the same annoyance and made a mental note to ask them next time they met. Perhaps the nomads had some sort of balm to ease the ache. She clung to Sophie, the woman's touch easing some of her doubts and apprehensions while watching the passers-by enjoying the festivities in the street. She longed to join them but was too tired, too drained to leave the stoop. Perhaps a nap would help. She excused herself and went upstairs to lie down for a while.

Danyl's corridor dream had invaded his sleep several times over the past few weeks, so much so he decided to speak with Zada about it. She listened intently as he recalled the endless gallery, the locked doors and the water dripping from somewhere off in the distance. His confusion concerning the direction he was moving in piqued her interest. The Herkah remained silent after he had finished reflecting over the words he had spoken.

"Many believe their lives are mazes they cannot escape from," she said. "In truth, a person's life is very simple and straightforward. We are all free to make a choice or choices in order to set our path right once more. The problem, Danyl, is that the option to escape their 'maze' is more daunting than the 'maze' itself. The doubt generated by leaving a known or accepted situation inevitably keeps them locked within the labyrinth."

"So my choices lie behind one of the locked doors?" he asked.

"Or at either end of the corridor." She gazed at him wondering if he understood what grew within him and how he would react once that truth revealed itself.

"Zada." He peered intently into her eyes. "What did you see the night I denied the demons in Ramira's soul?"

She should have anticipated his question but did not and therefore all she could do was to stare at him in silence for a long time. He knew she was a witness to what had happened that night.

"I was just so astonished by what had transpired, that's all," she replied honestly, but the prince refused to relinquish his gaze.

"Zada." He took her trembling hands into his. "Did something help me pull her away from him? Am I the bearer?" he asked quietly.

"What do you think?" she asked, her voice barely rising above a whisper.

He had been thinking about it since that night; there was no way for him to have possibly confronted the evil's power without any of his own. Also, since that night there had been a steady yet faint pulsing deep within him, as elusive as a summer breeze on a lofty branch. It subtly swirled deep within and just out of his ability to identify it but the one thing he knew was he had never encountered it before that night. The feeling he sensed was unfamiliar and intimate at the same time, but didn't cause him any undue concern. This presence, however, was not about to vacate his soul with which it had entwined itself.

"What am I supposed to do with it?" he asked in response.

"I don't know, Danyl, but I think you should keep this information to yourself for a while."

"Why?"

"Because you must be allowed to come to terms with what you house without any outside influences or advice. The Green Might is an extension of who you are, Danyl, therefore you must first be comfortable with who you are before you are able to wield the magic. The only person who can fully judge you is yourself and if you cannot do so, then the power will be useless."

"If it hadn't been for Ramira being poisoned by the Kreetch, I would not even know I had the might," he said after a long pause.

Zada thought about how she had approached the house and reacted with a single-minded determination to eradicate them. She had executed the Kreetch as if that had been her only purpose in life. She seemed to be more of a hunter as opposed to a protector and that thought sent a chill up her spine. The amount of venom inflicted into her should have turned her into one of the demons almost immediately, yet she not only survived but also showed no ill effects. None that were visible, anyway. What was it that allowed her to endure the demons and, in a roundabout way, ignite and endure the elven magic?

She glanced at a pensive Danyl, the burden he carried not one she would or could ever help him bear. She lifted his chin, the bewilderment on his face summoning forth an innocent cast to his features. He was like a small child given his first important task and wanting but not knowing how to accomplish it. The Herkah wished she could tell him something to ease his apprehensions and confusion, but he was the bearer and would have to figure them out on his own. The heaviest burden would fall upon his shoulders. She and the other leaders would lead their people to death; it would be his lot to brandish that final weapon. If he failed to find the courage necessary to allow the power to infuse itself into every fiber of his being, then they were all doomed.

"Danyl," she whispered. "Never forget that the Green Might chose you for a reason."

"And what would that be?" he asked.

"It will share that with you when the time comes."

She awoke with a start, her instincts fully roused as they sought to identify a presence lurking just beyond the edges of her perception. This sensation was different from the others and this time she did not ignore it. The voices' sinister echoes buzzed around her head like so many hateful flies she could not swat away; their angry wails growing with each passing moment. She was growing tired of these perceptions, wondering if she were going mad and, worst of all, she was beginning to believe these terrible things. They erupted at will, showing her horrible images of what had happened in the past and implying the same fate would befall those in Bystyn if she stayed. Ramira began to give credence to the promise of sparing the city if she abandoned it, too exhausted to fight their tenacious hold on her psyche.

She could not dislodge the obscure pledge from her mind. Her nightmares chipped away at her resolve, the dark advice pushing aside all reasoning. Was she willing to forsake this place and the people she had learned to love and respect? Was she ready to run away in order to draw its loathsome ire away from these gray walls? What then? Where could she go? She knew she could not head west or east and certainly not north into the impenetrable mountains. South remained her only option, but what if the voices were lying to her? What if they were nothing more than her own subconscious doubts?

She dressed then stood on the little balcony overlooking the wilting garden. The cold early morning air made her shiver as the first tinges of color stained the eastern horizon. She was a mystery even to herself, but she would not allow that unknown secret to jeopardize the lives of all of these good people. Her thoughts stayed with her all day and well into the next night, tormenting her with things she could neither prove nor disprove. The treacherous whispers seemed to sense her bewilderment, increasing the frequency of the images at a frightening pace.

All those she loved suffered horribly from every vile infliction known—their eyes firmly focused on her as they appeared and disappeared at will. Zada and Styph mingled with faces she did not recognize while Anci's emaciated body brushed past her to join them. Ramira felt something grabbing at her ankles and upon looking down, cringed. The elf and dwarf kings lay twisting on the ground, reaching up to her. Then the worst likeness emerged: Danyl. He had been torn apart by wolves and was covered with flies but managed to hold out his hand to her as he sought to pull her into this ghastly scene. She could take no more.

Sophie hummed softly as she set the table then stirred the contents of the pot hanging in the fireplace. She sampled the stew, added a few more herbs then mixed it a few more times. She wiped her hands on her apron, noticing how quiet the house was. Anci would be home from visiting her uncle soon and she had no idea where Ramira had gone off to. Perhaps she had run out to do an errand or two. Sophie's brows wrinkled, an unknown nagging tugging at the back of her mind. She shook her head and busied herself, placing a plate of freshly baked bread on the table as Anci walked into the kitchen and gave her mother a hug.

"Zada gave us these," Anci said excitedly, as she unfolded a neatly packed parcel. Sophie's mouth began to water at the small sweat bread drizzled with honey and nuts that was still warm to the touch.

"I'll have to repay her kindness. Did you see Ramira at the castle?" Sophie hoped Danyl and Ramira had been able to find some uninterrupted time together, a luxury of late.

"Danyl spent the whole day with Nyk and Styph," Anci replied, pouring mugs of tea.

"Did she happen to mention her plans for today to you?"

"No."

Sophie looked down at her daughter without really seeing her, a wave of uneasiness enveloping her thoughts. Ramira had appeared more tired than usual of late, the dark circles and withdrawn gaze a testament to the continuing nightmares she refused to discuss. Sophie marched upstairs and entered Ramira's room, noting how tidy everything was, except for a partially closed drawer Sophie pulled open. Ramira had kept the clothes she had arrived in within it and it now lay empty. All the other drawers were still full. She ran downstairs, the look on her face beginning to scare Anci. She flung open the pantry door, her eyes resting on the vacant hook that had held the travel pouches. Ramira had gone away.

"Mother?" Anci's timidity brought Sophie back to reality.

"Stay here," she told the girl, as she grabbed her shawl and headed up the avenue.

Danyl stared at her as perplexed as the others seated around the dinner table. Why in the four corners of the land would Ramira suddenly decide to leave? She had obviously planned her departure, slipping out into the night to go…where? Where was she heading and why? Sophie saw the look in his eyes and stopped him before he rode out to find her.

"I think her nightmares may have had something to do with her leaving, Danyl," she said, both hands flat against his chest to keep him from leaving. "She tried to hide it but it showed in her eyes."

"I should have been more insistent she tell me what they were," he said. He walked over to the window, straining to see a figure swallowed up within the darkness. He felt the first tinges of alarm worm their way into his heart, the guilt for not being there for her beginning to settle in his mind.

"She wouldn't have told you and you know it," she corrected him.

Zada's brow furrowed as she recalled the conversation she had had with Danyl another night and the thoughts those words had elicited. There was more here than they knew or understood. It wasn't so much that the pieces of the puzzle were missing, but they had yet to identify all the ones that were all around them. Ramira, she was sure, was a part of the mystery and had left Bystyn in the middle of the night to escape bad dreams. People had nightmares all the time but trying to run away from them was pointless. The bad dreams seemed to stow themselves away in their satchel along with a fresh change of clothes. Had the Kreetchs' venom intensified her nightmares? Were they calling out to her? Was she heeding that silent call? Is that why she left?

"Danyl," Zada asked. "When did you first meet Ramira?" He dropped his gaze and the room went silent.

"Tell them, Danyl." Sophie's voice urged him to the surprise of everyone gathered. Alyxandyr narrowed his eyes then stared from Sophie to his son as he waited.

"She is the one that saved my life months ago along the Broken Plains," he confessed. *I'm sorry, Ramira, but the time to reveal that secret has come to pass.*

The King raised his hand to still the chorus of surprised questions erupting in the room, watching Zada digest this information.

"She was in that cave before you got there?" she demanded.

"Yes, she woke up when she heard my cries for help. Why?" His anxiety grew with every beat of his heart.

"All of the caves we've found run from the desert straight through to the Broken Plains," explained Allad. "Some disappear into an abyss or underground streams but go through nonetheless."

"This one was blocked by rocks and debris and had been for a very long time," explained the prince.

"Did you see anyone else in that area while you were there?" Allad asked, his eyes bright points of light.

"Not that I can remember."

Zada sighed deeply. She saw how nervous and restless the prince was, for all he wanted to do was mount a search party. That was not a good idea, not quite yet anyway. Mahn had been probing for the Source in this area and she was sure more Kreetch would follow on the heels of their dead brethren. An indiscriminate hunt, therefore, would be foolish. The Kreetch had been virtually at the gates and that meant Mahn had already deduced where the Source was located. The elven power provided a sort of barrier against him, especially if his own power had not yet fully developed. He could not come and get what he desired, but he could have it somehow come to him. The woman with no past, tormented by nightmares and defiled by demons was suddenly gone, flushed out of Bystyn like a pheasant from the grass. She turned white and started to shake, the implications slowly manifesting themselves in her.

"Zada?" Seven called to her then glanced over at Allad, who began to move toward her, stopping only when she held up her hand.

"I think," she finally managed to say, "we had better have a very private meeting and you had best invite Gard."

There were twelve gathered in the King's private chambers, twelve who listened with varying degrees of disbelief as she told them what she believed was the truth. Their faces registered everything from dismay to impassivity yet none dared utter a single word while the Herkah spoke.

"Mahn became aware of the Source right about the time you were saved by Ramira, Danyl. He was unable to recognize it for what it was or he would have taken it at that moment. The same reason for him not detecting it allowed it to travel east to Bystyn. He must have taken control of Kepracarn then as well, because he would need a base to operate out of to fulfill his agenda. Once he had established himself he unleashed his ilk upon the land, seeking souls for his army while scouring the area for the Source. Not finding it near the desert forced him to broaden his search here."

"What are you insinuating, Zada?" asked Mason. The first advisor leaned forward as he studied the nomads' features.

"I think that Ramira houses the Source."

The ensuing silence was deafening and even Danyl was too shocked to voice his opposition to such a preposterous idea. The same thoughts and series of events played through all of their minds until they realized Zada's words made sense. The degradation of the land by the evil began when Danyl was nearly lost all those months ago. Ramira, apparently unaware she carried the Source, followed him to the city with the evil trailing behind.

Danyl could not believe the woman he loved harbored such evil. She had neither said nor done anything sinister since she came to the city. Quite the contrary. She had toiled long and hard to help everyone around her without ever complaining. The Source was supposed to be evil yet she did not appear to be corrupt. The prince could not look beyond her caring and loyalty to accept the logic in Zada's words.

"Now, I cannot even begin to figure out Ramira's past or anything else about her, but she does bear some Herkah traits. Her abilities with the knives, to an extent her choice in clothing and, according to Danyl, the briquettes she used in the cave hint at such a connection. The Herkahs, however, have never seen her before. Mahn does not know what she looks like, depending instead on the Source to guide him to her then send the Vox after her. They, too, will be forced to be directed by something else other than her appearance."

"Why do you believe he does not know who she is?" asked Styph.

"She has been wandering about the land since her emergence from the cave but has yet to be confronted by any of his minions, Styph. The Kreetch incident must have been purely accidental. Her brief connection to the evil via the poison confirmed the Source was in this area."

"That also might explain why the poison did not transform her into one of the demons," suggested Clare.

"It's entirely possible the Source negated their effect," offered Seven.

"Or maybe it absorbed their venom," muttered Gard, his animosity toward Ramira for bringing the evil into his home clear in his tone.

"That's not fair, Gard," Seven reminded him. "Regardless of how things appear, I doubt very much Ramira chose to be the bearer."

"Whether she embraced it or not is no longer an issue." Mason's deep voice stilled any further discussion about her guilt or innocence. "She has it."

"The nightmares, then, were focused in this direction, with Mahn hoping it would affect whomever had the Source and force them out into the open," stated Alyxandyr.

"Exactly," replied the nomad.

"So at this very moment he is hunting her but he still doesn't know what she looks like or which way she is going," added Clare.

"As long as she refrains from using the power, if indeed she is even able to, yes."

"So that brings us back to why she left," said Nyk.

"What would be the one thing that would make her leave, Danyl?" asked his father.

"She would only go if she thought any or all of us were in danger," he replied after a long while, his heart heavy in his chest.

"Mahn must have been sending her twisted half truths and outright lies, invading her sleep with horrible images. She took the only measure she thought would help us all," Zada said. The Herkah could not even begin to imagine what sort of horrors he had inundated her with and that, along with her unknown past, pushed her out the gates.

Lance and Sophie stared at Danyl, who had closed his eyes while Gard remained quiet in his chair, his anger focusing on Ramira. Zada thought back to when Danyl yanked her from the evil, realizing the Green Might had reacted to the Source yet it had not destroyed it. The elven magic had helped him avert a disaster but did not exterminate the Source.

"So," sighed Styph as he took in the magnitude of their dilemma. "What do we do now?"

"We have to find her," stated Allad.

"Find then kill her?" Gard asked, barely able to keep the bitterness out of his voice, ignoring Danyl's head snapping up at the suggestion.

"No, Gard," Zada explained. "We don't know how that will change the outcome, if at all. Besides, slaying her then finding out she would be more helpful alive is a mistake that cannot be undone."

"So what is to be done, Zada?" asked Mason.

"We have to catch her before he does, Lord Mason. The only advantage to her being out in the land is we will have more time and less eyes to watch the work on our own defenses."

"She bought us a little extra time," Seven mused out loud.

"Yes, Seven, but unfortunately, she shortened her own, which is why we have to move quickly. A small group with an experienced tracker should go after her, and I must insist at least two Herkahs go along to battle any demons that will surely be hunting her."

"Wait," she said, stopping them all from volunteering as she looked over at Alyxandyr. He would decide who went to their likely deaths.

"I think it is only fair since the outcome concerns all of us, that one from all the races gathered here should go, but each will choose who shall represent them."

"I would have no other dwarf take my place, and any arguments," Seven stilled many mouths that opened up in protest, "will fall on deaf ears."

Gard rose from his chair as did Allad and, of course, Danyl. Lance moved to take his place beside the prince.

"There stands before us more royalty than we can possibly spare," objected the King, as he looked from one to the other.

"If we fail we won't have to worry about that, now will we?" Seven locked eyes with his longtime friend, forcing the King to nod in agreement. They planned to leave at sunrise the following day, the impending bad weather a fortunate occurrence allowing them to ride out cloaked and hooded. Lance and Allad left to see to the provisions and the horses while the rest worked out a basic plan. Since only those gathered knew of the search, the group would be on their own, getting help from no one unless they happened upon a patrol.

"I cannot watch you with my inner sight, for Mahn will eventually sense it and take an interest in why I am scanning the land. I will, however, be able to see or feel any use of magic or whether or not you encounter any demons."

"Zada?" Danyl asked, as the two of them stood alone in the room. "If this Source is so sinister, why did Ramira slay the Kreetch? Why did the elven power aid and not destroy her?"

"I don't know, Danyl," she replied, as the memory of Ramira's single-minded determination to eradicate the demons filled her mind. The Source should have embraced the Kreetch and not turned Ramira into a killing machine, but she slaughtered the demons instead. She had failed to save the couple, the tears streaming down her face marking her grief while the vile blood of the Kreetch still dripped from her knives. The Source allowed her to destroy one moment then mourn the next…or did it? What exactly was this foul power embedded within the fair Ramira?

"What are the chances of encountering Vox, Zada?" he asked. She looked into his eyes, hers filled with hope that they would not, yet the chances of that happening were too great. He dropped his gaze, the thought of facing those vicious demons sending a shiver up his spine.

"You must not engage them if you do happen upon them, Danyl. Leave the fighting to Allad and Haban and heed their commands when they do so," she said, then touched his cheek before leaving the room.

Danyl poured a glass of wine and walked out onto the balcony, the crisp night air proclaiming a change in the weather soon. Winter's fingers stroked the land, preparing to smother it under a thick blanket of white while friends and family relaxed in their cozy homes. He had been looking forward to spending more time with Ramira during the long and dark nights but her flight had changed all of those plans. Why hadn't he insisted she reveal her nightmares to him? Why had he relented in allowing her to return to Sophie's home? Why hadn't he visited more often to see what was happening to her? This dire situation could have been avoided had he kept a closer eye on her.

They gathered together early the next morning, out of sight beneath the arches leading to the rear of the castle and the stables. Zada nodded at Haban then handed each member of the company a small scabbard they tucked away within the folds of their cloaks. They embraced each other then the members of the group mounted their horses, those staying behind staring up at them with concern. The time to leave was upon them.

"All Herkahs wear one of these," she explained in the crisp darkness. "If you are about to be killed by a demon, use it and spare yourselves the agony of becoming one of them. May your journey be swift and your hearts remain pure."

They urged their horses forward, exchanging silent farewells, then rode down the avenue and out the gates as a cold rain fell. More than one full day had passed since Ramira left, but she could not have gotten far on foot. With any luck they would be back by the following sunrise. Each rider was deep in thought with their own interpretation of what had and could happen but only one felt an emptiness in his heart.

Gard found the trail amid the rain and misty shadows and they ran, as they had surmised, south toward the Ahltyn River. They followed the trail until sundown but did not find Ramira. They made camp after dark sharing a meal and discussed how far she could have gotten on foot. Each also silently wondered if Ramira had any idea what she carried and prayed she would not be tempted to use it once she realized what she housed.

Part II

-7-

Ramira eyed the house as she went by, the memory of what had transpired there still fresh in her mind. She loathed the things that murdered the gentle old couple and whatever had sent the demons to fulfill that monstrous deed. The house remained unoccupied, boarded up as if to contain the horrors that had occurred within. Ramira could feel the bile rise up in her throat, the keen desire to inflict more damage onto the demons tempered only by their absence. There would be no mercy if she crossed paths with them in the future.

She turned south, crossing the Ahltyn by the light of the moon, now at its highest point in the sky. The first fingers of clouds began to obscure the moon and the change in the wind promised bad weather. She knew they would search for her but was determined not to be found, prompting her to cover a lot of ground by midmorning, even in the driving rain. She finally crawled into a clump of trees and brush to sleep for a few hours, exhausted from walking since late evening. She awoke to the sounds of thunder in the late afternoon and scrambled far enough out of her hiding place to scan her surroundings. Satisfied she was alone, she grabbed her things and set out once more, her mind on the friends she had left behind.

Was she doing the right thing by leaving them? Was Danyl's heart as heavy as hers? Would what she was doing really matter in the end, or should she have stayed and enjoyed the last days with them? It didn't really matter, for she was apparently the cause of not only this misery but the one from her past, too. People died, and worse, because of her and now the same fate hovered over the elves, dwarves, Herkahs, and Khadry. She was suddenly ashamed of having been intimate with Danyl, for she had done nothing less than taint him with her own brand of evil.

Oddly enough, the images and whisperings that had driven her from Bystyn were virtually silent out here, the only thing making her departure somewhat bearable. She could sense them on the edge of her consciousness but they did not torment her like they did in the city: it was almost as if they could not find her. The rain and impending darkness would make travel difficult, compelling her to find a suitable place to spend the night. She spotted a cluster of boulders under an overhang where she could remain dry and watch for any unwanted company. After a short climb, she settled in under the shelf and pulled her knees up to her chest. It had been two days since she left. Her exertions and the cold made her hungrier than usual but she forced herself to eat sparingly. She had provisions for at least another week but the unfamiliarity of the land demanded she ration her food. She had no idea what to expect in the south and did not know if the people living there would be hospitable to strangers. She ate without tasting the dried meat, fruit, and cheese, washing them down with water as she contemplated where she was going. How long would she be able to run, and how would that really affect the outcome to the north? Did she actually believe the evil would spare the city because she was gone? What exactly was she running from?

"You're running from yourself, you dolt."

She leaned back against the rock and drew her cloak more tightly around her body; the brittle night air balmy compared to the chill residing in her soul. She was still on elven lands and could easily march right back the way she had come and face Danyl's and Sophie's searing reprimands as she entered the gates. She smiled, admitting their scolding would sound like music to her ears, the ensuing embraces a balm to her troubled soul. She began to doze, the sound of the icy rain lulling her mind into restful darkness.

She awoke to a chilly and misty dawn, the rain gone but the earth damp and soggy. She stretched her cramped muscles and ate a few bites of food before starting off once more. She was careful not to leave too many tracks in her wake but knew the elves could trail her even if she left nothing behind. She did not vary from her course, walking steadily on as she tried to put as much distance between herself and her friends as she could manage. She kept near the tree line, her senses straining to capture any oddity that might be about. She heard hooves later that day and scampered into the brush, watching an elven patrol ride by. When they were well out of sight she emerged from her concealment and resumed her trek. She spotted no one else that day or over the next few days, their absence both a relief and worrisome.

She swung around a vast outcropping of rock, one driving her due east for nearly a half-mile before it disappeared back into the sodden earth. She came upon a thick stand of hardwood trees interspersed with pines and after taking a deep breath, walked underneath their boughs. The ground here was fairly level, although she had to be careful not to trip over an occasional root or fallen log. She remembered looking at the maps in Karolauren's study; the huge rock she had maneuvered around marked the edge of Bystyn's lands. If her memory served her correctly, there would be a neutral zone between the elves' boundary and the southerners where a traveler might journey without trespassing on either land. A crow landed on a branch several feet to her right then proceeded to caw loudly as she passed below it, its black brethren answering from somewhere in the distance. The sound was loud, echoing hollowly in her ears and through the endless rows of trees. It called out a few more times before flying away, but its absence did not quell the disquiet it had invoked within her. Ramira was able to hike for another hour before the light began to fade, her breath obscuring her view each time that she exhaled. She pulled her thick cloak more tightly against her frame to ward off the chill, her cheeks and nose beginning to take on a rosy hue. She wished she were trekking home to Sophie's house after a long day's work where the fire crackled and the aroma of simmering stew hovered in the air. For a brief moment the tired trees and bland boulders disappeared, leaving her within the confines of the kitchen until a root tripped her and jarred her out of her reverie. Ramira picked herself up off the ground, rubbing at her stinging elbow and knee, scanning the area to make sure no one had seen her careless blunder. Caw. She glared at the crow mocking her predicament. She squatted and picked up a rock, brandishing it at the coal-black bird which chose to stay and test her aim. She let it fly, watching as it skimmed along the bottom of the branch and ricocheted off in the distance. Caw.

"I would have hit you had it not been for the fading light," she muttered at the departing crow, grimacing with disgust as it emptied its bowels in response to her boast. The daylight quickly began wane, the pale gray giving way to the darker and more menacing black of night. Alone once more, she crawled beneath the drooping boughs of a pine for a few hours of rest.

The frigid air seeping through her blanket and clothes woke her near moonset. She sat up, pulling her knees to her chest and the blanket more tightly around her shoulders, her breath masking her view. She began to shiver with cold, a predicament that would get worse if she did not find some shelter soon. A few hours of rest in a cave or barn would be ideal. She gathered her few possessions and left her soggy refuge behind, carefully walking on the slick ground en route to, hopefully, a more suitable place. The land started to slope downward, making her footing more precarious, her backside becoming more and more familiar with the hard earth as she continued on. She rested against a tree and rubbed her backside, staring at the sun sluggishly rising behind a bank of ominous gray clouds. The wind bit into her dirty face and stirred her limp hair. Her gloved hand reached up and flipped her cowl over her head then tugged it closer under her chin.

"Come on, you don't have much time."

Ramira wound her way through a stand of oaks and maples, the thorny brush, roots and rocks hampering her progress. The frozen rain came down slowly at first then with greater force, coating her in ice within minutes. The extra weight on her exhausted and hungry body impeded her strides slowing her down. She passed beyond the last of the trees and stepped into a clearing. A large barn stood to her right and farther on was a farmhouse. She dropped behind a pile of wood as a door slammed, the rusty axe stuck in the chopping block impeding her view. She watched a man bundled up in a heavy coat head toward the barn.

"Uwing!" he shouted. "Uwing! Where'd that lazy little bastard get off to now!"

"Coming, Papa!"

Ramira spotted a small boy, his shirttails sticking out from under his short jacket. He ran over to his father, halting just beyond his reach.

"Those damn rats ate through the sacks again! You were supposed to keep an eye out for 'em, boy!" His hand came up and across the boy's face before the child could react and Ramira could see the red mark enlarging even from her vantage point.

"I'm sorry, Papa…"

"Get in there or I'll whip your hide!" The man grabbed the boy by his collar and yanked him into the barn.

The sleet began to hurt but she could do nothing but wait until the man was back in the house. She shifted her body, ignoring the subtle crackling of her cloak. Her fingers and toes grew stiff and unwieldy; her stomach growled from within her cramping midsection. Her eyelids drooped and only rubbing them kept them from staying closed.

"Now kill those vermin or else!" The man slammed the door behind him and headed into the house. Smoke curled up from the brick chimney. She imagined the warmth of the fireplace and the smell of food cooking in a pot hanging from the hook inside it. The memory of Sophie's kitchen filled her mind, tugging on her aching heart. Why did she leave?

Ramira waited for a while longer then cautiously crept toward the barn. She sidled up against the rough-hewn boards, inching her way to the window at the end of the building. She carefully lifted the wooden slat just high enough to peek inside, breathing a sigh of relief as she stared at the back of a beam. She looked around then sneaked into the barn, holding the shutter to keep it from banging against the window frame. She crouched down and remained still, listening for any sounds. She heard flames feeding on wood then a tap-tap-tap noise. She eased her way over to a punched out knothole and looked through it.

The boy, Uwing, sat in front of a potbellied stove holding a long, thin stick and letting its tip hit the worn floorboards. His nose was runny and the welt on his face covered his entire cheek. He wiped his nose with his sleeve and scooted closer to the stove, humming softly to himself. Ramira glanced over to the bales of hay stacked in the corner then at the sacks of provisions hanging out of the reach of pests. Small round protrusions...nuts? Larger chunks...potatoes? The rounded pouches might contain flour or meal—a virtual banquet dangling from the rafters. She exhaled slowly as weariness sapped the remainder of her strength. She crawled over to the hay, being extra vigilant as she passed by the opening to the main part of the barn. She quietly hastened to the bales and wormed her way behind them, pushing the front section forward to create a space for her to lie down in. Cold and hunger were her companions as she fell into a dreamless sleep. Ramira slept through the morning, never hearing the man chop wood or the squeal of the pig being slaughtered. She never knew the cows were being milked or the man coming in to spread out fresh straw for the animals.

He cut the twine on the bales then jammed his pitchfork into the straw to work it loose. His downward thrusts moved farther and farther toward the back then, when he had loosened enough straw, he tossed forkfuls over into the stall.

Ramira shuddered as the cold invaded her sleep. She forced her eyes open, the gunk nearly sealing her lids shut. Funny...she could see the back of the stable. A shape loomed over her holding something long and slender in his hands. Was that light reflecting off metal? She instinctively pushed herself against the uneven planks as the prongs bit into the hay where she had been a second before. Had she been found out? Was this person trying to kill her? She slipped into the space between the bales and the wall, praying that she had not been detected as the pitchfork stabbed down once again. Man...boy...barn...sweet mercy! Ramira was fully awake, her hands firmly gripping her hilts as one of the tines buried itself in her forearm. She sucked in her breath, the piercing bringing tears to her eyes, but not a sound escaped her throat. He brought the pitchfork down again and again, catching bits of her clothing but, mercifully, no more flesh. The man moved away and didn't come back—he was finished.

"Let's go, boy. Suppertime."

Warmth oozed from the puncture wound as she hastily bound it with a strip of cloth. She left her place of concealment, ignoring the nervous horse and cow. She peeked around the corner, grimacing at the throbbing pain in her arm. Ramira glanced at the milky light visible between the breaks in the barn walls then at the bags suspended from the crossbeams. She approached the ropes wrapped around the cleats and lowered each one, filling her pouch with as much as she could carry. She went over to the stove and held her hands out to the heat, squashing the urge to hug the glowing stove. The warmth made her fingers tingle and her face flush. It felt so good to be near heat…it made her want to lie down and sleep along side it. Her knees began to buckle and only the man's voice broke the stove's hold over her. She slunk out the way she had come, shivering as she disappeared into the gathering darkness.

The company set up camp beneath a clump of pines, their full branches arching and interlacing overhead like a natural, aromatic ceiling that kept out most of the sleet. They were already wet but the briquettes Allad lit dried them to the point of being comfortable as they shared bowls of hot stew and crusty bread. Their horses tended to and their bellies full, the companions, each lost in their own thoughts, sat around the embers.

"We should have found her by now," stated Danyl, troubled why their combined tracking skills had failed to find her.

"Evidently she does not wish to be found, Danyl," Seven reminded him, stretching closer to the fire.

"The few telltale signs she couldn't erase are all we have…she can't be too far away," interjected Allad.

"I'm sure we chose the right direction; it's just a matter of finding the hare before she hops down into a burrow," Seven said, passing an ale skin to Haban. The Herkah uncorked it and sniffed, then took a swig and shrugged in response. Seven shook his head in mock disgust.

"What does the land look like from here to…say another twenty miles farther south?" asked Allad.

"The forest stretches in a wedge shape to the west, growing wider as it heads in that direction," explained Danyl. "The land itself eventually turns into rolling hills with an abundance of rocks and boulders. The rivers and streams there are easy to spot because they are virtually enclosed within the trees."

"Sort of like the oasis in the desert," said Allad.

"You'll find fresh water and some food there," finished the prince.

"What of those who live on the other side of the forest?" asked the nomad.

"They do not mingle with those on the elven side of the woods," began the prince. "They are, for the most part, a sturdy lot eking out a meager living while trying to avoid scattered roving bands of marauders."

"Something to look forward to," muttered Seven from within his blankets, visions of rock lords appearing in his head.

"In any case they would be more apt to avoid rather than confront us," finished the elf.

"The bandits or the folk?" asked Seven.

"Both, Seven."

Gard and Lance took the first watch, the others seeking the warmth of their blankets yet sleep did not come easily for any of them. Her faint tracks told them she was heading steadily southwards, but she should not be that far ahead while making the journey on foot. Had they missed something? Danyl and Seven took over the sentry duty during the night while Haban and Allad stood guard in the wee hours of the morning, watching the pale sunrise behind a milky sky. They stretched their stiff and tired muscles and shared a quick meal before gathering up their gear.

"So much for finding her before sunrise," muttered Seven, as they mounted their horses on the sixth day out of Bystyn. The dwarf king could not fathom how someone traveling on foot in an unfamiliar area could so elude them. He as well as the others could not seem to shake the feeling she was nearby, but even with their keen eyes and sharp hearing they could not detect her or any other movement.

"We might have passed her by along the way," suggested Gard.

"Maybe," replied Allad. "But I don't think so. We aren't traveling very fast, and if she is in the area, it would not be difficult for her to keep pace with us."

"You believe she is shadowing us?" asked Danyl, turning in his saddle to scan the area for any sign of her.

"It certainly would be more difficult for us to follow the tracks that are behind us, now wouldn't it?"

They rode on for most of the morning, aware of the changes in their surroundings as they gradually crossed into the south. The watery sun trying to break through the thick clouds made everything appear washed out, a depressing sight to the frustrated trackers. They were mindful of the weather; more than one careless traveler had gotten themselves caught in a sudden storm. The company glanced at the line of short, rolling hills farther to their south interspersed with groups of stunted trees or collections of large boulders. The rocks, bleached by the sun, reminded them of pieces of bone sticking out from the ground. They were reminded that Bystyn's verdant plain might also appear in such a manner if they did not succeed in finding Ramira. Even if they did find her, that shared image might still come to pass. They stopped once to rest then resumed their search, coming upon a drab and dangerous-appearing town near sunset. Gard, Allad and Seven wormed their way between some brush on a hill overlooking the town and studied it.

The buildings were mainly one story and constructed of slats of wood with weathered tin roofs in need of repair. The lights shining through grimy windows fell in colorless pools upon the roughhewn boards of the sagging porches littered with debris and rickety chairs. A raucous group of men left a tavern, their voices reaching them from their place of concealment as they staggered into the street. A slightly built figure suddenly darted from an alleyway, immediately catching the attention of the group as it ran down the street. The inebriated men were unable to stay steady long enough to catch up, their cursing and shouting falling upon the escaping heels of the figure. Others ventured out into the street accosting the men and within moments fights broke out. The figure took advantage of the distraction and disappeared into the falling darkness.

"I think I prefer spending the night in the cold and dampness over that," stated Seven, jerking his thumb at the town.

"I agree with you," replied Gard, as the three of them returned to their companions and reported on what they had seen. They rode on for a little while longer, intent on placing a bit of distance between themselves and the collection of shabby buildings and short tempers. They found a place to spend the night, gratefully filling their stomachs with warm food, the night growing crisp and their surroundings very quiet.

They rose shortly before dawn and were about to mount their horses when a slight sound caught their attention. They pretended to adjust their equipment while Lance slipped away unnoticed, returning almost immediately with a struggling figure in his arms, his hand covering its mouth to keep it quiet. Danyl momentarily thought it might be Ramira but the girl in Lance's grasp was too slight and Ramira would certainly not grapple with the captain. Danyl approached the young girl and stared hard at her wide blue eyes and short-cropped brown hair, her defiance composed more of fright than bravery. The prince nodded to Lance, who grabbed her by the scruff of the neck and removed his hand from her mouth.

"Who are you?" demanded Danyl, trying not to laugh at her faltering bluster. She lifted her head with further bravado and remained silent until Allad came face to face with her. His hawkish features clearly warned her to respond or certain consequences would be unleashed. The nomad, too, worked hard to keep the amusement off of his face.

"He asked you a question."

"My name is Cricket," she finally managed to say, her nerve slowly waning.

"What do you want?" asked the prince.

"Nothing…I…" she sputtered, her hand nervously clutching at a little leather bag attached to her belt.

"You wouldn't happen to be a thief now, would you?" inquired Seven, squinting at the bag and remembering the group of men looking for a slight figure the previous evening.

"No! I'm no thief!" she replied defiantly.

"So why have you sought our company?" asked Allad.

"I just happened upon you, that's all," she said. She swallowed tensely.

"That scuffle last night would not have been due to you, now would it?" asked Danyl.

"Yes," she finally admitted after quite some time. "My brothers have little love for me."

"'Brothers,' eh? Well, Cricket, what do you want us to do? Maybe bring you back to them?" asked Allad.

"No. I can't go back or they'll kill me."

Danyl held her chin in his palm and forced her to meet his eyes and realized, family or not, those men would surely harm her if she went back or was caught by them out here. To take her along meant possible problems down the road if they were to meet up with the men, but he couldn't leave Cricket to face them on her own. He slowly shook his head back and forth because what could possibly make their lives more complicated than taking her along?

"What do you want us to do?" he gently asked the girl.

"May I stay with you?" she nearly begged in a small voice. "I promise I won't be a problem."

"What makes you think you can trust us not to harm you or bring you back to your 'brothers'?" asked Seven.

"Because you are not like them."

"Okay," said Danyl after a long pause. "You can come along, but the first mistake you make will be your last one, understood?"

Cricket nodded, the relief and abating fear in her eyes stilling even Gard's protests.

Danyl helped her up behind him as they resumed their search for Ramira, the day bright and clear cloaks pulled close. Cricket burrowed up against the prince's back, silently thanking him for trusting her. She knew the men would be looking for her and hoped her newfound companions would be able to protect her if or when the time came.

"What's to be found in these parts?" Seven asked her.

"You aren't from around here, are you?"

"If we were we wouldn't be asking you, now would we?" was Gard's terse reply. He did not think it was a good idea at all to bring this stranger with them. Their dire quest and the possibility of demons were enough to contend with without adding to the likelihood they would run into her pursuers. Cricket cringed as the dark elf glanced coldly her way.

"There are a few towns and villages like the one I left and some farms are scattered about." She eyed the Khadry but said nothing else.

"How do they react to strangers?" asked Allad.

"Not very well," she replied.

"What do you mean, Cricket?" asked the prince.

"There have been some odd things happening around here of late," she stated, the hint of fear in her voice muffled against the elf's cloak. "Even those who usually are to blame for such things don't leave town much anymore."

"Like your 'brothers'?"

"Yes. They can't bully what they can't see."

"What do you mean by that?" Seven stared at the girl then at his companions.

"Bodies have been found…horribly torn apart. No animal can do such a thing."

"Have you seen such things?" asked Seven quietly. Cricket closed her eyes trying to erase the images that would never go away. She vividly remembered one night a week or so earlier when she crept along the dingy alleyways behind the shops in search of anything of value when she stumbled upon two terribly mutilated bodies. She was so paralyzed with terror she could neither scream nor move for several long moments, then the sound ripping from her throat woke the entire town up. They raced to the alleyway silently staring down at the corpses nearly ripped to shreds, their dead faces contorted in sheer terror. Something other than a human or an animal had clearly killed them because nothing mortal could have inflicted so much damage. Everyone, even the worst of the bandits, had paled at the horrific scene in the alleyway. Danyl could feel her hold tighten on him as she spoke the words.

The King and the prince locked eyes for they had a good idea of what could have dealt such a terrible injury. Allad exhaled heavily, for it was apparent the Kreetch had invaded this part of the land too, and they would need to be extra vigilant in their travels. He fervently hoped Ramira would be alert, too, until he remembered what she had done to the Kreetch at the house. If there were Kreetch, the Radir and Vox would not be too far behind. They rode on in silence, the morning turning into afternoon before they stopped to rest for a while, Cricket never venturing far from Danyl.

"Cricket, have you seen any other travelers…a woman, perhaps?" Danyl tried to keep his voice casual but the young girl heard the yearning nonetheless.

"I've seen many women. What does she look like?"

"She has long red-gold hair."

"No," she replied after a few moments. "No one like that. She must be pretty special for you to be looking for her."

"Yes, she is," he said, his gaze dropping to the ground.

"Is there any place safe for a lone traveler in these parts?" inquired Seven. The dwarf frowned when she shook her head.

"Cricket, if you were a stranger in these parts and realized you couldn't go into the towns and villages, where would you go?" Allad asked quietly.

"I don't know, but there are a lot of places she could hide in like abandoned farms or the thicker woods in the south," she said, as she pointed to their left. "She could seek shelter among the hillocks that are common to the east of the town I came from, too."

"Where would you have gone if you hadn't found us?"

"The knolls."

"Why?" asked Seven.

"Because you can hide yet still see all around you." Cricket looked from one face to the next, noting they all shared a variation of the same emotion:

uneasiness. Allad's and Seven's concern was steeped in the urgency of finding a friend, Gard's held a tinge of bitterness; and Danyl's filled with sadness. In any case, they all wanted to find a certain woman as soon as possible. Why? Did she steal from them?

"Wasn't that the area where we last saw some of her tracks?" asked Gard, his gray eyes narrowing at the memory of the faint traces they had noted near the town. Ramira had undoubtedly scrutinized the collection of grungy buildings to determine if it was safe—and wise—to seek shelter there before coming to the same conclusion they had. He and his companions had continued to travel west while she had more than likely chosen a different path. The Kreetchs' handiwork told them the demons had penetrated the southland, but how far east had they traveled? How many of the evil ilk hunted for her here in the south?

"It was," confirmed Seven. "And it is only about half a day's ride from here."

They stopped riding and discussed what Cricket had told them, realizing in all probability they were heading in the wrong direction. Ramira would be seeking a place in which to lose herself but would certainly want to be able to keep an eye on her surroundings. There were many risks in going back, not the least of which was the possibility of running into the men Cricket had fled from and the Kreetch roaming freely there. If Ramira had gone the way they were now riding, they would lose a great deal of time by turning back and any signs she may have left along the way would surely disappear. This direction, however, slowly wound west and none of them, including Ramira, wanted to end up on Mahn's doorstep.

"Gard?" Danyl addressed the Khadry. "What do the others think about riding to the knolls?"

"I think we should turn back," Gard replied after a moment's hesitation.

"Allad?"

"If Ramira is trying to hide, then that would appear to be the best place to do so," replied the Herkah. Seven, Haban, and Lance agreed. Danyl nodded and they decided to turn back and head for the hillocks, a nervous Cricket clinging to the prince's cloak. No one needed to remind any of the others to increase their attentiveness as they rode back toward the town: the men would be the least of their worries.

Ramira rested in the shadows of a mound, a gnarly pine seeming to grasp its side as it bent out at an awkward angle. She opened her pouch and frowned: there was only enough food to last a few more days. She sighed and ate while surveying the area around her, the prospect of being hungry in this odd land hardly a pleasant thought. How far could she go before she ran out of earth to tread upon? Then what? Head back north to Bystyn to see if everything had settled back down to normal? Was she not shirking her duty to those whom she had come to love by abandoning them? Why had the voices become silent? They had not tormented her for many days now and that break left her mind free to contemplate how insane it had been to leave in the first place. She rubbed her face, her dirty hands smearing the road dirt across her cheeks and forehead while wild strands of hair flopped everywhere. She undid her braid and removed the hair clip, lovingly holding it between her fingers as she stared at the little bird in the apple tree. Jack. The kind elf's face appeared before her eyes until the tears welled up and blurred the image. She couldn't save them—she had been too late. The rage toward the demons began to roil deep within her once more. The memory of having to stab the gentle couple felt as if she had thrust the blades into her own chest. Her breast began to heave in unison with her increasing heartbeat as she fought to contain the hatred and loathing for those foul beasts that had slain them.

She forced the image away as she combed out her hair. Her anger, bitterness and sense of failure manifested itself in her strokes as she pulled out many strands of hair and tossed them on the ground beside her. Finally free of the tangles, she re-braided it and replaced the gift while apologizing to the couple and praying for their forgiveness. How many others should she be asking for mercy? She shook her head and got to her feet, resuming a trek to nowhere that had no reason, with a heavy heart and a lonely soul. She had just crossed over the next hill when the sound of hooves pounded toward her. She peeked from within her hiding place and spotted a group of riders approaching and immediately knew they were not elves. They were men, their menacing faces and array of weapons marking them as unfriendly. She cursed under her breath as they rounded near her cover and stopped. They argued violently amongst themselves, shouting and pushing each other until a fight broke out. The apparent leader ended the scuffle by grabbing both brawlers by their shirts and smacking their heads together. Bloodied and dazed, the aggressors glared at each other but refrained from throwing any more punches.

They were close enough for her to smell their sweat and other malodorous emanations as they scanned the area around them. Had they detected her?

Had she been so careless in her wanderings that she left herself exposed? She heard them curse then spit on the ground as they discussed a young girl, Cricket was her name, and what they were going to do to her once they found her. Whatever she had done had more than incited this group, for they were quite determined to find her at any and all costs.

The tallest of the men seemed to be the most irate. He loudly proclaimed he was going to enjoy whipping her once he had her in his hands, as if she could hear him. She had a feeling he was not going to stop with just a simple beating. Ramira slipped back farther into the brush, waiting until they were well away before continuing her own uncertain journey. Much to her dismay the men scattered and began to search the hills and brush in her immediate area and it didn't take long for one to approach her hiding place. He didn't dismount, taking advantage of his elevation while hunting for the girl. Ramira looked around for better concealment, spotting a fallen log over a small ditch to her right. When she tried to squirm in that direction, however, the strap from her pouch caught on a branch, keeping her rooted in place. She could move neither forward or backward without breaking the branch, the sound a sure beacon to the men. Ramira held her breath, the gap in the branches in front of her offering him a clear view of her predicament. She slipped the knives from their scabbards, preparing to cut the strap and, if need be, the man. The horse came nearer and nearer until it passed by right in front of her, her heart beating so loudly she was sure they would hear it. The rider went by never noticing she hid a few paces away.

"Not here!" shouted one of the men, who proceeded to ride on over to the next hill where the same procedure took place. One rider always positioned himself on a knoll to watch for anyone trying to scamper away from them. Ramira lay still, already realizing she would be spending the night here as the group moved farther and farther away. It was getting too dark to resume her trek and the men would not be far enough away. She sighed and was about to sit up when her instincts warned her of another presence nearby. She strained her ears but heard nothing, remaining stationary even though she needed to free herself from the branch. Her hands automatically tightened around her knives as that peculiar sensation she had experienced at the couple's home grew in her once more. This time the feeling was deeper, more sinister and made the hair stand up on her neck and arms. She waited then saw a pair of Herkahs walk in the opposite direction the men had taken, the urge to greet the nomads stuck in her throat as the wave of evil washed over her. It took all of her will not to rush forward and force an encounter with them, for the sensation welling up inside was nearly overpowering. One of the Herkahs paused momentarily as if sensing something moving away when Ramira quickly suppressed the reaction. She knew what they were, but what were they doing in the south? What were they looking for? It was becoming very crowded in this barren land and she vowed to head in a more westerly direction at dawn. She finally freed the strap then retreated as far back into the brush as she could wiggle, her eyes and ears straining to detect any more unwelcome visitors. The shadows around her grew longer, then her entire world resembled the inside of an inkpot as night claimed the land. She was safe within her thorny confines where any attempt to try to sneak up on her would have been impossible, but that did not calm her apprehensions one bit. The evil's vilest minions stalked the land, forcing her to reconsider her plans. She had to circumvent them, but how could she do that without knowing where they were heading? Was she foolish enough to track them, then head the other way?

Sleep did not come easily that night. She awakened every few minutes expecting to find the Vox' face inches from her own. She was not concerned about the men but the two high demons were another story altogether. As menacing as they were, however, she had wanted to challenge them with the same irrational impulse that had surfaced when she found the Kreetch. What stayed her hand this time was a mystery. She finally slept the last few hours before dawn.

Cricket pointed them south to the haphazard hills dotting the land and explained they ran farther south for about twenty or thirty miles. The members of the company each thought it would be impossible to find the elusive woman in such a broad expanse but their choices were limited. The trees wore dried remnants of their autumn regalia and that meant time was running out. If they wanted to return to Bystyn before the first snow fell, they had to do so soon. Once the land was blanketed in white, it would be very tough to try and survive, especially in an unknown land. They stopped amid a cluster of pines eating a quick meal while their horses rested. They walked around the closest hills for any signs of Ramira's trail, keeping a sharp eye out for intruders.

Haban slowly trod around the small hill examining every inch looking for any clues for Ramira's presence. A snapped branch and scuffmarks in the dirt made him pause and freeze as he carefully pulled the limb back. Someone had recently been here, and as he turned his head to alert the others, he discovered fine filaments caught in a bush. He leaned in and plucked the gossamer threads from the bough holding them up to the light, sucking in his breath as he recognized what they were.

"Allad! Arad mach-vee!" he shouted, re-emerging from the underbrush. Haban's companions came running skidding to a halt in front of him, their eyes wide with disbelief at what dangled from his fingers.

"Ramira's hair!" Seven said excitedly.

"Where did you find them?" demanded Danyl, then followed Haban back to the hill. They searched it again but other than a few more strands of hair and some boot marks, little else marked her presence.

"The trail is fresh, Danyl. She was here within the past day," stated Lance.

Danyl stared into the thicket, imagining her sleeping through the night, her nightmares her only companions. Their decision to return to this place had been the correct one, thanks to Cricket, and with any luck they'd find her sometime in the morning. He didn't know whether he should first hug or reproach her once she was found.

"We have company." Gard nodded toward the riders approaching them as Cricket disappeared into the thicket behind them.

They watched the men come closer and although they weren't sure if they were the same group from town, their unhappy faces certainly could not rule that fact out.

The riders reined up when they got close, glaring down at the odd collection of individuals standing before them. The biggest man in the group edged his horse forward, nodding once in greeting even though his eyes remained wary and unfriendly. They stared openly at the company seeking their leader.

"Seen a young girl, skinny with short brown hair, in your travels?"

"No," replied Lance, drawing the big man's eyes in his direction.

The man studied the captain, noting his ready stance and impassive features, marking him as a trained fighter who would not back down from a fight. A dwarf, some elves and a dark fellow made for awfully strange company in these peculiar times, especially traveling this far south. Their lot stayed on the other side of the forest and rarely ventured beyond it. They didn't look like outlaws, but he quickly surmised they wouldn't be easily intimidated either. He scratched at the scraggly growth on his dirty face, wondering what brought them here.

"Don't you want to know why we're looking for her?" he asked.

"No," Lance said in a disinterested fashion.

"Well, if you do run across her, she's a thief and has something of mine," persisted the man. "I want it back." He locked eyes with the captain then turned away under Lance's steady gaze before jerking his head to the side and riding away with the others.

The company remained where they were, watching as the men rode off in the general direction of the town.

"They'll be back," muttered Seven.

Danyl only half heard him, his attention focused on the silken hair he had taken from Haban. He had so many questions to ask her but the only thing he wanted to do was to hold her in his arms and never let her go. He didn't care whether or not she housed the Source or about the nightmares that drove her from the city. Wasn't it so much better to face their fate together? They were going to either survive or die trying, but at least they would be with each other.

They searched for Ramira all afternoon, their frustration at being so close yet coming up empty-handed etched across their faces. The long shadows spilled across the land, making the hills facing west glow in a soft orange light while the eastern sides were nearly lost in an inky blackness. Tired and disappointed, they decided to make camp for the night.

The men from town would undoubtedly observe, but they had no other alternative. Ramira was somewhere in the vicinity and those men were not going to stop them from finding her. A cold breeze blew across the open land, and if you listened, you could hear it moan as it brushed through the stunted pines dotting the landscape. The sound was disconcerting, reminding them of souls crying out over time and across a void that none were yet ready to traverse. Even the normally unaffected Lance surveyed the night around him with nervous glances every now and then, his hand never far from his sword. They took turns standing guard yet no one slept well that night.

Cricket reappeared well after dark and wriggled into Danyl's arms, her shaking due to the nearness of the men and not the chill of the night. The young girl was terrified of her "brothers," an emotion he could well understand considering their gruff and merciless manner. The elf knew they were no competition for him and his comrades, a fact Cricket had yet to discover. With any luck they would be able to avoid any conflicts with them, although he somehow doubted that. He felt sorry for the girl. She had evidently lived a rough life, a group of strangers her only refuge.

"What did you take from him, Cricket?" he asked.

"A stupid stone."

"A 'stone'? You mean a jewel, don't you?" He couldn't understand why a rock would make the man so upset.

"No, not a gem, Danyl, just a blue stone."

"Show it to me in the morning?"

"Yes," she said then fell into a fitful sleep.

Ramira sat with the blanket pulled close to her body, one that hadn't touched a tub of water in quite some time and wrinkled her nose. She guessed it would be even longer before she'd feel the steaming waters ease the dirt from her skin and relax her cramped muscles. The thought of being clean again only made her long for a bath even more. Her once bulging pouch lay flat against the ground, the few crumbs within barely enough to satisfy an insect. She had eaten the last handful of nuts early this morning, the mouthful of food leaving her hungrier than ever. She needed to find provisions and soon. She drank some water then placed the half-empty canteen down beside her. Sleep eluded Ramira even though her tired limbs and aching feet begged for it. She tossed and turned on the hard ground, the rocks and lumpy earth digging into her body. She gave up and sat with the blanket wrapped around her as she surveyed the land. The moonless night fused everything together, even the hand she held up in front of her face. She glanced up at the tiny pinpoints of light feebly twinkling within a sea of black then back out over the murky landscape. She jumped as an animal screeched with pain and panic, pushing back against the rocks as the mountain cat padded by just below where she sat. An owl hooted off in the distance and a wind began to whistle eerily through the scrawny trees, their sounds the loneliest ones she had ever heard. The Vox roamed somewhere in all that forlorn darkness, a fitting backdrop for such immoral creatures. She thought about the Vox and wondered what they were doing so far south from Bystyn. If there were Vox then the Radir and Kreetch would also be in the area, a thought that summoned her desire to kill them. It was, she realized, the same response she had had when slaying the red woman. She knew there was an inherent corruptness that rose to the surface of her consciousness whenever she was near the demons. It was a vile sensation, one she abhorred but one which she was powerless to fight. Was she nothing more than a demon hunter? Did the vile poisons she had been exposed to provoke her perverse dreams? She squeezed her eyes shut as if to force those thoughts from her mind.

The sun would rise in a few hours and she began to doze, her exertions demanding she rest for a while. She tried to remain aware of her surroundings but her mind and body had had enough and shut down her senses. She curled up, tugged on the blanket once or twice then gave in to her weariness.

The company awoke at dawn, the thick gray clouds hovering low over the horizon and the drop in temperature an unexpected, and unwanted, dilemma. The impending storm would reach them in a few hours, compelling the companions to hasten their search for Ramira. They shared a meal then divided up into pairs to search the area. Before they set out, Cricket reached into her pouch and produced the promised stone, one that Danyl carefully studied. It was the size of an egg, neatly fitting into his closed hand; its deep blue hue was unmarred by any facets. Then, with Cricket's permission, he handed it to the others to look at. None of them thought the stone was of much value but the prince did think it had a remarkable resemblance to the bracelet. He handed it back to the young girl then set out to find traces of Ramira.

They had been looking for several hours when Haban spotted a pair of Herkahs approaching them from the northeast and motioned to Allad. The nomad knew no other Herkah should be in the area, and as they neared the company, the hair stood up on his arms. He barked at Haban, the nomads removing their shirts as they prepared to face their ultimate nightmares: Vox.

Allad and Haban inhaled deeply, their eyes never wavering from the approaching demons as Haban's fingers twitched at his side. He had managed to battle and win against one Vox in the past but had barely escaped with his soul intact. Haban had removed Zada's knife and was about to plunge it into his own chest when the Vox slipped, allowing him one chance to twist around just enough to drive the blade into the demon instead. The memory lingered to this day, reminding him any mistake, no matter how insignificant, would prove costly indeed. Allad had fought several of the Vox and understood the necessity of slaying his own kin to kill the evil dwelling within them. It was a somber task devoid of satisfaction, for the men he executed were his own.

"Stay here and do not interfere," commanded Allad, his black eyes pinpoints of determination. "If one of us falls, ride away as fast as your mounts will take you." He nodded to an anxious Haban and the two of them walked over to intercept the Vox.

"Sweet mercy," Danyl barely exhaled. "Those things look just like our companions."

Lance, Gard and Seven formed a little group, pulling a terrified Cricket into their midst, their hearts pounding as fiercely as the girl's as they watched the Herkahs and the demons approach each other. All four studied their foes for a moment before the larger of the demon-Herkahs chose Allad, leaving the smaller one to face Haban. The ensuing clash was swift and frightening, as the two pairs lunged and wielded their weapons against each other. Those watching swore there was fire flying from their knives as they connected again and again. Allad kept pace with his demon, but Haban was not as adept as the master of the knives and began to retreat with each swing of the demons' blades. Haban did his best to deflect and attack but the demon was much stronger than he, and he soon went onto the defensive, parrying thrusts to save his life. Haban was one of the best, but Mahn had sent Vox that were even better. Allad faired little better but at least he was able to stand his ground.

Seven now completely understood why the Herkahs so feared the Vox; the high demons exuded a sense of power and doom. He could not even begin to imagine what the spirits of the Herkahs imprisoned within their own bodies were experiencing as they fought their kin. They undoubtedly prayed for freedom from the abhorrent parasites compelling them to further corrupt their clan. That liberation came with a price, one they were more than willing to pay: death. He glanced over at the impassive Lance, the stunned look upon his face gradually giving way to resoluteness. If one of the Herkahs fell, Lance would be the first one to defend him. Gard's gray eyes absorbed the skillful and deadly techniques used during this macabre fight as his friends sought to kill the Vox, who were determined to add two more demons to their ranks. He had seen the Herkahs do battle before but not at such a high level of mastery. The fierce fighting mesmerized Danyl, the graceful and fluid motion disguising the extreme intensity of the confrontation. The Vox wanted more than the blood of the Herkahs upon their blades and the nomads were resolved not to give in to them. He heard Cricket whimper with fear, her trembling body burrowing against his cloak as she hid from the horror. The young girl had seen plenty of terrible things in her life but none more terrifying than what now transpired. He slipped his free hand over her cold one, her fingers nervously trying to intertwine with his.

Ramira left the confines of her shelter, heading in an easterly direction and keeping an eye out for her next meal. With any luck she might catch a small animal or stumble across someone who would share some of his or her food. She would steal if she had to. She walked on, sipping from her canteen now and then, mindful of the gray day growing darker. The weather discouraged the woodland creatures from venturing too far from their burrows and she acknowledged hunger might be her companion again this night. A series of hillocks blocked her view, and as she rounded the nearest one, she discovered a large swath of trees choking beneath an onslaught of brambles. The way was blocked, forcing her to retrace her steps toward the north. She walked for several miles until she located a break in the barbed shrubs and decided to take a chance in maneuvering through them. The inch-long spikes exacted their payment for her passage as bits of cloth and blood adorned their points. Ramira finally made it to the other side, wiping away the blood trickling down her cheek with the back of her scratched hand.

"Wonderful," she muttered out loud. "More boulders and bony trees. Am I the only human here?"

She refilled her canteen at the nearby swiftly flowing stream, crossing it along the rocks poking up above the water. She almost slipped into the chilly water but managed to regain her balance, finishing the crossing with only a few wet spots on her garments. She glanced back at the thorn-encrusted trees running for several miles east, the stream flowing directly into the heart of it. It would have been a long trek had she chosen to parallel it. This entire area was composed of one barrier after another, hindrances that became more imposing the farther she traveled into it. The hills could be traversed without too much trouble, but the thorny thickets were another matter. They grew in clumps of varying sizes and widths: some no higher than her ankles, others larger than houses. She spent more time skirting them than she wanted to and made little headway as the day wore on. She finally broke free of them hours later, sighing with relief at the line of bent pines and slabs of stone directly ahead of her. Ramira glanced up at the bulky gray clouds pressing down upon the earth then over at the relative protection of the trees.

"Well, it's better than nothing."

Ramira heard the hooves and immediately hid within a cluster of boulders enshrouded within twisted bushes. Her first thought was of the men searching for Cricket and decided it was more prudent to hide than to incite a confrontation. She wormed her way forward and peered through the underbrush at the riders whom she recognized even at this distance. She had expected a search party but not one comprised of the individuals who slowly rode closer. Perhaps she was being too bold in thinking they were looking for her, maybe someone of importance warranted such a company. She wanted to drop her gaze yet a spark erupted in her breast, one fanned into a flame by a longing to be with her friends once more. She yearned for their contact then squelched that desire as the embarrassment of her actions surfaced in her heart. She should never have left and seeing them here amid the dangers lurking everywhere only made her feel even guiltier. She had done what she thought was right, but was it reasonable or did she just use that as an excuse? She glanced at Seven, the dwarf king's usually capricious demeanor replaced by a sterner and darker determination. Allad and Gard shared a similar expression while even the normally stoic Lance showed signs of trepidation and weariness. She did not know who the young girl was but the nervous and frightened creature kept close to a worried Danyl. She missed him the most. His presence had not just calmed her but had managed to chase away the foreboding shadows that stole her sleep.

It would be a simple thing to emerge from her place of concealment and beg for their forgiveness, but her shame kept her firmly rooted in place. She dropped her head in remorse and tried to block out their tired faces, tense postures and filthy clothing. She began to back away from those she loved then suddenly froze, that same sense of dark foreboding washing over her in repulsive waves. She scanned the area for the demons, detecting them as they rounded one of the knolls directly in front of the group. She watched with apprehension as Allad and the other Herkah removed their tunics and approached the demons with great courage. The Herkahs fought the demons with every ounce of their being but the dark spirits hacked and slashed at them with an otherworldly ease. The young nomad's desperate attempts to ward off the Vox' endless strokes sapped him of his strength and forced him backward to the group watching with horror. He was tiring and would soon be unable to defend himself any longer. The Vox feigned a blow to the right then slashed upward from the left, as Haban sought to block the blade, the searing pain dropping him to his knees. Blood poured from the deep gash to his side and Haban knew his time was almost over. He glanced over at Allad, wanting to help, but darkness began to blur his vision as the Vox surged forward to finish the nomad. The demon was about to recruit another Herkah. Haban had other ideas, however, mustering just enough strength to pull out Zada's knife and plunge it into his heart. The Vox' choked hiss of denial accompanied Haban's body as it fell forward in a heap at the demon's feet. To the dismay of the mortals, the demon began to advance upon the group clustered together near their horses. Allad had warned them but, danger or no, they refused to abandon him and drew their swords in unison to fight what would surely consume them. She looked over at the huge Herkah towering over Allad, whose daggers moved more slowly.

Ramira's head turned toward the members of the company. Her hands had already removed her empty pack and cloak yet she never noticed the chill in the air as she burst through the brush and planted herself between the demon and her friends. Hatred rose in her stomach, fueled on by the determination that these vile creatures were about to befoul her friends. She did not, could not look upon their faces as she raced over the uneven terrain. She heard their shocked and surprised reactions as she challenged the Vox, who focused all of his attention on her.

"You will not take them!"

Zada and Clare were making their way down the staircase to meet with the King when the nomad froze in mid-step, her eyes wide with alarm. She would have toppled down the stone stairs had Clare not grabbed her, immediately relinquishing the contact as the abhorrent feeling flowed from Zada into her. The dwarf queen shouted for the king, staying close enough to help Zada if she needed it. Alyxandyr and Styph came running but all they could do was observe the myriad of emotions and reactions distorting the Herkah's soft features. As the vision continued, they gasped at the toll it was taking on Zada. Her face became ashen and sweat formed in large beads that ran down her face and neck as she struggled to keep the image in her mind. She also had to fend off Mahn's foul presence.

"Vox...Haban has fallen...Allad is barely keeping the other one at bay," she told them in a raspy voice, the strain of keeping the vision for so long draining her energy.

"How many Vox? Are the rest hurt?" Alyxandyr demanded, as the worst of their fears manifested itself miles away to the south. He should never have allowed those individuals to go, losing them would be a huge blow in their fight against Mahn.

"Two Vox...the rest are alive."

"Have they found Ramira yet?" Styph's intense voice echoed in the stairwell. He wanted nothing more than to have his sword in his hands and stand beside his brother and friends to confront the evil advancing upon them. He hated this feeling of powerlessness and being forced to place his trust in fate.

"I..." She did not answer for her inner sense opened up once more, ruthlessly swallowing her up while forcing her to watch the continuing horror amid the hillocks and trees. She had been sucked into that black tide of energy where mortals were not meant to be and she prayed she had the strength to escape its grasp once the vision had ended. The journey back to the fight was akin to falling off a large cliff, the swift flight frightening her to the very core of her being. She sped across the plains with such velocity not one thing could be identified. Boulders, houses, trees and anything else along her path appeared smudged and indistinct, streaks of color without substance. She existed in that in-between place where the cries and shrieks of the damned accompanied her crossing, the indecent chorus a fitting backdrop to the insane passage she was rushing through. Then everything abruptly stopped.

Zada watched Ramira emerge from the edges of her vision, her features tight and reflecting a single- minded determination. Zada flinched at what she saw, the reaction much stronger than the day Ramira battled the Kreetch. For a brief second the brown woman appeared to her, her face lined with worry for, strangely enough, both Ramira and the Vox.

None but the Herkahs had ever seen the mindless ferocity of the Kreetch who fought with little regard for anything except their desire to inflict pain. The Vox battled to impose terror upon their victims. The bodies they inhabited had at one time been perfect fighting units and the dark spirits now occupying them added their own strength to them. Who better to send into combat than a Vox-possessed Herkah? A Herkah's technique, resilience and mastery with the blades were extremely difficult to duplicate, let alone defeat. Commanding one was the next best thing. The Vox sensed victory and planned to add the members of the group to their terrible fraternity.

Allad was immensely impressed with this Herkah's strength and skill. He was lightning fast, each swing of the blade meticulously timed and executed. He had to concentrate on the task at hand…losing was not an option. He glanced at Haban and cursed under his breath; if they were both to die, the remainder of the company would be in dire straits. The nomad knew even with his warning they would never abandon them. He grimaced as the demon sliced across his chest, the blood seeping from the wound mixing with the sweat and covering his entire abdomen. He feinted to the right then brought his blade up near the demon's side, but it sidestepped the metal and immediately recovered to stab back at him.

Haban panted, the exertion of fighting these relentless creatures wearing him down to the point where he could barely lift his knife. He knew he had only moments to live and decided to attack with whatever strength he had left. The demon, sensing his imminent fall, pressed harder, managing to carve several gashes into his midsection. Haban dropped to his knees and pulled out the small blade Zada had given to him, his eyes reflecting failure. He knew to do otherwise would make things even more difficult for his companions. He lifted the blade to his chest and called out to Allad, piercing his flesh just as the demon came crashing down upon him. Haban turned the blade upward, missing the Vox who brought his blades down into Haban's chest for spite.

Allad's resolve tightened: he was now on his own against the Vox. To his dismay the other Vox headed for his friends and there was nothing he could do to either stop him or order them away.

The demon rose and began to advance upon the others, its unfocused eyes intent on the group when a figure emerged from between the hills and scrubby pines. The companions gasped as Ramira placed herself between it and them, blades at the ready and feet planted firmly on the ground. She remained perfectly still except for a strand of hair lazily circling her face as the cold wind blew across the land. The demon took a tentative step to the side, cocking its head at this unexpected threat. The Vox wiped his blades on his trousers, the black garb camouflaging Haban's blood, the Vox' crude conduct more potent than a slap to the face. She set upon the Vox with a savagery stunning even the demon, her knives blurs of motion as she forced him to retreat.

She hacked and wielded at the demon, compelling it ever backward as it fought for its life against this unforeseen threat. It lost all the ground it had gained against Haban within moments. It was no match for the rigid woman pursuing it back to its companion with a ruthlessness making them all pause. The Vox was now on the defensive and the soul of the imprisoned Herkah knew its time was at hand to burst free and accost the demon from within. The soul could do little damage but it did distract the demon, allowing Ramira to dispatch the creature. She glared with hatred down at the twitching form then turned to the Vox holding Allad in its death grip.

Danyl and the others watched as the Vox lost all interest in an exhausted and wounded Allad, swatting the nomad away as it turned to face Ramira. Had the demon sensed the Source and was it intent on taking it for its own? Were the Vox capable of wielding it? Allad tried to intervene.

"Go! Take the others and leave!" she ordered, not bothering to look and see if he obeyed her.

Allad, like the others, was not about to abandon her: they would all stay and live or die. Allad staggered back to his friends, constantly looking over his shoulder at the drama taking place behind him. The confrontation reminded him of a brutal dance between an apprentice and her master. Ramira was much smaller and weaker than the demon, depending upon her resourcefulness to keep pace with the Vox. They battled back and forth, both sets of knives inflicting wounds bleeding freely while neither one gave any ground. The Vox finally outwitted her and in one swift motion grabbed her from behind with one hand and lifted his knife to her throat with the other. Allad could feel their mortality begin to slip away from them; if she succumbed to his blade they were all worse than dead. He heard Danyl give a strangled cry of despair, Cricket began to sob and Lance and Seven exhaled sharply.

Ramira somehow knew this thing's style and kept pace with the thrusts and parries and even though it had plenty of opportunity to kill, it bided its time. It was playing with her fighting as if this was nothing more than an exercise. She surged forward, initiating the attack then rolled to either side to thwart its advance, the combatants ending up exactly where they had started from every time. The final fake lunge caught her from behind so quickly its blade began to bite into her neck as it wrenched one of her arms behind her back. Her mind raced with information about how to defend this position when she noticed the Vox' hand.

The scars on her shoulder and thigh flared briefly in response to the likeness between his thumb and forefinger. Ramira stared at it without breathing, her eyes wide with incredulity at the coiled and hooded snake undulating imperceptibly in the spiritless light. Its movement mesmerized her, making her forget where she was and what she had been doing. Dumbfounded by what wavered inches from her face, she was powerless to stop her guard from dropping. She slowly began to sense the faint essence of what still existed inside the Herkah's body, a spirit ravaged by the presence of the Vox. It had never been quite extinguished, surging forward one last time to give her one small chance to defeat the Vox. And to set his soul free.

The Vox was surprised by its host's sudden resurrection, turning inward to eradicate it once and for all. Unfortunately for the Vox, the distraction lasted just long enough for Ramira to bring her free hand up and block the Vox' blade. The edge of her knife rested against his blade for a split second before the black dagger sliced cleanly through it. She twisted in its grasp and looked into the Herkah-demon's face, watching as the sinister light returned into the eyes. She felt no pity as she brought both knives down into its chest, remaining motionless as the demon violently grabbed at the air in front of her. The nearly dead-demon Herkah collapsed on top of her without warning, pushing her roughly to the hard ground. The impact knocked the wind out of her lungs and the added heaviness made it difficult to recover her breath as she hovered on the verge of unconsciousness.

Then the world she existed in disappeared. She felt the spirit within hover at the edge of her senses, the snake uncoiling and gliding toward where she lay. The serpent stopped then gradually rose from the ground, growing in height and breadth until it began to take on a human form, one composed of rippling muscles and sinew. Its black color melted into a warm brown hue covering the man from the top of his cleanly shaven head all the way down to his feet. The towering man knelt at her side, his large hand gently caressing her hot face, his black eyes radiating an inner peace. He looked up and beyond her for a second then returned his gaze to her.

Horemb?

I am free now, child. You do not have much time. Flee with your friends.

Horemb...please...

Go. Do not let us die in vain...

Ramira watched as he rose and began to walk away, dissolving into a fine golden mist before her eyes. The weight of his body began to crush the life out of her, but instead of trying to push him off, she weakly embraced him. For once she was able to physically cling to someone from her past, even if his spirit no longer dwelled within his body. A tear rolled down the corner of her eye as she fumbled for his lifeless hand, its warmth ebbing with every passing second. She clung to it like a small child holding fast to its father's hand, afraid if she let go she would become totally lost. Horemb's dead embrace kept her anxieties at bay, the feel of his stiffening body a link to her past. The world around her became fuzzy and indistinct as his corpse pressed down upon her yet she refused to relinquish the contact with her beloved mentor and friend.

Zada's rigid form finally collapsed into a heap beneath the strain of enduring the vision. The King carried her back upstairs to her room and placed her on her bed, Clare dabbing at her burning face and neck with a cool cloth. The nomad slowly began to recover and looked up into the anxious faces staring down at her.

"The Vox are dead and Ramira is now with the others," she told them.

"They will be heading back to us then," murmured the King.

"They are still quite a ways away, Father," Styph reminded him.

"We need to send out patrols to intercept them when they return to the lands."

"We don't know where they will be coming from, Alyx," stated Clare.

"Then we will have to guess."

Zada closed her eyes, relief and sadness flooding through her being. The evil had been denied the Source yet once again and she could well imagine how angry he must now be. He had sent his best and she had beaten them. No, that wasn't quite right, for the large Vox had revolted against its demon to aid her in destroying it. Her inner eye unveiled a thread of devotion between them. A headache began to pound in her head; the aftereffects of the extreme effort she had required to keep the connection open demanding she rest. Zada drifted off into an unsettled slumber.

She lay on the ground, the effort of fighting Horemb/Vox leaving her completely without energy and the knowledge, as little as it was, leaving her mind numb. Horemb had taught her how to wield the knives she had taken from the red woman and now she had killed him. Who were the others that had died for her? What part had they played in her life? Her mind began to reel, not just from the impact but from the information and the blood seeping from the lacerations the Vox had administered to her. It took several moments for her to realize the body had been pushed away and the faces gazing down were those of the very people she had abandoned. She tried to focus on them but the disconnected feeling between her body and mind left her unable to move. She closed her eyes, the only parts of her body responding to her command, and willed them to leave her alone. She didn't deserve their loyalty or understanding. They poured water over her face and neck, forcing her to return to the rolling plain where she had to face them.

"Ramira? Are you badly hurt?"

She looked up as the prince gently shook her back into the present. His face, as much as she wanted to see it, was the one making her cringe the most. She tried to turn her head, but he forced her to look into his eyes.

"Ramira!" he called to her again, as the opaque sun slipped behind a bank of dirty gray clouds.

"Get her up," she thought she heard Seven say as her body was lifted off of the cold ground and onto the back of a horse.

The land became clearer and more distinct with every passing mile, as did the cold no amount of clothing could keep at bay. She shivered even after Danyl wrapped her within his cloak, the tiny fingers of ice worming their way into her flesh to attack her bones. She felt Danyl's arms around her and the thumping of his heartbeat, her companions speaking of finding shelter from the threatening storm. The nervousness in their voices penetrated her semi-conscious mind, yanking her to the present with a start. The horses slowed then stopped within a clump of pines, their riders staring at a dingy inn in a little hollow about a mile from where they stood. An enclosed porch fronted the weathered L-shaped building and a covered walkway in need of repair led to the barn. The ground in front was so heavily used by travelers over the years that not even a blade of grass dared to grow there. A soaking rain would turn it into a muddy morass in moments. Lights shone through the thickly paned front windows and from one of the upstairs rooms and they could hear neighing from the barn.

"We have to take a chance and seek shelter there," Seven stated, the uneasiness in his voice as crisp and clear as the air around them. He glanced over at Allad and frowned. The Herkah needed his wounds attended to as soon as possible, as did a slumping Ramira.

"There doesn't seem to be too much activity," Lance said, his breath screening his face.

"Go down and find out," Danyl ordered.

Danyl held the reins loosely in one hand, his other holding her firmly in place as they anxiously waited for Lance to return. The prince glanced over at Cricket, who stared at Ramira with wide, frightened eyes then briefly met his with uncertainty. He offered her a little smile of encouragement but the young girl, confused at what was happening, clung to the dwarf king, who gently patted her hand. Seven had seen the fond look in her eyes prior to Ramira's return and understood Cricket's response to Danyl's genuine affection. Her confusion set in when he put Ramira in what she thought of as her place on his horse. The dwarf had seen the lack of attention in her life when they first met and decided to meet this newfound bewilderment concerning Danyl head on.

"I think we are going to be kept inside for several days."

"Maybe," she mumbled.

"It'll be nice to sit in front of a fire with a full belly, a drop or two of ale and a stack of winnings from a card game."

"There is no card game I can't win," she stated, her focus slowly being drawn away from Danyl and Ramira.

"Are you challenging me?" asked the King.

"Maybe."

"Such a young thing like you can't play anything but easy games."

"I've taken my share of coins," she rebutted, the dwarf's dare too much for her to ignore.

"Name your stakes," he chuckled.

"What have you got?"

Seven laughed, for the girl had no idea who any of them were or that the prizes would be more than she could ever imagine. She knew their names but nothing more. She had no idea she rode with a king, two princes, a lord, a high-ranking captain and the source of magic sought by the most evil of all creatures in the land. Seven liked the girl for she showed a great deal of pluck and character trying to hide her fragility behind a veil of bravado. He shrugged for most young people her age did the same, but she did it in a very charming sort of way. She had developed an infatuation for Danyl and was learning he would not be returning that emotion.

"When I peel off these filthy clothes and peer into my foul pockets I'll be able to tell you." She was about to answer when Lance returned.

"There are many rooms available," he began. "There are few people and the impending storm has kept everyone else at bay. There is a group of four already in the tavern and another pair were securing their horses."

"What did you tell them?" asked Danyl.

"Seven seek shelter. They demand payment up front for one night when we enter and everything else will be extra."

"Not very trustworthy, are they?" snapped Gard.

"Many don't pay in these parts," Cricket stated quietly from behind the dwarf king as a combination of snow and sleet began to fall upon them.

"Once the storm sets in few, if any, will be traveling anywhere, so I think we should be safe for a day or two while it lasts," added Gard.

"Then we should get going before we die in this snowstorm," Danyl said, as he urged his mount down into the hollow.

Lance and Gard took their horses to the barn, caring for the animals while the others entered the inn. The four other travelers were eating as they entered the building, the scrutiny between the party's brief yet thorough. The rotund innkeeper with the filthy apron welcomed them, the coins he was about to make already jingling in his pockets. His mate, a tired looking woman with a long face, came out from the kitchen wiping her hands on her apron as she eyed the extra mouths she would have to feed. She gave them a wan smile and invited them to the table in the far corner and placed bread, cheese and ale on it. She returned with plates and silverware just as Lance and Gard set foot in the inn brushing the snow off their cloaks before hanging them to dry by the fireplace.

"How skilled are you at sewing?" asked Allad, gripping his side.

"I once managed to thread a needle after only four tries," Seven stated, squinting as he mimicked threading a needle with shaky hands.

"Can you mend my cuts without sewing my tunic into them?" Allad watched Seven drink down an entire mug of ale then wipe the foam from his upper lip.

"I can now."

Seven and Allad disappeared upstairs, their companions grateful for the hot food and warm shelter. Ramira's stomach reveled at the food it was about to receive, growling so loudly in anticipation even Gard heard it from across the table. Her gaze never lifted over her plate as she took little bites and washed them down with tea. They ate in silence, looking up halfway through their meal as the dwarf and the nomad rejoined them.

"And?" Danyl asked Allad, the nomad's face less pain-filled than before.

"I will not have to wear this garment for the rest of my life."

They shared a rare moment of laughter, ignoring the sleet hitting the windows and the darkness that had nearly taken them.

"We made it just in time," Gard stated, filling his mug with ale. The howling wind smashed something against the outside wall, making everyone pause and look toward the sound then at each other.

The woman brought a large platter of steaming vegetables, returning with another laden with slices of meat. Ramira ate out of necessity though her friends could see food was the furthest thing from her mind. She knew she would have to explain her reasons for leaving the city: an act leading to Haban's death and placing all of their lives in great peril. They ate their fill then sat around the table, the smell of tobacco from Seven's pipe lifting into the air. Allad leaned back in the chair, alleviating some of the pressure on his wounds; Gard rested his chin on fists so tightly clenched his knuckles appeared white. Seven and Danyl were engaged in a discussion concerning their depleted provisions, the captain reminding them of things they had forgotten to add to their growing list.

"Good woman," Ramira called to the innkeeper's wife as she passed by their table. "A bath, please?" She crooked her finger and led her to the rear of the inn by the kitchen, opened a cupboard and handed Ramira a towel and a bar of soap.

She filled the tub twice before feeling clean enough to sit and soak in the waters warm embrace. The only sounds infiltrating the room were muted voices and the clanging of pots from the kitchen across the hall. Ramira quietly mourned Horemb's passing, killing the only link to her past before she could speak with him. Her mind replayed the moment she drove the blades into his chest, the pain exploding within her own heart as nothing but the hilts protruded out.

Horemb had saved her life by drawing away the demon and she had given him his soul back when she executed the Vox. Nevertheless, that did little to assuage her guilt. She closed her eyes and allowed the striking snake to fill her mind then gradually the hand became an arm and then a body. It relinquished its hold on her from behind and stood before her.

Horemb stood before her, his deeply tanned body glistening with sweat, gold armbands covered his bulging upper arms and flat golden earrings hanging from his ears. He wore a loincloth held in place by a leather belt, the many scars running along his body and weathered face a testament to his keen skills. He smiled down at her as his enormous hand reached out and cupped her chin. The image began to fade away, leaving her alone with a single tear running down her cheek.

Humbled and subdued by Horemb's sacrifice, she rose from the cooling water. She washed her clothes, hanging them on a clothesline strung behind the massive fireplace and changed into her spare clothes. She walked back to her companions, sitting down beside Seven as Danyl rose and headed for the bathing chamber. She knew they would go to their room afterward where she would have to explain her actions. In the meantime, the dwarf took her hand in his and squeezed it.

"It's good to see that you are well," he said meaningfully. "You are as hard to find as my concoction when Clare gets a hold of it."

"I'm sorry for all of the trouble I've caused. Why you think I was worth all of this trouble is beyond me."

Her companions exchanged knowing glances. She furrowed her brows and stared from one to the other as a sense of uneasiness began to grip her. Danyl would probably have come after her but not Gard; Allad and Seven might have sent men with the search party while remaining in Bystyn. She glanced at Gard, the unmistakable coldness shining from his eyes confusing her. *What did I ever do to you?* she thought. She turned her attention to Allad. The Herkah held her gaze, keeping his sentiments to himself. Her fingers curled more tightly around the king's hand as Danyl strode over to them, his features straining with controlled anger and the pain of betrayal.

The storm raged on, making the afternoon look like night, and the members of the company remained in their seats. The other travelers had retired to their rooms and the innkeeper and his wife were busy in the back of the building. It was time to plan their return to Bystyn.

"Cricket," whispered the King, "how far west have we come?"

"From what point?" she asked, keeping her voice low.

"From the eastern edge of the forest."

"About here," she stated, using the boards and cups on the table as vague reference points. Seven and the others immediately knew they were too far west to cut straight up and onto the plains. If Cricket was even remotely correct with her directions, they had to travel several days east then north just in case the enemy had infiltrated beyond the first third of the plains. They had been gone long enough for that scenario to have changed, a fact substantiated by the Vox they had already encountered. Mahn knew the Source was out in the open and somewhere here in the south. He had come very close to securing it and would undoubtedly be better prepared the next time the Source was flushed out of hiding. Would a day or two be sufficient enough to avoid Mahn and his army to the west?

"We should discuss this later," said Lance, as two of the other lodgers came downstairs to sit by the fire.

Danyl agreed and lightly nudged Ramira. It was time.

Danyl closed the door and immediately embraced her, the contact releasing the pent up frustrations, fears and doubts that had plagued them both for so long. She began to cry and he encouraged her to purge the darkness gripping her heart and soul. She began to weaken and he led her to the bed, continuing to hold her while gently rocking her back and forth. She finally ran out of tears and wiped away her grief, readying herself for the questions he was sure to ask. He did not speak right away, tending instead to the cuts inflicted by the Vox, satisfied none of them were serious.

"I cannot begin to apologize enough for the trouble I've caused."

"What made you leave?"

He listened to her speak about the whispers and the empty promises made by the unknown voices, her face pressed against his chest. She told him about her nightmares, the elf's jaw tightening with revulsion with every detail she revealed to him. She clung to him and he to her as he accompanied her through the terrible journey in her mind and her flight from Bystyn. Then quietly, almost reverently, she told him about Horemb. He heard the respect and love she held for him, clutching her more closely as she mourned his passing. The bearer of the most appalling of all powers in the land trembled in his arms begging for his forgiveness. He had two truths to tell her and wondered what they would do to her…to them.

"Ramira," he lifted her chin so he could look into her eyes, "I know why those things have been happening. You house the Source and the evil is hunting for you. He drove you from the city to make it easier for him to get it."

He watched her eyes widen and her mouth open in disbelief. The idea she was the cause of all of the death and destruction taking place was too much for her to bear. She could feel the bloody bodies bumping up against her legs and see their accusing faces staring up at her. She gasped as images of Bystyn crumbled beneath the weight of evil and its people being slaughtered by the Vox and Kreetch filled her entire sight. She began to shiver with helplessness and abhorrence as reality set in like an icy wind from the north. In essence, her dreams had revealed the truth and her friends, knowing the danger, came for her anyway. She felt his arms wrapping around her, holding her close as she grappled with the awful truth. Her head landed on his shoulder, her eyes wide with dismay as she stared unblinking at the worn wall behind them. She did not deserve such loyalty and dropped her head in shame.

"You shouldn't have come looking for me, Danyl. Now you are in even greater peril than before."

"Things will get worse whether we are here or back in Bystyn, Ramira, the only difference is the elven power will be able to keep Mahn at bay."

"You've found it?" she asked, her heart feeling suddenly lighter at the news.

The second truth was about to be revealed. He knew she would try to distance herself from him to keep Mahn from securing the elven magic. She believed Mahn would obtain Danyl's power through her and would do anything to keep that from happening. She avoided him back in Bystyn because he was a prince: what would she do once she found out he had the magic? He took a deep breath and made her look into his eyes.

"Yes. I'm the bearer," he said quietly.

"You!" Ramira stared at the elf then tried to break the contact between them. His grip remained tight, loosening up only when she began to relent. "Yes, me. I'm still the same person, just as you are, even though we both carry power. Ramira, the others know about you but not about me and it is best we keep this between us."

"Is the city not vulnerable now that you aren't there?"

"I think Mahn is so intent on finding you that Bystyn is the least of his concerns right now, but it is important we get back as soon as possible."

"That's why you were able to save me from the demons after the Kreetch poisoned me, isn't it?" she asked after a while.

"Yes. Your power ignited mine and it protected and guided me as I searched for you. If you hadn't been poisoned then who knows when the Green Might would have awakened. I'd hate to think what could have occurred if you hadn't heard me that stormy night along the cliff or if you had decided to travel elsewhere other than Bystyn. Fate, it seems, is determined to keep us together and I, for one, am grateful for it."

"You should be angry with me, Danyl," she said in a small voice.

"I would be lying if I told you I wasn't but things happen for a reason, Ramira. Reasons none of us can foresee but must simply accept. Promise me you won't run away again or use the Source?"

"I won't disappear and I don't even know how to wield the power."

"If you brandish it like you do your knives then..." He stopped for the image was too fear inspiring to accept, especially if Mahn was the one who controlled it. She gazed up at him, the innocent appeal to shield her from the evil an arduous task but one he was willing to accept. He kissed her forehead then tenderly traced the contours of her face with his finger. He offered her his quiet reassurance while she wrestled with the truths he had confessed. He somehow knew she would draw on her inner strength and courage to accept what had been imparted on them then place her trust in the bond that they shared.

"Danyl?"

"Yes?"

"No matter what the future holds for us I want you to know that I love you and I would never do anything to hurt you or anyone else. I don't know why I am the one that holds the Source, but I do know that I won't let him take it. This I swear to you here and now. "

"We all trust you, Ramira, and if we can't have faith and loyalty in each other then the evil has already won. As to your love..." He leaned forward and gently kissed her, the need for her closeness even greater now than before.

They both understood she was a danger to them all, but with her return to Bystyn she would at least be out of Mahn's grasp. He would come for her especially now that he identified the approximate location where his demons had been slain. The only thing hampering the immediate dispatch of more Vox was the weather. It would hinder both the pursued and the pursuers, but what would happen once they reached the plains on the other side of the forest? Zada, he was sure, had "seen" the confrontation and would have informed his father and the others about what had transpired. The most logical thing to do would be to send patrols to specific areas where they believed they might emerge from. What if they came out miles away and needed immediate help? There was nothing they could do but head back to the city as quickly as possible and hope for the best along the way. If they encountered any more Vox between now and then, they would have to rely on Allad's and Ramira's talents. They lay down on the bed together, the elf holding her tightly against him. She shivered beneath the blanket, her fingers fidgeting with his and her eyelids slowly sinking. Danyl fared little better but an undercurrent of need flowed from one to the other. Their union was brief and made them feel more whole about themselves and each other, an antidote for the emptiness that had haunted them for the past several weeks. The Green Might and the Source merged then separated, returning to their proper places once more but leaving behind a twinkling silver grain in their wake

Seven quietly entered the room with Cricket and walked over to the sleeping pair, the peaceful looks on their faces tugging at his heart. He missed Clare and would have given anything to curl up beside her. He rubbed his tired face and eyes and pulled the blankets up over their shoulders. He steered Cricket to the corner bed and patted her affectionately on the head before sitting down in front of the fireplace. Allad opened the connecting door between the rooms and glanced at Danyl and Ramira. The King noticed the imperceptible nod of his head and invited him to sit in front of the fire with him.

"I wish we had some news, any news about what is happening in Bystyn," said Seven as he poured them each a cup of ale.

"Unfortunately we are blind, Seven, and must therefore make more assumptions than is advisable."

"How much could have happened in the time we were gone?" asked the dwarf king.

"How much indeed," Allad muttered under his breath. He glanced past Cricket, who stood in front of the window looking out into the dismal storm. Bits of sleet whipped against the panes hurled about by the wind as it brought this part of the land to a standstill. At least they would be able to rest properly for a couple of days. They might need the extra energy for the return trip. How far had Mahn advanced upon the city during the time they were away? The Vox were already far to the east in the southern portion of the land and Allad believed it was not just to find the Source. They were scouring the area so the enemy could set up and control the forest separating them from Bystyn. Mahn would attack from the west and the south, hemming them into the city. He said as much to Seven, who agreed with his assessment.

"That would make the most sense, but will he be able to get enough bodies to do that?"

"The only thing he lacks the most are Vox," replied the nomad as his eyes locked onto Seven's.

"Well, he lost two and was denied two…I'd say we were most fortunate, don't you?"

"Absolutely, my friend. I know I am pleased to be sitting across from you right now," stated the Herkah. Both knew fortune would not always smile down on them and one day they would run out of luck. Allad checked his own injuries while the dwarf king stared off into space. His face suddenly lit up and a wry grin spread across his weathered features.

"Here." The King poured Allad a small amount of his potion from a flask he produced from within his tunic then filled one for himself. The Herkah shook his head and chuckled softly as they raised their glasses to one another then swallowed the drink in one gulp.

"Did you sneak this out while Clare wasn't looking?" he asked the King with a glint in his eyes.

"No, my friend," he grinned victoriously then refilled their glasses, "my sweet love packed it for me."

"She did, did she?"

"Yes, but I packed these!" he confessed with amusement as he pulled back the flap on his pack, exposing a half dozen more flasks carefully wrapped and securely tucked away.

"I've seen babies with less swaddling," stated the nomad with a stifled laugh so he wouldn't wake the sleeping couple.

"Drink up, Allad, and get a good night's sleep. We all could use one." The King finished his drink, grabbed his blanket, and followed Allad into the adjoining room, leaving Cricket asleep in her bed. She stared at Danyl and Ramira for a while with a tinge of disappointment on her face then sighed and closed her eyes.

Alyxandyr finished reading the stack of reports, tossing the last one on his desk; Mahn was already marching toward Bystyn even though he did not have the Source. The demons had ravaged and demolished everything in their path and those they had not slain were taking their chances hiding in the hills and forests surrounding their homes. They had lost four entire patrols and the city, now filled with all of the people who had lived in and around it, was getting nervous. He knew chaos was their worst enemy. He and the other rulers made it extremely clear that anyone found guilty of inciting disorder would be met with the harshest of punishments. He looked up as someone knocked on his door, greeting Nyk, Styph, Mason, Zada and Clare as they entered his private chambers.

"Any more visions, Zada?" he asked, her negative reply reassuring for that meant they had, for the moment, escaped any more Vox. He watched Mason unroll a map, placing objects on its corners to keep it from curling back up.

"What did you see in regard to their surroundings, Zada?" inquired the first advisor.

"Rolling hills…lots of stones and boulders all around…it was cold because I saw breath forming around their mouths while they were fighting. That's all."

"That would put them in this general area," said Styph, as he pointed to the map. "Nothing in that region but towns filled with thieves, murderers and the like."

"We know that Mahn has spread out to this point, and we have to assume he has managed to penetrate into the forest running east to west…the question would be how far?"

"We lost a patrol that was sent here." Styph pointed slightly west of the midway point along the woods. "So for now that would be his farthest push east."

"It's a two…two and a half day's ride from the northern fringes of the forest to the gates and they still have several days of uninterrupted riding to do before they even get to the woods," explained Mason. "We can't help them until they get to the plains, and even then they might be too far west for us to be of any significant aid."

"Mahn knows he has lost two of his Vox and he is also now aware that one of the companions has the Source. He will send more demons to find them, probably Radir, for he cannot chance losing any more Vox. The Radir are not as powerful as the Vox but they blend better into their surroundings and can be more easily replaced," stated Zada.

"Then Allad and Ramira will be even busier fighting them," muttered Alyxandyr.

"Not really, Alyx, for although they are formidable foes, they can be killed by those who are well versed in the art of warfare."

"That means the others can kill them, too?" asked the King, a positive piece of news finally presenting itself.

"Yes," replied Zada, "Seven and the elves are skilled enough to defeat them."

The noose was tightening around their necks and their only way of defeating Mahn was outside the rope. It was imperative Danyl and Ramira return to Bystyn before the enemy cut them off. The allies had lost control of half the plains to the west, making it difficult to gather information to prevent or plan any reprisals against Mahn. He glanced down at the map, his finger tracing toward the west until it rested on the spot marked "Kepracarn." Mahn originated from someplace in the desert but used Cooper's city as his point of attack. He would spread his armies to the northeast, the east then southeast, effectively engulfing them as the enemy closed their ranks on the other side of the city. Once that occurred, they would be isolated and unable to seek help. There had to be a weakness, though. There always was. Perhaps Cooper had some information that could help them. Alyxandyr sent four Herkahs to bring the King to his chambers, much to the dismay of those gathered.

"I hope you have everything you require." Alyxandyr greeted the King, offering him a seat and a glass of wine.

"Actually, my treatment is better than I had anticipated," he replied, lifting his glass to those present and ignoring their cold responses. He did not fail to notice the absence of the others. "Is there anything else you can tell us about Mahn?" Alyxandyr asked bluntly.

"A few of your kind came out of the hole, too." He glanced at Zada then immediately away from her hard gaze.

"'Your kind'...what do you mean by that?" demanded the Herkah, her heart beating strongly in her chest as she anticipated one of her worst nightmares.

"Vox." Cooper shuddered inwardly at the thought of either Allad or Zada being converted into demons, especially Allad. The Herkah was a formidable enough of a foe without the added impetus of a demon controlling his highly skilled body.

"How many, Cooper?" The King demanded.

"I'm not sure...a dozen, perhaps a few more."

"How many guarded you in Kepracarn?" inquired Styph.

"Two...two others escorted me out the gates."

"We've lost six of our people in the past few years," said Zada. "I can't imagine where he'd get the others from."

"Are there small groups of Herkahs living away from the tribe?" Mason asked.

"There used to be."

"There are two fewer Vox to contend with," stated Alyxandyr.

Cooper stared into the glass, the interrogation demeaning but necessary. He hoped he would discern things from them to help him with his own cause. They didn't have a chance against the evil even if it could never wield the power it sought. His gaze met each of those gathered and it began to dawn on him they were waiting for him to acknowledge something. He shifted in his seat then re-crossed his ankles wondering where the other leaders were. Clare was here but not Seven. Allad was absent as were Danyl and Gard. One or maybe two might be ill or off on some errand but all four not accounted for? And what did the King mean when he said there were two fewer Vox in the land? Who could possibly have killed those monsters?

"What's going on?" he asked, refusing to hide the suspicion in his voice.

"What do you mean?" asked Alyxandyr.

"Don't trifle with me, Alyxandyr." Cooper could feel the anger rising up his neck and into his face as he glared hard from one to the other, impatiently waiting for them to reply.

"What is it that you wish to know?"

"Where are Danyl, Seven, Allad and the Khadry prince?"

"They are currently busy with various duties," stated the King, pouring himself a goblet of wine. "Why do you ask?"

Cooper knew his chances of acquiring Bystyn as payment for his allegiance with Mahn were nonexistent and allying himself with the elves too galling. He would share in the elves' and their allies' fates. In short, there was nothing to gain no matter where he placed his fealty, an entirely unknown situation for the king. Cooper knew he would be dead in the end, whether it had been immediate in Kepracarn or later here in Bystyn. Cooper decided to play his hand, hoping he could bluff his way out of his situation.

"Are they out looking for the Source?"

"Why would they be looking for the Source?" asked Alyxandyr, his eyes narrowing to slits as he scrutinized Cooper.

"Because Mahn doesn't have it, and since he is concentrating on your city, I assume it must be nearby. You have it, don't you?" His mind began to establish a variety of scenarios and no matter which way he placed his suppositions, they all seemed to point to the same thing.

"We do not."

"But you know where it is."

"We do not," repeated the King honestly.

"Where are they, Alyxandyr?" Cooper saw the concern flicker in his eyes, a reaction the others shared as well. For the first time Cooper felt a stab of panic in his chest. The only way to beat Mahn and save his own skin was to have the Source at hand…any hand other than Mahn's.

"Alyxandyr, Mahn is also searching for the Source, and once he has it we are all beaten. You are obviously quite concerned about it, but you don't show any signs of alarm and that tells me something else is going on. Now, where are they?"

"At what point did you became the inquisitor?" asked Styph, not bothering to hide the danger in his voice.

"When my life became an issue."

"Why I should tell you anything? What could you possibly reveal to us that would help our situation?" inquired the King, contemplating Cooper's reactions.

"Because the last thing I want is to become like them!" he hissed between his teeth, pointing to the west. Those gathered stared hard at the undisguised candor not only in his voice but on his face as well. None of them wanted to become a tortured tool of the evil, either.

"What do you know?" the King persisted, his patience wearing thin.

"When Mahn sent me to you, a contingent left at the same time heading south, following the forest eastwards. He can't go through you but he can go around and search for what he wants. Now you."

"We are aware of that, Cooper."

"Mahn has plenty of power."

"We know that."

"He can't use his might without this Source."

"We know that too," replied the elven king.

"What don't you know?"

"Why all of this is happening."

Cooper had no idea why Mahn chose this time and place and suddenly didn't care. His ruse had failed in obtaining any information that would help him out of this dilemma. He was very tired of everything and wanted nothing more than to return to his prison and sleep. Would he have been better off had he made a pact with Mahn like Antama had? The red mist engulfing her filled his mind, reigniting the hatred he felt for her.

"Cooper?" Mason's voice cut into his thoughts like a knife.

"Antama made a…bargain with Mahn. I think the crimson haze might have been yet another fiend."

"Something else to contend with," muttered Styph, staring hard at Cooper.

"So it seems," replied Cooper, draining his glass then setting it on the table beside him. "I'd like to leave now."

Alyxandyr glared at Cooper and saw a King bereft of his city, followers and all that he acquired, even if he had forcefully taken them and felt a pang of pity for him. Mahn would have wrested away all Cooper had, regardless of how intelligent the king was. The evil could not have inflicted a greater emotional and mental pain upon him using any other method. Cooper deserved to be humbled but not in this fashion. Alyxandyr nodded and the Herkahs escorted him back to his room.

"Antama finally found her road to power," Mason said in his deep tones. "Her knowledge, fighting skills and lack of remorse make her a menacing foe, and I am not surprised she has allied herself to Mahn."

"I don't think anyone 'allies' themselves with Mahn, Mason. I tend to believe he has some use for her down the road," replied Zada. She was at a loss to explain this red demon, for she had never sensed it before. What else had been awakened in that foul hole?

"We all have much work to do if we are to survive," said the elven king, rising from his seat. The others followed suit, silently resuming their duties, their minds subdued but their spirits determined.

Mahn surveyed the army standing silently before him from atop a mammoth black horse, their eyes blank and minds controlled by his. The Vox were stationed along the edges of the huge group like dogs keeping a flock of sheep in line waiting for the signal that would send them east. Mahn wondered what had killed the two Vox he had sent in search of the Source. He had sensed no power being wielded, only an increase in exertion then a sudden separation from them. That meant there was someone out there with the capacity to beat them in combat, an unexpected revelation, one which troubled him but not enough to alter his plans. The third Vox was already in place and would remain there until the fighting began, for it had only one purpose, one that would devastate the hated Herkahs. A low hiss of anticipated satisfaction issued forth from the cowl as he imagined the Vox completing his task.

Mahn opened his mind and scanned the land for any magic but found nothing; there wasn't even a flicker of green from the city. The elven magic had flared briefly but its current peculiar dormancy since the Source departed the city mystified him. He tapped the pommel of his saddle with a gloved finger, the bottomless blackness issuing from his cowl pointing in Bystyn's direction. He converged all of his appalling energy into a point and let it fly straight into the heart of Bystyn. The arrow of darkness darted past trees and over the cold ground then up the main avenue to the castle. It sliced through the thick oak doors and up the staircase, impaling Zada with its despicable barb. Mahn sneered with pleasure as he watched the Herkah witch clutch at her chest and gasp for air. Her face turned nearly purple and, as his power dissolved, she collapsed in a heap. He saw no more, careful to refrain from using too much of his might too soon.

The Green Might, however, did not respond to his probing. It remained silent, almost uninterested about his attack on the city. It did not matter if it was in the city or not because the Green Might alone could not harm him, especially if he had the Source. Besides, he planned on extracting the Green Might from the bearer and adding it to his own. The thought of so much power inside of him fine-tuned every muscle and fiber in the body he inhabited, sending his senses to their maximum limits. He could hear his army breathing and smell the sweat and death permeating the edge of the plains and. He focused on their vacant faces, every pore as deep as a crater and every hair as tall as a tree. Their leather jerkins creaked loudly in his ears and the faint scraping of their weapons as deafening as steel being sharpened against a stone. He sensed the souls imprisoned within the demons, their silent screams echoing hollowly within their bodies. They howled in bitterness, fear and hatred, but all yearned for death, an end he was not about to grant. Soon he would have scores more to torment: an eternity of spirits to break.

He nodded toward the Vox. They herded the vast army east as he followed behind them. The weather was cooperating at this point but he sensed it would soon change. He was unconcerned for the black horde spreading out before him like some hideous disease; they would drive on, heedless of hunger or exhaustion. He turned toward an approaching Vox.

"The Radir are in the forefront," it wheezed, then rode back to the army.

The evil was pleased. The first wave of his army would be able to inflict a great deal of damage on the defenders. He relished the thought of demonizing them and the ensuing chaos that would erupt in the city. Such a plan would have a devastating effect on the others and would stir up old animosities amongst the races. It would be difficult enough for the allies to fight his army without the added burden of cutting down their own men. Mahn pictured the turmoil and dread that that would cause and wished the moment were before him now.

Soon enough, he hissed with satisfaction, *soon enough*.

They all met for the morning meal at the same table from the previous evening, grateful they had found shelter from the storm still raging outside. Two of the four men were seated at the other side of the room talking with each other while the others must have been still in their rooms or out in the stable checking on their horses. Allad and Seven had already done so and now enjoyed steaming mugs of tea to ward off the chill. The woman placed fresh bread, cheese and a variety of sliced meats on the table then refilled the teapot before busying herself in the back of the building. The innkeeper brought in armfuls of wood for the fire, filling up the bin after several trips outside.

"It felt great to sleep in a bed," stated Seven, helping himself to the food.

"I think you'll get the chance to do that for at least one more night," Allad informed him. "This storm won't stop before late afternoon."

"That didn't seem to hinder two of our friends from leaving early this morning. Must have been a damn good reason to go out in this weather," said Seven.

"We'll have to be extra vigilant, won't we?" said Danyl.

"I asked about getting some supplies from the innkeeper," Allad stated, reaching out for another slice of bread. "He told me he could spare maybe a few days worth if we were willing to pay for them."

"I expected nothing less," muttered Danyl, placing his fingers around his mug for warmth.

"Do you think the weather has affected Bystyn?" the nomad asked the prince.

"No. The storms usually swing south first then slowly move northward. We are running out of time because the last place I'd like to be is outside the city when the weather does change."

"Perhaps we can leave if this clears up no later than early afternoon," suggested Seven. "I know we'd all like to get back as soon as possible."

"I agree," said Gard. "It'll be just as difficult traveling regardless of when we leave."

They kept themselves occupied most of the morning doing everything from playing cards to tending to their gear while they waited for the weather to break. Danyl and Ramira managed to get some private time together while the others were downstairs, the ever-present Lance sequestered in a corner of the hall where he could discreetly guard them. It began to get lighter late in the morning and the snow finally stopped altogether around midday and the company, well rested and provisioned, headed out. Thoughts of seeing the gray walls of Bystyn filled all of their minds. They saw no other travelers during the afternoon and decided to head in a northeasterly direction back toward the city. They spoke very little, keeping a sharp watch on their surroundings, Cricket riding behind Danyl and Ramira on Haban's mount beside them. They continued on until the sun began to set, its colors muted by the dirty gray clouds stretching from horizon to horizon. They made camp along a small hill sprouting pines along its slope and shared a meal. They assigned sentry duties amongst themselves before rolling into their blankets to seek out what little warmth they could.

Ramira hesitated as Danyl held up the corner of his blanket. She still felt guilty for putting them all in jeopardy but the elf insisted and she complied. She was grateful when his arm slipped over her; she placed his hand against her heart, the feeling reassuring to them both. She turned to look him full in the face.

"I'm going to lock you in my chambers when we get back to Bystyn," he whispered in a half joking manner.

"Wouldn't a partially mad woman with a pair of knives make you think twice about such a foolish endeavor?".

"I'd take them away from you."

"You'd still have to contend with my madness."

"True, but I'm sure I can deal with that before it flares out of control."

They were both very quiet for a few minutes, growing comfortably warm snuggled together.

"Danyl?" she whispered.

"Yes?"

"When this is all over, can the two of us go somewhere…anywhere for a while?"

"I think that can be arranged," he replied, pulling her closer. All he wanted was to be somewhere else alone with her.

Seven rested his head on his hands and studied his companions. Danyl and Ramira were where they belonged, together; Gard and Allad were guarding them from somewhere in the shadows. Cricket, he noted, had been watching the pair but soon grew either too tired or resentful and turned her back on them. The girl had grown quite fond of the elf; it was apparent he had been the first to show any trust in her. The prince undoubtedly elicited a variety of feelings from the young girl, emotions she had never known. He guessed she was about Anci's age and the two girls would get along well with one another, if they got back to the city in one piece. The King wondered if they were bringing her to an immediate death or saving her from one that would take longer if she remained here in the south. There were going to be some very frightening and trying days and weeks ahead of them. If they managed to get back to Bystyn with Ramira at least they would have some chance against the evil. If they failed or if Mahn took her, then all they could do was to fight and hope for a miracle.

Was there anything about her magic or any other kind of power that predicted how it was to be used? Mahn, after all, was destructive but Ramira, who held the power within, was not. Granted, the young woman could destroy demons with a hunger alarming even to a seasoned veteran like himself, but her loyalty and dedication were not rooted in evil. She had not abandoned them, for although the nightmares had become too oppressive, she had left because the voices threatened to demolish the city and all those who lived within it. She did not believe she was running away from her dreams as much as distracting them away from those she loved. Did that mean the magic she held reflected what was in her heart? If the Source was purely evil and she only a reservoir for it until the intended user came along, would not that evil somehow taint her heart and soul? Seven knew individuals who were steeped in corruption showed no signs of guilt or remorse. They could also never love. He saw all of these things in Ramira, and not just for Danyl but for them all. Seven rolled over onto his back and stared at the intertwining branches over his head and sighed. Were not all of their lives woven together like those limbs? Each tree was capable of supporting itself but an entire forest of trees could provide shade and comfort for a myriad of creatures. And each other. The strength of the oaks and the graceful birches would stand beside the fragrant pines and the sturdy maples. Seven liked being a part of the forest and with that thought breathed deeply and fell asleep.

They resumed their trek at dawn, carefully avoiding groups of men they'd sporadically encounter during the course of the morning. The companions picked their way over fields of stone and boulders then ducked their heads as they moved through broad stands of trees. They jumped a stone fence and cut through the farmland, staying hidden amongst the plant growth as they passed by a house to their left. They heard pigs squealing and cows lowing near where smoke curled out of a chimney sticking up above the treetops. Chickens squawked with indignation as something chased them around the yard, the excited barking of a dog pointing to a likely culprit. A woman called out and a moment later children answered from a distance. The noises became indistinct then faded away as they maneuvered past hedges festooned with fat red berries.

Seven plucked one from a branch and immediately regretted doing so. The berry was sticky and it took several quick flicks of his wrist to get rid of it. He watched the berry arc gracefully and land on an unsuspecting Allad. Cricket shook her head and smirked at the dwarf king who held his stained finger to his lips and rolled his eyes at her. I might just tell on you, she mouthed at Seven. He winked at her then became absolutely serious as Danyl glanced over at him.

"Behave or I'll tell Clare," Danyl playfully whispered to him.

They stopped at the edge of the haphazard row of shrubs staring at the dark canopy on the horizon to the north. The forest separating the elven lands from the south appeared like a smudged line of green and brown stretching in nearly a straight line from the east to the west. Barring any unforeseen problems, and with a little luck, they would be on the other side within a day or two.

"Danyl," Lance warned.

"I see them, Lance. Remember, we are just a lowly group of travelers." They rode on nonchalantly, casually glancing at the approaching men and silently cursing their imminent arrival. They would be outnumbered two to one if forced to fight. He recognized some of the men and Cricket's whimper confirmed his suspicions as she pressed her face into his back. The strangers continued to angle toward them, finally stopping and waiting for the group to intercept them. The large man reined in his horse several yards away and nodded tersely at Lance, his eyes glittering dangerously.

"We meet again," said Lance.

"So it seems," he replied then spat on the ground, the disgusting stain standing out sharply on the snow. A lecherous look crossed his features as he glanced over at Ramira, a reaction becoming even more depraved as she defiantly glared back at him. She shifted her gaze to his men, staring hard from one to the other while ignoring the perverse proposals they offered her. Her hands snaked down to her blades, the sudden sensation to hunt taking over her. Her companions and even the men wondered what she was looking for but only the former knew why: demons. Now would not be a good time for a confrontation with the men let alone the demons but the dark look on her face would not go away. Her attention became fixated on two men at the rear of the group, their coarse smugness indistinguishable from their companions. It took every ounce of willpower to keep her hands from instinctively sliding out her knives. Ramira didn't know what he was; she only knew he stirred the same reaction in her the Kreetch and Vox had and that she needed to destroy them.

"What do you want this time?"

"Who's behind the elf?" demanded the man.

"A fellow companion."

"I'd like to meet this 'companion.'"

"I don't think so."

"You gonna stop me?" he barked at Lance, urging his horse forward only to have Ramira intercept him.

"I will," she warned, pulling back the edges of her cloak.

The man laughed at her.

"Not likely," he replied as he reached over to grab her. He immediately winced in pain as she swung her blades up and across his hands, the motion so swift all anyone saw was a streak of black, then the slow oozing of red as his blood seeped through his shirt. Hands dropped onto pommels and the sound of metal scraping leather scabbards filled the air.

"If that's the little thief then you will all die," he growled as he and the men converged on them.

The company formed a loose circle and faced outward, the clanging of steel on steel ringing abruptly beneath the milky sky. The men realized they faced well-trained warriors, their numbers meaning nothing to the group. They decided this battle would not fall in their favor, tripping over their dead comrades as they hastily retreated. Ramira waited for the demon to dismount and approach her.

"Vox, Allad?" asked Seven in hushed tones.

"No, Seven, Radir. Don't, Danyl." He cautioned the prince who moved toward Ramira. She had thrown her cloak over the saddle, her knives held loosely in her hands, her face firmly set. The nomad took his outer garments off as he readied himself to help her if she needed him.

The Radir was a demon with characteristics of both the Vox and the Kreetch. Although able to occupy and properly use its host, it stayed unrestrained like the Kreetch when it came time to destroy. This demon abandoned the normal movements of the body it occupied and began to flail and slash at Ramira with glee before her swift and fluid motions killed it within moments. She turned toward her horse when a form flew at her from behind a cluster of boulders while a third appeared from out of nowhere from the right. Allad was immediately on the ground helping Ramira, who had succeeded in deflecting the demon away from her at the very last second. She slew the Radir in rapid fashion, but not quickly enough to dodge the sword it swung at her. The weapon glanced along her side, slicing through her tunic without penetrating too deeply into her flesh. Allad took a few moments longer to dispatch his demon then called to Ramira to see how badly she was hurt. She shook her head and hurried to her mount. They raced as one for the dark line of trees that were still too far away.

So many and such a variety of demons in this part of the land meant the forest could very well be teeming with them as well. Time, they knew, was running out for them. They had many miles to go before they passed through the woods and onto elven lands. What, they wondered, would they find on the other side? They urged their mounts on, not stopping until early afternoon and only then because the animals were exhausted. They rubbed them down then rested for a spell, three pairs of eyes continuously looking in every direction.

"Radir can be slain by anyone skilled with a weapon but you must be careful: they as dangerous as the other demons," explained Allad. "The best way to slay them is by slitting their throats."

"I've seen men like that in the town," Cricket said in a small voice. "I just thought they were the crazy sort and avoided them." Cricket remembered seeing them scattered in the city shunning everyone, even each other. Their faces were vacant but something lurked just beneath the surface of their skin, something warning her to stay away from them.

"They were in your town before we met?" asked Danyl.

"Yes, for about a month or so. "

Seven exhaled sharply then lifted his heavy eyebrows, for the news was dire indeed. If they were already prevalent in these parts then it made sense they would stumble across more of them before they got back to Bystyn. Their trip through the forest would be an interesting one to say the least. Their choices, however, were limited. They had to take a chance and follow the most direct route back or they would only further endanger their lives by trying to dart here and there in hopes of evading any more demons. At least they could fight the Radir and not solely depend upon Allad and Ramira to do all the work for them.

Gard kept the anger he had for Ramira locked away. They were in this predicament because she had fled the city, and he resented it. Granted, they would be taking back a great deal of information, but it didn't appear as though they were going to make it back, so the news was a moot point anyway. She had what the evil wanted and he wondered again why they couldn't get close enough to Mahn and let her unleash her might into him and get it done with. She was unwillingly enticing him to the very gates of the city and he was sure Mahn would rip apart every last wall in order to get to her, killing many along the way. The odds of their demise had increased dramatically over the past few days and would escalate before they reached the elven plains. And for what? To protect one form of evil from an even greater one? What if she had to be killed? He was the only one in the group, except for maybe Lance, who could drive his sword into her. Even Allad had hesitated after the Kreetch had poisoned her. He glanced at Ramira, the morose look on her face and slightly stooped shoulders signs he had not wanted to see. He noticed Allad staring at him, the Herkah's steady gaze making him turn away and finish adjusting his saddle.

They rode for several hours then rested for one, the pattern never varying until the forest loomed ahead of them in the growing light of day. Their doorway to safety lay on the other side of this brooding line of trees, their roots barely visible from within an undulating mist. The gnarled roots reminded the men of crooked fingers beckoning them into the gloom of the skeletal trees standing at the edge of the forest. They could almost hear the beguiling voices calling out to them, promising a favorable path through. They imagined menacing shadows following them from one tree to the next using the fog as cover, the prospect of riding within that eerie labyrinth of tree trunks not one they looked forward to.

"This feels wrong," stated Gard, scanning the area.

"I agree," agreed Lance. "We could ride east another day then take the same route north we took to come down into the south."

"A good suggestion but a bad idea," said Allad, pointing through the branches of the trees toward a large group of riders heading in the direction Lance had indicated. It was becoming very crowded in this area—too crowded for their liking. The drab, homespun clothing and large horses identified them as men similar to Cricket's pursuers, who would certainly be interested in following them. They could also be part of Mahn's conscripted army. The companions wanted no part of them regardless of who they were.

"Is anyone else feeling as concerned as I am at this very moment?" asked Seven as they waited for the men to disappear before emerging from their hiding place.

"I get the distinct feeling we are being hunted," Danyl stated, watching the riders heading farther south toward the town Cricket hailed from.

"They might have been roused by the two men that disappeared from the inn," suggested Lance.

"Those 'men' could have been Radir," stated Allad, studying the land around them.

"They could have been a lot of different things, none of which I care to think about so far from home," Danyl muttered out loud.

"Cricket? Are there normally so many people traveling in these parts this time of year?" asked the King.

"No."

"Well, trap or not, we have to get to the plains," said Danyl, looking across the now empty area. "Let's go."

They surged forward, watchful of every tree and cluster of rocks as they raced toward the dark line of trees. The fog seemed to writhe the closer they came as if it had a life of its own until the rising sun burned it away. Its departure was not reassuring but at least they'd be able to see what littered the ground as they rode through the woods. They entered the outer ring of trees and were immediately aware of the silence hanging beneath the boughs. Nothing flew or scampered out of their way as they continued on through the unusual stillness. The only sounds they heard were the muffled pounding of their mounts' hooves, their nervous snorting and their leather saddles creaking underneath them as they galloped over the terrain. Cricket was terrified and clung to Danyl with every ounce of her strength, everyone peering into the dark shadows for any signs of danger. It didn't take long to reach the center of the woods; this end of the forest tapered until it was no more than a few miles wide. Gard, the most experienced tracker, chose the best pathways that would lead them to the plains. They had been riding for little more than an hour when the trees began to thin out up ahead. A brief surge of relief washed over them, for the elven lands were only moments away, when a rustling sound on their left caught their attention. The same noise came from their right and the word "ambush" suddenly erupted in all of their minds. They urged their horses to run faster with a renewed sense of urgency as snapping and scraping sounds began to increase all around them.

Shadows darted amongst trees and brush, appearing then disappearing at will from every direction except in front of them. There was nothing they could do but hope to outrun the specters remaining just beyond their sight. The phantoms could just as easily have confronted and annihilated them within the trees yet chose not to, content in just herding them out to a specific point. The very point that a distressed Gard was forced to lead them to.

"Don't stop and do not get separated from each other!" shouted Gard as the trees gave way to the plains.

Ghostly riders moved out from within the darkness of the trees and converged on the company seeking to escape them. Allad and the others surmised they would be confronted once they reached the plains, their tired horses unable to outrun the fresh mounts waiting for them on the plains. Fighting such a large host was obviously out of the question. There were wider swatches of open ground around the trees now and the nervous horses, sensing this change, began to accelerate. They hurdled over the occasional fallen trunk or clump of bushes to escape the threat, needing little prodding from their riders. The plains gave the companions a renewed sense of hope, an optimism that was, unfortunately, short lived.

The companions burst through the last line of trees and finally touched the snowy plains as their hunters closed in on them. To their dismay a line of black-garbed riders surged toward them from the west, forcing them to angle farther to the east. It would only be a matter of time before they were overtaken and what would befall them then was something none of them cared to think about. Cricket hung onto Danyl, her eyes focused on the black horde closing in on them as they passed through the trees. She stared wide-eyed at her, the grim determination chiseled on her friends' faces, their free hands resting on their swords. Panic began to grow in her stomach, branching out to her limbs as the cold reality of their predicament began to take root in her heart. She had seen much death and despair in her short life but they had manifested themselves in ways she could understand, like being felled by a sword or being beaten. These demons and those things now pursuing them were unlike anything she had ever seen before and would be impossible to stop. There was nothing she could do now but to place her trust in the people around her and pray that some kind of miracle would happen to save them.

Gard stared hard at the riders and cursed under his breath for the thing he worried about the most was coming to fruition. Outnumbered and atop tired horses, the group from Bystyn was riding into death. No, there was one option, although that was the very thing they had to avoid to have any chance of beating the evil...or was it? He glanced over at Ramira, noting her tightly pressed lips and the fierce resolve glittering from her eyes. She looked past him at the advancing enemy, her features blazing with the same coldness she bestowed upon the demons. Gard was momentarily paralyzed with dread and awe at the power he could feel but not see. It reminded him of the electrical current in the air before an impending storm. He second-guessed his desire for her to wield the Source, but what choice did they have?

Ramira realized time was running out for them. There were too many to fight and the horses were already lathering down their necks and across their legs. She had to do it...she had no choice. She closed her eyes, daring to face that which delved deep inside of her. It responded by pulsing to life and filling her entire mind with an image lasting no more than a few seconds.

She stood on a balcony overlooking the sparkling white sands the full moon had ignited until she gazed upon a sea of shimmering diamonds, amethysts and sapphires. She was naked and the cool night air touched her skin. She felt three different hands lightly resting upon her shoulders, their size and pressure telling her they belonged to three different people. They spoke to her in unison. *The moment of truth has arrived, Ramira, for when you wield what lives inside of you, it will reflect which is in your heart. Will your fire be black or will it be amethyst...*

Ramira knew the moment she used the Source the evil would swoop down and snatch her away to his loathsome lair. Not using it would insure a fate worse than death for her friends, and if Danyl was also taken then Bystyn would be bereft of its protective magic. Even if Mahn were to take her, he would still need time not only to move his army across the plains but also to wrestle the Source from her and that, she swore, would be no easy task for him. Ramira inhaled deeply, hoping and praying that she was doing the right thing.

Ramira caught Lance's attention and motioned for him to keep riding and to make sure Danyl and the others did not stop. The captain stared hard at her for a few moments realizing she was going to confront their pursuers. He was about to protest but the look on her face forbade any argument. She caught Allad's attention and conveyed the same thought to him before suddenly reining in her nearly exhausted horse, dismounting before it even came to a complete halt. The group had ridden for about a quarter mile before Danyl noticed her alone before the oncoming horde, his horrified shouts muffled by the thundering hooves approaching her. She took off her gloves, removed her cloak and closed her eyes, summoning the power from deep down inside of her.

Initially there was darkness and a stillness that alarmed her. If she could not coax the Source to life then they were all lost. She search frantically for it, not quite knowing what it looked like but desperate to find it nonetheless. She finally sensed a faint pulse and concentrated on the twinkling deep down inside within her soul. She could not determine any of its characteristics in the gloom, fervently trusting it would not betray her as she began to rouse the slumbering power to life. She gathered her courage and confronted the might and was shocked at how benign it seemed. She had expected a raging inferno, not the subtle emanations from a seemingly innocuous ember pulsating from within the depths of her spirit. She reached out and touched the spark, the immediate reaction unsettling her in ways she could not even begin to imagine.

The Source sprang to life in her midsection and felt as if she had swallowed an entire skin of Seven's concoction. It spread outward to her arms and legs then up her neck and into her head, its heat threatening to burn the flesh from her very bones. It momentarily blinded her then, when she was able to see again, watched as the black-garbed riders approached her in slow motion. Their mantles billowed up behind them like great black sails while clumps of frozen snow and sod, kicked up by their horses, arched sluggishly upward behind them. The sound of the horse's hooves striking the hard earth echoed hollowly in her ears and matched the rhythm of her pounding heart. She dared not turn around and look back at her companions, especially Danyl. She planted her feet firmly on the ground, gradually bringing her arms up then forward until the palms of her hands touched. What color will the Source be? Black or amethyst? She pulled her palms apart and felt the fire concentrating in her hands. Black or amethyst? She took a deep breath and let the fire explode from her fingers and into the onrushing riders, the power so incredible it blinded her. *I am not like you!* She let the Source rush forth from her body.

Danyl howled with fury and fear. It would be a simple thing for him to pluck her from the plains and yank her back into his lair. The very thing they had tried to avoid all this time was happening and there was nothing they could do to stop it. She had promised not to use the power and subsequently broken that vow. He had to get to her before her fire became a beacon for Mahn, who would surely take the opportunity to capture her and further his hideous plans. He felt the tendons and muscles on his neck and face expand as he screamed at her to withdraw her power. His cry was drowned out by the roar of thunder accompanying the dazzling light accelerating toward the line of black riders. It never occurred to him to use the Green Might which remained idle deep within his soul. He was held back by Lance, Gard and Allad as they watched her stand alone against the horsemen. Flames so bright they had to shield their eyes, erupted from her hands: the brilliant lavender fire ripping into and completely disintegrating the hunters.

Zada gasped then collapsed as the Source tore into her inner sight, its potency stealing her breath and turning her legs to rubber. Zada felt the eruption scorch every fiber of her being. She was buffeted by the powerful winds of magic, abandoned in a raging blizzard composed of raw energy ripping at her psyche even at this distance. Zada sensed the ancient crafts responding to it, rising like mammoth waves from the recesses of time. The longer Ramira wielded her power the more likely they were of being drowned by those magic surges. She slid to the tiled floor in shock. An attendant shouted for help, then carefully tried to prop the nomad up against the wall, backing away instantly as the residue of her vision seemed to burn into his mind. Fear and awe flushed his features yet he did not abandon the Herkah. Seconds later Styph, Clare and Mason crouched down beside her and one look at her shocked features told them something awful had occurred.

"She used it..." she said, her voice thick with distress as she tried to recover from the disastrous illusion.

"What?" asked Mason. "What did you say?"

Zada shuddered as she saw the dismal mist race over the miles to that coveted prize on the edge of the plains, the implications spelling their doom with every passing second. She sensed the maniacal glee that existed within the fog, wincing as it closed the distance. This was the moment it had been waiting for and in mere seconds it would have the ultimate treasure, and their destiny, in its grasp.

"Ramira wielded the Source and Mahn is speeding across the land to get her."

"Sweet mercy," muttered Clare, wiping away the sheen of sweat from her pale face.

Mason stared at Zada, her words turning his countenance ashen; their very survival depended on the company bringing her back into the safety of the city. Ramira was their trump card and in a few brief moments she would be in Mahn's hand, a hand that offered no mercy but plenty of woe.

"Why is she wielding it?" he demanded.

"She destroyed the riders sent by Mahn...horsemen wanting to bring back the group on the plains."

Mason nodded. The havoc that would produce would be unimaginable. The loss of the dwarven king, the Khadry, the Herkah lord and the elven prince would seriously affect their respective people. He could only imagine what would happen if they were turned into demons and stood facing them in battle. It would be difficult enough to fight without them, but to battle against their demon-occupied bodies would be disastrous. If the remainder of the company managed to make it back to the city then they had a chance, admittedly a small one, but a better one than had they been taken by the evil.

Ramira may have allowed Mahn to take her but she also gave them a chance where none would have been if she hadn't used the power. Things were bleak but not disastrous.

Ramira dropped to her knees, the unfamiliar power too much for her to bear, as it gradually returned to its resting place inside of her. She inhaled deeply then tried to remember what color her fire had been, but she had been unable to see anything at all. *I am not like you*, she thought, struggling to rise, the horrible dreams and visions beginning to stream into her mind as she reeled from the might that had erupted from her soul. She finally managed to stand but wavered as she turned around and watched her companions riding toward her. She needed Danyl to hold her and quell the terrible things burning in front of her eyes and making her stagger even more. She thought she saw them coming nearer, but before they covered half the distance, a black cloud composed of what looked like millions of flies tore across the land. She tried to run away from the whirring mass, managing a few steps before falling hard on her elbows and knees. Panic began to take hold of her as the edges of the buzzing fog reached out to her then engulfed her. Its horrible touch and foul stench were so overwhelming she lapsed into unconsciousness and fell to the ground, disappearing moment's later.

An odd silence descended upon the land as if the earth itself held its breath. The company reached the place she had occupied but it was empty and lifeless, a cloak and a pair of gloves the only evidence she had ever stood upon the soil. The companions could only stare at the spot then irrationally searched for her as if she had merely moved instead of vanishing. The only thing they learned was they were, for the time being anyway, the only ones on the plains. Gard exhaled sharply while Lance continued to search the area, the Herkah and dwarf just sitting in their saddles as the ramification of their situation seeped into them. It was then Danyl jumped off his exhausted horse, his frustration finding no suitable escape as he paced heavily back and forth with fists so tight his knuckles threatened to break through the skin.

Cricket clung to Seven while the others tried to calm the livid and frightened prince who wanted nothing more than to go after her. It was a foolish thought but he had to release his emotions or they would never get him back to the city. After several long minutes he finally quieted down and listened to reason.

"There is nothing we can do for her now, Danyl." Allad made the elf look into his eyes while he spoke to him. "Ramira sacrificed herself for us and now we have to get back to Bystyn and prepare for the worst."

"We have to do something!"

"What? What shall we do? Perhaps five exhausted and starving men with a small girl can ride up to Mahn's gates and demand her back?" retorted the Herkah.

"Mahn knew the Source's general vicinity and effectively flushed it out into the open," began the King, placing his big hand on the elf's shoulder. "I think he expected it to be wielded to protect the bearer from capture, but I don't believe he realized who it safeguarded by being used."

"The only thing worse than having lost the Source to Mahn is having our Vox-possessed bodies free to roam within the city," stated the nomad.

"A disagreeable predicament," added Lance.

"Here." Gard handed Danyl the gloves and cloak he had retrieved. "We are in grave danger here, Danyl. We must leave."

The prince stared down at her things, his mind reeling with possibilities, none of which were pleasant. They were right, and as he regained control of his emotions, he mounted his horse and headed north, his companions following behind. They rode on well into the night, wanting to put as much distance between themselves and Mahn's minions as possible. They rested for a few hours shortly before midnight, eating the last of their food but unable to close their eyes for even a minute of sleep. They were up well before dawn, riding on while keeping a sharp eye on their surroundings. The main question each asked was what did this journey actually accomplish? Their goal had been to find and bring Ramira back because she housed the one thing the evil needed the most. He had it now so where did that leave them? They were alive to lead the fight but would all of that be for naught if he had the Source? They stopped around midmorning and rested, their growling stomachs reminding them they would not eat again until they either ran into a patrol or entered the city. Gard passed around the last of their water, the canteen barely half full.

"I hope you brought plenty of your poison, Seven, because I could use a huge draught."

"I'm sure there is plenty, Allad, for I doubt even Clare would be so cruel as to deny us after such a long trip."

"We should be there before sunset," stated Lance, staring northeastward.

"Danyl?"

"Hmm? Thank you," said the prince, taking the water from the captain. He stared at it for quite some time before drinking a few sips then handed it to Gard. They mounted up and were on their way again, all of them eager to get back to the city. They rode on until they ran across a patrol an hour south of the city. It wasn't long before they could see the gray walls of Bystyn looming off in the distance and relief flooded through all of them, even Danyl. At least now they could come up with a plan to help Ramira. Danyl's mood, though, remained dark.

Part III

-8-

They rode under the gates, ignoring the people welcoming them as their horses trotted up the main avenue. They had failed in their quest to bring Ramira back and the horrors they had encountered along the way only added to their sense of foreboding. Even the relieved faces of their friends and families waiting for them at the castle could not still the trepidation they felt as they dismounted. They exchanged warm embraces then were ushered into the castle.

They ate because they had to and bathed to refresh their filthy and sore bodies before meeting with the others for a briefing, offering little in the way of good news. Mason reminded them Ramira had allowed the heart and soul of the people gathered within the walls to return thereby averting certain disaster. The members of the company weren't so sure, especially Danyl, who sat glumly at the conference table listening to what had transpired during their absence.

"We obviously must rally around each other," began Alyxandyr. "For to do otherwise would be instrumental in our own demise, even without the help of Mahn. He has the Source but he must also extract it from Ramira, and I firmly believe it will not be such an easy task."

"How can you be so sure?" demanded Gard, his bitterness at Ramira eliciting several looks from those gathered around the table, most notably Danyl.

"Her extreme loathing for his minions is no secret, Gard," Zada said. "It only makes sense her feelings for the evil surpasses even that hatred."

"How can you be so sure?" he persisted.

"Because she promised, that's why!" Danyl slammed his hand down on the table as he rose, his glittering eyes challenging the Khadry. She had also agreed not to wield the Source or abandon him. Even if her actions had, for the moment, helped them, her betrayal still ripped into his heart. There was nothing he could do but to try and prepare for the inevitable and understand her decision out on the plains.

"That's enough!" roared the King. "I will have no bickering!"

Styph and Nyk pushed their brother back down into his seat, their hands feeling the knotted muscles on his shoulders slowly begin to smooth out as the elf's fatigue took control of him. He and the others needed a few hours rest and it took a great deal of urging for the members of the group to sleep for a while. Danyl returned to his chambers, the very rooms he had threatened to lock Ramira into when they returned. He flopped down on the bed, closing his eyes immediately and was meet head on by the annoying stone maze in his mind.

The elf ran down the stone hallway, stopping at every door along the way. He tugged violently on the locked doors then banged on them with his fists until his hands were raw and bleeding. He shouted and screamed but the echoes mocked his dilemma. He began to run down the hall, stopping now and then to try the doors, but they remained shut, and he subsequently became lost in a maze that was nothing more than a straight line…

He awoke with a start, his body covered in sweat as he peered out the window at the bland light seeping in from between the drawn curtains. He exhaled slowly as he remembered the evil had her, and what plans he had for her he couldn't even begin to imagine. She was gone. He lifted his shaking hand and pushed a section of his light brown hair from his forehead then buried his face in his hands. He sat that way for a long time, trying to purge the emotions threatening to overwhelm him. The empty feeling became numb as a tendril of the Green Might reached out and tried to soothe him, refusing to withdraw even as Danyl lashed out angrily at it then at himself. Why hadn't he brandished his power to save her? He rose and dressed, then poured himself a cup of water, drinking it down in one gulp. He wondered what he could possibly do for her then shivered with horror at what he might have to do to save her and everyone else in the end. Perhaps he could avoid that if he could only find the answers somewhere within himself or these gray walls. He headed for the great hall and the tapestry.

He stared up at it, willing it to tell him its secret, but the woven fabric remained silent, the moment frozen in time offering many yet no solutions at the same time. The first king continued to gaze at him while his people moved on toward their final destination. Alyxandyr was watching someone, of that Danyl was sure, for he could see the concentration in the king's eyes as he strained to peer into the far left corner of the tapestry. Who hid within the branches and brush? He must have told the queen what to weave, but did he also tell her what lay concealed within the shadows? Somehow he doubted it.

He and Karolauren had combed through every possible tome, diary and list that existed within the library and had found nothing.

You are looking too hard.

"What...who's there?" he demanded. He was in no mood for pranks. He saw no one and the voice remained silent. He was tense and tired, his mind beginning to play tricks on him, so he rubbed his eyes to clear away the exhaustion and string of emotions.

You are looking too hard.

Danyl did not speak nor did he look around the room. He knew the voice existed only inside his mind. Where were the answers he was looking for? Were they with the historian? Did he overlook a tome or map? Did he not listen well enough to his lessons? He glanced up at the image of the long dead king and realized how similar their features were and that both possessed the Green Might. He held his hands up and stared first at the palms then turned them over. Ramira had brandished the Source with her hands. He closed his eyes and concentrated on the mysterious ember intertwined with his spirit, first willing then begging it to rouse itself. The magic would not budge. He tried again and again until he ran out of ways to encourage it to life and was about to give up when the voice returned.

You think too much.

"I am a descendant of the first king and I house the Green Might: I demand that it fly forth from my hands!"

Do not be arrogant.

"I am not arrogant!"

Danyl dropped to his knees, realizing he was more than disdainful for his attitude bordered on stupidity. Who was he to assume he could use the elven might at will? He was nothing more than an ordinary person composed of flesh and blood. His only distinction in life was the title before his name, a title passed down through his family and not one he had earned. What he supposedly housed was a precious responsibility, one he should honor and respect, not one he could wield whenever he chose. He should hold that privilege in the highest regard and not treat his legacy lightly, trying to command it as if it were his plaything. It was a deeply intertwined part of his being, a birthright from the land that had spawned it eons ago. He should be humbled by its presence, not disrespectful of it.

He sighed, rising to his feet with his head down and eyes focused on the floor. This is where he believed they belonged. He stood in the midst of his ancestors, individuals greater than he ever could aspire to be. He suddenly felt ashamed and wished for nothing more than to take his contemptuous presence away.

He headed for the huge double doors leading into the hall. He tried to open them, but they would not budge. The lesson was not yet over and the elf turned to face the judgment of the kings and queens who had gone before him. They remained silent yet he could feel their presence everywhere. Their thoughts, emotions and unfinished deeds hovered in the hall. They no longer walked the land but their spirits, still resonating with their beliefs, prevailed. Their emotions were by far the most prevalent traits still continuing because those had been the very things that had allowed them to complete their duties during their lives. He felt them surge all around and through him like some unseen wind blowing from a distant place. Isn't that what set them all apart in life? Wasn't that the very nature and drive of their souls? What was his passion? What made his spirit soar? Up until a few months ago his obligations were the driving force of his soul, but then Ramira entered his life and changed his perspective about his existence. She had unassumingly taken his feelings to a new level, making him a better person even though she had struggled to keep him away from her unknown past. She had only partially succeeded for a while, but she could not escape the ultimate emotion: love.

Sophie grew to love Ramira as each day went by, treating her like her own child. Seven adored Ramira, as did the slain couple. His own passion toward her could never be fully explained even if he were to live for a thousand years, but the one thread binding them all together was their faith in each other. He looked over at his mother's bust remembering how animated his father had been while she lived. His love for his people and friends had not abated but the light that had flared in his heart had been reduced to an ember the day she died. Her quiet strength and gentle presence had offered him more courage than he could ever know. Now bereft of her presence, his father faced their terrible fate without her kindhearted guidance. What would he have to confront without Ramira's presence? Indeed, what would he have to do in Ramira's presence when Mahn eventually brought her to the gates of the city?

You must believe.

He did believe…in her, his friends, and family and in the strength and conviction of those who were about to face their most trying hour ever. The question was, how much did he believe in himself? Did he think he would falter when the moment came upon him? He could not afford to fail. Too much was at stake, but what would happen if he did? What would the consequences be of his inability to summon forth the power or his incapability to wield it in the way it was meant be used? The great hall began to flicker and dim, replaced by a vision that made his blood run cold.

The great hall was vacant and crumbling as if it had been abandoned for countless years. The windows were broken and the items that had sat upon pedestals and hung from walls lay strewn on the floor. He looked down at his mother's broken bust and took a step backward as he sought to escape the glare of her one remaining eye. The tapestry of the first king was nothing more than a few tattered pieces held against the wall with rusting nails. Vegetation grew along the broken stones and dirt; dust hid the fine granite floor. A haze spread its cheerless light into the corners of the nearly destroyed room, illuminating the ruins in a macabre sort of way. Danyl did not know if this was what could or would happen to Bystyn and its people, but the sight made his spirit shudder. It took all of his will to wait and see what the vision wanted him to know. It didn't take long. Soon the grayish light began to penetrate the dark recesses of the chamber, scattering shades that had sought solace within the shadows, apparitions Danyl did not yet recognize.

Was this what would happen if he was unable to wield the Green Might? Would he be unable to use it because of his arrogance? Was this their future because Ramira was incapable of keeping the Source from Mahn? What was he being shown? To Danyl this was as frustrating as that damn maze and...the maze. It was as enigmatic as the hall. Force could not open the doors nor could it point him in the right direction to compel the magic to set free its fire. The only time he was able to wield the power was when Ramira began her headlong spiral into the waiting hands of the evil. What had activated the magic and allowed him to retrieve her from those apocalyptic hands? What was the catalyst? Was this what would happen if he and the others failed? Would everything they had built be reduced to ruins? Would the same fate affect the dwarf city and all of the other cities and villages in the land? Danyl heard the lock open on the doors and knew the lesson was over. He bowed respectfully to his ancestors and left the hall, the unmistakable throbbing of the Green Might alive in his soul but apparently still out of reach, for now, anyway.

Ramira roused herself from the horrible experience on the plains and opened her eyes knowing full well where she would find herself. *Please let them have escaped*, she silently implored. She rose unsteadily to her feet and stared at her strange prison, sensing the demons skimming along in the darkness just beyond the strange light glowing all around her. She stood on a round platform, narrow and twisting staircases sprouting everywhere and disappearing into the inky heights above her. Blood red curtains woven of the lightest of fabrics hung down all around the ascents, their origins somewhere high overhead. They stirred and floated independent of any breeze, partially obscuring the steps whispering "this way out" to her. One of the staircases led back to the world of light but there were dozens tempting her to try them. They mocked her predicament as they stretched upward into a blackness throbbing with evil.

She glanced down at herself and saw a black, long-sleeved dress composed of the same material as the curtains, its touch making her skin crawl. No amount of effort could remove it from her body. She pulled on it then tried to rip it off but the gown remained in place, relishing its repulsive contact by clinging even more tightly. She ignored the attire and decided to try one of the stairs. She approached it and heard claws skittering across the stones somewhere just beyond the light. The staircases were well guarded by a variety of demons. She reached toward her knives, smiling glacially at the feel of the cold blades. Her knives would draw a great deal of blood before she succumbed to whatever awaited her.

Her attention returned to the plains and her friends. She had been so blinded by the Source's light she did not know if they were alive or dead. She was here so that part of the outcome was no mystery to her, but what had happened afterward?

"Much occurred after your departure," a smooth voice hissed from beyond the light.

Ramira started, for that voice could belong to only one creature: Mahn. She turned trying to distinguish from which direction it came, but it seemed to issue from nowhere and everywhere at once.

"What do you want?" she demanded, continuing to spin around, knowing full well what the evil coveted.

"You have eluded me for a very long time but that only makes this moment so much sweeter," he replied while ignoring her question.

"I will not give you what you want."

"'Give'? Of course you won't 'give' me what I want. I will simply take it when I deem the moment is right to do so."

A tall and burly figure cloaked in black slowly walked onto the platform and approached her. Every step bringing him closer made it more difficult for Ramira to breathe. She gathered her courage and tried to peer into the black cowl but could see nothing within its ominous depths. The demons haunting the edges of the darkness stirred at his presence but Mahn ignored them. His entire being concentrated on the woman composed of the hues of the setting sun. His gloved hand reached out to her, compelling her backward, an act eliciting a deep and dangerous grumble from within the depths of his hood. He sensed her fear and repulsion and nodded in satisfaction; those responses would be quite useful when the time came to rip what he desired from her. He hissed with delight.

"Your mind and soul were tainted by those who thought to spare themselves from what you contain. The high priestess learned her lesson too late and paid for it with her life, losing the very implements that would have made the power's retrieval easier."

"What are you talking about?" she said, as the vision of her slaying the red woman and taking the blades surged into her mind.

"They were foolish in believing they could avoid the inevitable by teaching you about 'good,' for they disregarded one basic truth."

"What is that 'truth'?" she said in a voice smaller than she had intended, for her uncertainty gripped her heart once more.

"The 'truth' is that no amount of 'good' can wash away the black fire residing within you."

Ramira stared hard at the evil, her uncertainty gnawing at her once more. She had not seen what kind of fire exploded from her hands nor even if she had destroyed only the black horde upon the plains. Had she obliterated everyone, including her companions? She truly did not know, but she did know that Mahn would attempt to plant any and all doubts into her mind, uncertainties she could not counter. They had to have survived. She could not, would not, ever harm any of them. She watched as Mahn backed away the way he had come, and as repulsed as she was by his presence, she needed it. She could sift through his lies and piece together enough information to make up her own mind. The dais was hers once more and she stood there searching for the good in her life to thwart the depravity echoing all around her. She sensed Mahn was somewhere in the shadows, leaving her to drown in her own doubts and apprehensions. Every face she tried to conjure up to quell her fears was somehow affected by the evil until it was less painful to erase them all from her mind. She remembered the "they" Mahn stated tried to teach her about good and concentrated on the few memories she did retain. She recalled the warm feeling of the brown woman and the gentle satisfaction Horemb bequeathed onto her. She envisioned the warmth of Sophie's kitchen, the well-worn wooden table a beacon for those seeking comfort and companionship. Then there was Danyl.

She had tried not to get involved with him but that which bound them from the very beginning would not falter in the face of her own wishes. They overcame numerous obstacles along the way and ultimately accepted their fate. She could not say whether that was a good or bad thing, but she did know there would have been no way to escape that eventuality.

You were instrumental in the downfall of your own people and I will have the pleasure of watching you perform the same accomplishment on those in the city.

"I am not like you!" she protested in the eerie light.

You are quite correct, Ceraphine, for I am like you.

"What did you call me?" she asked in a whisper.

Ceraphine.

"What does that mean?"

It means "queen" and you, Ceraphine, are the last one from your city.

"I am no more a queen than you are merciful," she snarled. Her patience, her very tolerance for this evil was beginning to slip beneath the waters of her own self-doubt.

Do you not remember the pact you and I made?

"I would never bargain with you."

You told me that if you gave me the Source I would spare your people. You reneged and therefore forced my hand to obliterate everything. If you repeat your mistake this time, all you know will be gone.

"No."

You are in no position to negotiate with me, Ceraphine.

"I am not disputing you, I am telling you!" She suddenly stood erect, daring Mahn to gainsay her.

That same pride cost the lives of your people, those on the plains, and will doom those in the city.

She forced him from her thoughts, wondering if he might be telling her some measure of truth. Her nightmares revolved around death and destruction yet her mind would not open up to show her what had really transpired. Had the guilt of having inflicted the devastation from her dreams locked her memories away? He called her a queen, yet there was no way for her to have ever held such a position; in fact, he had made the title sound so…terrible. She sighed and sat down upon the smooth floor, drawing her knees to her chest and burying her face in her arms. They had to have survived! She couldn't have killed them, too. She lifted her head and stared hard at the staircases taunting her, the crimson material still undulating without a breeze. She fingered her dagger hilts, her mind wondering if she should risk exploring a way out. As long as she was with the evil, those in Bystyn had a better chance to prepare for what lay ahead. She knew her past would eventually come to light and hoped she would be strong enough to face the truth when it finally did surface.

Zada stared out into the gloomy darkness pondering Ramira's fate while fretting about their own destiny. Her actions had allowed the Green Might to return to Bystyn and she shuddered to think of what would have happened had Ramira obeyed the order not to use the Source. She had given them all more than a chance to succeed, but it remained to be seen if that was enough. The evil's vast army would arrive on the outskirts of Bystyn within the next few days, laying siege shortly thereafter. Mahn would make quite an entrance but she doubted he would tear the Source from Ramira prior to his arrival. She guessed he would do so in front of them all, further shredding the already fragile confidence keeping the allies together. That, too, granted them an edge, but they had to make sure they did not squander the precious time they had managed to acquire. She saw Danyl's reflection in the window as he came up behind her, placing his hands on her shoulders to comfort her.

"I should be the one consoling you, Danyl."

"Your presence is soothing enough, Zada."

"I know this is hard to believe, Danyl, but she gave us a chance," said the nomad after a while, hoping to ease his loss.

"I know, Zada." The reality of Ramira's actions, as painful as they were, had finally set in. He was distressed by her imprisonment, his inability to help her gnawing at his heart.

"I don't think he will take the Source from her until he arrives. That sight will be detrimental to the spirits of those who will face him and his army."

"He plans on inflicting every possible horror upon us, doesn't he?"

"Yes."

The Herkah turned around to face him, studying his features and looking deeply into his troubled eyes. The bulk of the responsibility lay upon his shoulders. She was sure he would be able to handle his part, but what if he had to destroy Ramira in order to defeat Mahn? Was he capable of such a thing? Could he be convinced that doing otherwise would effectively assure their defeat?

"I have tried unsuccessfully to revive the Green Might."

"All things will fall into place when the time is upon us," she said, then gently touched his cheek.

"I dreamt of the maze again, Zada. It seems the doors are more firmly locked than before and my reaction to them is becoming rather violent."

"Perhaps you should not fight it but let what is meant to be shown to you converge on its own," she suggested, then patted his arm before leaving him to his thoughts.

She returned to her rooms and stuck her hands in her pockets, her fingers finding the bracelet which she pulled out and held up to the light. Enough beads had been broken to reveal gaps in the bracelet yet a silent voice urged her to break another one. She remembered the brown woman's warning, but time was running out and they needed any sort of answers that would help them. She took a deep breath then sat down and smashed one of the beads. For a moment nothing happened then her chamber disappeared.

She was back at the platform in the desert just before sunset. It stood tall and proud as it was when first built even though Zada thought she would again see its destruction. The place of the Horii remained whole. A slight breeze lifted up from the desert, carrying with it a most wondrous fragrance. She could discern spices and perfumes of blossoms, the scents intoxicating her even within this memory. She lifted up her arms and tilted her head back, inviting the perfume to invigorate her soul as she stood upon the sacred dais. She brought her head upright and glanced down at herself, astonished to see the plain homespun clothing that seemed so very out of place here. She believed she should have been clad in the finest attire but whoever had owned the bracelet did not feel the same way. The bracelet. She lifted up her arms and there, on her left wrist, was the trinket. Her skin was not quite as dark as she had thought it would be and the soft red and golden hues of the setting sun turned it into a rosy-brown shade. What was the bearer of the ornament doing at the place of the Horii? It was a hallowed site, one that did not respond kindly to those who were not deemed fit to stand upon its ancient stones…

The image withdrew, leaving Zada with more questions than answers. The Horii had accepted this woman or she would never have been allowed access to the sacred ground. She knew the beads showed only snippets of this woman's life, but it was becoming quite clear she had occupied some powerful position. Her clothing and the fact she preferred the warmth and love of the humble brown woman told another story. She thought of Mason and Sophie and how Cooper would undoubtedly have permanently removed them had they not gone to Bystyn, a situation often accompanying those born into power. Could this woman also have faced the same sort of situation? She was kept at arm's length from those who ruled and that, in turn, allowed her to live. The woman favored these circumstances over the ones that would have given her the chance at power. Zada gritted her teeth and crushed one more bead, knowing full well she might become entangled in its memories.

She stood in a stone chamber where wonderfully painted river scenes seemed to come alive along one side of the room. There were tall reeds filled with waterfowl hunting the painted fish swimming in water so blue she was tempted to dip her fingers into it. Blossoms floated upon the water, their pale petals standing out against brilliant green leaves. The colors were vibrant, their rich hues soothing to the eye. A series of pure white, nearly transparent drapes made up the other wall and just beyond them was a wall composed of mirrors. She could see her shadowy form as she moved along the flowing fabric and Zada silently pleaded with the indistinct woman to part the curtains and stand before the mirror. The woman, however, was not interested in seeing her reflection and continued to tease Zada as she walked parallel with them. Zada approached the end of the row of curtains, her heart racing in anticipation as a gap appeared between the curtains and mirror. She was about to unmask the woman's identity, but the woman turned the corner and the vision faded…

Zada's frustration at coming so close to seeing who this person was almost brought her knife down on another bead. The visions, however, were taxing and she knew to pursue these images in her tired condition would lead to problems. She rubbed at her face, stared at the bracelet again then placed it back into her pocket. Perhaps there were other images that would fully reveal who this enigmatic woman was, but she did not have the strength to seek those answers just yet. She sighed and wondered what was keeping Allad. He should have been back from the meeting with the King quite some time ago. She left her rooms and went out into the hall, heading downstairs to the council chamber only to find it empty. She assumed he must have gone with Nyk and Seven and was about to go back upstairs when she espied the historian, stick-like arms laden with books, disappearing into the library. She rapped on the door and entered the chamber, barely able to see him over the piles of books on his massive desk. She smiled in greeting, marveling at how much energy and enthusiasm he had for his tasks, even if he did mutter and grumble about them.

"Good evening, Zada."

"Good evening to you, historian," she replied, sitting down beside him. "What keeps you up so late?"

"I wanted to finish the inventory of the scrolls," he responded, pushing his list aside and openly staring at the Herkah.

"What?"

"I would like to write down your histories, if I may, after all of this nonsense is over with. I think it will be important for both of our descendants and everyone else, too."

"You are saying that it might help others from developing an imaginative description of my people?"

"Yes, yes in a manner of speaking."

"Won't they be disappointed that we do not eat our young or use the skulls of our enemies to drink out of?" She laughed softly as his face reddened.

"Well," he sputtered, "those without the benefit of having met you might think of things along those lines."

Zada laughed and Karolauren's face soon mirrored her mirth until she noticed the fragile glass holding the deeply hued liquid. The historian followed her gaze and gingerly picked it up from its safe place on the shelf behind him, carefully handing it over to her. She deftly pulled out the stopper and sniffed the contents, her brown eyes growing so large they nearly fell out of their sockets.

"You plucked the plug from the bottle as easily as that damn girl...Zada? What is it?"

With trembling hands, the Herkah reached into her tunic and drew out a small phial that hung from a silver chain around her neck. She placed it on the desk then uncorked the delicate glass vessel holding it up for him to smell. She swapped her phial with the perfume bottle, watching for his reaction.

"That is queen's blood, Karolauren. The dried residue along the sides is all that remains and has been passed down though the generations. Where did you get that bottle?"

"It has been so long I have forgotten...would you like some of it?" he asked, as he handed her the narrow mouthed jar, watching her painstakingly and reverently fill her container. She beamed with gratitude, embarrassing the historian who pretended to shuffle some papers.

"Queen's blood, historian," she began to explain as she repositioned the treasure against her skin, "is the rarest thing in the land. Those who first combined the extraordinary ingredients are all gone, and the elements needed for its making are no longer available. From what I understand, even when it was being made it was a scarce and highly prized thing, worth more than all the gold and jewels in the land. It has not so much become a symbol of the Herkah power but a link to our past."

"I never thought of perfume in that way before," he muttered more to himself as he stared at the bottle.

"Karolauren…who was the girl that removed the stopper?"

"Hmm? Oh, Danyl's companion," he replied, distracted by something other than paper.

"Ramira?"

"Yes, which is why it stays in my sight all the time."

"What was her reaction when she sniffed it?"

"She seemed to enjoy the fragrance…that was all," he replied, as Zada slowly nodded her head.

"What do you know about this bracelet?" she asked, removing it from her pocket, hoping he would not become angry about the missing beads. He sucked in his breath then murmured several words in the old elven tongue as he turned it around and around looking for any other damage. Zada revealed the visions she had seen, the historian never blinking once the entire time.

"The beads have somehow been able to retain the memories of its wearer and these recollections are released, so to speak, when they are broken."

"Who else knows about them?"

"Danyl."

"I should have known that boy would somehow be involved."

"Don't blame him, Karolauren, for he only did what it asked him to do just as it beckoned me, too."

"I suppose we should break the rest of them then," he mumbled almost sourly, taking out a small knife.

"No, historian," Zada said, stopping the point from breaking one of the beads. "It's a little more complicated than that."

"How do you mean?"

"There is a chance that whoever smashes the glass might well be stranded in the memory and therefore be at the mercy of whatever destroyed the owner."

"We have to tell Alyx, Zada."

"I know. Why don't we go to see him together?"

The King and Mason listened to what they said then called for Danyl to join them. Alyxandyr was unsure as to how important the bracelet was in the scheme of things, but he didn't like being left in the dark about its existence, especially during these trying times.

"I suppose you are willing to part with this bauble, Karol?" he asked the historian, who shrugged in assent.

"You realize we may well have to break the rest of the beads," Zada said to the stick-like figure nearly lost in the chair across from her.

"Yes...yes..." he grumbled.

"Are you strong enough to shatter one in front of us?" the King asked the Herkah.

"Yes," she replied, then took the offered bracelet, placed it on the table and broke the tiny stone closest to the clasp.

The wearer stood upon the side of a mountain overlooking a most impressive city with its high, cantilevered walls glowing like pearls, its main gate flanked by a dozen tall pylons. The pennants aloft were multi-colored and flapped in the breeze as they stood guard over the gentry streaming into and out of the rectangular entrance. Watchtowers were situated on each of the four corners of the broad complex and they, too, sported bright standards as guards patrolled along the parapets. Two main avenues, not unlike those existing in Bystyn, intersected in the center of the city, but that is where the comparison ended. Bystyns streets were open to all, but this city kept the majority of the population cordoned off behind a massive brick wall. The upper portion of the city was dazzling to behold, especially the palace. It was a monumental structure atop steps too numerous to count, accessible by a road lined with crouching figures interspersed with fountains. Tile-covered conduits paralleled the streets and fed the fountains and vast tracts of greenery. Sunlight reflected off capstones adorned with beaten gold and made the granite pulse with a soft pinkish hue. The lower half of the city was a completely different story. The narrow and winding streets were crowded with people, carts and animals, the rooftops covered by ragged awnings. It was almost impossible to keep the alleyways clean and that squalor spilled out into the streets. People moved slowly, stopping occasionally at a pushcart to purchase items or backed up against a wall to let wagons pass by. No precious metals shone from the drab walls...

Zada remembered the plain garments the brown woman had worn, how callused her hands had been and the sparseness of her home. Those were signs of a people who labored for a few privileged individuals and were not allowed to partake of the bounty they worked so hard to provide.

"There is no more?" asked the King, his eyes riveted to the spot where the vision had been moments before.

"No, Father, there are only brief flashes of time."

"I'd like to see more," said the historian, looking around for a continuation of the image.

"The city was as beautiful as it was ugly," Zada breathed for those that had nothing lived in the indulgent shadows of those who had everything.

"It seems as though those who ruled had not learned, or had forgotten, the lessons taught to all who must care for their people," began Alyxandyr. "That usually means a collapse is imminent."

"Mahn evidently found the lack of a pulse in this place and used it to his advantage," stated Mason, silently questioning what he had just seen.

"Or perhaps he had been awakened by someone who sensed what was happening to use it to their advantage," suggested the King.

"What do you mean?" asked Danyl.

"The city was evidently in a state of decline," his father explained to him. "I cannot even begin to guess at what was transpiring within those walls, but Cooper experienced the same thing when he had his father killed and took control of Kepracarn."

"He's right, Danyl," confirmed Mason. "Our father became disinterested in everything other than himself, and Cooper, along with a few other determined individuals, used that to oust him and make himself king. The people of Kepracarn had to believe things would improve with Cooper, and although they did slightly better than with the other king, they found out Cooper liked to indulge himself, too. The only difference was my brother understood he had to make some concessions to his people in order to retain control."

"The owner of this bracelet evidently saw things quite differently than what was happening in the palace, but I have to wonder, what could she have done about it?" asked Alyxandyr.

"Probably nothing," conceded Zada. "Except for the fact that Mahn arrived and hastened the decline."

"Then why was her bracelet found amongst the first king's things?" asked Danyl. "That's what is such a mystery to me. He either took it from her, found it, or she gave it to him." Danyl could not stop the tapestry from filling his mind as he stared at the king's face from within the woven trees and bushes.

"The elves passed near that city when they were heading to our present location at about the same time it was destroyed," stated the historian.

"You don't think she warned him of what was happening there, do you?" asked Mason.

"I think there was some sort of contact between them, yes," stated Karolauren. "Or we would not have this in our possession today."

"If we speculate she did warn him, knowing her city was doomed, then she effectively saved the elves from the city's same fate."

"True, Alyx," Mason commented. "And that would explain the Herkahs, too, for did you not say your origin lies within the city, Zada?"

"It does, Mason. It also means perhaps she also helped those unaffected by the ruler or the evil to flee the city before it was laid to waste."

"We are making a lot of assumptions out of one vague image," said the historian.

"Indeed we are, Karol, but these guesses are making the most sense," the King argued.

Zada stared at the trinket, its fragile blue beads as much a link to her past as the queen's blood yet Karolauren was right in saying they were reading too much into one vision. If indeed they were real to begin with. He slid the ornament over to her and she cracked another one of the beads before anyone could stop her.

The owner of the bracelet walked up the avenue ignoring the extravagant objects flanking her. The splashing fountains, crouching lions with human heads and human statues with animal heads were invisible to her. She never looked down at the cobblestones, their herringbone design drawing her toward the palace rising up in the distance. The great complex at the end of the avenue bustled with activity. The guards gave her a wide berth as she reached the wide stone steps leading up to the colonnaded palace. She entered into the cool darkness escaping the sun's heat, but she had not come here to refresh herself. The reaction of those she passed said as much for no eyes dared to meet hers. She gazed neither left nor right but headed straight down the airy hall, forced open a tall set of richly carved black wooden doors and let them slam behind her. She stood in front of a throne embellished with gold and jewels and finely painted jars holding tall, blue-green feathers clustered around it. Behind the throne was a wide balcony and beyond it a lush garden where broad-leafed trees and bushes kept out the heat of the sun's rays. The image of the Queen standing victoriously over her enemy, her foot placed on his neck and her hand holding a scepter had been painted on the wall to the left of her throne. A figure emerged from one of the rooms to the right of the dais, the look of loathing so intense those watching through the unknown woman's eyes squirmed in their seats. In fact, the closer the bearer came, the more the red woman began to cringe, but her eyes never faltered from those of the approaching woman…

"That was interesting." The King exhaled with some apprehension.

"The ruler of the city?" asked Mason.

"I don't know…perhaps," said Zada, picking up the bracelet.

"Zada? Is there any way, any way at all, you could see how Ramira is faring?" asked Danyl.

"If Mahn has her it would be very difficult, Danyl, especially if he is preparing her for his final assault on us."

"You mean poisoning her mind against us?" inquired Mason.

"Something like that," she replied quietly.

"So," the King recounted what they had all seen from the bracelet's memories, "we've seen the city, this confrontation, the brown woman, the place of the Horii twice and also the bald man. Danyl explained to us how Ramira had seen the man who had taught her how to fight. Could it be possible that Ramira is the wearer of the bracelet?" he asked after several long moments. "After all, her memories of her past are unavailable to her..."

"Then maybe they were kept in a safe place for her in order for her to survive," Zada finished for him. How very clever—being oblivious to who she was and what she housed prevented her from exposing herself to Mahn.

"That way she could avoid being beset upon by the evil until everything fell into place for Mahn to be effectively challenged," added Mason.

"That would make her a thousand years old!" Danyl exclaimed, unwilling to accept the fact that the woman he loved came from another age.

"Yes and no, Danyl, for the Source would have contained her in a way that, well, basically stopped time for her." Zada's excited voice filled the room as the pieces of the puzzle began to fit together. If their theory was correct, Mahn was finishing what he had started centuries ago. Ramira and the Source had been concealed from Mahn until a power equal to his could arise and challenge him. Fate had decreed that that time was now. Destiny had set the stage for the ultimate battle but could not move the pieces.

Ramira might not have heeded Danyl's cries that night. She could have chosen not to follow him to Bystyn. Allad had taken great risks in allowing Nyk and Ramira to live. Sophie could have turned Ramira away instead of letting her live in her home. There were so many variables, each decision based on emotion—the hardest thing of all to predict. They now stood at the edge of their existences but their circumstances seemed less dire than they had first believed. Mahn had what he wanted, but was it what he expected? What exactly was the Source? Was it as evil as Mahn made it out to be? Would that not make Ramira just as depraved? That was one thing Zada could not understand, for how could the bearer of the Source, a magic steeped in all things amoral, burn with an amethyst fire instead of black? What had transpired to change it? Did fate somehow intervene? Zada thought the brown woman, the bald man and the spirit tainted by the Vox were in some way involved, but she could not quite place those pieces together. They appeared to be very prominent in her life, if indeed this was Ramira's life. It had to be, for nothing else made sense even though this, too, seemed highly unlikely. She looked over at the prince who stared at the floor between his feet, the information frightening him in a way she could not even begin to understand. He and Ramira had formed their bond long before each knew what the other housed. They would have to hold fast to what they learned about each other if they were to survive. She did not envy their positions and hoped that very connection would give them the strength to do whatever fate had in store for them.

"You give new meaning to loving an older woman, son," the King gently teased him. Danyl dropped his head to his chest and closed his eyes, envisioning her in his arms, in the darkness of Sophie's terrace, the warm summer night filled with the sounds of insects and birds. Could she have been kept alive by the magic for all of those centuries? He knew the bearers of the elven magic lived longer lives—providing they survived wielding it. If it was true she warned the first King then…was that what he was staring at in the tapestry? He rose without a word and returned to the Great Hall, planting himself in front of the mural while staring hard at the king. He inhaled then exhaled several times then opened his mind to the past. Nothing happened for a while until he thought he saw the dead king smile.

Nyk and a group of guards saw the black mass camped several miles away and watched them for a while. They took notes of what equipment they brought along and approximately how many made up the army. They brought large structures to batter the walls and they knew there had to be other weapons of war too small to be seen at this distance but no less lethal. A quick guess told them they would be outnumbered at least four to one, and coupled with Mahn possessing the Source, their outcome seemed rather bleak.

"We are going to have our hands full," muttered the prince, studying the vast gathering.

They had prepared a multitude of defenses including digging traps on the plains, readying vats of oil and stringing razor sharp wire along the least defensible sections of the wall. Mahn had plenty of soldiers to break through the city's defenses; the only question was how long they could hold out until he did. The well-seasoned veterans could easily keep pace with their vastly outnumbered foes but not with the demons and the Source. They would fight well but without an edge of their own would not be able to hold out too long, maybe a few days at best.

"I count about a dozen catapults and rammers," his captain informed him.

"Our walls can only take so much pounding before the stones begin to crack and splinter," stated Nyk, jerking his head to the side, ordering them to head back to the city. Unfortunately, not even the mountains could hold out forever against such an assault. They would have to destroy or at the very least disable those machines before they could be used, a task requiring a great deal of courage. He tried to envision where they would place those things for maximum efficiency. Their range would depend upon what they intended to hurl at them: something large enough, he surmised, to inflict the greatest damage. They could set them up from any direction or they could concentrate on a specific area, heaving stones against the city walls until they weakened and finally gave way. That would be the course of action he would take if he were on the attack. Even if they only managed to undermine the structure, they could then turn to the rammers and create a rift in Bystyn's proud skin, a split large enough to let Mahn's minions pour through.

"They don't seem to be in any hurry," noted his captain.

No, thought Nyk, of course they aren't because Mahn has Ramira and he intends on using her to obliterate us all. If an entire army was under his control, what made any of them think that she could somehow withstand his manipulations? Nyk did not like the fear beginning to gnaw at his heart, carefully concealing it from the others. The last thing they needed was to see him lose faith in this all-important campaign. They rode on, Nyk glancing more than once over his shoulder, disguising his uneasiness behind a stoic countenance.

Ramira rose to her feet and looked around. Nothing except silence greeted her even though she knew things lost in the shadows were watching her. She could sense the Kreetch everywhere, their nervous scurrying becoming more noticeable as she approached the staircases. Was one of the staircases an escape, or were they just there to torment her? She stopped at the nearest one and craned her neck upward to see if she could see anything, but it ended in a forlorn blackness. She repeated her action on several more, all with the same results. It would help if you had some vague idea as to where you were, she thought. This place, except for the staircases and drapes, left her with the sensation she was drowning in doom. Danyl had saved her from this place while she battled the Kreetch poison. This was where she would have ended up had he not braved the frigid horror surrounding her, but this time he could not save her. Or could he?

She closed her eyes, emptying the evil from her mind and refilling it with the last time she and Danyl had been together. Their spirits had intertwined and become one, taking them to the top of a pale blue mountain surrounded by a softly shimmering silver mist enshrouding them from the world. A full moon, flanked by sparkling stars, hung within a sky the same shade as the mountain. She experienced a bit of respite from her terrible predicament but the moment was too brief. The image began to fray and shred, the bits and pieces blown away by a foul wind. Mahn violated her sanctuary with horrible impressions, yanking her back to reality with a hatred that made her cringe. These visions filled her with despair and there was nothing she could do to stop them. A city died beneath a conflagration; people seeking to escape were cut down by her own hand; children desperately clawed at her legs begging for a scrap of food, and the ghastly faces of people sick with the worst diseases threatened to press their pus oozing bodies against hers. All eyes stared accusingly at her. And the vilest of them all was the death of Jack and Ida. She slew them or they would have been enslaved by the master of evil, forced to rise and serve in his army of demons. She had slit their throats, slipping in their blood as she struggled to rise, her eyes filling with tears of anguish and remorse. The demons had nearly torn them apart but had left the most terrible job of all to her, a task that would haunt her for the rest of her life. Even now tears slid down her cheeks as she remembered the warmth and compassion they radiated, teardrops Mahn ridiculed and disrespected as his hideous chuckle filled the cavern. She fumed with hatred as the black cloaked figure emerged into the peculiar light.

"You!" she hissed with loathing.

"You betrayed your entire city, yet you let two insignificant lives trouble you? How absolutely delightful," he laughed.

"I did no such thing!"

"Quite the contrary, Ceraphine."

She stood upon a balcony, her perfumed skin glowing with oils that had just been applied to her by her handmaidens. She scowled down upon those toiling beneath a merciless sun that baked what flesh wasn't flayed from their backs. Their skeletal forms strained with the burdens they carried but none dared look up at her as she sneered at their puny existence. She watched unemotionally as a woman went down under the weight of her crude basket. One of the overseers immediately began to whip her, shredding her brown garments even further until only strips remained. This woman, however, did look up and for a moment her brown eyes locked with Ramira's, telling her in no uncertain terms what she was doing was a wickedness that would haunt her forever. She glared back down for a moment then nodded to the overseer who proceeded to take the woman out of her earthly misery…

"No!" Ramira shrieked. "I would never allow that to happen!"

"You sensed the other magic and sought to ally yourself with it even though it cost your people their very souls. I must confess I find that to be quite fascinating. That would make you and I the same, don't you think?"

"I am not like you!" she shouted, even though she wasn't so sure any more. Something had happened to steal her memory and her mind chose to shut itself in rather than face the truth.

"You have darkened the Source for me quite nicely, and when the time comes, you will remain inside of me, forever sharing with me all I will do. By the way, did you know your power obliterated everyone on the plains? I see, you didn't." Mahn slipped back into the shadows, leaving a stunned, confused and bereaved Ramira alone.

She couldn't have killed them too, she silently wailed to herself. She had been aiming her might away from them. He was lying so she would lose her will and desire, leaving the Source even more readily available for him to rip from deep within her. Her steadfast conviction and a sudden obstinate feeling erased his words from her mind. If she only knew what color the fire had been. She stood tall and proud, willing the Source to stir within her but careful not to let Mahn sense its presence, then closed her eyes and flew down inside of herself. She was well aware of the fact he was watching her, but she also knew he could not see what she was doing. Or so she hoped. She drifted farther and farther down until the sensations crowding her prison receded far off into the distance leaving her truly alone.

There were no ghosts or nightmares here, for they shunned that which she sought, and although surrounded by blackness, she was totally unafraid. She soon sensed a low thrumming sound and followed as it guided her even deeper inside revealing a pale glow. She angled toward it, the light growing brighter but not increasing in size until she faced the brilliant core floating in the darkness. Pulsing with a deep lavender light, the Source hovered before her as if waiting for her command. Ramira reached out with trembling hands and warily touched it with the tip of her fingers: it felt cool to the touch. If she hadn't wielded it on the plains, she would be very surprised such a little thing could be so powerful; but she had and therefore knew its size was deceiving.

She was about to coax it into her upturned hand when it suddenly sped away. It was time to go. She had seen what she needed to and began to retreat when she noted another shimmering form. It was small, nearly lost in the darkness, but it burned with a power all its own. Ramira stared at it with wonder then instant devotion for the tiny seed brought joy and strength to her very soul.

Zada smiled at Cricket as they joined the King for the evening meal, pleased the young girl had recovered from her perilous journey. Sophie and Anci had also been invited and it seemed as if the two chatting girls would become fast friends. Cricket had spent so much time surviving she had been bereft of such friendships and clearly enjoyed being with someone her own age. Danyl and Karolauren entered the dining hall and took their seats just as the servers began to bring out platters of food. Nyk, Allad and a few others wanted to decline dinner but the King, sensing there might not be too many more shared meals, would not accept their refusals. There would be plenty of time to continue preparations for the attack later. There was some small talk while they ate, but it was mostly silent as each thought about what they were to face. The meal ended and they retired to an adjoining sitting room where they shared glasses of wine and ale.

"Danyl tells me you have an interesting little bauble, Cricket," said Zada, breaking the silence. "May I see it?"

Cricket reached into her pouch, pulling out the blue stone and handing it to the Herkah. Zada stared into the stone, raising an eyebrow at how closely it resembled the beads on the bracelet. The egg-shaped stone was polished so smoothly it nearly slipped out of her grasp as she held it up to the lamplight. Deep blue swirls curled slowly within its lustrous surface like an early morning mist in the middle of summer. What sort of memory could you house? she asked herself, then handed it back to the young girl.

"The army is encamped a day and a half from the city, Father," said Styph. "They seem to be waiting for their leader to arrive."

"I don't doubt that will take too much longer, but I believe they will attack before he gets here," stated Seven.

"Inflict as much damage as possible before he arrives?" asked Nyk.

"Yes," replied the dwarf king.

"Then when we are dazed and battered by his army he'll...sorry, Danyl, he'll finish the task with Ramira," said Styph.

Danyl remained distracted and apart from the group, his eyes looking beyond the gloom of the balcony window at the snow beginning to fall softly down upon the city. It would, he guessed, be over within the week. They would pick up the pieces of their lives and go on or they would not have to worry about anything anymore. He rested his forehead against the cold glass, its frigid touch soothing against his heated forehead, remembering the promise he had made to her near the end of their journey.

When this is all over, can the two of us go somewhere...anywhere for a while?

Yes, we can and we will, Ramira, that I pledge to you here and now, and nothing, no one will stop us.

He closed his eyes and blocked out everything except her face, willing her to hear his silent words, words originating from his heart. He didn't care that each of them bore their respective powers nor their possible annihilation only days away. He concentrated on what they had vowed to one another and sent that conviction west, trusting she would somehow know his declaration even if she were deep within Mahn's lair. He slowly opened his eyes, the whites gone, replaced by a brilliant emerald hue glittering with determination. They stared unblinkingly into the night as a vague shape began to materialize outside the window. It appeared to be a hazy collection of colors that had no defined edges, developing the faintest of outlines as it drew closer. Then, her face hovered just on the other side of the glass. Tell me how I can help you, he begged of the fluctuating image.

His heart beat wildly in his chest; the only thing he wanted to do was reach out and grab her, even if the likeness was composed of memories and desires. She came closer, placing her spectral hands against the window and prompting him to do the same. He stared into her eyes, willing her with all his might to take shape and return to her flesh and blood form. He gazed into her shifting features and felt a tear slide down his cheek at the fear and resolute conviction on her face. She had chosen her fate not upon the plains but on the night in the cave when she had pulled him, and with him, the elven might to safety. No matter what was to occur in the future, she was willing to challenge it with every ounce of her being. She began to dissolve into a million sparks, leaving him staring into the snowy vista once more. His breath condensed on the window, obscuring the night but not the face permanently etched into his mind and heart. He removed his hand from the glass and rejoined his companions.

Ramira felt a peculiar yet cherished sensation touch her, much to the dismay of Mahn, who instantly roared to life in response from somewhere within the shadows. She ignored his objections and threats, focusing instead on the unexpected feeling flooding through her, following its gossamer connection to a place far away from this terrible place. The tether extended out from this horrid abyss, pulling her through the frigid night past stars resembling streaks of light and over the dark land. She flew through time and space until a vast shape even darker than the night loomed ahead of her. Then a large window appeared, the light filtering out into the snowy night illuminating the terrace and outlining a lone figure with his head pressed against the glass. Danyl. She floated closer then reached out to him, taken aback as his green eyes bored into hers. He wanted to help her but there was nothing he could do right now. She placed her hands against the glass then smiled as he pressed his against hers. She had so much to tell him but what traveled to Bystyn was not composed of flesh and blood and could therefore not speak.

Infuriated beyond belief, Mahn shattered the connection and yanked her back to her dungeon. He violently severed her from her stony prison, ramming her into the foul depths of his cloak where she shared his hideous existence with the tortured and tormented souls he had devoured over the eons. They pulled and clawed at her from every direction, some beseechingly others out of sheer hatred and loathing, their accompanying shrieks forcing her hands to her ears to block them out. The air was fetid and heavy like having her face pushed into a vat of rotting meat. As if those horrible things weren't enough, he began to assault her mind with more images of the death and destruction he claimed she had caused. The howls and screeches of the souls around her multiplied dramatically in response, their cacophonous screams compelling her to do the only thing that would keep her sane. She disappeared into herself, taking comfort in the radiant silver sparkle next to the Source, the only place offering her any sort of sanctuary from the vile corruption surrounding her. She curled up amongst that which made up her whole world and waited to be released from the bowels of Mahn's malice.

Time seemed to stand still for her as she endured the constant battering of both Mahn and the loathsome things around her. The evil forces encompassing her left her unable to wield the Source. The Source was now caged. Mahn's arrogant plan to wrest it from her in front of Bystyn would be a horrifying spectacle and she shuddered to think what that effect would have on the allies. Ironically enough, Mahn was powerless to seize the Source even though she was deep within his foul robes. Perhaps he wasn't helpless but just bided his time. She brought her knees to her chest in thought. In essence, Mahn already housed the Source since it now resided deep in his repulsive robes, but he still had to retrieve it from within her. She had had to delve deep down within herself to secure it. How would he seize it? She would not willingly cede the power to him and the nearly constant barrage of horrors he inflicted upon her could not dislodge it, either. The Source beckoned like a gold rich vein deep within a mine, a tunnel he would have to lower himself into to obtain it. The notion of his loathsome presence deep inside of her made her shudder with revulsion, turning her stomach while her skin erupted with goose bumps. She knew all too well what his presence within her mind caused, likening the physical assault to a violation without equal. Just the mere thought of him ravaging her on his way to securing the Source...she smiled for the answer manifested itself before her. The only problems were how to convey her solution to the others and how to coerce Danyl into fulfilling his part in the evil's destruction.

-9-

The first skirmish began early the next morning, as nearly a hundred horsemen were beset by a large contingent of the enemy several miles west of the city. The battle was brief yet incredibly violent, with many of Mahn's men killed. Those from Bystyn had fewer losses as they repelled the demon-prodded army. They were able to retrieve their dead and dying, bringing them back to the city before rounding up fresh men and horses and returning to the same area. They battled twice more before the evil's army simply retreated from the conflict, the act unusual but not unexpected. Things remained quiet until dusk, when another wave of attackers confronted the horsemen, fought briefly, then withdrew once more.

Nyk watched as they pulled back, their hit and run tactics serving no other purposes than to test the allies or distract them. The latter thought prompted him to send a patrol both north and south of their present position with strict orders to report anything unusual. Gard took the northern route and Seven headed south.

The prince spat upon the bloodstained snow, keeping a watchful eye on the western horizon, waiting for signs of another assault. Nothing moved except the cold wind.

Seven could clearly see the shapes moving about through the woods bordering the plains and knew they were spreading out along the line of trees. The enemy wound its way east without bothering to conceal themselves, a fact making the hair on the back of the King's neck stand up. Their brazen disregard for the patrols paralleling their advancement told him Mahn planned on sacrificing any and all of his men to take Bystyn. They were being surrounded while their attention was diverted by the brief skirmishes. Seven surmised Gard was witnessing the same thing a few miles to the north. They would soon be cut off from any help, and then the evil's army would converge upon the city like some giant noose, strangling it at his leisure. Their only course of action would be to maintain a buffer zone around Bystyn, keeping them at bay for as long as possible before the inevitable retreat behind its gray walls became necessary. Help at that point, if they were fortunate enough to receive any, would be futile. The situation then would be dire indeed. He sent a messenger back to Nyk with the information and continued his vigil.

Gard's thoughts mirrored those of the dwarf as the vague shadows spread eastward through his home. The Khadry felt the bile rise into his throat. He could well imagine what they were doing to the forest as they expanded through its once-bountiful ground. They would undoubtedly slaughter everything in sight then raze whatever the Khadry had left behind, forcing them to start all over again once this dilemma was over. If, of course, any of them survived.

All for one woman with a magic as evil as Mahn's. Gard seemed to be the only one who thought her existence was nothing less than a bane to them all. He had kept silent during the meetings but the hatred building up inside for her could no longer be ignored. He swore to himself if Mahn succeeded in destroying everything using Ramira's power and he, Gard, survived, he would hunt her down and kill her. Indeed, if given a chance now he would do the same, regardless of the cost to his own life. Or soul, for that matter. Her evil, he determined, was enshrouded in a deceitful beauty that had charmed most of whom she had come into contact. Was he the only one who had somehow managed to avoid the spell she had cast on the others? Danyl's deep affection for her worried him the most because he knew that, without a doubt, the prince would protect her with his very life. Those thoughts turned the Khadry's face dark with unease. He pushed the vehemence he felt for Ramira into the back of his mind, focusing instead on the danger all around them. His plans for her would have to wait. He would continue to stand by the others, for to do otherwise would mean they would be lost. He, too, sent a courier to the prince and waited for a reply.

Nyk and a handful of others waited for darkness then slipped away from the city, riding south toward the fringes of the enemy camp just as the snow began to fall. The weather would allow them to remain hooded without causing any undue suspicion, prepared nonetheless if a challenge arose. They had smeared their faces with grime and dressed in well-worn homespun clothing making them nearly indistinguishable in the night from the enemy. Their mounts, too, had been transformed, wearing bridles, blankets and saddles taken from enemy horses that had fallen in battle on the plains surrounding the city. The prince decided the best course of action would be to ride directly into the camp along its edges then casually merge with the enemy. There would be precious little time to wreak as much havoc as possible before retreat became a necessity. It was a dangerous plan, but if they failed to destroy at least a few of the machines they would be in deep trouble indeed. Nyk's concern revolved around the demons. Mahn would surely have sprinkled them amongst his men, making their task even more daunting. Allad had insisted he go with them but Nyk refused, citing the devastation that could occur were he taken and metamorphosed into a Vox. The Herkah conceded, then offered them each one of Zada's knives. Nyk wished Allad were riding by his side; he greatly respected his fighting capabilities.

The elves took several deep breaths to steady their nerves as they reached the enemy camp then split up into pairs. Nyk and his captain rode their horses in as far into the camp as they could, then loosely tied their mounts' reins before walking aimlessly amid the shadows toward the nearest hurling machine. The captain hunkered down beside the guard while Nyk disappeared into the machine's silhouette, nimbly climbing up along the crossbars until he reached its apex. The prince remained absolutely still for several moments then reached into his cloak to pull out his knife. The entire machine was held together by ropes as thick as his arm. He had to slice through enough of the fibers to keep the machine from falling apart during transport yet render it useless at the first volley. He sawed through them, cutting deeply enough to satisfy him. He replaced the knife and descended the structure. One down. He resumed his listless state as he and his captain walked indifferently to the next apparatus.

They had covered half the distance to the next one when a peculiar feeling touched him, one he had experienced before. It wormed its way into his stomach, squeezing it with dread and fright. Demon. It would be hard to recognize by sight. Nyk headed for one of the fires, sitting down beside it, staring into the flames while stretching his senses to their limits. He could smell the sweat on the unwashed bodies around him and hear the enemy coughing and sniffling. A quick, piercing cry off in the distance made him freeze in alarm but the camp did not erupt in chaos. The unnatural feeling subsided and the elves rose to their feet to continue on to their next target. The captain again sat beside the guard while Nyk scampered up the tower slashing at the ropes binding it together. He was about to go down when a large contingent of soldiers approached, their drawn weapons, a clear indication things had gone awry. The brief shriek he had heard in the distance echoed within his mind, sending a shiver of dread down his spine. Nyk watched a group advance from out of the darkness and pressed his body against the beam. His captain followed the guard's response, scrambling away like some tormented animal and lifting his arm up in mock defense as the gang stopped yards away from the catapult. All but one of the soldiers dispersed, the remaining one standing completely still as if gauging his surroundings. Nyk's eyes narrowed for he knew what it was.

The hooded figure slowly craned its neck first right then left until it focused on the guard and the captain. To his credit, the disguised elf kept calm, continuing his deception even though the terror he felt lodged like a stone in his chest. The black form advanced upon him, forcing the elf to crawl backward until the massive tower blocked any further retreat. Nyk watched helplessly as the demon scrutinized the elf then surged forward, grabbing the elf by the neck and lifting him high into the air. The fiend pulled him closer and yanked the hood back, exposing the captain's filthy features. A hissing sound of satisfaction escaped the dark cowl as it slowly crushed the life out of the elf, but the captain was not about to die without a fight. His charge lay concealed in the darkness above and he was not about to let this creature live to take him. He fumbled with his scabbard then gathered all of his remaining strength to push Zada's blade into the Vox then into his own chest. Nyk looked on helplessly; his face draining of blood as his captain jerked several times then went limp in the enraged demon's hand. The Herkah blade had hurt, but not killed, the Vox. It dropped the dead elf and began clawing at its wound, collapsing to the ground as it wheezed and hissed in pain. Two more screams exploded into the night, leaving Nyk with the feeling he was soon to be on his own…if he survived.

A vile wind blasted through the camp, the air so fetid it nearly knocked Nyk off the beam. His eyes watered and the morbid cries of the souls imprisoned within his hatred filled his ears. The frigid air bit into his flesh and bones, numbing his hold on the beam, his fingers gripping not wood but a slab of ice. Nyk gritted his teeth, watching as the black gust encircled the distressed Vox and whisked it away. Sweat poured down his face as he quietly gulped in air and regained his composure. That was as close as he ever wanted to come to the evil. It was time to leave; the extra guards posted around the machine and undoubtedly the other towers posing a problem. He desperately needed some sort of distraction. He checked the area as best as the darkness allowed, looking for anything that would give him those precious few moments to escape. The tree line loomed in the blackness a short sprint away to his right, taunting him with its nearness. It might just as well have been on the other side of the earth. He waited for a while listening for any of his men, slowly realizing he was probably the only one still alive. He was on his own. The sentries faced outward, their attention on the woods and brush around them and not on the catapult. He could clamber down without alerting them, then time his move to join them in their sentry duty. He slithered down the crossbars keeping to the shadows, his perfect timing allowing him to join the pacing guards. He participated for a while then indicated he needed to relieve himself, disappearing into the bushes before they had a chance to reply. He hastened to his horse, mounting it then heading back to the city before all hell broke loose. Two other riders materialized from out of the night. At first Nyk drew his weapon in anticipation of a fight then recognized his men. He made them cut themselves with the Herkah blades to make sure they were not demon-infested then the three of them rode back to the city.

They met with the others, divulging what they had seen and heard in the camp. They had managed to tamper with five of the towers, leaving seven to be destroyed later once they were within range. The prince reported on the physical and mental makeup of the enemy and also on the fetid mist that came to get the wounded Vox.

"They are swinging up and around us," reported the prince. "My guess is that Mahn is on his way and has ordered them to assume their attack positions."

"I agree," stated Gard. "They are using the forests to the north and south to hide their men, hoping to draw us into the trees to fight. That would be a perfect way to increase their demon count."

"They are going to have to get close enough to use their hurling devices, but they will be well guarded. Attacking or disabling them will be quite the challenge if we choose to do so," added Seven.

"I think they have learned their lesson," stated Nyk.

"How many of the traps have been set?" asked Alyxandyr.

"Several," replied Mason, unrolling a map of the area. "There are three along the forest to the west and north." His finger traced the locations. "Ditches have been dug along these two lines just south of the edge. If they decide to bring any heavy equipment or come by horseback, they will find themselves several feet down, the steep sides impeding their ability to escape.

"We also dug channels that can be filled with oil and lit in crossing patterns all along the plain. Thankfully the snow has hidden them, but I don't think it will hinder the incendiary nature of the oil. We could do little in the south, but we did manage to set a few traps to the east."

Alyxandyr absently tapped the map then looked up as Zada joined them, her face haggard and shoulders stooped.

"How are you feeling?" he asked her as she sat down beside Danyl.

"Fine," she replied with little conviction. She listened while he updated her, taking deep breaths as she braced herself for another round of images beginning to build inside her mind. The blank look on her face alerted the others and they became silent as the Herkah began to receive more disturbing visions.

There was chaos all around her, the uncountable souls screaming and clawing in this netherworld agitated by her presence. She could smell their rank odors and feel their ghostly forms as they crowded around her. Zada guessed Ramira was somewhere deep within that obscene darkness, and how she was able to withstand those horrors was beyond her comprehension. Zada was on the fringes of this appalling maelstrom and could barely tolerate it and would have to break the contact soon. She had only a few moments and took a chance by sending a message to Ramira, one she more than likely would never receive. To her complete surprise, she acquired one from Ramira, the lightning-fast vision initially confusing until she broke the connection…

Zada sat utterly still as Ramira's feeble thought took hold within her mind, grateful there wasn't a sound in the room. The fading vision Ramira sent showed a mighty tree sprouting from the trough of a snow-white dune, fully developing in seconds before her eyes. Its sturdy roots disappeared down into the sand, snaking outward and into the dunes around it. Puddles of blood surrounded the roots wherever they penetrated the sand, the bright red fluid trickling away from the tree like crimson tears. The great canopy of leaves blotted out the sun, and as the shade spread, so did the vision dim. Zada smiled tiredly.

"Zada?" Allad softly brought her back to the chamber.

The nomad nodded to her mate then reached out for his hand. His touch had always soothed her even after the worst vision and this one, although filled with hope, was no less taxing to her. She sat down in front of the fireplace to chase the chill from her bones. She gazed at the flames flickering and snapping upon the grate, holding her hands out to absorb the heat. A movement to her right caught her attention. It was the specter of the brown woman.

Tell me about Ramira.

Not here.

The ghost dissipated before her eyes, Zada's heart constricting at the sadness in the other's brown eyes. The spirit clearly loved Ramira, accepting of her part in the scheme of things but still afraid for her. They all were, but this long dead woman continued to haunt the land, refusing to rest until Ramira was safe. Zada doubted the brown woman was her mother, but that didn't stem the emotions keeping this shade in the present.

It occurred to Zada Ramira was not the only one for whom the brown woman was concerned. If the living failed, the dead would never achieve an eternal peace. Zada was better able to "see" the ancient spirit because of her inner sight and the fact that her roots were inextricably bound with this distant ancestor. Her eternal destiny hinged upon their success in destroying the evil because the dead were powerless to confront and vanquish Mahn. Or were they?

That fate rested on two shoulders and the strength and courage of many arms: arms that would wield their weapons against an enemy none could have envisioned. Ramira had only momentarily hampered Mahn's plan centuries ago when she disappeared; the battle would eventually take place in another time. Evil thoughts and deeds never disappeared but regrouped to arise once more. It always found a host, nurturing and preparing its minions to perform wholesale destruction without any regard for anyone or anything. There were plenty of weak and empty-headed marks for it to home in on. The best individuals to defile were those already corrupted: the greedy and power hungry. Its insatiable appetite to inflict death and misery was devoid of mercy and conscience. She stared at Alyxandyr and wondered who he would lose in the coming days. Zada looked at the rest in turn for they, too, would lose friends and family. And herself? Who would she lose? What would be birthed in the end when it was all over? Would the evil rule the devastated land, or would the allies live? Her gaze returned to the fire. She fervently prayed she was not seeing Bystyn's future within the orange flames as they fed off the wood cradled upon the grate. One of the logs popped and fell, sending embers out onto the slate floor near her feet. The image Ramira had sent to her burned in her mind, most notably the immense tree squeezing the blood out of the desert.

They stood within the watchtower looking west upon the black plague spreading as far as the eye could see. The same scene played itself out to the south and along the foothills of the mountains to the north and west. There were a few pockets of the enemy in the east, too. The adversaries swarming along the forest to the south could easily ride up to prohibit any messenger sent to alert the remainder of the dwarves in Evan's Peak. Seven rubbed his chin while Gard stared at Mahn's forces with crossed arms, his keen eyes absorbing every detail before them. They watched with a sense of fascinated horror as the rear of the army began to part as if a gigantic pair of hands had pushed them aside.

A knot of riders rode down the middle, the enemy pouring back into the breach left in the wake of the black group heading toward the city: Mahn. The time was at hand and he was bringing his prize to the gates where he would tear the Source from Ramira and use it to obliterate them all. The sight of him wending his way through his army of demons was frightening, but it did not shatter the resolve of those who witnessed his dreadful entrance.

"Well," Seven watched the dramatic approach, "we all know what his presence means."

"Do you think Ramira is on one of the horses beside him?" asked Gard, as he, too, measured the effect Mahn's appearance had on the black host spread around him. One true arrow could end her life and Mahn's ability to take the magic, he thought. He noted there were no cheers or even one word spoken as the evil passed through his army. They remained in place, their features blank and their armed hands hanging limply at their sides.

"I doubt he would take that chance, Gard. My guess is she is contained within his bulky black robes," replied Mason.

Mahn halted near the middle of his forces, the riders at his side remaining for a few moments before riding off. He stared up at those gathered on the battlements from within a circle no one dared to venture into. His army was so densely packed few could move about freely. They stood shoulder to shoulder garbed in everything from leather to homespun, some with shields, most with nothing more than a sword. There were legions of archers and phalanxes of spears occupying the forefront; groups of cavalry rode at the ready along the sides. The lack of armor was prevalent throughout the ranks. Their lives were meaningless to Mahn, shells of flesh and blood whose only purpose in his plans was to wear down the allies. The blank features of the thousands were the most frightening of all. They had no concept about what was happening to them and it was debatable whether or not they even realized where they were. Their minds and bodies were no longer their own and they would endure whatever Mahn ordered them to do.

"Where could he have gotten all of these people from?" asked Styph.

"Many lived in Kepracarn, and don't forget the towns and villages scattered throughout the land," stated Alyxandyr. The King noted their varied attire and recognized how busy Mahn had been conscripting people from the south, Kepracarn and places he could not identify. His recruitment had been indiscriminate.

"Are they all inhabited by demons?" asked Mason.

"No, I don't think so," replied Allad. "They have been exploited by him and could return to normal once he is defeated, that I've seen before. See there," he pointed to small groups of figures moving about in a jerky sort of way, "those are Kreetch and over there," he directed their attention along the sides of the army, "are Radir." He surveyed the groups of foot soldiers, horsemen and those specializing in swift attacks and retreats.

"And the Vox?" asked Nyk, looking around for the elusive and deadly demons.

"They have already been dispatched to target Herkahs, I assume," replied the nomad in low tones, trying to pinpoint the loathsome demons. At this point they would be easy enough to distinguish amongst the rest of the army, but the problems would begin once they managed to infiltrate into the allies' ranks. One Herkah demon could cause a great deal of damage amongst his people and throw the allies into complete chaos. His face darkened at the thought of a Vox within the gates, freely feeding upon the nomads at will until fear and terror crushed those who so courageously battled to defeat the evil. Their vigilance, therefore, must be increased tenfold to avoid such a devastating scenario and it was up to the Herkahs to insure that didn't happen.

"Wonderful," said the King, sarcastically.

Danyl stared at a knot of figures toward the middle of the army, noting how unaffected they were by everything around them yet studying their surroundings nonetheless. He sensed Mahn there and if he were there then Ramira would be with him. She had managed to elude him for a thousand years and saved countless generations of a fate worse than death, but the evil had to be confronted eventually and now seemed to be that moment. Why now? What was it about this place and time prompting such a challenge? What pieces fell into place, and would they be beneficial to them or to the enemy? He sighed and pulled his cloak tighter, for the day was bright but the sun provided no heat. Winter had finally claimed the land from autumn.

"Can you 'see' her, Zada?" he asked the nomad standing beside him.

"She is there, but he will not let me penetrate into his gloom."

"They are starting to move forward," said Nyk, then he and several others descended the stone steps and jumped onto their horses. Whether they were fully prepared to meet the horde or not, the time to defend was at hand. Every member had a specific duty to fulfill and, although many wanted to join the impending battle, they remained at their designated stations.

The gates opened and several hundred riders rode out into the early morning light to join in the battle. They ignored the fact that nearly twice as many of the enemy awaited them. Nyk and Allad rode directly west while Gard led a contingent slightly northward. Seven and Styph headed south toward the trees. Alyxandyr watched with Clare, Danyl and Zada, their minds assimilating every detail on the plains. They looked for weaknesses and possible strategies they could use during the course of the upcoming confrontation. Eliminating the Radir and the Kreetch would give them an edge, but the amount of strength and stamina needed to fulfill that task would leave them vulnerable to the mortals under Mahn's control. Besides, the loss of life in striving to achieve that goal would have been more than they were willing to gamble on. Allad had assigned Herkahs to each of the groups. They were to confront the demons using training much better suited to defeating the demons. That also gave the evil a chance to procure more Vox if they were unsuccessful, but their choices were limited indeed. The nomads were well aware of the fact that more than one of them would succumb to the evil and be forced to fight against their kin and friends.

Few of those standing against the demons had witnessed their terrible wrath and could not truly understand what they were fighting. The Herkahs had attempted to prepare them, but any training would not be sufficient in exorcising the fear they would face once they confronted them. Zada desperately wished she could supply each member of the allies with a blade to counteract the poison, saving many who would succumb to the evil's venom and join that horrible brotherhood. They watched as the towers of destruction were pulled closer to the city. The robust horses strained under the immense weight, the muscles on their necks and shoulders so taut they nearly burst through their hides. The machines creaked and groaned, inching slowly forward as the soggy ground sucked at the huge wheels. The snow-covered earth only delayed the inevitable. The archers awaited the signal to rain a volley of arrows into the animals once they were within range, a futile endeavor considering once the horses were within range so were the towers. They looked down at their men dispersed below them, warriors waiting for the giant wooden devices to be set into place. The plan was to try and draw them to these furrows and use them to their advantage without falling prey to the catapults. Part of Mahn's cavalry rode toward the allies but none of the foot soldiers followed suit. They remained rooted in place as if cast in stone. Their time was not yet at hand.

The wait turned into hours, the enemy taking their time in setting up their implements of destruction. The first volley of rocks were hurled at the city near midmorning, falling shy of the walls but not of the riders. The crash initially spooked the horses but the horsemen regained control of them, repositioning themselves as another barrage impacted at their forefront. A large contingent of demon-possessed men followed in its wake, their silent throats and vacant eyes devoid of the normal emotions that drove a warrior into battle. They shouted no battle cry. Mahn's army fought not for revenge, protection of their lands, or for spoils. They had neither goal nor choice in the matter. Those anticipating their arrival stared at the eerie advance then toward their leaders. Allad, Seven and the others were equally perplexed as their men, keeping their features tight and unperturbed as they studied the advancing units. It was time. The horsemen kicked their mounts' sides and rode forward to meet the enemy, the violent encounter taking place about a half mile from the gray walls of Bystyn. The fight for their lives and very souls had begun.

The furious battle lasted for nearly an hour, the clashing of sword against shield punctuated by the screams of the dying and rocks whistling overhead hitting the earth with thudding sounds. Pieces of the shattered rocks peppered the warriors cutting any exposed flesh, the large fragments as deadly as any blade. These pierced into horse and man instantly felling them where they stood. A second set of catapults was being set up behind the first, their trajectories aimed at the groups of fighters on the plain. Mahn was going to smash into both sides heedless of the deaths of his own men. The enemy released the thick ropes around one of the catapults. The bucket for the debris came crashing to the ground, killing all standing beneath it. Alyxandyr stared at the huge arm teetering back and forth then collapsing forward. There were four more disabled machines out there, but would they be the ones Mahn ordered onto the field? The King signaled for the red flag to be hoisted over the parapets, preferring retreat to watching his men getting crushed beneath the debris Mahn was about to fling at them. The soldiers and horsemen did not notice it for several minutes, minutes that ended up costing many lives as the rubble crashed down around and upon them. The elves and their comrades extricated themselves from the fighting, retreating back into the city and slaying many who sought to keep them in the open field. Oddly enough, however, Mahn's army did not follow them to the gray walls, withdrawing instead back to where they had started. Mahn wanted this bloodbath to continue for as long as possible, playing with them like a cat with a mouse trapped between its paws. When the final warrior entered the gates, the defenders slammed them shut.

The fighters' hearts were heavy with bitterness and sorrow. They could do nothing for the dead and dying littering the plains around them. They grieved for their fallen comrades, vowing to seek retribution against the evil that had descended up them. If Mahn hoped to demoralize the protectors of the city by inflicting such horrific injuries, he was sadly mistaken. The newfound resolve and determination springing forth from their souls was greater than any evil he could heap upon them. The light burning in their eyes promised as much. They silently endured being stitched and salved, knowing full well they would need more attention after the next battle. The physicians were kept busy tending to the wounded while the Herkahs kept a close eye on them to make sure none had been poisoned. The nomads were forced to slay a half dozen of their comrades in arms, their normally dispassionate faces filled with emotion as they carried out their unenviable duty. Some of the witnesses rubbed the backs of their necks; others swallowed hard and took a step backward as the possessed bodies writhed in agony then became still. When the grim task was finished, the warriors exchanged unspoken vows to seek revenge upon the evil and his minions.

Seven, Nyk and Gard stood on the parapet with the others, pointing out a host of possible counterattacks, ignoring the healers attending to their injuries. The three brushed them off, ordering them to care for those who were in dire need of aid as they continued to look for weaknesses in Mahn's strategy. The catapults were becoming a problem, one that had to be addressed very quickly. Mahn could easily keep pressing forward, forcing the elves back until the devices literally smashed into the walls of the city. He chose not to do so, creating a momentary stalemate upon the plains. This would not last. With every skirmish fewer defenders were left alive to withdraw into the city. They had to do something about the hurling devices even though they were heavily guarded and too far for the elves to throw flames upon them. Nyk's earlier sortie, although successful, had made little impact on the amount of damage the remainder of the catapults delivered. Barring a miracle, they would have to endure the aerial assaults.

Danyl stared hard at the scene before him, knowing he held the Green Might, a power that could reach and lay waste to the machines if only he could let it rip from his body. He sensed the power whirling and swirling within but try as he might, it would not fly forth. He could cause so much destruction with it, saving all of these good people. The magic would not acquiesce to his demands, continuing to smolder and curl inside. He glanced at Zada and immediately looked away.

"It will come when it deems the time to be right," she whispered to him while gently gripping his hand.

"So many will die needlessly in the meantime."

"I know, Danyl, but you have to remember the magic responds to things no one can understand…just like it did when you saved Ramira's soul after she was clawed by the Kreetch. It came and accomplished its goal then and it will do so again."

"It's so hard to just stand here and do nothing, watching and waiting as the slaughter goes on."

"Have faith, Danyl."

Faith. The word stuck in the elf's mind like a bone, taunting him just as the magic seemed to as he glanced from injured elf to dying dwarf. Their courage and determination were steeped in the faith they held for each other and in the belief that the elven magic would save them. Danyl held up his hands, staring in disgust at them and at what would not burst forth. For a brief moment an image formed: his blood-covered hands dripped into a pool at his feet, each droplet falling with such force it splattered him all the way up to his face. He recoiled at the contact, cringing as he felt the crimson rivulets running down his cheeks and mingled with his tears. The sound they made as they fell echoed the dripping he had heard in the maze. Was that the meaning of the labyrinth? Would he remain incapable or unfit to wield the might locked away in the maze while the sound of death trickled down into his stone prison? The vision dissolved away, leaving him standing beneath the sun's cold glare, oblivious of Zada's concern as she stared at the darkness that had settled upon his face.

Ramira stirred from her temporary haven sensing most of the horrific souls tormenting her were elsewhere. She left her sanctuary, rising to consciousness, probing her black prison to insure she was indeed alone. The fetid silence increased her wariness as she checked the darkness in which she was restricted. She suddenly sensed Mahn. He immediately wrested her from her foul confines, thrusting her into the bright light, the violence with which he extracted her equal to the impact of the blinding daylight and noise. She shielded her eyes but could not do the same for her ears as the furious sounds of battle assaulted them. Her senses, accustomed to the gloomy prison in which she had been isolated, overwhelmed her and she began to topple to the blood and mud encased ground. She felt a vise-like grip reach out, grabbing her by the scruff of the neck, and jerk her erect. Mahn was not about to allow her to miss one moment of his triumph. She saw the horror upon the snow-covered plains surrounding Bystyn, as she became accustomed to the sunlight. The terrible carnage stole her breath and brought tears to her eyes.

Debris crashed down upon the plains, smashing into friend and foe alike. The ear-shattering sounds of metal clashing against metal and the screams of men and horses filled her ears. The black army surged forward. She looked over her shoulder and saw another wave waiting their turn to fight those who valiantly strove to protect Bystyn. She blanched in horror as Mahn's forces tore the dead and dying into shreds, their companions unable to stop them. She noted the bitterness, determination and grief marking their bloodstained features as they clashed with the enemy. She felt anger and hatred rise in her midsection as she looked back toward the black cloaked shape sitting on the horse behind her. She peered up into his cowl and saw only a vague mist, one even darker than his garb. She reached back to thrust her hand into that horrible void, but his gloved hand caught it, his grip nearly breaking her bones as he squeezed her wrist.

"In due time you will be reaching for your friends," he hissed at her, his words infuriating her much to his profane pleasure.

"I will not relinquish what thrives within me," she growled at him.

"Of course you will..."

"Never!" she shrieked, her tone so venomous the Vox turned to see what was transpiring behind them. Their disinterested looks returned to the battle at hand and, without a word, they rode away. She watched as they split into pairs, each of the three teams heading in different directions. She knew where they were going: they were hunting for Herkahs. Ramira hated Mahn and his minions more and more as she watched them kill the elves and their comrades as well as each other. The catapults indiscriminately flung their deadly cargo into the midst of all those battling on the plains. She vowed to put a stop to the carnage unfolding before her. Ramira began to summon forth the Source.

Mahn immediately recognized what she was doing and assailed her with vicious and obscene images to stop it. They were so intense he could not have inflicted greater damage had he pummeled her with his gloved fists. Her eyes went wide with horror but she managed to thwart the visions and proceeded to gather the power within her once more. The images were losing their effect, compelling Mahn to squeeze her innards in a desperate attempt to regain control. His fierce retaliation was so swift and cruel she could feel the blood trickle down her chin as the standoff between the two continued: she had the Source and he had his iron will. She would not give an inch of ground. Sensing her stubborn determination, he commanded the evil souls to torment her once more.

This time she did not hide within herself. She flung the Source at the horrible shades with a vengeance, incinerating one disturbed soul after another. Mahn hissed with pain and rage as wayward bits of the power struck him. He exploded at her defiance, bringing his fist down across her face and sending her into unconsciousness. The master of evil glared down at her with a mixture of hatred and fear, sentiments hidden deep within his cowl. Her ability to control the Source disturbed him, his growing inability to restrain her using the images becoming an obstacle to his plans. How long would he be capable of suppressing her with brutality before that too became ineffectual? For the first time since he snatched Ramira from the safety of this accursed city, doubt began to creep into his mind. Time was no longer a luxury.

Zada watched the sudden eruption occurring in the midst of the army and suddenly smiled. Mahn had lost control over Ramira. He had made the mistake of allowing her to see the bloodshed on the field, expecting her to be too stunned to do anything about it. He had also not anticipated her being able to handle the Source. She would not go quietly and that made the Herkah feel a certain sense of hope, even after she watched him strike her into senselessness. Ramira's sense of duty and loyalty clearly lay with the Bystynians.

"Why the smile, Zada?' asked Danyl.

"It seems as if Ramira has seen the carnage on the plains and is trying to use the Source to stop it."

"Can she do that?" he asked, his features losing some of the tension in his face.

"I'm not sure, but she certainly has given Mahn something to think about."

"Wouldn't he be able to take the power from her if she brandishes it?"

"No, son. As long as she wields it, he is at her mercy. The bearer controls it."

"Then why take the chance? Why not take it from her before she annihilates him?" The elf stared hard at the knot of darkness, though try as he might, he was unable to distinguish Ramira. Her vow to keep harm from descending upon the city echoed in his mind. A wry grin lit up his face for he was well aware of how trying she could be once she made up her mind.

"Think of it as hunting with a hawk, Danyl. The bird of prey is cunning with sharp claws and a beak capable of ripping your flesh to shreds, but once it lands on your arm and you place a hood over its eyes it becomes submissive."

"Mahn can't get the hood over her eyes, can he?" He spoke almost as if to himself, his gaze never shifting from the black group across the plains. The evil had her within his grasp, the desired power at his fingertips, yet it might just as well have been a thousand miles away. Or a thousand years. Her obvious success in eluding him over time was not anywhere near as frustrating as her refusal to cooperate. Well done, my love.

"Danyl." She pulled him to one side, for it was time to tell him of the image Ramira had sent. The nomad's clear and firm voice forced the elf to focus on every word she spoke.

"I had brief contact with Ramira yesterday when she showed me a huge tree beginning from seed then growing tall and sturdy from the desert sands. You, I am convinced, represent that tree and she the white sands. I don't know how that will be achieved, but your powers are to unite somehow and defeat Mahn." Zada searched his face, finding only the look of despair at being unable to wield his power. His demeanor darkened at the knowledge she gave him and further eroded his courage and conviction. His inability to summon forth the power was steering him farther away from the sacred trust imparted unto him. His anxieties and doubts manifested themselves in subtle ways: the nervous rubbing of his thumb and forefinger together and the inability to make eye contact. The elven might burned like fire through his body yet it would not allow itself to be set free. Not yet, anyway.

"What if the Green Might has other plans?"

"You are trying too hard," she replied, her words echoes of what he had heard in the great hall. The memory sent a shiver up his spine.

He stared at the knot of black amid the enemy, noting it was once again calm for Mahn had managed to suppress Ramira's rebellion, for the time being anyway. His mind drifted back to the vision she had sent Zada and wondered how they were supposed to combine their powers to defeat Mahn. Would the Green Might cede to such a fusion? He had to trust Ramira's insight, though, for she was in a position to see and know what they could not. She had told him she would do everything in her power to keep from ravaging any of them and he believed her even though others, he suspected, did not. He glanced at Gard, the Khadry's face not bothering to hide the resentment he had for everything swarming within the blackness, including Ramira. He had vocalized his distrust on more than one occasion and Danyl could not really blame Gard for feeling this way.

The Khadry had chosen isolation and had lived in relative comfort within the forest until Ramira came, followed by the menace that had destroyed their homes. All of this was happening because of her, but she, like all of them, was at the mercy of an evil that would never rest until it had the Source. This confrontation could have happened during her or any other's time, but it transpired now and they had no choice but to defy it or perish. As distasteful as Cooper was, he had lost his entire city while countless other villages perished under Mahn's relentless pursuit of the Source. The King deserved a great deal of misery for his recklessness but the price he now paid was unjustified. His city was his soul, his reason for being, and to be bereft of it, especially under such circumstances, had to tear even at his cold heart. The destruction and sorrow would continue unless Mahn was stopped here before Bystyn fell as well. Danyl filled his lungs then exhaled, his breath momentarily concealing the terrible scene below.

Cooper stared out of the barred windows, the battle sounds detected even through the castle's thick stone walls. He had been largely ignored, which allowed him a great deal of time to plot his life after the fall of Bystyn. He thought about the best way to sneak out of the city, where to hide and what people he could subjugate. He had to find a way back to Kepracarn and unearth his hidden treasure trove to buy…to buy what? There wouldn't be anyone untouched by the evil left in the land. He'd be a rat slinking from cave to deserted village searching for food, always looking over his shoulder for the inevitable fate to come crashing down on him. There'd be no one left to hate! There'd be nothing to enjoy either, like women or fine wines or those delicious little songbirds marinated in spicy oils. No more elves or dwarves…not even a stinking desert insect to chase after! Cooper's face abruptly lost all color, his jaw slowly dropping to his chest. Those whom he hated and had betrayed would be stalking him, never giving him a moment's reprieve. His dry lips twitched as he imagined Allad trailing him from one end of the land to the other, at no time tiring in his pursuit to turn him into one of the lesser demons. The Herkah would torment him for all eternity. He scratched at the stubble on his chin, rethinking his escape plans.

He knew the only reason Mahn let him go was to do more than bring information to the elves; he had brought something with him to aid Mahn from within the city.

"Hmm. Allad killed the horse and I carried nothing from Mahn with me…what in the four corners does he want me to do?"

Cooper slapped his forehead as the truth began to manifest itself in his mind. Mahn depended on Cooper's hatred to perform certain deeds, which would make it even easier for him to demolish the walls of the city. Mahn wanted Cooper to kill all of those whom he hated, and what better weapon than the King who had always lusted for what his enemies possessed? Slay the leaders of those gathered here and seek revenge upon the despised Herkahs, starting with Allad, the most detested of all.

The King would harbor no regrets in performing such tasks and indeed had looked forward to such an opportunity for a long time. Things were different now because those he had scorned the most were also the only ones who could save his skin. The only problem was he had to tell them about his revelation, and once he told, they would only place more guards and tighter bolts on the door. No, he had to devise a plan to get free, an extremely difficult maneuver. The Herkah guards would not listen to him and the few others who were allowed contact with him would be equally disinterested. His own reaction to such words would be to execute the messenger regardless of the reasons behind such a message. Rulers rarely survived if they did otherwise. That was the main problem: what would they say—or do—after he revealed why he had been sent? That he had a change of heart and wanted to live and would lend them his sword to fight for their survival? He laughed at his own thought so he could well imagine how they would react, but he had to try nonetheless. He banged on the door, waiting for the small panel at eye level to be pulled back, his mind made up, his conviction unchallenged. A stoic face nearly covered in black stared in at him.

"Speak."

"I need to see the elven king or Zada. It's very important."

The nomad stared at him with his black eyes for a moment then slammed the trapdoor shut. Cooper did not hear any footsteps in the hall. He sighed. Those involved in the fighting had more important things to do than to dote on the wishes of an imprisoned king. Cooper sat and waited, his thumbs drawing nervous circles around each other as the minutes ticked on by. The wait seemed like hours but finally he heard the lock snap open and in walked Danyl, flanked by two Herkahs. The prince studied the King for several long minutes before Cooper could speak.

"This may sound contradictory, Danyl, but I think I've figured out why I was sent here," he began hesitantly, not expecting the elf to believe a single word he was about to say.

"You? Contradictory?" Danyl was in no mood for Cooper's games, the acerbic tone in his voice conveying that thought to the king.

"Yes." He tried to ignore the sarcasm and continued. "Mahn expected me to not only fulfill his desire to have the leaders here slain, but also expected me to carry out my own wish to see the same thing happen." The Herkahs immediately surged forward held back only by the prince's raised hand.

"What is your point?"

"Look, Danyl, I don't want to end up as some filthy demon any more than you do, so let me help in the fight against Mahn."

"You first tell me that you were sent to kill us then you have the audacity to ask for a sword and be allowed to roam freely in our midst?" he asked, a look of astonishment on his face.

"Well...yes."

"Why should we trust you not to carry out your assigned task?"

"Because if I do that then I'm a dead man, and I am not yet ready to depart this world!"

"Mahn would have expected you to be isolated, locked up and well guarded, so where did you get the idea you'd have access to my father, Zada and the rest?" demanded Danyl.

"Because my innermost feelings toward you are...were his most potent weapons, weapons he could never have contrived or instilled into me."

"Mahn judged you well."

"I've lost my city, my people, my riches and I could be turned into one of those repulsive creatures. All I am asking is that you give me a chance to at least put up a fight and save what shards of my life there are left!"

"You are Mahn's puppet, Cooper."

Danyl's accusatory glare only intensified the powerful emotions surging through Cooper as the King's volatility smoldered then burst into life. Cooper had had enough and rushed forward not to harm the elf but to drive his point home. The Herkahs immediately placed themselves between the prince and the King, their weapons drawn, their faces set with Cooper's fate.

"I will not bow down to him or anyone else!" Cooper was livid. He despised being exploited and not taken seriously by anyone, including his enemies. His defiance had turned him into the perfect pawn for Mahn. Cooper was absolutely in control of his own soul, the rage radiating from his body borne of the indignity caused by Mahn.

Danyl stared at Cooper's clenched jaw and the veins straining along his neck and face. The King's emotions were raw, unfettered even within this prison. The King had been singled out by Mahn because of his duplicity, a trait the evil relied upon to complete his plans, but what he did not anticipate was as much as Cooper hated those who fought Mahn, he despised the evil even more. Danyl knew in order to deal with the elves and the Herkahs, Cooper had to live and that meant aligning himself with those that fought from the city. What was murky was how much influence Mahn held over the King. The decision was not his to make nor did he want that responsibility.

"I will speak with the others," he stated curtly and left, the King staring after the retreating prince.

Cooper stood in place for a long time, fists clenched and eyes boring into the thick oak door. He had done his best to persuade the elves to let him free but that did nothing to quell the nervousness in his stomach. What if this was also part of Mahn's plan? Was he thwarting his intentions or merely helping them to fruition? Doubt gnawed at him for the first time since arriving in the city, leaving him strangely exposed and completely unsure of what to do. His hands slowly unclenched as he dropped into a nearby chair, his fixed stare never wavering from the door.

"What the devil is he up to now!" barked the King. The last thing he needed was an added distraction. Alyxandyr never lost the scowl on his face while listening to his son recount Cooper's words.

"I don't know, Father, but he did seem genuine when he revealed that information to me," finished Danyl.

"He wants us to know he was sent here to kill us and by the same token he wants us to free then arm him so he can help? I don't like that at all," stated Styph, gathering his weapons together to return to the fight on the plains. His father, Zada and the others would have to make that decision, but he could not help but insert his thoughts before he rejoined his comrades. The crown prince was not about to battle death and worse only to find the leaders murdered from within the walls. He stopped at the bottom of the staircase and looked up first at his father then at Zada before disappearing around the corner. The Herkah's eyes lingered for a few moments where the prince had just stood. It would be a perfect coup for Mahn to slay them within the protection of the city's walls while their warriors died outside of them. What Styph overlooked was the fact that Cooper, as blameworthy as he was, had had no choice from the moment Mahn arrived at his gate.

"Styph is right, Alyxandyr, but Cooper has lost much and, like us, stands to lose more," Zada said.

"Are you suggesting we take such a chance and free him?" asked the King, unsure why the Herkah of all those gathered held any compassion for him. After all, Cooper had made it a point to hunt the nomads in an almost sporting-like fashion, and she could be excused for wanting him dead. There had been many times he himself had wished that fate on the king.

"I'm saying that Cooper has not been tainted by any demon and is therefore making his own choices."

"One more sword being wielded will not turn this tide," he said, quietly watching more and more of their people fall lifeless from their saddles as they valiantly fought against the enemy.

"Perhaps he is not meant to take his place on the field, for fate has always set forth strange assignments."

"Do you think it is fate that will have you die from his weapon?"

"There is a reason for everything, Alyxandyr. I do not think he will slay me, not yet anyway. You forget that Cooper's only motive to ally himself with us is to resume the life he once led and if that means standing by my side then he will tolerate that." Zada was sure of her words even though the King's suspicions were clearly obvious.

"For now."

"Yes, for now. You disregard one very crucial fact, Alyxandyr," she said softly. "You can put many safeguards into a situation, but there is always something you cannot foresee, therefore you can never control everything. Mahn knew what kind of person Cooper was, but what he couldn't predict was how someone as uncaring and greedy as Cooper could develop a conscience, as thin as the meaning of that word is in his case."

"You think he has his own peculiar destiny linked up with ours."

"I do."

Alyxandyr didn't want to be bothered with Cooper right now. The fierce clashes occurring below them had resulted in many senseless deaths on both sides. Such a waste of life greatly disturbed the elven king. Zada had every right to insist on an increase in guards around the King yet the Herkah gave no such indication. The elven king studied her strained features looking for any evidence of fear or doubt but saw nothing more than certainty reflected there. They had trusted her counsel from the moment she came to the city and there was no reason not to do so now. After quickly conferring with Clare and Gard, Alyxandyr reluctantly ordered his release. Cooper would be allowed his freedom with the stipulation he would be slain immediately and without question if he made even the most innocent of false movements.

"Zada...have you sensed the elven power yet?" he asked after several long moments. The elf king's tired expression appealed to her for any measure of hope.

"It is nearer than you think," she replied, knowing full well what was going through his mind. The same thought haunted his son, the bearer of the Green Might who stood beside his father. She glanced over at Danyl, who reddened with guilt as his eyes met hers for the briefest of moments.

"Do you suppose it could be conjured up to help us?" he asked, unaware that Danyl had been trying to do just that since the moment he found out he housed it.

"It, like Cooper, has its own part in all of this too," she replied softly, offering Danyl a slight smile of encouragement. It did nothing to assuage his sense of helplessness, compelling him to avert his eyes from all those standing around him. Danyl's father's next words stabbed at his heart and all he could do was grip the balustrade tightly and squeeze his eyes shut.

"We could sure use it about now." He spoke so quietly they could barely hear him but the tone in his voice grieved for the dead and dying that littered the snow-covered plains amid puddles of red blood. The King knew the horror would not only continue but would worsen until the Source and the Green Might were wielded by their respective bearers and propelled them to their final outcome.

Alyxandyr was convinced the Source and the elven magic were opposites and would be brandished against each other until only one bearer remained standing. He wanted to gain as much edge in the conflict at hand as he could before that happened yet that did not seem to be happening on the plains. It certainly wasn't due to the lack of courageous actions by the warriors battling for their future. What did he really know about Ramira? He did not know her well enough to assign any confidence in her and assumed that Mahn would be victorious in taking the Source away from her. He kept these thoughts to himself because to air them would only cause pain and resentment, especially with his son who loved Ramira very much.

Alyxandyr looked upon Danyl's face and saw a great weight within it that seemed to spread out to his shoulders and down through his body. It suddenly occurred to him that the heaviness that forced his body to stoop was not just about the loss of the girl but of something else. He looked into Danyl's eyes and saw they had changed almost as if he were being consumed by a thing not of this world. He was about to speak when he noticed his eyes had lost their whites and nearly pulsed with an emerald light, and it was then the King, standing there shocked and speechless, understood. Zada saw the same thing but did not register the same astonishment. She felt a sense of awe at what was taking place beside her. She and Danyl knew the truth yet had kept this extremely vital piece of information from them, all for reasons the King was about to demand.

Danyl felt a sudden surge of power as it reacted to something on the field, and looked toward Mahn. The black power incited his own and it began to burn through his veins, scorching muscle, sinew, bone and blood. It raced to his eyes, enveloping everything in an emerald mist then slowly cooled until it felt like ice in his veins. He shivered beneath its touch then grimaced with disgust as Mahn's voice filled his mind, his tone deep and mocking.

Do not fret for her, for she is nothing short of my kin.

You lie!

Think about it, bearer, for how else could she survive fighting the Vox and the other demons?

You will not convince me, Mahn.

Do you know what the Source actually is? It is all things dark and horrible compressed into a force that will only perpetuate all things terrible.

That is what you are.

And what she is.

No.

Her memories were so tainted by her evil acts her mind had to suppress them or go mad.

So you say.

Break some more of the beads and find out for yourself...

Mahn released him from his mental hold and as Danyl glanced over at Zada, he could see she had not been privy to their conversation. She had, however, sensed the communication with him. Mahn knew who bore the Green Might. Did he do so to toy with him or was Mahn worried that Danyl and his power could overwhelm him? Was he therefore planting seeds of doubt and despair into his mind to hinder such an encounter? Perhaps Mahn thought Danyl to be weak and preyed on that very flaw to gain an edge over him? He felt the fire burn brighter and more intensely in response to the echoes of his words but somehow they made sense even if he chose not to believe them. Mahn knew about the bracelet...what exactly happened after breaking the beads? Did those actions send a signal to Mahn? Had he somehow planted that trinket for that specific purpose?

"Danyl…" Zada began to speak, but he held up his hand to both her and his father who had joined them.

"He knows, Zada, and now, Father, so do you. I house the Green Might and no, I cannot wield it right now."

"Your eyes have not yet changed, Danyl," Zada reminded him, the astonishment in her voice barely checked. "They appear just as they did the night you pulled Ramira from Mahn."

Danyl realized the power still thrummed within his veins and wondered why it did not seep away as it normally did. He then raised his hand in front of his face, concentrating on the flow of power as it began to course down his arm and into his fingers, the tingling and burning making his skin itch. The magic had firmly and formally manifested itself to his flesh and bones. The elf determined it would soon be time to use it in a way that frightened him, for he would have to face the Source and Ramira. Would he be able to harm her knowing full well it meant destroying Mahn? He needed to find some answers.

"Why would he contact me, Zada?"

"Intimidation, I assume."

"It's not going to work," he replied, the depth of his commitment shining from within his eyes.

"Why didn't you tell me about this when you first learned you had the Green Might?" the King charged. He was very upset, wondering how differently things could be now if his son, his son of all people, had wielded the magic. He glanced over at a motionless and ever-present Lance, the captain watching from a short distance away. He had known about Ramira from the start and of several other "secrets," therefore it wouldn't surprise him if he had been privy to this one, too.

"We didn't mention anything to anyone because we believed the fewer who knew about it the more of a surprise it would be." Some "surprise": the evil already knew he housed it. "And obviously due to my inability to use it."

"Is that changing now?" snapped Alyxandyr.

"Yes. Father? I apologize for not informing you, but that was a decision we thought would be the best one."

"I do not agree but I would appreciate being informed of any other bit of information that you might have." The statement was more of a chance for them to confess, but neither Zada nor Danyl had anything to add to the conversation.

They stood together, the winter chill making them shiver, the furious battle sending an icy touch into their hearts. The afternoon sun cast long shadows, turning the macabre scene before them even more ghastly. The wind blowing from the west brought the cries of dying men. It was redolent with the smell of death that washed over those standing on the parapets as they witnessed the continuing carnage below. Alyxandyr ordered replacements for the men on the plains so they could eat and rest for a while. A fresh group of fighters rode out from the city, but instead of replacing their exhausted comrades, they fought by their sides. Sensing their weariness, the black plague had surged forward, pressing hard to push the allies farther and farther toward the walls. They pushed forward but the valiant efforts of the allies kept the enemy from gaining too much ground.

Finally the sun began to set and the combat began to diminish. Alyxandyr sent out fresh forces to patrol the area around the city while those that had fought long and hard came in for food, rest and attention for their wounds. He, Clare and Zada listened to their reports and the approximate numbers that had fallen during the battles, realizing the roughly two hundred that had perished would not be easily replaced. The elven king watched the stragglers enter beneath the gates, their heroic efforts to destroy the enemy coming at a high price. They had killed many but the sheer number of foes replacing their dead made it seem as if none had perished. If they continued to lose men at this rate, they would be in serious trouble within two or three days. The only thing that could both save and end their existence was the clash of the two powers.

Cooper heard the lock snap open and jumped to his feet as four Herkahs entered the room, jerking their chins for him to follow them. He had wholeheartedly agreed to the stipulations Alyxandyr had set forth and sighed with relief that he was at least going to be able to see what was transpiring outside of the city walls. He was led to the dining hall where many scrutinized him as he entered and seated himself at the end of the table. The Herkah guards planted themselves within a few feet of him, their unassuming stances belying their readiness.

"I appreciate your trust," he said, offering them a little bow.

"Trust has nothing to do with it, although I am surprised by your patron," the elven king said, his eyes warning him that any false move would lead to an unhealthy end.

"Who…" he began to ask, then locked eyes with Zada, Allad glaring at him from beside her. Although the Herkah guards stood at his shoulders,

Allad's gaze warned him he would reach his throat first if he made any move toward his mate or anyone else seated at the table.

Cooper could not hide his incredulity and nodded toward her, making sure he did not meet Allad's stare. Zada's mate was the best warrior in the land and, as a Herkah of high stature, he would certainly be welcome in Mahn's presence. Even now, after all of the fighting, there were few wounds on his body and he seemed as fresh and strong as ever, a fact impressing even Cooper. Nyk and Gard appeared a bit worse for wear but still capable of fighting nonetheless. The unflappable Seven moved about with ease though he had a head wound and bandages poking out from beneath both of the dwarf king's sleeves.

The meal was eaten in silence, the short time they shared together afterward spent more in contemplation than conversation. Everyone was very concerned as to what the next sunrise would bring. At what point would Mahn determine those from Bystyn had suffered enough before he ripped the Source from Ramira and completed his horrible task? Cooper looked from one to the other, and although they were quiet and pensive, none showed signs of giving up.

"There is a large contingent of Vox and Radir just south of the edge of the forest," Allad stated, accepting a small glass of Seven's concoction. "I'm not sure what they are planning but I do think we should find out."

"The perfect trap," said Mason, his steel gray eyes locking onto his brother. Cooper subtly flinched beneath his gaze, knowing full well that Mason would not think twice about killing him if the need arose. Mason was just as adept with a weapon as anyone else.

"Mahn would not risk so many Vox in one area without a reason, and that is incentive enough to hazard a look," replied Allad.

Cooper began to squirm in his seat and not because anyone was staring at him but in response to a vague yet familiar sensation creeping up inside of him. He could not quite pinpoint what it was only that it made him tense and uneasy, attributing it to the fact that he was amid so many of his enemies. He took a deep breath and ignored the feeling.

"I'd sleep better if you took more elves and dwarves than nomads, Allad, just in case it is a trap," suggested the elven king.

"I agree," said Seven. "Perhaps King Cooper might like to travel with you?"

"I spent a year with those miserable things," muttered Cooper. "I don't think another day will matter much." He kept his eyes averted to avoid anyone seeing the unpleasant thoughts running through his mind. The idea of being near those monsters again sent the bile up into his throat.

"I believe you should stay here," stated Styph. "That way one of us will have the pleasure of killing you when you finally act on your orders from Mahn." Styph's undisguised mistrust silenced the room. Cooper may have dined with them but that did not mean he was accepted.

"I have no orders, Prince Styph," he countered, glaring at the crown prince.

"That's enough," said the King, scowling at his son.

"We have a great deal to plan, Alyx," said Allad, rising from his chair. "And the sooner we start the better. Nyk?" The prince joined him and the three of them left the room. Alyssa, Seven and Clare followed not too long afterward, leaving Danyl, Mason, Alyxandyr and Cooper alone in the room.

Alyssa had been kept extremely busy, as she took control of the city making sure those within the walls were properly cared for. She took her responsibility seriously, discarding the silks for tunic and trousers and making her presence felt in every corner of the castle and city. She no longer fretted over trivial details, concentrating instead on the basic needs of several races. Alyssa, like her brothers, had been well schooled in the art of war, ruling and a host of other important duties, for the King had made sure any one of them could rule if something befell him.

"Mahn would like nothing more than for Allad to become one of the Vox," stated Cooper, staring into his goblet of wine.

"You believe it is an ambush, brother?" Mason asked him with a modicum of skepticism.

"Don't you?"

"Perhaps," replied the first advisor, scrutinizing his brother. Mason knew, as did Cooper, that he would have had no problem in gaining the throne, ruling Kepracarn far differently than his brother. Mason chose to extricate himself from his birthplace, instead ending up as the elven king's friend and counsel. Thinking back on his decision all those years ago, he wondered how altered their present predicament would be had he chosen to stay. His relations with the elves would have been warmer and Mason would certainly not have hunted the Herkahs. The first advisor realized he would have made a better king than Cooper but fate had determined his purpose lay in Bystyn.

"What will you do when this is all over, Cooper?" asked Alyxandyr.

"What indeed? If my city still stands and there are enough people left to return to it then I guess I'll be starting over, now won't I?"

"And if that is not what awaits you?"

Cooper had thought about that, too, but everything was out of his grasp until the final battle decided what alternatives he had, if any. His mind conjured up Antama and his lips pulled back into a snarl, for she had been the one to coerce him into following the stranger who turned out to be Mahn. He doubted he could have avoided the inevitable, but her alliance with the evil still made his stomach sour to this day. He knew she was out there somewhere on the plains and vowed he would find then tear her asunder piece by piece.

"Who do you hate so much to make your face contort with such loathing, brother?"

"Antama. I will not rest until my hands are around her throat."

"You may get your chance, Cooper." Mason's deep tones filled the silent room.

Yes, I will.

Zada handed Allad a glass of wine when he finally returned to their room later that evening, the concern for their predicament firmly etched into his hawkish face. They had noted a number of good changes in their companions. The Herkahs knew each and every one of them would step into their roles with a gritty resolve that would not easily crumble beneath adversity. Death and destruction awaited them yet they fought with a spirit that threatened to be literally torn from their bodies if they failed. They sat down in front of the fire, their arms around each other, absorbing the rare moment alone. Their souls drew strength and courage from each other as they realized this might be their last night together in this world. They let go of everything but each other as they stared into the fire. They rose after a while and sought solace in each other's special embrace, a scene that was repeated in Seven and Clare's room as well.

Danyl stood on the balcony, the cold night air not penetrating into him for the Green Might pulsed with an internal energy that kept him warm. He could feel it building and shifting within him and swore his breath was tinted green as he breathed evenly in and out. He felt strangely calm even though his heart ached for Ramira and all of those who would face the severe challenge in the days ahead. He closed his eyes and waited for the maze to reappear as it always did, tormenting him with the truth he could not understand.

It did not emerge this time, although he could hear the dripping echoing in the back of his mind and the dank smell permeating the corridor. Then another scent began to seep in. He could discern spices and unearthly flowers that bloomed only by the full moon and was quickly enveloped by the fragrance, a perfume he knew all too well. He smiled at the memory. She was with him just as he was with her, and nothing was going to separate them, not now or ever. The magic swelled briefly, as if confirming his thoughts, offering the prince some measure of comfort. For a fleeting moment they were both in accord.

The Herkah guards left the barracks and headed toward the castle to relieve the pair guarding Cooper's chamber. They walked along the path between the barracks and the residence, the unusual quiet making them hesitate. There were no lights shining from the windows overlooking the walkway. There should have been sentries posted around the building yet passed by no one. They stared ahead at the archway looming darkly, ominously before them. Where were the torches and lamps? The night was utterly silent. A movement to their right caught their attention, a rustling to their left made them stop in their tracks. Scrawny trees and bushes growing in beds against the gray walls, their roots hidden beneath the snow, could barely hide a bird let alone a person. But there was someone here. The Herkahs could sense it. They withdrew their weapons and spun around until their backs touched. As one they slowly turned looking for the source of danger. They exhaled in unison, their breath creating a ring around their heads. The seconds ticked by, each stroke verifying the dreaded idea forming in their minds.

"Kee-yat," one of the nomads swore under his breath, the fear worming its way into his wildly beating heart.

A shadow detached itself from the black recesses of two adjoining walls and penetrated into his chest. He briefly flailed his arms and legs at the impact, his swords clanging loudly to the flagstone ground. It happened so quickly that he didn't even have time to scream. His comrade fared no better, the strangled cry remaining firmly lodged in his throat. He fell in a heap to the ground a moment after the other nomad. The eerie shape reappeared and knelt between the two bodies, one gloved hand placed around their necks. The form began to rise, pulling the Herkahs' limp bodies up with it. It held them aloft as if they were no heavier than a feather hissing with satisfaction. It carried the Herkahs over to the dark recess beneath the archway where two muffled shrieks escaped into the night. One of the nomads resumed his trek into the castle.

He entered through the heavy doors, the occupied elves barely acknowledging him. The nomad/demon walked down the long corridor toward the nomads standing watch in front of Cooper's room. He offered them a curt nod.

"Where is Ramsat?" asked one of the Herkah's guards. "You know better than to walk this place alone."

"He was momentarily detained."

"Stay here," he ordered Tutmas. "I'll see what's keeping Ramsat."

The Herkah guard moved a few steps away from the lone nomad and rested his hands on his knives. The Herkah/demon remained motionless and calm. The minutes began to accumulate yet neither Ramsat nor the other nomad returned. Suspicion began to seep into the guard's mind. They should have been back by now. He glanced at his relaxed friend then back up the hallway.

"Zada will have to be informed about this," he said.

"She will," it replied, the faint wheezing barely perceptible.

The hairs on the back of Tutmas' neck stirred and the first bead of sweat slowly trickled down the side of his face. He said a little prayer, swallowed hard and pulled out his knives. He opened his mouth to shout a warning but the Vox was upon him before a single syllable could escape his throat.

Cooper shifted in his bed, that peculiar crawling sensation keeping him awake. He tossed and turned several times, scratching at the imaginary itch that would not go away. Frustrated, he rose and poured himself a glass of wine, looking around the room for the annoying insects invading his slumber. His tired mind tried to tell him something but the only thing he wanted to do was lay his head on the pillow and close his eyes.

"I thought those damn elves would at least be able to keep the vermin out," he muttered with distaste, then drained his goblet and headed back to bed to a fitful sleep.

-10-

Karolauren looked up as the sound of books toppling from somewhere in the back of the library caught his attention. He exhaled, cursing at the carelessness of the scribe who had placed them on the shelf, and rose to investigate the sound. He walked past row after row of bookcases and saw nothing and was beginning to think he had imagined the noise when he noticed the fallen stack at the far end of the last row. Still muttering he headed for them. He squatted painfully beside the fallen clutter to pick them up when he caught a movement out of the corner of his eyes. The ancient elf was too slow to keep the blades from nearly severing his head from his shoulders. The shadow stood darkly over the body, the knives slick with the historian's blood as it dripped onto the stone floor. The dark shape followed the hall to the back of the library, where it forced open the massive doors, grabbing a torch before entering the room. It scanned the chamber then froze as it saw the fragile glass bottle carefully tucked on the shelf. The silhouette grabbed the queen's blood then slipped from the historian's realm.

A silence descended upon the chamber as if the histories mourned the loss of the one who had so lovingly cared for them. Karolauren's blood seeped away from his body, following the grooves in between the stones until it reached the fallen pile of books. It then wended around them as if the dead elf embraced his treasures for the last time, touching that which had driven his spirit for so many years. His fingers twitched once then the sparkle in his blue eyes finally went out.

Allad and Nyk rode off with their men heading toward the Vox; Styph and Gard led a large contingent back to the west while Seven headed back south to contend with the enemy that massed near the Ahltyn. Danyl had ordered Lance to accompany Gard and his brother, but the captain was reluctant to take up a position between the two princes. Lance hesitated for the command Danyl gave him went completely against everything he had been trained to do. It was hard for Danyl to explain to Lance that the magic surging within him effectively made Lance's capabilities obsolete.

"Danyl," his tone bordered on defiance, "my place is beside you."

"I know, my friend, but you must trust me and go with them."

Lance looked into Danyl's eyes carefully, studying the secret they strove to keep. The captain's demeanor veiled the vast amounts of information he processed in his mind, and right now his reasoning told him something that saddened him more than anything else. His thought centered on his lifelong friend and the burden that weighed down upon his shoulders, an onus he could not help him with. It made perfect sense: Ramira housed the darkness while he harbored the elven magic.

"My lord has a new captain to protect him," he said after a long pause.

"There will always be only one captain, Lance." Danyl placed his hand on his friend's shoulder, nodding for him to join the princes. The elf disappeared after a few seconds, linking up with his new charges as they headed out the gates.

Cooper, still plagued by that nagging feeling, remained in the castle with Zada and Alyssa, the Herkah guard watching his every move. This annoyed Cooper, for he was not a threat to any of them, at least under these circumstances. He checked his tongue, however, fearful of being locked up again. He cast a sly glance over at the unsuspecting princess, the thoughts he had had about her surfacing again until Zada broke into his lustful reverie.

"I would think that would be the least of your worries," she reprimanded him.

"What...?" he stuttered, as the Herkah's intense stare locked onto him like some razor sharp steel trap. Alyssa looked over at them but Cooper had by that time hidden his lecherous expression. Now is not the time to fantasize about the elf princess, he sharply chided himself, vowing to restrain his hunger.

"What did he do?" demanded Alyssa, the fire in her eyes making the King smile. Her spirited energy was nearly as exciting as her beauty.

"You should be more careful or find yourself back in your chambers," the nomad stated, her words laced with a sharp warning.

"Why did you stick up for me?"

"I believe we all have a part to play in this, Cooper."

"You should be consumed with hatred for me."

"'Hatred' is a very strong emotion, Cooper. It serves no real purpose."

"It's kept me going all these years," he muttered under his breath.

"Why do you hunt us?"

There were many reasons and there were none at the same time. Herkahs were the ultimate prey: evasive, perilous and extremely deadly. The pursuit made him feel alive. Victory sent a thrill down to his very core. He thrived on that excitement, especially considering finding his quarry was so incredibly difficult. Cooper glanced over at Zada. She sat patiently awaiting his response, curiosity the only expression on her face. He looked down at his fidgety hands. They had killed three Herkahs…members of this woman's tribe. She had every right to reach out and slice his throat open. She would be doing him a great favor about now.

"If we survive and I return to rule Kepracarn that will change, Zada." I'll amuse myself with the people in the far southwest instead.

"I will hold you to that, Cooper."

The King inclined his head and smiled.

Alyxandyr had taken up his position on the battlements, watching the impending battle with Danyl. He looked over at his son and realized how much he, of all of his children, resembled his mother. He remembered that although she never favored one child over another she did regard Danyl with something he could never identify. The Queen had been a direct descendant from the first king and he deduced he had received the Green Might through her. She probably knew all along. She never mentioned anything to him either and apparently believed, as Danyl and Zada did, the fewer who knew the better. Either that or the knowledge would somehow change Danyl, leaving him confused or arrogant and therefore incapable of wielding it if and when the time came. He spotted Allad and Nyk heading north and silently wished them well, his anxiety for their welfare chiseled into his face. What they rode off to face was almost as perilous as Mahn. Alyxandyr felt a knot form in his midsection and it took all of his will not to shout out for them to turn back. He had to believe, just as they did, that the only way to fulfill their destinies was to face the unknown with courage and determination. There was nothing he or anyone else could do or say to stop Allad and Nyk from riding toward the Vox.

Nyk and Allad rode side by side as they made their way to the dark line of trees a mile to the northwest. They and their men were quiet, their minds reviewing what they could and could not do once they confronted the vicious demons hovering like malevolent shades beneath the skeletal shadows of the forest. They could sense them even from this distance and the anticipation grew into apprehension with every hoof beat that brought them closer. Zada had provided them each with a poisoned blade, but that did not ease the tension in their chests. They faced a foe resembling the only Herkah in the group, the very one all of them had grown to respect and admire.

Nyk glanced over at his friend remembering the first time they had met and how Allad had saved his life and the souls of his men out on the Broken Plain. He had become a different person while recovering in the Herkah camp; Allad's and Zada's guidance had opened his eyes to himself. He understood and highly regarded the Herkahs and a part of him wished he could roam the Great White Desert with them. He had yet to repay Allad and vowed to protect the nomad with his life. Allad turned his head and met the prince's gaze, his features calm and sure. They urged their horses to run closer together and reached out toward one another, grasping each other's hand. The contact sent a surge of energy from one to the other and to their men riding behind them. Killing the Vox would not be an easy task and many that now rode toward the fiends would not return. They reined in their horses about a hundred yards from the knot of evil and studied their enemy. The Vox tarried, speaking amongst each other and occasionally pointing at the intruders. Allad narrowed his eyes at the overt communication then scanned the area around them for a trap.

"Something over there is of far greater interest than us and I, for one, can't think of a single thing of what it could be," stated the prince.

"Neither can I, Nyk."

They took their time but the group of demons finally decided the newcomers were worth a moment of their time and turned their dead stares towards the horsemen, chiefly Allad. He felt a chill run up his spine and knew this was indeed an ambush. They would have to retreat and rethink their strategy. The Vox had other plans and immediately headed for the elves and the lone Herkah, mounting their demon steeds in the blink of an eye and racing toward the allies. They wanted Allad and would settle for the prince.

Nyk ordered an instantaneous retreat and as one they swung around and kicked their horses into high gear, but the demon steeds were well rested. Spurred on without the use of whips, the animals quickly caught up to them before they had traveled halfway back to Bystyn. They knew they would soon be overtaken but hoped they could get close enough to the city where reinforcements might come to their aid. The Vox, however, had other plans, fanning out and around them to cut off their evacuation. With Bystyn looming up before them, the noose was set and their way to safety completely cut off, forcing them to rein in their terrified mounts.

They jumped off their horses, Nyk barking orders at his men as they formed a tight circle facing outward. The Vox advanced slowly, deliberately allowing the prince a few precious moments to gauge his men. Pride flooded his features as his men stood tall and resolute against the evil that should have made them cower. They drew their weapons, bracing for the horror that was about to descend upon them, yet none flinched as the demons advanced. The elves cut and slashed at the demons, wounding the bodies but not the monsters thriving within. The Vox, in turn, hacked and killed their way through them, their only goal to get to Allad. Three Vox stepped over the bodies of nearly twice their number of highly skilled elves, disregarding the three Nyk and Allad had slain. Allad managed a look of praise for the elf prince as he fought the demons, combating the fiends as if he had been born a Herkah. The last of the elves fell around them and Nyk and Allad were the sole survivors. The Vox did not immediately set upon them, standing around and staring at them for several long moments instead. The elf and the Herkah pressed their backs against each other and pulled out the small knives Zada had given them with one hand and clutched their swords in the other. They were prepared to deny the Vox and Mahn two extremely desirable bodies.

"Sweet mercy!" whispered Alyxandyr, his white knuckles clinging to the edge of the parapets. His son and Allad were on the brink of their mortal lives, the black chasm on which they teetered crumbling beneath their feet. The King could not breathe or move, so transfixed was he by the distressing sight.

"We should have listened to Cooper," stated Mason, watching the carnage with the King.

"They wanted Allad all along," whispered Danyl. He knew that Allad and Zada would be as much of a jewel in his crown as Ramira was, and there was room for one more gem: himself.

They watched as Styph rallied his men, riding hard to get to his brother and the nomad. Those watching on the battlements screamed for them to stop, for they too would meet the same fate once they arrived. Styph could not hear them nor did they look up at the tower for the flag ordering them to pull back. The King looked over at Danyl, his horrified gaze beseeching his son to do something to help. Losing Allad and Nyk would be a terrible blow to the allies, adding Styph to that list would be even worse.

Danyl pleaded with the power, begging it to rise up so he could help his brother and the others, but it refused to heed his appeals. The elf felt the bile of hatred for it rise in his throat, leaving him feeling powerless and to some extent foolish. He had the power but not the resolve to brandish it and that was more painful than watching the carnage near the trees.

Zada and Clare had not seen the historian all morning and decided to pay him a quick visit. They entered the vast chamber and found it empty and cold, the eerie silence broken only by the pages of an open book flapping near the open window. Clare closed the book. Karolauren was an old man and would hardly allow the cold winter wind to penetrate the library. They called out his name several times, their echoing voices filled with uneasiness.

The two women unsheathed their blades and began to search the library. They guarded each other's backs as they made their way past the rows of bookcases, nervously licking their lips and gripping their hilts tightly. They squared around toward a noise in the front of the room, remaining immobile for several long moments before resuming their search. They tread beyond a row of shelves and stopped, inhaling sharply at the ancient elf crumpled in a bloody heap amongst a pile of scattered books. They could not believe anyone would harm the old elf, redoubling their vigilance against the danger that could possibly still be lurking in the library. Clare kept watch as Zada crouched beside the historian, pushing back the blood-soaked strands of white then flinching at what she saw.

"Zada?"

"The strokes are from a Herkah blade." She could barely speak above a whisper, for none of the nomads would ever do something like this.

"But..." she protested.

"I know, Clare. There is a Vox in the castle and we have to find it." Zada caressed Karolauren's lifeless cheek then closed his eyes, whispering a Herkah prayer to him before rising to her feet.

They left Karolauren where he had fallen and headed back out into the hallway, their minds benumbed with the dreaded information, their hearts grieving for the gentle soul that lay dead behind them. They emerged into the main entrance, Clare calling over one of the elven guards to inform them what they had discovered. Zada, meanwhile, scribbled a note to the King before sealing it and ordering the elf to take it to the King without delay.

"How many Herkahs have access to the castle, Zada?"

"There were six, Clare. Allad, myself and the four guards that are assigned to Cooper."

"One of the guards..."

"So it seems. Do we wait, or do we lure them down here?"

"I take it you are as capable with those blades as Allad?" asked Clare without any hint of disrespect, her face set and her hands firmly clasping her weapon.

"I am not as fragile as some suppose."

"That thought never crossed my mind, Zada."

"We'll give Alyxandyr a few minutes then we go upstairs…" Zada began then spotted Cricket and Anci heading for the stairs, Cooper and his escort walking toward them from the opposite direction. The girls took one look at their faces and froze and only Clare's urging sent them running downstairs and out the door as the five men began to make their way down. Zada studied each of the nomads very carefully as they approached, ignoring Cooper's confusion at seeing the two armed and charged women. It occurred to Zada that it was highly doubtful only one of the Herkah guards would be a Vox. Initially, perhaps, that was true, but it would be a simple thing for one to take the remaining three bodies. If that were the case then they were in very dire straits indeed, for two women, a handful of elves and Cooper were no match for them, regardless of their skills. She glanced at the King who finally realized what that odd feeling was and he, much to his credit, kept calm and very alert. His complacency within Alyxandyr's protection did not stem the feeling but had dulled his awareness of its origin. The result of his ignorance now threatened them all. Cooper silently blasted his stupidity, hoping they would all emerge unscathed from this desperate predicament.

Zada barked out several words in the Herkah tongue and watched all four react without stopping. They continued their approach, their fixed stares firmly focused on her. Clare heard her curse under her breath and the dwarf queen realized all four of the Herkahs were possessed by demons.

"Sweet mercy," she muttered under her breath, as death in four forms advanced upon them. Clare took a deep breath to help steel her resolve, for flight was not an option. Clare hoped that Zada's message would reach Alyxandyr in time for help to arrive. Every second counted. Staying alive would be a monumental task at the very least.

The elf and the nomad brought the blades to their throats, the demons only a dozen paces away from them. Their time, it seemed, was nearly through. Their backs touched and they shared a peculiar comfort from that contact. Facing certain death together made the inevitable less lonely and frightening. They were both proud and honored to die together.

"I am a better man for having known you and your people," said Allad, his voice clear and strong as he faced his last moments on earth.

"As I am, Allad," replied Nyk. The elf could feel Allad's muscles bunching against his back, the heat from his body felt even through the heavy woolen tunic. They lightly bumped skulls and pressed the knives into their throats. They strained to break the skin on their necks, craving nothing more than to feel their blood pour down their chests. They dropped their swords, adding a second hand to the hilt with the same result.

"Nyk!"

"Allad…why…?" The elf could barely breathe, for although the blade did not bite into his flesh, the pressure he applied to the knife risked suffocating him. He and the nomad sank every ounce of strength into their mortal task but the edge refused to budge. The more energy they applied to their weapons the more resistance they encountered. Panic began to take hold of them as the Vox loomed over their prone forms, their bodies blotting out the ineffectual sun.

Allad faced his worst nightmare with uncertainty, his only way out of this terrible predicament impeded by the will of his enemy. He was afraid for those whom he loved and who would be subjected to his unwilling participation in the evil's plans. He sensed the frosty haft in his cold hand, his fingers numbed by the air and his foreboding. The Herkah lord spurned the idea of just sitting here waiting for the Vox to take him and the elf.

"Nyk?"

"Yes?"

"We need another strategy."

"I'm open to ideas," he panted.

"What if we…"

Allad never finished his sentence. Two of the Vox yanked them to their feet and grabbed the wrists holding Zada's knives, squeezing them until the daggers fell from their lifeless fingers. Allad and Nyk tried to bring up their other weapons but the third Vox quickly disarmed them. The Vox held their prizes up in the air and began to immerse themselves into the elf and the Herkah.

Allad felt the icy breath envelope him, the horrible hissing streaming into his ears and permeating his mind. He stared at the face distorted by the evil parasite living within, recognizing the nomad named Bahnal who had been lost two years ago. Bahnal's hand reached up to his face, grabbing Allad's locked jaw with an iron grip and forcing his mouth open. The nomad began to breathe heavily, loathing the creature that was about to violate him in the worst possible way. The Vox turned toward one side, allowing Allad to see what was happening to Nyk. The elf was in the midst of being overrun by the other Vox, his distended features brimming with repugnance and agony as the Vox poured itself into him. The tendons and ligaments around his face and neck nearly burst through his skin; tears streamed from his wide eyes as the repulsive monster oozed into him.

The Vox' subjugated features replaced the elf's tormented countenance. Allad flinched as the Vox closed the distance between them and opened his mouth, helplessly watching as the Vox vomited his essence toward him. The sickly yellow haze appeared as polished as a finely honed blade one moment then flared like fire the next. It flowed into his mouth and down his throat, slicing and searing everything in its path. Allad jerked and twitched, gagging on the foul taste as it spread outward from his torso to his limbs. It pierced his organs and burrowed into his muscles then seized the core of his being. It settled upon everything except his mind like some loathsome blanket composed of rotting flesh and the dankness found in long forgotten tombs. The malignancy began to swell up into his head, rounding up his spirit and slamming it against the back of his skull. The appalling mist formed a netting around his soul, keeping it imprisoned but permitting it to witness the horrors it would unleash. Allad's spirit would not cede quite so easily. He rose up and retaliated against the Vox with such intensity the demon lost control of his soul. Allad's will was greater than the Vox' and he began to drive the demon from his body. The loathsome monster had never encountered such determination before and only Mahn's interference kept Allad from prevailing. The Herkah had no choice but to relent beneath the overpowering black might battering him from without. Allad ceased his uprising and returned to his prison, a single tear running down his once proud face.

Styph watched with dread as Allad and Nyk rose amongst the other demons gathered around them. They were too late to help: to attempt a rescue now would mean adding their bodies to that terrible group. He gestured for them to break off the attack and head back to the fighting, his heart and mind numbed by the loss of his brother and the nomad. His eyes scoured the parapets, and to his dismay, he saw his father staring at what Styph rode away from. Danyl's unmoving form stood near the King. Where was that damn elven magic? It could have saved them! It could save them all!

Styph felt the fury within and spurred his mount on, needing to release that frustration in the most useful sort of way. He neared a cluster of enemies, raised his sword high into the cloudless air and roared with rage, his men following suit as they thrust themselves into their midst and hacked at their foe. Their ferocity became infectious and soon the outnumbered allies began to push back Mahn's army; those who refused to give up ground were slain where they stood. Each of the races shouted their own particular war cries, sharing the words until elf praised Herkah and dwarf celebrated the Khadry. The words drifted back and forth across the bloody and mud-covered snow then flowed back to the city walls, where those upon the battlements heard them. They called back down to them, encouraging them with shouts and raised fists. The momentum shifted and the allies, filled with a renewed sense of strength and courage, rallied against the dark force that threatened their very existence.

Alyxandyr's heart stopped beating in his chest as the hated demons took his son and Allad. Though his mouth was partially open, the King could not breathe nor blink his eyes so transfixed was he on the horrifying scene on the plain. He finally managed to glare at Danyl as if their deaths were somehow his fault, but the angry helplessness he reflected stilled his slowly recovering tongue. He snapped his attention back to the Vox glowering with hatred as they disappeared into the trees, their indifference ridiculing those that watched. He seemed riveted by the awful memory, initially ignoring the soldier who desperately sought his attention. The elf had to physically rip him from his trance.

"My lord!" shouted the messenger as he tugged on the King's cloak while hurriedly pressing the note into the King's hand. Danyl watched his father's face as he read it. The King turned pale and barked several orders, nearly flying down the stairs, a contingent of Herkahs and elves right on his heels. He shoved his anguish into the back of his mind as this new and greater danger took precedence. He grabbed Danyl by the arm as he began his descent, the group quickly jumping onto waiting horses and racing up the main avenue to the castle. People scurried away from the speeding group, watching with trepidation as their king accelerated up the avenue cloaks parallel to the ground. The Vox had taken his son and friend but they would not have Zada and Clare. They rode at full speed, scattering soldiers and citizens alike.

A half dozen of the royal guards formed a protective circle around Clare and Zada as the Herkah/demons advanced upon them. The nomad watched as Cooper, forgotten by the demons, slipped down the hall and out of their sight.

He had, apparently, succeeded in executing Mahn's assignment and left them to their fates. Her eyes lingered for a moment at the spot where he had disappeared before focusing on the urgency at hand.

"Coward," hissed Clare, as she surged forward and joined the elven guard in combat.

The Vox were fierce fighters, their skills borrowed by the bodies and souls of those they occupied. Clare's expertise and determination, the elven guards resolve and Zada's own abilities, however, did not allow for an easy victory for the Vox. The elves managed to kill one, as did Clare, but the cost had been all but one of the guard, and the injuries Clare had sustained were beginning to sap her strength. The last elf went down, leaving two unharmed Vox facing one injured and one tired woman. The odds were against them, and as each Vox rushed forward to one of the women, a blur materialized from behind the one seeking Clare. The unsuspecting demon fell to the ground a second or two after his head, his companion hissing with hatred at Cooper and his blood-stained sword. The King did not shrink back, raising his weapon in defiance, the cold determination blazing from his eyes sending a shiver up even Zada's' spine. The Vox, however, would deal with him later, for his main quarry was the injured and worn Herkah standing a few paces away.

It lunged at her then parried the strike Cooper swung at him. The King attacked several times and only a ringing blow to the head dazed him long enough for the Vox to concentrate on his prey. It surged forward, overwhelming the Herkah with lightening fast strokes that Zada managed to ward off while retreating back one step at a time. Clare endeavored to rise and help her friend but her wounds betrayed her, stealing what little energy she had left. All she could do was watch in horror as the Vox systematically overpowered Zada, finally succeeding in pinning her against the wall next to the massive doors of the castle.

"Cooper!" she shrieked at the King as he labored to his feet.

He managed to gain his feet but swayed unsteadily as he took a step in Zada's direction. He wanted nothing more than to slay the demon. He tried to distract the Vox using any method his impaired body and mind allowed, including shouting and cursing at it. It ignored him, the prize seconds away from being in his possession. Cooper lurched forward and fell painfully onto his knees. He staggered to his feet, shaking his head to keep the room from spinning. He dashed toward the Vox, slipping on the bloody floor and falling in a heap upon a dead elf, panting for air and fighting the urge to retch. Can't...let it...have her! His mind demanded that his body rise and defend Zada, but it was not to be.

"Zada!" he shouted, his blood-laced spittle spraying the dead around him.

The Vox brought its dagger up just as the King and the others burst through the entrance, crushing both combatants between the door and the wall. The heavy oak portal hid what transpired behind it, the ensuing silence deafening to those who waited for it to close. They could do nothing but stare in dread at the gruesome scene before them. Clare sat bloody and crumpled on the ground amid the bodies of the elves and three Herkahs, while Cooper, sword in hand, swayed over her. Their eyes were glued to the closing door, the creaking noise it made while closing grating their nerves. The door closed with a thud, revealing Zada, her back to them, and the Vox up against the wall, locked in a hideous embrace. The Vox stared down at her, their hands hidden between their bodies. Zada stepped back slowly, haltingly her rigid body quivering. The demon did not move, immobilized by the dagger buried deep in its heart.

Zada shuddered with revulsion as the damned darkness came to claim her soul. Her strength nearly gone, she reached into her tunic to retrieve the only thing that would save them from that terrible fate. The message she had sent the elven king would not bring help in time, and neither Clare nor Cooper was physically able to come to her rescue. They had all fought valiantly, even the king, and she rued the fact that they too would be consumed by this evil. She had to use the small blade on the Vox to avert that disaster. The Vox was upon her and she shivered as the evil permeating it gushed over her. It filled her nose and throat with such foulness she began to gag. It seeped down into her stomach then radiated into every fiber of her being, the need to spew out the abominable sensation a priority. The Vox was not yet ready to inhabit her, for it wanted to inflict her spirit with one final blow. It revealed what had befallen Allad and Nyk. She converted the anguish lifting up from her soul into a weapon the Vox had not anticipated. She drew strength and courage from her loss, determined not to spend an eternity with Allad in a place devoid of love. She gritted her teeth, her face contorted with revenge as she centered her hatred and self-preservation into the blade, thrusting it half way into the Vox' chest. The demon grabbed her by the throat and began to squeeze the life out of her. Her eyes watered and her skin started to turn blue as she struggled to breathe. She began to lose consciousness until the sudden impact of something slamming against her back pushed her against the demon. The impact plunged the knife almost through the Vox' body.

"Zada?" Clare called out to her, her voice shaking from fear for the nomad and the effects of the fighting.

"No!" Cooper held his hand up as the elven king began to move toward her. "We have to make sure she has not been affected by the demon!"

Danyl understood Cooper's fears but ignored him and walked up to Zada. He lifted her chin with his fingers, feeling the heat and sweat of her exertions while watching her take deep and painful breaths. Did the Vox poison her before she killed him?

"I know…what they did to…Nyk and Allad." Her voice was barely audible. "It showed me…for spite…" Tears flowed down her cheeks, mingling with the blood and perspiration as she collapsed against him. He collected her in his arms and carried her to a chair while the King, his grief as fresh as hers, went over to the dwarf queen.

"How are you faring, Clare?" he asked, squatting down next to her to check the gashes on her arm and along her midsection.

"I will heal but…" Her eyes traveled over to Zada, for they did not know of Karolauren's fate.

"But what?" asked Danyl, the unspoken knowledge leaving him with a hollow feeling in his chest. What else did the Vox do?

"They killed Karolauren," Clare said, as she ignored the pain throbbing from her wounds.

"They did what?" Alyxandyr's eyes went wide with disbelief as the news sank in.

"We found him…in the library…that's how we knew the Vox were in the castle."

"You will have to tell the others about Nyk and Allad," Cooper said. His hand pressed against the deep cut on his forehead as he tried to stem both the bleeding and the nausea. His wounds were insignificant compared to the dilemma they were in.

"Yes, I know," said the King. "Danyl, pass on the news." They had lost Allad and Nyk, and Zada narrowly escaped that same terrible fate. Cooper and Clare survived yet could just as easily have become members of that dark brotherhood, too, leaving Alyxandyr unsure of what to expect next. He looked over at Cooper; the King's face smeared with blood, his eyes devoid of their trademark arrogance. Mahn had demeaned him in so many ways yet he had risen above that humiliation with noble acts even he did not know he possessed. Cooper exhaled slowly, momentarily closing his eyes in relief as Zada regained her composure. Alyxandyr left Clare and stuck his hand out to help Cooper to his feet, checking on the gash on his forehead.

"You'll barely notice it when it heals," stated Alyxandyr. He held Cooper's baffled gaze for a moment then subtly nodded at him.

Ramira fumed and shrieked at what Mahn was doing and every time she tried to wield the Source he assailed her with everything in his power. She was extremely difficult to restrain and there were times that he thought he was losing control of her, prompting him to be more careful. It was almost time anyway, and soon she would be nothing more than one of the thousands of souls existing within his tormented domain.

Nyk and Allad were worse than dead and all because of her. So many had been slain because of what she housed. How could she ever face any of them again? How would she be able to endure their accusing eyes? She could feel the Source reacting to her rage as it rose from the depths of her soul like some phantom whirlwind seeking to destroy that which caused so much pain and sorrow. She could have helped them just like she helped Danyl and the others that day on the plains. She had to cling to those things that offered hope like the fact he had not been able to turn Zada into a Vox and that Clare survived the battle. He had sent some of his best to acquire those bodies and had failed because Zada, Clare, the elven guard and even Cooper rose above the fear and threat to defeat the Vox. And what had she done that could be even remotely comparable with their courage?

Come, Ramira, leave your petty musings behind and greet your friends…

Mahn deposited her onto the plains to stand before the vacant-eyed Herkah and elf, hissing with pleasure as she mourned for them. Allad's dignified features were distorted by the Vox struggling to keep control of him just as Nyk's demon endeavored to suppress his resolute spirit. Ramira saw that these two, like Horemb, would never fully relinquish themselves to the evil that had invaded their bodies and would wait for the right time to be set free. She fingered her blades, her desire to set them free the only thought in her mind. She moved with incredible speed, managing to catch Mahn completely off guard as she lunged forward and slew Nyk. He fell in a heap, the fleeting look of gratitude radiating from his soul negating the gaping wound across his throat. Allad's spirit came to life within its prison as he tried to manipulate the Vox into position so she could grant him the same end. The demon grappled with its host, losing ground until Mahn interfered. His gloved fist came crashing down on her cheek, the impact so severe she immediately collapsed into a heap on the ground.

Mahn was beside himself with anger. She had denied him the elf and would have stolen one of his greatest prizes had it not been for his supreme overconfidence. He could not take the knives from her nor could the demons, for their touch was now an anathema to them. The dangers she posed became evident, compelling Mahn to hasten his plans. He glared at another hooded and cloaked figure standing by his side, forcing its head up until the light penetrated the gloomy cowl. A woman's ultra pale face with crimson eyes stared ahead waiting for her master's command. His hatred-filled spirit bored into her with such vehemence her body trembled at the intrusion, but her features never exhibited anything but apathy. The high priestess had made a terrible pact with the ultimate evil a thousand years earlier and he was determined to extract a severe payment for her past failure. Her tainted soul shared the body of another corrupt individual, one craving the same chaos he intended to inflict upon the land. The high priestess' desire for glory beneath Mahn's black rule paled beside that of Antama's, who dominated the host body. Ina, weakened by her failure centuries ago and no longer protected by Mahn, would be no match for her. The hiss of spite escaping from within his hood scattered his timid minions and prompted the woman to carry out her assignment. She walked away, disappearing within a knot of fighters as they turned to confront a band of elves.

Father and son stood next to each other upon the ramparts, the setting sun unable to impart any of its vibrant hues onto their pale faces or penetrate their heavy hearts. They watched their enemies start their fires and knew there would be no rest tonight. They had lost so many good men and women. Reason told them the enemy would attempt to gain access to the city and terrorize it from within. Although Alyxandyr hoped his son could find some way of wielding the Green Might, he never vocalized his thought; he knew if Danyl could find any way of doing so he would already have tried. He could not even begin to imagine what his son was going through while the power surged within him. The King looked up to accept a message from an exhausted and bloodstained dwarf who turned back to continue to fight.

"What does it say?" asked Danyl.

"All of the units are being forced to retreat. At this hour, Seven, Gard and Styph are still live."

"Mahn will come to the gates tomorrow."

"How do you know that?"

"I feel it," he replied, then left his father and headed back to the castle.

Styph met up with Seven just inside the barracks after the sun had set. Their filthy and sodden clothes hung limply from their bodies, appearing as tired as their wearers. Alyxandyr had sent out the last fresh group of soldiers to relieve them, and unless a miracle happened and a large host of friends suddenly appeared over the horizon, there would be no more men to challenge Mahn.

"We lost Nyk and Allad today…they were taken by Vox," Styph sadly informed the dwarf king as they stripped off their armor and accepted mugs of tea.

"I heard. Zada and Clare also had their hands full," replied the King, as he sat down on the makeshift table across from the prince. He sat and stared at his clasped hands, disregarding the dirt and blood he thought could never be washed away, then closed his eyes. He thought of Allad and Nyk and gripped his hands more tightly together, the pain of losing them ripping into his heart. They ate stew and fresh bread without tasting them, washing them down with hot tea.

"They managed to get into the city, and who knows how many more of them are lurking about. We've lost so many, Seven, and I doubt we can protect the city if we lose even a fraction of that tomorrow."

"Where is the elven might, Styph? Why isn't someone brandishing it in our defense?"

"I wish I knew, Seven. It falls onto our shoulders to buy as much time as possible until that happens." Time, the prince realized, that was nearly expired.

"And Ramira? When will he drive the stake into our hearts with her?"

Both of them thought about the one person who was the reason all of this was happening, but neither one could blame her; she was as much a pawn in this terrible game as they were. Even though many had died on both sides, she had been able to keep him away from the Source, an act monumental in itself. They looked up as Gard joined them, the Khadry's face as dour and fatigued as their own. Styph updated him on what had occurred during the course of the day as they finished their meal.

"Losing those two does not bode well for us," Gard remarked around a mouthful of food.

"Zada and Clare, with some help from Cooper of all people, were able to kill four Vox—Vox that had been assigned to guard Cooper," Styph told him.

"How in the four corners of the land did four Vox accomplish that feat?" asked the Khadry.

"We don't know, which leads us to believe other demons may already be in the city."

"Wonderful. And what of Cooper? Did he atone for all his sins by saving them, or are you still considering him a tool of the darkness?"

"He could just as easily have killed them and no one would have been the wiser, Gard," Styph pointed out.

"Which means they weren't his only prey."

"Zada and Clare would certainly have been worthy trophies," corrected Seven.

"That is not what I meant, Seven. I meant there is something else he seeks either to gain or to destroy."

"The elven magic."

"Exactly," said Gard, as he used the end of the bread to sop up the rest of the stew.

"Zada had said that Mahn could take it too, once he had the Source, but he could not take them at the same time; he has access to one and must therefore know the other no longer slumbers." Seven looked down into his mug of tea, the faint candlelight reflected off of its dark surface like the moon on the river by the home he left behind. If he could just sit on the top step leading into the hall with a pipe in one hand and a glass of his…he forced the foolish thought from his head.

"Well, whoever it is," said Styph, as he stretched out and tried to rest his weary bones for a few moments, "he or she had better befriend it quickly or there won't be anything left to save."

Gard said nothing in response. His ire was still focused on Ramira, the reason all these people were dying in the first place. And what of the elven magic? Where was it and why hadn't anyone used it yet? How many more would be slain before it surfaced? Gard didn't have the optimism to think about what his people would do once this was over because, if tomorrow were a repeat of the past two days, none of them would have to worry about that. He sighed and extended his aching arms and legs as he, too sought a few minutes of rest.

-11-

Zada lay curled up on her bed staring out into the dismal morning with red-rimmed eyes. She sniffed and reached out for the empty pillow beside her, gently caressing the place Allad's head had once rested. She tiredly got to her feet and dressed. She stuck her hands in her pocket and felt the bracelet wrap itself around her fingers as if demanding her attention. She took it out and stared at it. The tiny beads gleamed dully in the light, reminding her that they were still fighting for their lives.

"Well, Zada," she took a deep breath and collected her scattered emotions, "you can't help Allad or anyone else by sequestering yourself in this room all day." She answered the knock at her door, graciously accepting the tray of food the elf brought her. She sipped her tea, feeling the hot liquid warm her cold and empty insides.

The Herkah armed herself, sliding blade after blade into small scabbards on her arms, legs and around her waist. She gained a sense of purpose with every click of a knife snapping into place.

She stood in front of the floor length mirror and smoothed out her garments, gauging her worthiness when her sight became active. She gazed beyond her own reflection at the nebulous haze beginning to concentrate behind her. It congealed to form the brown woman who drifted over and enveloped her with heartfelt sympathy.

I am called Oma.

She gratefully accepted Oma's ethereal embrace, the brown woman's warmth and caring soothing her broken heart. Zada's inner sight began to open, allowing the cold air of the in-between world to stir her clothing. She would be withdrawing from her chamber but not through the door leading to the hall.

Time is growing short, child. Do you have the strength for the journey?

Yes.

Are you afraid, child?

No.

Good. Do not attempt to make any contact or interfere with what you are about to see. These things happened long ago and if you try to communicate you will leave your world forever and exist in a place that is somewhere in between.

I understand.

You will experience everything, child, but will remain unseen.

Zada took Oma's extended hand and felt her entire being dissolve into glittering dust. She was aware of every single one of the sparkling motes and of Oma's essence that merged with hers. Her room turned gray and grainy then disappeared into a smoky haze and, as it did so, the world around Zada became muffled then silent. She was lifted up then pulled into an unknown direction where the air was cold, the dizzying impression of speeding through time as numbing as the frigid surroundings. They hurtled past points of light or did the lights flash by them? The Herkah's nervousness began to manifest itself but she held fast to her trust in Oma, who sped her into the distant past down this eerie corridor. The nomad was frightened but she had already begun the journey and there was nothing she could do to stop it. Nor did she want to. Time seemed to stand still and the blackness continued to roil around her as she hastened on, her anxiety and curiosity growing the farther she went.

The light-less corridor finally began to lighten, turning first dirty gray then to a creamy shade before exploding into bright white. The sudden cessation of movement and the blinding light combined with the extreme heat paralyzed her. She began to falter, losing her bearings and, more importantly, herself in this strange place. Oma squeezed her hand reassuringly and waited for Zada to settle down. The Herkah relied on all of her other senses as her sight gradually began to clear. Waves of cool air touched her hot skin, the unmistakable scent of incense clinging to the breeze a pleasure to inhale. She heard scuffing sounds and people talking, the feel of cloth as they brushed past her. Hooves pounded on stone, and somewhere off to her right the sound of a child screaming over its mother's admonishment. Her feet were uneven and she cautiously pushed the higher of the two forward, her toe abruptly finding an obstacle. Her vision began to clear, the scene stealing her breath away.

She stared upward trying to absorb the magnitude of what towered before her. Massive columns shouldering monumental stones fronted a structure she could never even have dreamt about. The colonnade continued on in the middle of the huge building, disappearing into the darkness that seemed to stretch forever. The sides flanking the gallery were enclosed, the stone carved with gigantic images of battles and persons on thrones. Oma nodded to the huge entrance, catching a stumbling Zada several times as the Herkah craned her neck to absorb the awesome sight before her.

Zada marveled at the brilliant images painted all along the pillars. There were birds flying over and landing on a reed-enclosed river so blue she reached out to dip her fingers in its cooling water. A tall, white crane watched her walk by, its painted beak longer than a lance. She furrowed her brow at a column filled with peculiar black symbols neatly divided by deeply incised panels.

She finally took notice of the people walking past her. The men wore white linen kilts; the women donned flowing gowns of the same material, their well-oiled nut-brown skin a perfect contrast to the snowy fabric. Both men and women shaved their heads, some wearing braided wigs bearing gold sheaths at the tip of the plait. They accentuated their costumes with gold bracelets, earrings and rings, each piece marked with the same strange characters Zada had noted on Ramira's blades. The shade of the brown woman penetrated through her awe, reminding her that this was no time for sightseeing.

Where are we, Oma?

Welcome to your roots, child...

Dar-Ahnet strode through the palace as if she were already ceraphine and all those she passed bowed low to her. Her head remained erect as she cast disdainful looks down at the backs of the servants' perspiring skulls. Her perfumed skin glistened with oils, the pure white linens covering her slender limbs so finely woven they were nearly transparent. Jewelry crafted of the finest gold and encrusted with brilliant gems glittered upon her dark skin. Her lovely features suffered beneath her arrogance, leaving her with a constant contemptuous expression.

The ruling ceraphine's decline into death was taking longer than Dar-Ahnet had anticipated. Her mother's refusal to die would not put a wrinkle in her plans. Dar-Ahnet fingered the vial hanging from a chain around her neck as she entered the ceraphine's chambers, dismissing everyone but the high priestess, Ina. The woman clad in red robes inclined her head in greeting then joined her beside the bed. The ceraphine lay in a semi-lucid state, her face pale and a silken sheet covering her gaunt body. The high priestess grabbed the woman's jaw and forced it open, waiting for Dar-Ahnet to pour the liquid down her throat. Dar-Ahnet drained the small bottle and watched as Ina closed her mouth to prevent the ceraphine from spitting out the bitter liquid. She convulsed and clawed at the air around her, her face turning first crimson then purple before becoming wan once more. The ceraphine twitched twice more then lay still.

"We've managed to gain an extra week, Ina. Go and prepare the Blood Prophecy…I'll meet you in a little while."

Dar-Ahnet stared down at her mother's lifeless body, the feel of the crown already heavy on her head. She crossed her arms and closed her eyes, her hands grasping an imaginary gold flail and crook. She heard the roar of the crowd as they chanted her name over and over again, immediately silencing them with a wave of her hand. She had so many changes to make, starting with the demise of her siblings to dissolving the council. She planned to invade the water dwellers in the far south and go after the strangers heading toward the east. All of this was possible because she housed the greatest power in the land. Ina had told her so.

The leader of the strangers, according to the high priestess, teemed with power, a might she intended to assimilate with her own. The main obstacle to her objectives had been eliminated and soon anyone else with rights to the crown would meet the same fate. She inclined her head to the dead ceraphine, her eyes narrow and her mouth turned up in a sneer.

Dar-Ahnet strolled out of the ceraphine's rooms, following the endless corridors leading down into the bowels of the palace. The beautifully painted limestone blocks found in the upper rooms diminished in decoration at every level down, becoming giant cubes of unfinished stone at the foundation. The fit between the stones was perfect and not even a sheaf of paper could fit in the barely discernable gap. Torches jammed in wall brackets provided the only light; smoke from the oil soaked tops blackened the wall around them. The brands near the airshafts flickered, casting eerie shadows along the angular walls. Dar-Ahnet coughed and brought the edges of her gown up across her nose and mouth to filter out the heavy incense confined to these dank depths. She sniffed and wiped away the tears trickling down her cheek, anxious to cleanse the musty taste from her mouth.

She descended the last few steps and saw the massive doors at the end of the dim gallery, their hinges as long as a man's arm and the iron rings wide enough for her to slip her entire body through. Two hooded priestesses effortlessly pulled open the portals, bowing as she walked past them into the immense chamber. It was empty except for a large altar surrounded by stands bearing torches.

"I've come to see the blood, Ina."

"You will see it, Dar-Ahnet," she replied in a low and flat voice. She clapped her hands, summoning two vacant-eyed priestesses bearing a chalice of silver encrusted with sapphires and diamonds. They handed it to her, averting their eyes as they walked out of the room backward. Ina poured the thick blood mixed with things she would never disclose onto the corner of the altar, watching it flow down the main channel. The mixture zigzagged over ancient symbols, a few rivulets dripping down one of hundreds of canals carved by some unknown force countless years ago. It seeped this way and that until it finally drizzled off the end into a waiting vessel. The high priestess took the urn and lifted high over her head then looked at the pattern on the altar.

"What...?" Blood filled every furrow and continued to ooze out onto her feet from the spout that had fed the urn. It overflowed the grooves, cascading over the sides at an alarming rate. It lapped up against her ankles then her knees like some ghastly red tide rushing in to drown everything in its path. It whirled around her waist, climbing steadily upward to her shoulders and neck and finally filled her mouth. Ina dropped the urn, the echo of shattering pottery breaking the hold the image had over her. She wiped away the sweat with trembling fingers, her lungs aching for lack of air. She dared to look at the altar top and began to pant with relief at the blade-like imprint created of blood.

"Is something wrong?" demanded Ahnet.

"Ah...no, Dar-Ahnet, the reading is quite clear."

"What does it say!" snapped the other impatiently.

"You will be ceraphine."

"That is all? I came down into this...this place for four words?"

"They are important words, Dar-Ahnet," she replied with the utmost of reverence, her black eyes staring at the trail on the stone. Ahnet turned on her heel and left, the trek down to this loathsome chamber hardly worth hearing the report she had already surmised years before. When the massive stone doors swung shut, Ina cursed everything under her breath. She had chosen poorly, applying her dark secrets and energies on the one that did not house the Source. What had she overlooked? What hint or clue had she ignored? What could she do now to correct her mistake? He was to awaken soon and would not be overjoyed at her error.

She had ten to select from and Ahnet seemed the most logical of the choices yet she had erred, so who held the power? She had less than a week to rectify her mistake, for once the strangers passed it would be too late. She had already awakened the evil and he expected the Source at the apex of the full moon when she was to sacrifice the bearer and allow him to take the power. He would not know of her mistake until then, but she was not about to waste any time amending it. Her failure, she knew all too well, would be punishable in ways she did not even want to imagine.

She paced back and forth, willing each of the ceraphine's offspring into her mind then eliminating the least capable of them until four remained. The only sure way to know which one held the power was to perform this very ritual, but how was she to explain their presence during this ceremony? Dar-Ahnet would find out and attempt to prevent her from carrying out her task, killing her siblings before she could even read the blood. She had to get all four into this inner sanctum at once, a difficult challenge indeed. She needed an excuse, a very good one, even if she were the high priestess able to function in the city without having to justify anything she did.

She left the damp chamber behind and walked steadily upward until daylight made her squint. She stopped as one of the four family members she had decided upon turned the corner in front of her. This child frightened her for reasons she could not explain and was the only one who dared to show her contempt openly. The high priestess bowed to her; the fear and hatred for this woman barely kept in check.

"Why are you out of your snake pit during the day?" she demanded, not bothering to conceal her loathing for the high priestess.

"Many pardons, Dar-Ramira, but I have important business to attend to."

"Whose mind are you intent on poisoning now?"

"Please, Dar-Ramira, my entire life is devoted to your family and the city." Her words prostrated themselves in front of Dar-Ramira.

"Then why have you spent so much time at the black well?" Ramira flexed her fingers, the desire to wrap them around Ina's neck nearly overwhelming her. The high priestess quickly glanced at them and took a step backward, swallowing hard at the remorselessness radiating from Ramira's eyes.

The black well was located north and slightly west of the city at the northern edge of the trees paralleling the mountain range to the east. It rested upon ground that had long ago ceased to sustain growing things, becoming a swampy place surrounded by a foul yellowish mist the sun could not penetrate.

"You must be misinformed, Dar-Ramira, for that place is forbidden..."

"My eyes do not deceive me."

"In truth," the high priestess began, seeking to extricate herself from Ramira, "I needed a specific kind of root that grows only near its border."

"Really?"

"Yes," she replied, kowtowing to her with clasped hands. My work will be so much more arduous if you are the one. Although the pleasure your terrible death will bring me will make it all worthwhile.

Ramira said nothing. She continued on down the corridor knowing the only reason the high priestess would go to the black well was because of what lay imprisoned within the noxious morass. The high priestess was determined enough to toy with something that was beyond her comprehension and power. Dar-Ramira was just as resolute to keep that from happening. The high priestess was responsible for making the ceraphine lose sight of her duties, then subverted Dar-Ahnet to believe she was going to be the next queen. Those that lived and worked within the palace were more concerned about retaining their stations and would follow whoever sat on the throne. They latched themselves onto the high priestess thinking she would be the one to propel them into higher positions. The dangerous games being played within the palace prompted her to seek companionship outside the polished limestone walls. She continued to walk its stone corridors, however, to observe and, if necessary, to intervene. She had accepted that responsibility from Imhap, Horemb and Oma without question.

Ramira abandoned the cool confines of the massive stone walls and stepped out beneath the searing sun. She adjusted her head covering, descending the wide staircase leading to the thoroughfare lined with statues and fountains. Trees, flowers and shrubs clustered around those life-giving waters as they braved the hot breath of the desert and the blistering sun slipping into the west. She headed for the crowded section of the city that housed all those who toiled for the palace, their bones and muscles weary as they huddled inside their Spartan mud homes. The delineation between the two was immediate, made even more so by the thick wall separating the two classes. The side facing the palace displayed richly painted scenes heralding the ceraphine's achievements; the other was composed of adobe bricks partially covered with crumbling plaster. The narrow alleyways abounded with wares, food, weaponry and other goods, not including the carts that zigzagged between people and animals. Barking dogs and clucking chickens mingled with the bickering merchants trying to earn a few pieces of silver as they argued under drab awnings. She passed by clay jugs filled with wine, baskets of fruit and vegetables and tables laden with copper bowls. Marinated meats on long sticks simmered over open pits and aromatic spices clung to one's clothing with the tenacity of a small child seeking its mother's attention. Life continued as it had for centuries. They labored until their bodies gave out yet never shared in the bounty they reaped. Ina, through Dar-Ahnet, would make their lives impossible. Dressed in loose trousers and tunic with her hair hidden under a head covering, she passed virtually unnoticed through the constricted streets. She took several twists and turns before ending up in front of a nondescript house deep within the packed quarter.

"Oma?" She smiled at the brown woman beckoning her into the small kitchen.

"Good evening, my sweet," she said, hugging Ramira. Her work-hardened fingers reached up to push a few red-gold strands of hair back as she studied Ramira's tense expression.

"I need to speak with you." Ramira helped herself to a plate of honey and date treats the other had placed on the table. She lifted the delicacy to her lips but the bile still burning in her throat from the encounter with Ina took her appetite away. She replaced it on the tray then folded her hands on the table.

"Go on, child," Oma urged, wiping her hands on her apron. A bad feeling began to gnaw at her as she looked at the crimson staining Ramira's cheeks and fire blazing in her eyes.

"I think the high priestess is trying to awaken that which is imprisoned in the black well."

"Yes," sighed Oma. "I thought she might."

"What are we going to do? No one else in the palace cares or is aware of her plan, and I don't know how far she has gone to resurrect it."

"If she has already been there then I believe it is already astir, child. That means she has focused on the Source which it needs to become as powerful as it once was." Oma spoke very slowly.

"Source? What are you talking about, Oma?"

Oma knew this day would come. She took Ramira's hands into hers, gazing tenderly at the woman she had helped bring up. A slow, sad smile spread across her plain features as memories of the little girl curled up in her lap filled her mind. How many times had she held and rocked her, humming a tune into her ears as she drifted off to sleep? How often had she dabbed at the scrapes and bumps on her elbows and knees? Even as a small child, Ramira had sought to escape the dishonesty prevalent within the palace and, fortunately for them all, she chose to go to Oma. The brown woman had been present at her birth, cradling her in her arms the moment her mother released her into the world. Oma had continued to hold and coo her even after the birthing chamber emptied out. The baby girl was ignored, forgotten and abandoned by almost everyone except the three who had accepted the lady's daunting behest. Now the grown woman before her would be told of the truth hidden from her since the instant she was born.

A low, melancholy sound traveled through the city, silencing everything in its wake. Birds took flight from rooftops and dogs whined. Vendors and buyers stood motionless, the former with their hand out to accept pieces of silver for the wares the latter clutched against their chest. People looked from one to the other, their faces registering both mourning and apprehension. The Thebans resumed their activities; their voices, when they spoke, were hushed. They glanced about nervously; mother's calling to their children and men taking deep, tense breaths.

Oma closed her eyes as the horn's echoes ended. She looked over at Ramira to gauge how she took the news of her mother's death. Ramira stared past the wall and toward the palace, her features cold and unforgiving. Oma shivered, the warmth leaving her limbs.

The ceraphine had been wasting away for weeks now, with Dar-Ahnet handling the palace affairs. The high priestess, initially a shadowy form behind the throne, became more active in the day-to-day activities. The trips to the black well and the ceraphine's death did not bode well for Thebes or her people. Ina was under the assumption that Dar-Ahnet held the power and would, through her, advance her own objectives. Her miscalculations would, with any luck, buy them some time.

"Ramira." The words were thick in the woman's throat. She had kept this information from her, fearing the day when she would have to explain the dark truth to someone she had grown to love as her own child. "You house the Source."

"Me?"

"Yes, my sweet, you."

"Why didn't you ever tell me about this before?" Ramira just sat there, her fingers nervously plucking at her sleeves. Ina's image formed in her mind, the corners of her mouth turning down, her hands flexing around her invisible knives.

"Because we thought that you'd be better protected if you didn't know and..."

"And what?"

"We hoped the Source depended upon the disposition of the bearer to keep it in check. Imhap, Horemb and I decided to teach you, interact with you so the power would not corrupt you as you grew older."

The Lady of the Sands had called to Oma, guiding her to the dais in the desert where she told Oma of the Source and where it resided. The Lady had presented Oma with an alternative, one that might keep the power from falling into the wrong hands. The Lady believed with the right training, discipline and teaching, Ramira's spirit would be able to withstand the Source's influence and keep its evil intentions in control. There were no guarantees or assurances they would have even limited success with what was being proposed, but they had to try and Oma and the others took on that immense task.

"Are you saying that the Source is evil, Oma?"

"Yes, child, the Source is, but you are not and that eases my apprehensions. We are not worried that it resides in you, for we believe you will not use it to destroy, whereas if it dwelled in anyone else..." She could not finish for the very thought of Dar-Ahnet housing the power was too much for her to bear. Her lack of insight would allow Ina and the evil to easily wrest it from her, brandishing the power to smite everything in their path.

Oma could only watch as Ramira gazed down at her hands as if she were waiting for the power to spring forth from them. Her lovely features rippled with awe then dread, her simple appeals for help heartbreaking to the other woman. Ramira had been virtually ignored all of these years and it remained to be seen if the course they had charted when she was born had been the right one. Desperation had driven the three to confront the Source, the initial fear of doing so quieted but never completely lost over the years.

"What do I do now?" she asked in a small voice. Ramira had trusted Oma her entire life and saw no need to cease doing so now.

"Continue to behave as you have and do not tell anyone that you have it," warned Oma. "If the high priestess begins to suspect you might be the bearer, you must take any and all precautions to insure she does not get an opportunity to acquire it." Horemb's part in tutoring her with the blades was an essential ingredient in preparing Ramira: lessons she had learned well and would need in the not-too-distant future.

"Oma?" she said softly as she sat on the bench beside the brown woman.

"Yes, child?" she asked, as she placed her arms around the now grown woman. She held her tightly, kissing her forehead while fighting tears.

"Things are going to change now, aren't they?" she asked, her voice quaking at the thought.

"Yes, my sweet, they are." She absent-mindedly turned the bracelet on Ramira's wrist.

She returned to the palace, entering the royal wing just as Dar-Ahnet and her perfumed entourage were leaving her rooms, the looks exchanged between the two women anything but cordial. Dar-Ahnet dismissed her retinue and faced an unemotional Ramira.

"I will be ceraphine," she hissed at Ramira. "And the first command I will give is to have your head presented to me on a platter of woven of reeds."

Ramira ignored the insult, inwardly preferring a tray of rush to one composed of gold and precious gems. Ahnet discerned as much, which angered her even more.

"Thank you for the warning," Ramira replied, the desire to slay Dar-Ahnet nearly overwhelming her. "I'm curious, Ahnet, what honors will you bestow upon the ceraphine during her entombment?"

"She will be given the proper respects then placed in her crypt within a few days."

"You are foregoing the customary week of mourning?"

"The high priestess Ina has seen dark days ahead and has counseled me to expedite the services."

"The two of you can't wait to establish your plans, can you?"

Ahnet stared at her half-sister, her features darkening with every passing second. Ramira pretended not to care for the mantle of power. The moment Thebes' crown rested upon her head, her half-sister would plot to take it away from her. Her nonchalance failed to mask the conspiracy already hatching within her black breast, one Ahnet would thwart before Ramira had the chance to act. The eternal night already beckoned to her other siblings, but Ramira would be much more difficult to dispose of, a detail she and Ina had previously discussed. The high priestess, probably Ramira's greatest adversary and most hated of all people, wanted that assignment, one Ahnet was loathe to give up. Dar-Ahnet would grant Ina that honor with the stipulation she was able to witness the murder. *I will throw a festival on that day celebrating your death by re-enacting it!*

"I understand you have taken a great deal of interest in the trespassers." The silken words oozed from her mouth as she watched Ramira's reaction.

"I am merely curious," she responded, refusing to fall into Ahnet's trap. Ramira openly accompanied the scouts assigned to tracking the strangers' progress as they made their way east along the southern boundaries. Her nighttime excursions to study them on her own, however, remained unnoticed. Subtle undertones of aggression against the outsiders permeated the air, the nuances of deceit rising thickly with the incense from within the bowels of Ina's chambers. Ramira had seen nothing from the group indicating an invasion, leaving her wondering what they possessed to capture the high priestess' attention.

"Perhaps we can capture a few and allow them to entertain us."

"Maybe you and the high priestess could prod them with your forked tongues."

"How dare you!"

"I dare, Ahnet, but you do not have the stomach to play that game; you leave your dirty deeds to others."

"I could have you executed for uttering such insults!" she shrieked, her face turning crimson with rage, hatred and fear.

"My point exactly," retorted Ramira, as she turned her back and walked away.

"I did not dismiss you!" Dar-Ahnet proclaimed at the unresponsive woman striding down the hall.

"I didn't ask for permission," Ramira muttered to herself as she disappeared around the corner, her half sister's denouncements fading away.

Ramira changed into traveling clothes then packed a small bag in case she would be gone for more than a day, her eyes disregarding the luxuries that surrounded her. Beautifully carved boxes of fragrant woods held the finest of linens while equally elegant stands held perfumes, aromatic oils and a variety of cosmetics. The walls held painted river scenes so lush that they made one forget the city stood on an immense desert. Ducks flew in between reeds over fish swimming in sparkling waters beneath pure white blossoms floating upon emerald lily pads. She ignored the canopied bed, its silken sheets and softest of blankets as appealing as a bed of nails to her. The statues and busts and other fine pieces that filled her chambers meant nothing to her as she turned her back on the opulence and sneaked out of the palace through a maze of hidden halls. She exited the vast complex via the garden to the east then vanished into the city and headed out to find the strangers.

Ramira rode south and west, keeping to the brush and trees as she watched for the large group of travelers making their way across the rolling meadows. Her curiosity and something she could not quite identify drew her on while the revelation of the Source's location reverberated through her mind. If Oma knew then so did Imhap and Horemb. Her entire life had revolved around these three individuals and even knowing what she housed had not lessened their affections. She swore she would do everything in her power to keep them from being found out, regardless of the cost. Imhap had encouraged her to glimpse the strangers as they passed by, heightening her curiosity with bits and pieces of information. They were heading for some unknown destination, the keen interest shared by Dar-Ahnet and the high priestess in their passing not lost on Ramira. Ahnet and Ina had no intention of welcoming them into the city but rather of harming them somehow and that was something Ramira was not going to allow.

She spotted their trail about an hour later, pursuing the large group of travelers for several miles as they wound their way eastward. She could tell they were approximately a mile or two ahead of her and would, if her calculations were correct, be near the line of trees running perpendicular to the mountain range. She cleared a little rise and could see the end of the undulating line of wayfarers in the distance as they pressed on. Her inquisitiveness and excitement grew with every passing second as she tried to imagine what the outsiders looked like. Would they be dark or fair? Thin? Heavyset? Learned? What language would they speak? Would they be friendly or hostile? She tracked them within the concealment of the trees well into the early evening, thankful when they finally decided to stop for the night. She dismounted and rubbed at her sore muscles, her eyes never leaving the scene below her.

Dusk camouflaged many of their details but that did not discourage her from inching closer and closer to the camp. She moved soundlessly down the rounded hill and hid herself in the last series of brush and trees near the base of the hillock. Some of the travelers tended to their horses while others checked the wagons for wear and tear. The campfires sprouting up in the darkness cast a soft light on the figures sitting around them eating their meals and talking amongst each other. She guessed there were at least several hundred encamped below, then wondered if more were bringing up the vanguard intent on meeting up with them farther along their trek. One of the strangers caught her attention as he moved from campfire to campfire, speaking with nearly everyone as he made his way through the encampment. He would lend a hand when needed then proceed to the next group huddled around the flames as he made his way to the rear of the assemblage. She watched as he walked well beyond the edge of the camp and placed his hands on his hips, the full moon eliciting an almost unearthly glow about him. Ahnet's words of capturing some of the strangers echoed in her mind and she could well imagine what horrors Ina would inflict upon them if they managed to seize one of the outsiders. Ramira would not allow that to happen. She estimated a group of this size would be beyond Thebes' borders in a couple of days, but how far had preparations by Ina evolved in capturing one of them? Should she warn the strangers or take the chance they would be gone before anything happened?

She watched the man turn around and slowly make his way back into camp, his head turning this way and that as he studied the dark land around him. His gaze seemed to linger in her direction, prompting her to let the leafy branch she had pulled away to observe him to resume its normal position.

She decided to convey a warning; if nothing else she would at least appease her curiosity. She rose to her feet, brushing off the dirt and leaves stuck to her clothing, her eyes searching for the man working his way through the group. He had disappeared from the camp. He couldn't have gone too far; perhaps he had stepped beyond the firelight into the darkness. She watched the far edge of the camp for several long moments before spotting him looping around and heading in her direction. Ramira remained rooted in place, her feet unwilling to carry her toward the outsider. Her mind tried everything from ordering to cajoling her feet to move, but they refused to yield to any of her demands. A slight rustling sound from behind increased her heartbeat and urged them into action. She dropped down into a crouch, hoping the brush concealed her when an iron grip grabbed her from behind, but it wasn't just his strength that subdued her. She felt a peculiar stirring react to his presence, one that reassured her in a way she could not describe. Unafraid and strangely calm, she allowed him to turn her around to face him.

The full moon cast its silver light upon his features, illuminating eyes filled with wonder and astonishment as they unabashedly studied the creature in his grasp. The scrutiny was mutual; she had never seen such an unusual man before, her own eyes tracing the elegant arch of his brows down his noble nose then over to his gracefully pointed ears. Silence claimed the hillock as their gazes met and held. Horemb would have been dismayed that she had not drawn her knives to protect herself from this stranger, but her instincts detected no threat. She sensed a sort of current running from him through the contact on her wrist, one burrowing into her flesh then vanishing down into the depths of her soul. It spiraled downward like some mighty bird of prey and she swore she felt the tips of its extensive wings brushing against the sides of her very existence. Then, as if spotting its quarry, it swooped down to a specific point within her, folding back its great wings as it dove onward. She suddenly realized what that target was and immediately broke the connection. She took several steps backward, noting how he watched her, his intense gaze riveting her to the ground.

"Who are you?" he demanded, his body poised in readiness in case she decided to bolt away.

"I...I have come to warn you," she replied, her voice suddenly very faint.

"From what?"

"You cannot stay here, for there are those whose interest in you is far from civil."

"From that city?" He pointed toward her home. Patrols had informed him of its presence long before they traversed its southern perimeter. He had had the opportunity to send an emissary there but something advised him to forgo that plan. This woman seemed to corroborate his decision to ignore the city and give it a wide berth instead.

"Yes, Thebes, and it is about to receive a most unpleasant and unwelcome visitor, one that you don't want to be near."

"I sensed an evil as we passed by," he said. "We need to restock our provisions and have many repairs to make on our wagons before we can go on."

"You must go...tonight...now." She turned to leave but his hand grabbed her wrist; he wanted to know more about Thebes and the people living there. She twisted just enough to escape his hold, withdrawing into the shadows. She could hear him pursuing her but familiarity with the mound allowed her to elude him. She had mounted her horse and ridden down onto the flat ground before he had the chance to catch up.

He stood in the darkness watching the night devour the dark shape, his mind taking her warning seriously. He had sensed an odd emanation from her, one he did not recognize yet respected nonetheless. He sighed, narrowing his eyes at a form he could no longer distinguish, then returned to camp, her forewarning resonating in his mind.

The high priestess had surreptitiously tested the last of Ahnet's siblings, yet none of them exhibited even the faintest hint of the Source. She became concerned, for she had to complete the final spell tonight in order to free Mahn. He was already loose in the land but needed the Source to complete his transformation from phantom to utter power wielder. The red woman was in a dilemma. She could do nothing to prevent him from coming to Thebes nor could she turn to anyone else to help her destroy him. If she could locate the Source then perhaps she could brandish it and defeat Mahn. Who was left?

The high priestess cringed, realizing who the bearer might be, and it could not have been a more hated enemy: Ramira. It had to be inside her! Ina realized next to Mahn, Ramira was her most formidable foe, one that was even more relentless with her hatred than the evil she had aroused in the swamp. She would be difficult to trick and it would be nearly impossible to extract the Source from her if she knew she carried it...but if she didn't know, then Ina's task was that much easier. Who would know of its existence other than herself?

The red woman thought long and hard about who else would be aware of the Source then remembered Ramira spent little time at the palace, choosing to live amongst the residents of the city. One of the houses she frequented belonged to Oma. Ina tapped her tight lips with a gaunt finger, her eyes half closed as she analyzed what she knew about the woman. The jeweler's widow lived alone and had been present at Ramira's birth, taking care of the child within the palace until Ramira was old enough to walk. Oma had never done anything out of the ordinary, instead cared for Ramira according to the rules that had been set down within the royal residence.

"Why you? Who choose you, a member of the lower class, as guardian to a royal child?"

The high priestess scowled for the one person who could answer her question lay cold and stiff in her tomb. The ceraphine must have selected Oma to watch over Ramira...or did she? Two others also interacted with Ramira: Imhap, the vizier, and Horemb, the general of the army. She shook her head, for they were also responsible to teach all of the ceraphine's children. Imhap taught them from the scrolls and tomes, Horemb to do battle.

Ina walked over to the altar, the memory of drowning in blood still fresh in her mind. She stared at the hundreds of small channels making up the maze on the altar top for so long they began to shift and change before her very eyes. The edges of the grooves began to blur, their borders' sharpness becoming rounded then flattening out. It began to ripple and flow like a tiny lake, complete with shadowy reflections along its "shore." She reached out a trembling hand and hesitantly dipped her finger into the black water, immediately recoiling as the water both burned and froze her. She grabbed her finger wanting to massage the life back into it but the blistering pain stopped her. She lifted it up and stared at the frostbitten digit bearing multiple welts. They gradually disappeared, leaving her finger as before. Was this a warning or an omen?

Whether Oma and the others were innocent or not was no longer an issue. She had to find out what, if anything, they knew regardless of the consequences. He would soon sweep across the desert and into Thebes, taking what she had promised him. The end result of her failure to deliver her end of the bargain would be dire indeed and she was not about to allow that to happen.

She hurried to her chambers, changed into simple clothes and headed out. She blended in perfectly with the denizens who carried out their arduous chores to keep the city and, more importantly, the royalty, comfortable and wealthy. She made her way through the crowded streets, taking several twists and turns before ending up in front of Oma's home, and knocked on her door. The brown woman recognized her right away but admitted her anyway, ignoring the sick feeling beginning to grow in her stomach.

"What do you want?"

"What have you told Ramira about the Source?" demanded the high priestess, spurning even the vaguest hint of civilities.

"You haven't found it, have you?" Oma crossed her arms in defiance, her usual gentleness replaced with an air of utter control. She stared hard at the high priestess, meeting her gaze with one that challenged the hatred blazing from the other's eyes.

"Does she know she houses it?" the high priestess furiously hissed, hiding her desperation and growing fear of the woman who began to loom over her.

Oma continued her silence, watching Ina's face taking on a crimson cast and the nervous twitching of her hands. Beads of perspiration formed on her forehead, trickling down along her sharp cheekbones and collecting along her bony jaw.

"What will you tell him when he comes, Ina?" asked Oma in a calm voice.

"What?"

"How will he react when he finds out you are incompetent?"

"Ramira has it...doesn't she?" snarled the high priestess, fumbling within the folds of her clothing.

"Ramira has many things."

"I know of one thing she will no longer have."

The high priestess brought out a dagger and promptly buried it in Oma's chest again and again. The brown woman's gaze never left Ina's, even as she fell in a heap to the floor. The red woman rested one knee on the floor, her features cold and unrepentant as the life flowed out of Oma and stained her cleanly swept floorboards. Ina impatiently waited for her to die, containing the desire to slit her throat to hasten the process then decided it was more satisfying to watch her die slowly. Blood dribbled from the corner of Oma's mouth, retreating behind her ears and accumulating on her disheveled hair.

Her hand reached out and grabbed Ina's thin wrist with a strength that surprised even the high priestess, who cringed beneath the contact. Oma's breathing became ragged, but she did not relinquish her hold on Ina. The high priestess wished she could be here when Ramira found her as she tried to extricate herself from the brown woman's powerful grip.

"Hurry up, woman, I have things to do!"

"You...have already...failed..." Oma winced as the high priestess brought the blade across her neck then ripped her hand free of the dead woman. She rose to her feet and glared down at Oma with contempt and a hint of fear crowding her countenance.

"I have not faltered," she disputed, the corpse prone on the floor, trying to ignore the chill suddenly settling into her body.

She headed back to the palace, the searing rays of the sun unable to penetrate the gloom taking root in her soul. Her black clothing obscured Oma's blood but it could do nothing to ward off the growing truth of her words. She hadn't failed but simply miscalculated her plans. She had plenty of time to rectify her mistake, and two more individuals could help her. Ina took a left at the corridor beyond the entrance to the palace, ignoring the stately columns and open air rooms beneath them. She disregarded the scribes with shaven heads and writing surfaces placed across their crossed legs. They busily dipped their reed styluses into wells of black ink, entering information onto sheets of paper from the lists handed to them. She walked on and entered the plant-enclosed courtyard at the end of the hall, where she found a skinny little man sitting in front of a fountain. He stood up in one fluid motion and offered her a polite bow, his black eyes devoid of emotion as they scrutinized her garb.

"My presence doesn't seem to surprise you, Imhap."

"Neither does the ceraphine's passing."

"She was quite ill."

"And so are the tidings you bear, yes?"

"Where is Ramira?"

"She is not scheduled for any teaching at this time."

"Where is she?"

Imhap folded his hands in front of him, his fingers clutching a sheaf of documents. He had observed Ina taking Ahnet under her wing, indulging and training her from the moment she was born. The young girl had been corrupted over time, growing up on the bitterness and arrogance that Ina had disguised as tutelage. Ahnet was a willing student for him, ravenously devouring everything he had taught her. She memorized the maps and histories and paid special attention to the races living around Thebes. The ceraphine was dead and the high priestess wore common clothing flecked with blood. The self-proclaimed ceraphine was an intelligent, albeit self-centered, woman who was about to plunge Thebes into darkness with the help of the high priestess.

"I do not know."

"Guess!"

"My guess is that she is beyond your influence and control."

Ina muttered unintelligible words under her breath as the little man calmly frustrated her attempts to gain information. He mocked her without appearing disrespectful, made her feel insignificant and worthless. Malice rushed through her at lightning speed, carried on the back of the beginnings of panic. Her constricting chest muscles squeezed at her lungs and her stomach pumped bile into her throat.

"Damn you!"

Imhap stood motionless as the blood spurted from his throat down his wiry chest and followed the contours of his arms onto the papers. He never raised his arms in defense nor tried to run from the knife-wielding high priestess, which infuriated her even more. She glared at his crumpled body, gasping for air as her options dwindled down to one man. She did not relish confronting the mighty Horemb.

The unseen witnesses followed the course of events, Zada's hand covering her open mouth during all the incidents, especially the murders of Oma and Imhap. The spirit of the brown woman wiped the tear running down Zada's cheek then gently patted her hand. Oma inclined her head to the dead vizier and closed her eyes as if in prayer. She remained that way for several long moments then took a deep breath to face the next series of circumstances.

This was the easy part.

Easy? Oma, how can you say such a thing!

Because it's the truth.

Sweet mercy! The things that were done to you, Imhap...the whole city!

It gets worse, child. Come.

Oma directed her to the exercise grounds behind the palace where soldiers practiced beneath the midmorning sun. Groups of well-muscled men in loincloths sparred with swords, lances, axes and other weapons under the command of one man standing well above them all. His legs were like oak trees and his solid body seemed chiseled out of a single slab of granite. His arms bristled with sinew, the veins barely able to encompass his brawny build. Horemb's glittering eyes caught every movement from every man without ever moving his head even an inch.

"Falit! Keep your sword up or he'll cut you into pieces! Sentet, what have I taught you about gripping your hilt? Vesna! Rest the back of your shield against your forearm and upper arm or it will completely break apart with your enemy's first strike!"

Horemb walked into the midst of the gangs who moved back respectfully, listening and watching to everything he did or said. He moved Sentet's fingers along the haft of his sword for a better hold, scrutinizing Sentet as he manipulated the blade in the air in front of him. He repositioned Vesnet's shield, nodding as the man deflected blows from another man without the discomfort he showed before.

The high priestess glared at Horemb from behind a succulent bush full of pale pink blossoms. Ina could not simply walk up to the general and challenge him like she had the others. He would be as unwilling to reveal what he knew as Oma and Imhap had been. She crossed her arms and bit her thin bottom lip. She needed an appropriate punishment for him, one that would haunt him for an eternity. She nodded to herself as she remembered the special demons that would accompany Mahn from his morass, demons that thrived on the physical capabilities that defined Horemb. She grinned wickedly then frowned. Why hadn't she thought of that before killing Oma and Imhap? Well, she wasn't about to let this opportunity pass her by. She scanned the practice yard and spotted Horemb's water jug. She grabbed a pail and worked her way along the edges of the training field filling up the containers. She may be the high priestess but she had no privileges to be on the field. She shuddered to think what Horemb would do to her if he caught her. She finally approached Horemb's jug and added a few drops of a pale blue liquid along with the water. She held her breath, her hands trembling as they finished their task, and casually strode back to the well and replaced the pail. She returned to her vantage point and waited.

Horemb finally ended the exercises late in the afternoon, a sweat-drenched high priestess glowering at him from behind her concealment. *It's about time, you fool!* Ina used a sodden corner of her head covering to wipe away the perspiration, watching intently as the general neared his water and dipped the ladle into the opening. He lifted it out and put it up to his lips, the high priestess leaning forward without breathing. She scowled as Sentet marched up to him and engaged him in conversation, the dipper momentarily forgotten. Horemb dropped the scoop back into the vessel and held up his hand, showing the novice an imaginary grip that Sentet copied. The general nodded with approval, slapped the young man on his shoulders then raised the dipper to his lips. He tilted his head back and emptied out the scoop, the high priestess smirking as he dipped it into the water for more. *Easy, Horemb…I want you awake so you can appreciate my little surprise.*

Horemb picked up his gear and walked toward the building near Ina, his initial steps steady until he reached the bush she hid behind. He stopped, wiping away the perspiration suddenly pouring down his face, then rubbed at his eyes. He began to stagger and dropped his equipment, barely making it to the stone bench just feet away from the red woman. Ina scanned the area to make sure they were truly alone then joined the ailing general.

"My lord does not feel well?"

Horemb noted her casual attire and the hood framing her gaunt face. She was out of her temple during the daylight hours and sat fearlessly beside one of her adversaries, the feigned looks of concern awkwardly twisting her features. He could only inwardly recoil from the arm she placed around his burly shoulders, its cold and prickly feel inducing gooseflesh even beneath the hot sun. She sneered at him as he tried to lift his hands to crush the life out of her but the effort unleashed nothing more than a torrent of sweat.

"You foul and purposeless fiend…"

"You flatter me, Horemb."

"I'll…kill…you…"

"You've had plenty of chances." She leaned over and kissed him on the lips, the low, cackling sounds issuing from her throat grating on his ears.

He mustered up enough spit to wash away some of the repulsive aftertaste clinging to his mouth. It dribbled down his chin and dripped onto his glistening chest. Hatred and loathing formed a knot in his breast and began to radiate outward. It strengthened every fiber of his being until each and every muscle strained against his skin. Ina's eyes went wide as she shrank back and fumbled for her knife as Horemb labored to stand up. He managed to gain his feet and reached out, grabbing thin strands of hair and ripping them from her scalp as he tumbled forward. She yelped with pain then kicked the sweating man panting on the ground before her.

The high priestess tied a rope around his ankles then hoisted him up into the back of a cart, carefully concealing the unconscious general with an old blanket. No one paid any attention to the spare figure on the rickety wagon pulled down the main avenue by an old horse with a limp. The dray creaked and rumbled unevenly over the stone boulevard, every bump dislodging rusting nails or pieces of planking. Ina prayed that the wheeled crate would hold together long enough to get her to her destination.

The sun descended, sending long shadows over her like a black awning. By the time she reached the main gate, the bottom of the smoldering orb touched the horizon. She yanked on the reins then smacked them down on the horse's hind quarters, urging it to take a northwesterly direction toward the mountains. The hot winds pressed down upon the sands then rose again as the cold night air began to seep across the desert. Sand devils erupted at will, the swirling sands towering into the star encrusted heavens or barely reaching the knees. They emitted high-pitched whooshing sounds as the fine grains brushed and beat against each other in their frenzied dance lasting only moments. They became less frequent the farther she ventured from the desert, the mountains an imposing wall the winds could not penetrate.

The changes in her surroundings marked her entry into the evil's domain. A sickly yellow mist swelled in front of her, obscuring everything around it. The air grew foul; the ground to either side of the narrow path she followed became more viscous and slimy the closer she came to the edge of his dominion. The branches of leafless and twisted skeletal trees, bent as if in agony, loomed on either side of her, their tortured roots trapped in the quagmire that belched up gasses in spurting sounds. The mushy, slurping noises it made while reabsorbing its own waste made even Ina queasy. The air was thick and heavy. It pressed down with such palpable weight it threatened to break every bone in her body. Her neck and shoulder muscles ached as they fought the pressure and kept the terrified horse from bolting into the marsh. She had numbed its senses with potent herbs but even the strongest potion could not completely buffer it from the evil lurking within the swamp. Her previous trips had been difficult, but now that he was about to rise and assume his full power it became nearly impossible. She forcefully turned her head to look over her shoulder just as the evil fog swirled to hide the night. She pulled on the reins and stopped the wagon, managing to calm down enough to be able to convince him that everything was proceeding as planned. The wait was interminable, the mist disturbing as the droplets clung to her exposed skin like leeches seeking blood. Brushing them away, she knew from experience, worsened the situation because once the beads were broken, they formed an icy layer that seeped into your very soul. That mistake forced her to spend days beneath a mountain of blankets, and even the searing noonday sun could not penetrate that malaise. She shivered at the memory then froze as a deadly silence settled down upon the marsh, stifling even the horrible sucking sounds.

A shape began to materialize within the fetid mist, its shifting form human one moment then massive without delineation the next. It ambled toward her, bringing with it a stream of odors so disgusting even the fen quaked with repulsion. It stopped just beyond her ability to determine its details, the soupy haze veiling something she was glad she could not discern. The high priestess felt her blood stop within her veins, fearing the evil would find out about her failure.

"What have you brought me?" he hissed from deep within the noxious mist clinging to her skin with such tenacity she swore it was composed of clammy hands that reached out to torment the living.

"My lord needs warriors," she bowed low to him, "and I, your humble servant, thought this one might be adequate enough to fulfill that role."

"Indeed…" Mahn parted the mist and the high priestess cringed. The undefined specter moved forward and brushed against her, its touch scraping and burning her skin. She fidgeted with her cloak, backing away from the shape hovering over the prone Horemb. The Theban general's eyes were open, staring up at the monstrosity filling up his entire vision, his fingers digging into the greasy ground. Mahn opened his nebulous robes, letting them billow in the still air and form a tent around him and Horemb. The evil's head tilted back, his lengthy arms elevating until they seemed to scour the very universe. He shoved an indistinct shape into the general, his movement lightening fast and filled with a depraved glee. Horemb convulsed, his purplish features stretched to the limit, his back so arced Ina believed the general was about to snap in half. Mahn violated the general for several long minutes then departed his body as abruptly as he had invaded it. The high priestess stared at Horemb's lifeless form, her brows wrinkling together, her fingers ceasing to knot her garment. She dared to look over at Mahn, who stood unmoving several paces away. Did she bring Horemb here only to have Mahn kill him? She opened her mouth to speak then jumped as the general's eyes snapped open and stood erect as if yanked to his feet like a puppet.

Mahn walked around the partially suspended man, nodding with approval as he looked at him from head to toe. The evil tore a strip of cloth from his robe, wrapped it around his hands and pulled tightly on it. The cracking noise it made sounded like thunder reverberating through the swamp, and sent unseen things scattering into the mist. He placed the piece over Horemb's shoulder and stepped back, whispering words under his breath while waving his hand to the subtle cadence. The section of fabric began to expand leaving Horemb clothed in black within moments. Mahn reached over to the man and flipped a black cowl over his head, blocking out the hatred burning from Horemb's eyes. *I will have an entire army composed of creatures like you!*

"You have done well. How goes the preparation for the Source?"

"Everything is on schedule, my lord."

"Good. The moon will be full soon and I still have much to do in readying the transfer of the power to me." Mahn turned without another word and disappeared back into the fetid haze, taking his new prize with him.

"Yes, my lord," she replied, bowing low. She carefully turned the horse around, resumed her seat on the wagon and headed back to Thebes. The breath she exhaled seemed to last all the way back.

The passing miles increased the distance between her and the newcomers but did not decrease the sensations still flowing freely through her mind. His appearance and the electricity that emanated forth from him captivated her and she rued the fact she would never be able to learn anything about them. They would face enough trials and tribulations on their journey without having the added pressure of contending with Thebes' problems. Perhaps when things settled down in her city she would have the luxury of meeting up with them one day and exchanging information about their respective people. In the meantime, however, she had her own problems awaiting her when she returned, issues that would only became more apparent over the next few days. The sun was just painting the morning sky as she re-entered the city and stole back into the palace, her vigilance increased due to Ahnet's very real threat. She disappeared into her rooms, checking every corner for signs of an assassin and only then was she satisfied that she was alone.

She bathed, then dressed and was heading down the brightly painted stone corridor when she suddenly doubled over in pain, dropping to the floor gasping for air. She looked around to confront whoever had delivered such a vicious punch to her midsection but found herself alone. She crawled over to the wall, using it for support as she rose unsteadily to her feet. A white-hot fire burst deep inside of her, squeezing her lungs and heart with such force that her face turned bright red and her eyes began to tear. She continued to wheeze as the hallway began to spin and blur, and it took all of her will to keep from fainting.

A sensation began to flow through her, drawing her down into the bowels of the palace, her feet unwilling to heed her mind as it screamed for her to stop. She walked on in an almost trance-like state, the sounds of the living slowly diminishing as she disappeared down into the deepest section of the palace. Her bare feet did not feel the cold seeping up through the stone floor nor did she gag on the pungent incense hanging heavily in the darkness. Her hands forced open the massive doors shutting out the world of light from the high priestess' lair. The high priestess stood at one end of the altar; her arms overhead as Ramira interrupted her in mid incantation, the look on her face bordering on panic. Fully in control of herself again even though the pain still threatened to tear her apart, Ramira noticed the thick, incense-infused blood slowly seeping down the top of the altar and heading for a pair of black daggers. The viscous liquid began to turn black and effervesce the closer it oozed to the blades and soon tendrils of steam lifted up from the altar. The sounds of moaning and shrieking could be heard somewhere far off in the distance, the eerie echoes of tormented souls screaming for release. The torches began to flicker, the flames undulating wildly then turning bright red. Ramira had no idea what the blades were for but everything the wicked woman in red did revolved around evil. The spell Ina was casting over the knives wormed itself into Ramira's midsection stimulating the pain that had brought her here. Ramira ignored the stabbing pain, closing the span between herself and the daggers. The high priestess spoke faster, trying to hurry the process along before Ramira could react, but her victim had other plans. The daggers were key to extracting the Source and would be of little use if they weren't fully saturated with the potion. Ina's voice began to falter, her hands shaking as they frantically waved over the blades. Ramira was within arm's length of her.

Ramira reached out, snatching the blades before they were defiled by the concoction running down the channels, the hilts feel cold yet oddly revitalizing at the same time. Something began to surge through her hands and up her arms until the feeling not only saturated her entire being but also seemed to interact with the Source. The power sprang to life within her, coursing through her veins like liquid fire, invigorating her in ways she could not even describe.

The high priestess shrieked in denial, racing around the altar to take back the blades and complete her invocation. Failure meant having to face Mahn, and she had little time before he arrived. She labored to keep the hysteria at bay, watching the potion nearing the end of the altar top. She took a step toward Ramira, shrinking back as she brought the blades up, daring Ina to take them. The chamber became deathly still. Plop. The high priestess' face started losing what slight color it had. Drip-drip. Ina cringed at the sound and stared at the solution pouring into the stone vessel from the corner of her eyes. Panic took hold of her, sending its roots deep into her black soul.

"What have you done! Let me finish or he'll kill me!" she screamed as she lunged for the knives.

"I will slay you, but first you will tell me what you did!"

"He is the lord and master and will take what you have then rip the power from the strangers," she shrieked, her wild stare and grabbing hands closing in on Ramira.

"When?"

"Tonight," she replied, her eyes never leaving the knives in Ramira's hands.

Ramira held the implements of her own death within her hands. The reason behind their creation should have appalled her yet she gripped the hilts more tightly instead. A strange connection began to form between flesh and metal, one that brought on an odd sense of confidence within her. Her mentors had instilled that same sort of conviction into her, placing their trust in her ability to draw from the lessons she had learned from them. Failure was always a factor. Ramira had had little time to think about the Source or its reason for existing within her, relying instead on her instincts and training. Killing Ina became a priority, one emanating from within her glittering eyes as they stared into the high priestess' black ones. Ina stood her ground, afraid yet driven by the thought of what the evil would do to her if she faltered. The red woman was running out of time but then again, so was Ramira.

The high priestess was being uncharacteristically open in providing her with this information, turning suspicion into caution. Ramira carefully walked around the altar, forcing the red woman to follow suit as she scanned the dark shadows permeating the vast chamber. They were alone yet that did not alleviate the sense of foreboding flooding into her mind. The red woman was stalling her and Ramira knew she had to leave as soon as possible or fall prey to her schemes.

"You have betrayed your people and now you are on the threshold of doing the same to the evil. How very fitting of you." Her dark tones seemed at home within the dismal chamber as they echoed thickly off the ancient stone walls. The hatred she felt for the red woman radiated from her face burning and singeing Ina's corrupt soul. Ramira had not forgotten her treachery as she spun the ceremonial daggers in her hands. Ina's face drained of blood, her fingers twitching nervously as Ramira's statement settled upon her skin like the noxious mist in Mahn's realm. That haze was preferable over the murderous gleam now shining from Ramira's eyes. A sense of desperation leaped to life in her breast as she sought to delay Ramira's departure and save herself from Mahn's wrath.

"I care nothing for anyone, least of all a group of vagabonds! Give me the knives, Ramira."

"I think not. You will undo the bargain you made with Mahn."

"It's too late! He will come no matter what you do and will take that which you house!"

Ramira glared at the traitorous woman who slowly began to close the distance between them, her red-rimmed eyes ablaze with malice. The loathsome bargain the high priestess made with the evil was about to reach fruition and the only thing it lacked to complete its abominable transformation was the Source. The power Ina sought came at a price too high for Ramira to accept, and although most of her people were doomed, at least the strangers had a chance to survive. When she was finished here, she would find a way to help at least some of the Thebans escape the impending devastation Ina assisted in orchestrating. The high priestess gathered together the last shreds of courage and stood in front of Ramira. She licked her dry lips, discreetly slipping her hands inside her blood red gown, but she never had the opportunity to pluck out her knife.

"I don't think so," snarled Ramira, bringing the blades down across the high priestess' throat. Ina's hands reached up frantically trying to stem the torrent of blood covering her fingers, her wide eyes focused on the glacial look on Ramira's face. She crumpled to the ground, twitched several times then lay still.

Ramira stared at the dead woman whose blood was indistinguishable from her gown then turned around to make her way up out of the dank stone halls. She extinguished every torch along the way, fighting the urge to wield the Source and bury the evil lair beneath tons of rock and debris. She was sure that, deprived of his prize, the evil would fulfill that temptation for her. Mahn would rise from his sulphurous realm tonight, leaving her precious few hours to help those who could escape. She headed to Oma's home. People scattered away in terror from her as she walked down the street, the high priestess' blood staining her clothing and skin and her wrath glittering from her eyes. She arrived to warn Oma of the impending evil and to gather as many people as possible to escape from the city. She entered the home, her foot bumping into something positioned on the floor just inside the door. She looked down and felt every ounce of strength flow from her body.

Ramira could not believe what she saw and dropped to her knees beside the corpse, her eyes filling with tears, her throat unable to utter a single wail. She held Oma in her arms, rocking her just as the brown woman had done to her since the day she was born. Her silent grief spilled over the body in huge waves, nearly cleansing it of the blood that had begun to dry. The tears finally abated and Ramira leaned forward kissing Oma on the forehead while hugging her close to her body. She finally understood what had happened and gently deposited the woman on the floor, letting out a moan that carried to every corner of the city. It resonated with an anguish steeped in the loss of a beloved one but was carried on the wings of bitterness and vengeance. Dogs scurried away with their tails between their legs and their ears pressed against their heads. Mothers collected their frightened children in their arms and ushered them indoors. Men took a step backward as if they had been dealt a blow to their bodies. Soldiers automatically drew their swords trying to ward off an enemy their blades could never penetrate. The entire city trembled beneath the onslaught of those fierce emotions. Ramira knew this same fate had befallen Imhap and Horemb, too, and she would avenge their deaths in ways that would make even Mahn cringe. There were only three people in her life that meant anything to her and now they were all dead.

The sun began its descent as she emerged from Oma's home, blood soaked and raging with fury at the grave injustices ripping her city apart. Veins and tendons stood out along her crimson neck and face as she struggled to control the feelings that seemed to chain her to the street. The high priestess had doomed Thebes by making her evil pact with Mahn, and Ramira could at best reduce the damage that bargain had caused. She had to calm down and think clearly and try to take advantage of the fact that Mahn was temporarily ignorant of Ina's shortcoming. She could not afford to make any mistakes. She forced the chaotic eddies of emotion into a corner of her mind, seized the nearest horse then sped through the city heading for the main gates.

She raced out of the city, glancing toward the northeast where a yellowish glow could be discerned against the impending darkness. Time was running out. She had to make sure the strangers had heeded her warning, and forced her horse to sprint to the last place she had seen them. The ride seemed to take forever. Ramira's mind whirled, conjuring up their death and destruction. The vision became sharper and clearer with each passing mile until she returned to the knoll from which she had first observed them. To her relief, the wagons and tents were gone, the trampled grasses marking their progress through the verdant plains heading east. She hung her head, the tears forming in her eyes running down her cheeks as she looked back to the yellow haze. It had intensified and served as a beacon to call her back to complete her duties. She wiped away the teardrops and turned to remount her horse when a shadow detached itself from the darkness.

"What is going on?" he demanded, catching her wrist to keep her from fleeing.

"You should not be here…your people…"

"They are gone many hours," he stated. "What is that?" His tone cut through her uncertainty, its strength and fortitude shoring up her slowly crumbling resolve as they watched the unhealthy light spread to the outer walls.

"Death," she replied in a small voice, her eyes wide as she watched it touch the city. She was too late and too far away to help. She had failed.

"I sense its evil…" he began, but she wrenched her arm, loosening his grip just enough to escape, jumping upon her horse to race back to Thebes.

Despondency clawed at her soul as she dashed back to the city in a foolhardy attempt to do something…anything to stop Mahn. Her breath stuck in her throat as the sickly luminescence hovered over then plunged into the palace where it would discover the truth. She kicked the animal's sides, disregarding the foam spreading from its mouth, down its neck and across her legs. Its ragged exhalations kept time with its pounding hooves but Ramira refused to relent to its exhaustion. She heard the stranger pursuing her, cursing under her breath for the very thing she did not want was for him to be near the ill-fated city. She shouted back at him, nearly shrieking for him to turn away, but the stranger only followed her with more determination. He finally caught up to her and grabbed the reins, keeping her from plunging heedlessly to her death. He forced her off of her horse and was about to reproach her when a sound filled their ears, a sound that made them freeze in their tracks. The noise sounded like bones being broken as the evil shattered and pounded the very stones composing the buildings, walls and foundations of the city.

The devastation began in the palace, the destruction continuing unabated as Mahn followed the main avenue south to the main entrance. His enormous smoldering shadow demolished and consumed everything in his path grinding stones to dust beneath his feet then incinerating those remnants until nothing but ash remained. Fire exploded everywhere, the screams of the dying reaching their ears above the hellish cracking and grinding. Mahn shattered the gates with one tremendous burst of power, its pieces raining down even upon the pair watching with dread. Spooked, the horses disappeared into the night, stranding Ramira and the stranger. Ramira knew Mahn had found the high priestess and with that discovery he also uncovered her failure to secure the Source. She had inadvertently done Ina a favor by slaying her, for the evil would certainly have severely tortured the red woman for her negligence. She tried to rise and retrieve her mount but his strong hands pulled her back and down into the concealment of a nearby ditch. Fire consumed the night, the flames extending into the dark heavens as they fed upon the carcass of the burning city. It spread quickly, engulfing everything in its path as it feasted on wood, oils, canopies, and, worst of all, human flesh. The intense heat carried that horrible smell to the pair hiding in the darkness. The hatred borne upon a foul wind rushed toward them, stilling her protests as she grabbed the other's hands in fear. Mahn, she was sure, was about to find them.

Mahn swooped down into the bowels of the palace anticipating the feast he was about to enjoy. Once he had sated himself with the Source he would hunt down the other power that existed in the land. The souls imprisoned within him felt his excitement, feeding off of it as they began to scream and pulse with anticipation. Soon countless others would join them in their insane realm of darkness. They looked forward to the new arrivals; they would torment them just as they had been when they first entered this appalling black kingdom.

He flew through the unlit corridors, quickly reaching the huge stone doors separating him from his prize in no time at all. They were ajar, the silence issuing forth causing him to hesitate. He paused; the empty silence and lack of burning incense sent waves of apprehension through him. He forced the doors open and stared dispassionately at the slain body of the red woman. He glared at the altar, watching the last of the liquid dripping into the carved bowl. The daggers were gone.

"You will not escape through death, for I command you to rise…rise and face your master!"

The red woman began to twitch then slowly rose to her feet in jerky movements, her eyes wide open and filled with fear. He had called her back from the only place she could hide. She began to change, the human emotions surging through her cold soul replaced with nothing but a need to serve the evil she had delivered from the stinking swamp.

"Where is it?" he hissed.

"She escaped...she went to warn the strangers..."

"You managed to deny me both prizes?" He fumed with such an intensity the very walls around them shook with his ire. Mahn, the high priestess firmly in his grasp, rushed up the stone corridor. His passing scorched even the impenetrable granite walls of the hallway as he hurried to salvage his plans. Mahn refused to abandon his scheme even if it meant laying waste to everything within his reach. He exploded out of the palace, the cacophonous cries of the imprisoned souls wailing and shrieking in accompaniment to his own thunderous rage. He landed at the base of the great staircase into the palace, the high priestess dangling limply from his black gloved hand, his hooded head snapping back and forth in search of the Source. He sensed nothing.

He deposited her unceremoniously upon the sands then prepared himself to destroy the city. He sent mighty pulses of black power into everything, heedless of the falling debris raining down all around him. Obelisks cracked and collapsed down upon themselves and mighty facades built centuries ago shattered and crumbled onto the streets. Well-tended trees and shrubs burst into flame as did the pennants hanging from the poles both inside and outside the city. The ground shook and vibrated, further destabilizing the foundations and sending what barely remained balanced into the street. Great billows of dust rose up, mixing with the smoke, obscuring the entire city and most of the evening sky. When it finally cleared, the devastation Mahn wreaked could not have been more complete. Once great buildings and the outer walls of the city lay in smoking and charred ruins while every living creature succumbed to his power as he smote them with his passing. Except for the occasional cracking of stone or the popping of fire, there was total silence. He could not sense the Source within the city so he turned his vengeance onto the plains on the other side of the mountain. He vacated the city gates heading south then backtracked, always sweeping the land for any sign of the Source. He roared over the peaks as if they were no bigger than anthills, sending his fury into the trees and brush as he passed over them. He burned and singed everything in sight, forcing large chunks of earth to erupt, and filled the plains with his venom. The poison began to sear the soil until it could no longer sustain a single living thing.

Still he was not satisfied; he knew the others had succeeded in moving just beyond his power and they, for now, were out of his reach. He turned his attention back to the city, continuing to search for the ultimate reward, obliterating anything he had left even remotely intact as he scoured the remnants of a once proud and powerful city.

And so Thebes was no more, child...

The gray mist closed in on Zada, mercifully concealing the horror she witnessed. She returned to the present, the journey into her past leaving her reeling with emotions and many questions. Oma had shown her the demise of the city from where the Herkahs hailed and revealed it was the Lady of the Sands who bestowed the inner sight upon her. The stone pavilion marked her realm and it was from here that she, and those who came before her, was judged and deemed worthy by the Lady. How far did the Lady's power and influence extend? Zada suddenly remembered that "other" sensation she had experienced, the one that stayed just beyond her sight. Was the Lady watching from a great distance?

What of Ramira? How did she end up housing the Source? Oma had shown her the deception by the high priestess but had failed to inform her how Ramira first ended up with it. Did it travel through the generations like the Green Might did or was it somehow infused into her? If the latter, then when? Just prior to the high priestess' betrayal? At birth? Where would it go when Ramira died?

Zada dropped her face into her hands, her exhaustion sapping her mentally, emotionally and physically. The strain of the past few months culminated in the journey back to her roots and she was sure Oma wanted her to discern something her tired mind could not quite grasp. All she wanted to do was sleep. She painfully rose from the chair and headed to her room, a room that would forever be devoid of her love. There were few about the castle and those that remained kept at a respectful distance from the nomad as she tread through the hallway. She entered her chamber and closed the door, collapsing onto her bed. Her last thought before falling into a deep sleep was of Allad...

-12-

The prince tried to rest but his mind reverberated with thoughts tied to the power vibrating within him. He tossed and turned but the magic grew more insistent with each passing second. It first heightened then dulled his senses until all he could do to keep still was to clutch his blankets. He got up and poured himself a glass of wine, his shaking hand threatening to spill the contents all over the floor. He took a sip then grimaced at the bitter taste. He put the glass down and walked out onto the balcony, the cold night air washing over his heated body making him shiver, but it also chased away the frustration gathering in his soul. He went back inside and sat in front of the fire, staring into the flames until the flickering orange glow disappeared, leaving him within the maze once more…

The corridor was as before complete with locked doors and the dripping sounds echoing hollowly in the distance. He glanced upward and saw the infinite blackness stretching far away over his head. He looked down both ends of the hall that appeared to lead into infinity in both directions. He cocked his head to the side pondering the meaning of the doors. They were of wood and as ancient as this place yet sported no handles or locks but did have hinges. He approached the nearest door and gently pushed against it then tried to pry it open without any success. He lifted his hand and knocked, slightly embarrassed by this behavior; did he really expect someone to open it from the other side? The rapping, however, echoed hollowly beyond the door.

He sighed then felt the Green Might begin to twist as if in response to something. Danyl began to smile for the key to unlocking this maze he realized, was the power and he let go of it, allowing it to explore the surroundings without hindering it with his doubt and frustration. To his amazement the magic began to shift and change. It altered his psyche in the process as it tentatively, then with greater certainty, challenged the portals by slipping underneath and taking him with it.

Danyl found himself looking down upon the dwarf king, the Khadry and his brother as they slept fitfully within the barracks. Their shredded and filthy clothing spoke volumes of their tireless efforts and incomprehensible losses. While he stood upon the parapets these individuals and others like them took a physical, mental and emotional punishment he could barely comprehend, the Green Might refusing to be summoned forth to help them. That situation made Danyl sick and he vowed he would raise his sword in battle rather than stand idly by while they were systematically slain. Now as the power began to confirm itself within him, he understood wielding a weapon of steel would not be necessary. Or so he hoped.

Gard woke first and stretched, never acknowledging Danyl who stood only a few paces away, his breath visible as he sought to warm himself with a mug of tea. Danyl tried to speak to him, but even though his mouth opened, no words left his lips nor did any breath materialize before it. He exhaled harder and still no mist appeared, leaving him confused then wondering if he were dead. Was his shade gazing down upon his companions? He reached out to touch the Khadry but his hand disappeared right through the other's chest as if he weren't there.

What…?

Danyl stared in shock at the scene taking place before him. Warriors who had died on the plains outside the city walls filed past him as if they had returned to eat and rest before heading out once more. Elves, Khadry, dwarf and Herkah moved silently by, their hands and quivers empty because they had fought until no weapons remained. Danyl's brow knitted in quiet grief as each of the shadows glanced over at him, nodding in recognition as they passed him by. He had failed them yet none accused him of causing their deaths. He stood there mouth agape with a bewilderment bordering on horror as so many ghosts passed by until his gaze fell upon Nyk. A sob lodged in Danyl's throat as Nyk halted in front of him, the urge to hug his brother overwhelming. He had escaped the ravages of the Vox because Ramira had severed that horrible bond with a stroke from her knives, but she could do nothing for his bruised soul. The Vox' touch would stay with Nyk for eternity. His eyes reflected the repugnance he felt for that brief merging yet they also radiated a great sense of concern for those still defiled by the demons, especially Allad. Danyl's eyes glittered a promise that he would do anything he could to help those who were still under the Vox' influence. Nyk lifted his hand, placing it against his brother's heart and flooding him with a variety of emotions. Love, gratitude and that powerful connection that exists between siblings surged from Nyk into Danyl, their intensity bringing the younger brother nearly to his knees. Tears formed in his eyes as he grieved for

Nyk, his shaking hand slowly reaching up to touch the spectral one resting on his chest. The Green Might flared as it sought to cleanse the last vestiges of the Vox' contact, leaving Nyk completely free of its corruption. Nyk offered him a sad smile, one that Danyl could barely see through his tear-stained vision but felt in his heart. It was time for Nyk to go. The dead prince followed the other apparitions as they disappeared into the darkness beyond the barracks, leaving the distraught elf little choice but to stare after them. If he were dead then why was he not following them? If he were alive then why could he not touch Gard? Was he somewhere in between? Danyl raised his hands to his face and stared for they were fully enveloped in the green mist as were his arms and, he was sure, the rest of his body. The Green Might was fully awake and began to saturate his form, the reason he was able to exist in this in between place. He hovered backward and out into the corridor once more.

The door slammed shut and the dripping sound growing louder. He ignored the doors showing the living and dead in one place, a place that he did not want to revisit. Why had the might allowed so many to die before it was willing to be wielded? He glanced down both sides of the corridor then slowly lifted his head upward. Darkness greeted him as he craned his neck, staring into a nothingness that seemed almost oppressive. It dared Danyl to probe its obscurity, mocking his doubt and trepidation. The memory of his brother's touch and the hope in his eyes materialized briefly in Danyl's mind, reminding him time was running out. He gathered his courage, positioned himself as close to the center of the corridor as possible, took a deep breath and willed the might upward into the daunting blackness…

Zada woke with a start, the sudden ignition of power exploding into her inner sight and momentarily blinding her. She gasped for air, shielding her eyes as the waves of energy pummeled her mind and crawled like insects across her skin. The prickling sensation surged through her mind and out her body, manifesting itself in the floor beneath her feet. It began to vibrate then shake, radiating outward until the bottles and books began to dance and fall off the shelves and tables. She reached over, clinging to the bedpost as the jolting peaked then subsided and, for a moment, all was still. Then a massive thunderclap exploded overhead, its residue sizzling electricity that gradually abated long after it finished reverberating throughout the city. She smiled. She rose and walked out of her chamber, seeking out the elf in his room but not finding him there or any other place he usually frequented. Of course she would not find him for the magic, she was sure, had taken him to a different level and it would only relinquish him to the land of light when the transformation was complete. She passed by a window and noted that the sun would soon rise and the fighting and dying would begin anew. This day, however, would not be like any other day. She took a deep breath as she stared at the gold, lavender and pale pink pastel hues gently tinting the horizon.

The elf prince surged upward with it, his body weightless, shifting with the Green Might as it flowed and swelled toward the very heavens. The Green Might felt as if it were slithering through his body like a snake weaving its way through the grasses. It looped around his bones, in between the fibers of his muscles then amid the myriad of tendons and veins. It encircled his organs, lingering around his heart, before diving where his soul awaited its inquisition. He held his breath as it hovered over his spirit, sensing the souls of those who had wielded it in the past. Some had wilted beneath its potency while others gained strength from it yet all had endured its intense scrutiny. He could not shake the feeling that they now watched his reaction to the power to see how he would fare under its mighty influence.

He was anxious and tentative but he also knew what would happen if he failed to live up to its demands and accepted whatever it commanded of him. He released all of his apprehensions and doubts, flinging away all of his wants, desires and emotions to make room for it. He could not, however, abandon one thing: love. He needed to cling to the love of his family, friends and all those who inhabited the city, and it was absolutely essential in maintaining the bond he had created with Ramira.

Let go of it all.

I can't.

You must or the metamorphosis cannot be completed.

No...

Danyl knew he had to heed the power but what kind of person would he be if he relinquished all that he was? Would he be lost forever? The magic became insistent; he could not turn back from the road he was now on. Not fulfilling the transformation would be disastrous because then the might would be set free. Mahn would scoop it up as easily as picking a stone up from the ground. The Green Might showed this to him, and with a reluctance that nearly ripped his heart into shreds, he cast aside everything that bound him to the world on the brink of destruction. The effect was immediate and threatened to render him limb from limb as the power burned into his spirit.

It incinerated his memories and links to all those in this and the netherworld until he became nothing more than an empty vessel. Then, when it had completely expunged all that he was, it began to pour back into him. The power rushed into him with a mindless intention, spreading to every corner of his body, flowing into every nook and cranny until the elf thought he would drown. He remained as calm as he could, allowing it to wash over and through him, feeling as if he could not hold one more drop of the magic. Then and only then did it finally stop.

He waited for whatever it would do next then sensed his memories and emotions being returned to him, but the power kept the essences of who he was carefully stored away where they would not interfere. Danyl waited for his instructions but none were forthcoming. The elf realized he was on his own...

Danyl opened his eyes and found himself in the great hall standing in front of the tapestry, his ancestor seemingly evaluating him through the line of trees. The prince sensed the souls within the hall but they were silent. The dreams, duties and desires of his predecessors had brought him to this point and it was only fitting he should stand before them brimming with the power they had brought from their original home. Their lives had determined this moment and it was appropriate to show them the homage they so righteously deserved. The prince knelt down in the middle of the hall, placed his crossed arms over his chest and bowed his head in reverence to his ancestors. They emerged one by one from their places of honor to stand around him in a circle. The last two to approach were the first king and a beautiful woman clad in a flowing blue gown.

My lord...my queen.

Danyl was ecstatic as he beheld Alyxandyr the First and his own beloved mother. The King's piercing green eyes bored into him while his mother's benevolent gaze soothed his racing heart. Instead of uttering a single word, they descended upon him as one, forming a macabre cocoon around him that nearly suffocated him. He remained motionless, although the eerie handling by the dead intimidated his very senses. He strained to keep still, the beads of perspiration upon his forehead dripping upon the stone floor. When they were satisfied, they all floated back to their displays except for the first king and his mother. They stared down at him for another moment: his eyes filled with anticipation while hers brimmed with love. No matter how difficult the impending battle was to be, Danyl knew he would not face the evil alone. That thought wiped away the sweat and the drip-dripping sound stopped. He rose to his feet and left the hall.

Seven, Gard, Styph and the other warriors were in the process of dressing to face another day when the explosion that rocked the city startled them all, each one imagining it to be a harbinger of evil. They exchanged perplexed glances then grabbed their weapons as they headed out beneath an inky sky painted with the first tinges of the rising sun. Alyxandyr and Clare met them as they rounded the corner near their horses, their features reflecting the same reservations.

"What in the four corners was that?" asked Clare as she stopped adjusting Seven's leather breastplate. Her hands clung to the straps in anticipation of another concussion.

"It arose from within the city," added Styph, glancing at the buildings and shops for any signs of damage. His first thought was that Mahn and his forces had managed to hurl rocks from several catapults over the walls, but he could discern no sabotage to the structures or any fires caused by their passing.

"You don't think…" Gard didn't need to finish the sentence for if Zada were under another attack, one spearheaded by the darkness looming on the plains outside the city, she would be powerless to stop it. Moments turned into minutes as they sought to find the source of the concussion. No smoke rose over the roofs from an impact nor could they see anyone running toward a particular collision spot.

"I'm going to…" The elf king did not finish his sentence for he and the others watched with confusion then awe as a rider enveloped within a greenish mist galloped up to them. Unable to move, they stared at the figure silencing the city with his passing, the faint yet unmistakable glow pulsating from his body giving him an ethereal quality. They recognized the rider as he neared them, their incredulous stares tempered only by the feeling of hope they now all shared. Danyl halted a few paces away, dismounting his steed while patiently waiting for the truth to sink into those who stared in wonder. The optimistic hope that the elven power might stem the tide of death permeated the air in and around the plains. It radiated from their faces and renewed their energy to fight.

"You…?" was all Seven could muster. His tongue could not decide what words to say. He reverently absorbed the magic throbbing from the elf, his mind telling him he stood within his mighty shadow. His heart, however, brimmed with pride and the confidence of knowing Danyl would not fail them. The dwarf king looked into Danyl's eyes but the hard and unforgiving look staring back at him forced him to turn his gaze away. The magic had firmly infused itself within him, the resulting coldness emanating from his face sending a shiver up the grizzled veteran's spine.

"Yes, me," he replied in a detached tone as he stood before them, his impassive features acknowledging family and friend.

"What will you do now?" his father asked, studying his child who had grown into a man and then into something completely unfamiliar. The King would never have guessed such a moment would ever arise in his lifetime, but it had and they must now each acquiesce to what destiny had in store for them. Fate chose various individuals for reasons only she knew, reasons that would only make sense in another time and place. Mere mortals had no hand in altering that destiny. His child had become a thing of legend and now stood before them awash with his own legacy to fulfill whatever destiny had deemed.

The sun chased away the shadows and promised there would be no snow nor would a single cloud mar the sky. This sign suddenly seemed heartening to those who were already fighting for their lives and for those who were about to join them. Zada arrived and beheld the prince's subtle radiance, which she knew would become something none of them could ever have imagined.

"Nyk is dead, Father," Danyl said, the image of his brother touching him still fresh in his mind.

"No, Danyl, a Vox took him," was Alyxandyr's grief-filled reply.

"The Vox had him but no longer," he clarified, the power not allowing him to share in his sorrow. His reaction drew perplexed stares because those standing before him were unaccustomed to an emotionless Danyl.

"The only way for Nyk's spirit to be released from the demon would be..." began Gard.

"Ramira. That was what that commotion was all about," Zada finished for him. "She must have tried to help Allad, too, but Mahn...he must have punished her severely for her act."

A part of Gard questioned his harsh judgment concerning Ramira, the established blame he had placed on her for causing all of this devastation beginning to waver but not disappear. His intolerance for her existence was only slightly eased by her merciful act but then his rationale returned, reminding him that Nyk and Allad wouldn't have been taken by the evil had she not lived in the first place. He found it difficult to share in his friends' faith in her, his unwillingness to let go of the one thing that made sense to him in all of this madness. He flinched as Danyl's cold, hard glance penetrated his thoughts. He looked away, the struggle to give Ramira the benefit of the doubt knotting his brow and turning down the corners of his mouth.

"We have to go," said Seven, as the sounds of metal clashing upon metal and the screams of the wounded and dying filtered into the city. It would, they knew, be the last day to do battle out on the plains. Today they would either stand in mournful victory or become a part of the black army pressing toward the city. They said their farewells; they exchanged embraces solid, heartfelt and filled with their love and appreciation for each other. Those who remained watched the retreating backs of their companions as they headed out to meet their individual destinies.

"Go with them, Lance," ordered Danyl, and, for once, his captain did not argue. Although awed by the prince, the captain stuck out his hand to his lifelong friend, gripping it tightly. They acknowledged their feelings for each other then Lance turned and followed the others out. Danyl sighed; the burden of their existence depended upon his ability to wield the elven magic. Death and despair would not wait for him to perfect his skill with the power. He would have one chance only.

The Source responded to the Green Might flaring in greeting and infuriating Mahn. He repeatedly thrashed her with horrific images agitating the most appalling of the souls into tormenting her while he pondered what to do with this new adversary. He knew it because he had come so close to extracting it from the other bearer and that failure still left a bad taste in his mouth a thousand years later. It was imperative he take the Source soon or the other magic would become too overwhelming for him to overpower. Mahn decided he would allow the decimation of the elves and their allies for a few hours more before striding forward and drawing forth the Source. He would then concentrate on obtaining the other power before obliterating every living thing on the plains. He hissed with satisfaction, imagining himself towering so high in the air that he could plant one foot on each side of the city. He would glare down upon the mortals, squashing them with his heel as if they were nothing more than insignificant insects. He would then turn his wrath upon the witch that had hidden the Source from him all of these years, hunting her down to teach her a lesson.

She had managed to make things difficult for him for all of those eons, thinking herself clever by concealing it out in the open. The high priestess had been fooled, just as he had, but she could obscure it no longer. He stood on the brink of total victory while she concealed herself within the silver sands. He would poison everything with his hatred and would leave no living thing in his wake.

He watched as both good and bad fell beneath each other's weapons, gradually riding closer to the gray walls now pitted by the debris hurled at them. His huge steed had to pick his way over the fallen bodies the closer he came to the turmoil, but Mahn's cold eyes never looked down. He focused on the figure that had emerged from beneath the gate, a lone rider taking up position on a small rise in front of the city. There was something different about this bearer than the one he had sensed so many centuries ago and Mahn mulled over what that could be. The magic itself was essentially the same, as was the force driving this one to protect those gathered on the field and in the city. Yet he could perceive something else.

He narrowed his eyes, straining to discern who was beneath the simple brown hood. He noted nothing more than a patient restraint. He had misread the Source and been forced to wait all this time to retrieve it and would not overlook anything ever again. It had somehow protected the Source a thousand years ago and could just as easily impede him now. Mahn decided to test the bearer.

Do you actually think you can defeat me?

Mahn sent the thought into the rider as swiftly as an arrow but he remained silent. He assailed him with the same images he had tormented Ramira with and again the horseman did not so much as even flinch. Mahn stared at the unemotional figure, the uncharacteristic response an enigma he would try to deal with in another fashion. He grabbed and displayed Ramira to him, her face contorted with the pain he inflicted upon her with hand and mind and still the rider appeared not to care. Mahn was used to toying with emotions and feelings because they provided him with the greatest of responses from his victims, yet this elf seemed oblivious to his treatment of Ramira.

I will eat the flesh of your father and drink the blood of your friends.

You will choke on both.

Ah! It has a voice and it sounds as if it belongs to a little boy!

Mahn waited for a reply but none came. Urgency began to grow within him as this magic calmly challenged him from beneath the shadows of the gate to the city. He urged his mount on a bit faster, his presence creating a crease through both sides of warriors as he passed them by. He stopped on a slight rise where everyone could see him. He had to rip the Source from Ramira soon but he could not help making sure that all who were present watched him transform himself into the ultimate power. He sat up straighter in the saddle, his head tilted arrogantly to one side as he absorbed the fear lifting from the plains like the shimmering heat waves in the desert. He glared at his men, the fear of reprisal clearly etched on their possessed features then over at the allies who wore expressions of determination tinged with dread. They hammered away at his army, desperately trying to keep at bay the terrible consequence of faltering beneath their enemies' blades. He reveled at the panic and horror contorting the faces of the elves and dwarves as they fell beneath his army's swords, consuming their emotions as if dining at a sumptuous feast. His hunger, however, would not be appeased until he dined on the banquet's main courses: the Source and the green magic.

Each one of the companions pondered what they had seen as they rode out to battle the enemy once again. They shared their amazement and disbelief that Danyl housed the Green Might, hoping perhaps now so many would not have to die. They all wondered why it had taken so long for it to surface and how long he had known that it thrived within as they neared their opponents and drew their weapons.

Seven and his men returned to the southern portion of the plains, the King remembering the stoic look on the prince's normally emotional face. How much had the magic to do with that? The prince had always been compassionate, quick to lend a hand and openly showing his feelings toward those whom he cared for the most. He had gazed down upon them with a far-off, almost detached look, as if the power had somehow dulled that which made him Danyl. The dwarf king hoped and prayed today would be the day that the powers engaged each other. So many had died, leaving too few to continue this fighting.

Seven had a great deal of faith in both Danyl and Ramira. After having seen the prince's transformation and Ramira's deep and abiding love for him and her friends, he felt as if Mahn had no chance to defeat them. If they survived, would they be able to gather their deep feelings for one another and persevere? Seven's musings were forced out of his mind as they began the exhausting battle once more. The dwarf king and his men clashed with their foes and were still amazed and alarmed at how they simply thrust themselves upon their blades, heedless of the death the warriors dealt to them. The King brought his sword down, nearly cutting a man in two only to find another ready to take his place. Mahn did not care if he won with his army for they were nothing more than an amusement to him and a way of eroding the spirits of those who fought for and with Bystyn. Seven, who had been gone long from his own city, wondered how it was faring and hoped the evil had not reached it, for there were few dwarves left to defend his home. He thought about his home and how badly he wanted to sleep in his own bed and listen to the children as they squealed with delight while playing down by the river. His mouth watered as he thought about the marinated meat cooking in the fireplace and the stout ale with which to wash it down. It would all be gone if he did not start paying attention and focus on the bloody task at hand, and as he chanced a glance at Danyl sitting unmoving upon his horse, if he failed.

Styph turned his head and watched Lance catch up to him. The sight of Danyl's protector so far away from his brother only accentuated the fact that his brother was beyond the aid of those composed of flesh and blood. The crown prince gratefully accepted Lance's presence for the captain's abilities, heightened by the training he had received from the Herkahs, were formidable indeed. The fact that Danyl no longer needed him spoke volumes about the power he held and Styph realized that he was not one bit envious of his brother. He was sure Danyl did not particularly relish what he housed but destiny had decreed otherwise. The crown prince gave his brother a lot of credit for handling it as well as he had. The black line grew and swelled, stirring the elf's training into action. His eyes narrowed as they sought out where to attack the weakest section of the opposing army while he pulled his sword from its scabbard. The invading horde stretched from the forest in the north down to the knolls in the south then westward for as far as the eye could see. Lances and swords reflected the sunlight no matter which direction he looked while cavalry units broke through the ranks of foot soldiers. Mahn was sending every available body at them. Arrows fired from both sides whizzed by his head forcing him to lay low over his horse's great neck, his sweat mingling with the steeds as they surged forward. An arrow lodged itself in the saddle beside his knee and another whistled through his tunic without penetrating his flesh. His luck, he knew, would not hold out forever and no sooner did that thought erupt in his head when a barb bit into his thigh. Inhaling sharply, he reached down and wrenched it free, the pain pushed to a corner of his mind as he and the others engaged the enemy. The morning sun continued to climb into the bright blue heavens, offering some measure of warmth as it illuminated the defenders gradually being pushed back toward the gray walls.

They fought hard but the sheer numbers of their opponents began to overwhelm them. Many had already been lost and it would only be a matter of time before the enemy held the upper hand. Gard, Styph, Seven and all the others who knew of the Green Might kept looking over at Danyl, but the prince had not moved since posting himself on the little rise in front of the city. Couldn't he see those that fell dying upon the plains? Why wasn't he wielding the power to stop the slaughter? What was he waiting for?

Seven quickly deduced that the enemy swarming from the forest's edge was about to overrun them and called for a retreat. The blackness streaming forth forced them backward to the city, herding them like cattle towards Styph and Gard. It was clear they would all meet before the sun rose too much farther. Those fighting were too exhausted and wounded to shout out any battle cries, managing to just grunt with the effort of wielding their weapons. Seven bellowed over the clanging noises, ordering his men to sever contact and head for the closest knot of fighters, then brought his sword down upon the helmeted head of a foe. His blade sliced through the armor and skull, ending up at the base of his shoulders. He pushed his men on, chancing a glance at the unmoving figure, watching the battle from atop his horse. Come on, boy. Do something!

Alyxandyr and Clare, pale with fear and disbelief, stared down at the waves of friend and foe that began to wash up along the gray walls like some terrible tide. They could no longer stand idly by, grabbing their weapons as they ran toward the gate. The King shouted orders over his shoulder as he and the Queen mustered whoever was capable of lifting sword or longbow to follow them. They left the city and headed for their nearest comrades, slashing and cutting with a vengeance that caught on all around them as they helped push back the enemy. They were at a critical juncture where saving themselves from death was a moot point: there would be no one to rule if they stayed on top of the battlements. Their heart and determination caught on and they succeeded in regaining some of the lost ground. That changed as Mahn urged his army on until the allies were forced into the defensive once more. Clare and Alyxandyr lost track of one another during the fighting. The blood and mud covering them from head to toe concealed their identities from each other and everyone else around them. They became just two more bodies in a sea of thousands. The enemy fanned out and began to push inward and those who valiantly fought on the plains knew without question the noose was tightening.

Zada stared as if hypnotized at the ferocity taking place on the plains as she searched the surging mass of flesh and metal for any sign of her companions. They were indistinguishable from the masses hacking and chopping away at each other. The elven archers, fearful of hitting their own kin, descended down off of the ramparts and took up their swords, flowing out of the gates and onto the churned up field. The only ones left in the city were the old, infirm and the children. The nomad ran along the parapets dodging arrows loosened by the enemy, searching for a position where she could see both Danyl and the approaching Mahn. The evil casually rode closer to them as if he already tasted victory. His massive steed carried him over the fallen, Mahn somehow parting the combatants staring wide-eyed at the monstrosity that had initiated the fighting.

She silently implored Danyl to do something, begging him to make use of the power coursing through him, but the prince watched blankly as the evil advanced. She could sense Ramira within the dark cloak but could not tell if Mahn had subjugated her to his will. The Herkah had no way of knowing how powerful the elf had become nor could she tell how weak Ramira was. She could clearly sense the black force straining in Mahn. His enormous cloak billowed insanely as if some monstrous storm raged within its blackness determined to burst out and sweep away everything in its path. Ramira was stranded somewhere within that terrible tempest, enduring things Zada did not even want begin to imagine. *Hang on, child!*

Cooper descended the castle steps armed and ready to join the fighting. He reassuringly touched the small blade strapped near his chest then grabbed the reins of a loose horse, mounting it in one motion. He kicked its side and raced toward the gate at the end of the avenue. He was about to pass the intersection when he caught sight of an odd shape keeping to the shadows of the buildings as it flitted along the street. It disappeared then reappeared from within shops and storehouses, its movements feral in nature. Cooper reined in his mount fearing more fiends had infiltrated the city, but this person did not act wild like the lower demons nor did it have the cunning stealth of the Vox. The King had no idea who it was or what it was looking for. He was about to investigate when the shape spotted him. It became motionless and fixated on the King, wanting to approach him yet loath to abandon its purpose for being in the city. The King rode over to it, halting a few feet away.

"Who are you? What are you doing..." Cooper glared as the figure pulled back the cowl to reveal a deeply tanned woman with short-cropped hair. A red mist pulsed from where her dark eyes should have been, the corrupt haze matching the hatred forever chiseled on her features. Antama. He dismounted, withdrew two daggers and walked toward her. The savage look on her face did nothing to deter him nor did the brutal swings of his blades as he bore down on her. She deflected his blows with ease but could do nothing to parry the vehemence attached to every stroke. It wasn't enough for him to cut and slice into the traitorous wench and whatever thrived inside of her. Cooper used the blunt end of the hilt to pummel her whenever he had a chance, disregarding the slashes she administered to him.

"You fight like a woman," she taunted him.

"You filthy wretch! You will not live to see the end of this day."

"You think to kill me with those ineffectual weapons?"

"No, Antama, but I believe this will suffice." He feigned to her left, dropping one of the blades and wrenching out Zada's knife. He lunged forward and buried it into her throat, the look of surprise giving him a moment of satisfaction. His expression turned to bewilderment when she pulled it out and dropped it at his feet, none the worse for wear.

"Is that all you have?" she scoffed at him.

What sort of demon had filtered into her body? Not a Vox or she would at least have appeared distressed even if it didn't kill her. Not a Radir, either, for she remained lucid and focused. The red mist he had seen stream into her wasn't a demon then but something else…Cooper cocked his head and pursed his lips then did something Antama didn't expect. He smiled at her. The curious response made her hesitate long enough for the King to raise his sword and bring it down on her neck where it met at the shoulders. Her head fell on the cobble-stone street with a heavy thud, rolled several feet and came to rest face up, her mien frozen in a look of dumbfounded outrage.

"That's what I've got, my love."

Cooper spat on her then kicked her head over to her body. He was now ready to meet up with the allies but stood over the corpse, the lingering question of what possessed her still occupying his attention. He was about to squat down beside her when the red haze oozed out from her pores and floated over the remains. The King took a step back, swallowing hard as he tried to identify what he had released. Not a Vox or Radir but belonging to Mahn…what else could you be? Come on, Cooper: think! The King's gaze fell on Zada's knife. He picked it up and slashed through the vapor, sucking in his breath as his hand and arm felt as if he were hacking his way through blistering briars. The haze separated wherever the Herkah blade touched it but did not succumb to what little of Zada's blood was left on the knife. It suddenly formed a spear point and shot away toward the gate before Cooper could vex any further. Cooper watched it cut through the air, fervently hoping it wasn't seeking another host. *I'm going to get blamed for this, too.* He glanced down one last time then mounted up and continued his ride.

Zada's knuckles were in danger of splitting open as she grasped the edge of the bulwark and stared down into the melee pressing up against the walls. There was barely enough room to swing a sword, and those who fell beneath a blade remained propped up against those who still wielded one. Warriors from both sides tripped over arms and legs, grabbing anyone around them to help break their fall. Those pushed up against the wall were in the worst shape, for the sheer number of combatants shoving against them crushed the life out of those trapped against the bulwark. They disappeared beneath the rush, replaced by another group who would meet the same fate.

She turned her attention to Danyl. He brought his hand up and for a moment Zada thought he would let the Green Might fly but all he did was reach into his cowl and scratch his face. She looked over to the stairs and made up her mind. She refused to watch any longer and took a step toward the riser. Her inner sight clicked on and turned her toward the impending danger. She opened her mouth but no words came out as the red arrow sped in her direction. Her feet merged with the gray stone below her, her eyes growing wider the closer the glittering substance came. Her heart beat wildly in her chest for although she wanted nothing more than to be reunited with Allad, she did not want to do so in Mahn's dark realm. She sluggishly raised her trembling arms, the effort futile for they would not stop the inevitable. The evil cloud passed over the barracks, crossed the alley between and dove straight at her, a choked cry escaping her throat. Zada crossed her arms in front of her and braced for the impact.

The haze was mere inches away from her when a brilliant green bolt enveloped it, blinding her and grinding the red particles into dust. The mist's annihilation broke the hold it had on her and she toppled to the floor, scraping her elbows and knees. She breathed in deeply trying to regain some measure of control then rose shakily to her feet and stared at the elf prince. His impenetrable hood pointed her way for a brief moment then turned back to the monstrosity that had taken up position across from him. Zada left the ramparts on rubbery legs and headed out of the gate.

Mahn finally stopped and dismounted near the southwest corner of the city. He grunted with displeasure as the bearer denied him the Herkah witch. He was untroubled by this for he would seize her once he conquered the elf and took his power. There would be no one left to help her then.

The combatants, momentarily free of the iron grip he had over them, sensed the impending confrontation. Mahn had abandoned them to fully concentrate on this last task. The fighting continued for several long minutes until it dawned on most of Mahn's army that they were no longer under his control. Individuals, then groups, withdrew pushing away the allies as they retreated away from the evil standing completely still upon the plain. They looked at each other as if awakened from a long nightmare, their human needs finally registering in their benumbed minds as stomachs growled and injuries ached. They soon ceased fighting, drawn to watch what was about to unfold, the cessation of striking metal leaving an eerie silence that was not broken even by the cries of the wounded and dying.

Seven grunted with pain as he toppled from his horse and landed on his shoulder, the unmistakable snapping sound followed by a piece of bone sticking up through his sleeve. Grateful that it wasn't his sword arm, he rolled to his feet and fought on. Every stroke of his weapon made him wince and soon the aching that began in his shoulder worked its way down into his body. He was growing weary and the small knot of men that remained to challenge the enemy became fewer and fewer as time ticked on by. He quickly glanced over at the disturbance to his right and saw Mahn about to commence the final stage of this conflict. His attention returned to the struggle at hand and none too soon, for he blocked a blow that would have decapitated him. He managed to jam the other's weapon but not enough to keep it from striking his wounded shoulder and deflecting it up against the side of his head. The blow knocked his breath away, sending the dwarf to his knees. He looked up shakily at the shadows around him knowing he did not have the strength left to save himself. The blood from his head wound ran into his eyes as he endeavored to rise but was too dizzy and in pain to find his feet. A black silhouette towering over him with sword held aloft marked the end of his time and all Seven could do was grasp his sword in a feeble attempt to protect himself.

Styph and Lance began to merge with Gard and the remainder of the Khadry's men. The sheer numbers of the enemy forced them to rally around each other much like Nyk and Allad had done the day before. They were about to die together as comrades. The enemy had moved the catapults close enough to hit the solid gray walls and the continuous thudding and cracking sounds soon filled the air around them. Loose debris would rain down upon them and more than one man dropped to the ground with a gaping hole in his head.

The luxury of looking around to see how the other units were faring had ceased. Most of the morning had been devoted to keeping one's head intact. Except for the warriors in the immediate area, none of the combatants on the plains knew how the others were faring. The only thing most of them knew was that Danyl waited outside the main gate and they anticipated him using the power to avoid disaster. The enemy swarmed around them and began to slaughter those on the edges as they worked inward to the princes.

"Do you see any place to retreat to?" shouted Styph, warding off one potential blow then thrusting upward with a dagger at another attacker.

"We're completely surrounded…just like everyone else on the plain!" Gard replied, then grunted in pain as the flat end of an axe smacked him in the back. He recovered and blocked a blade that would have landed on the back of Lance's neck.

"What in the four corners is Danyl waiting for?" cried the crown prince, severing the hand of one of Mahn's puppets.

"I think his wait is almost over."

One of the Vox spotted Styph and headed for him, the Herkah/demon's attraction to the prince alerting Lance. The Vox sprang forward, cutting apart all those who were in his way and was about to launch himself upon the prince when Lance propelled himself at the creature while pushing Styph into Gard's arms. The two princes watched with horror as the Vox' blade passed completely through the captain's chest and came out the other side. Lance, however, was not about to leave this earth without taking the hated demon with him. With bloodstained and trembling hands, he grabbed the Vox' tunic with one hand and yanked Zada's knife out with the other. With the last of his strength, the captain jammed the blade into the demon's throat and the two of them fell into a heap at the prince's feet. Styph and Gard, fearful of another Vox attack, spun about, their backs touching as they prepared to make a last stand, a quick image of Nyk and Allad darting through their minds. They had no intention of meeting that same fate.

-13-

Danyl stared at Mahn and the rigid form he yanked out from within the folds of his cloak, the expression on his handsome face devoid of emotion. The Green Might had scattered that which had once been the high priestess before she had a chance to infect Zada and it now roiled to face its ultimate challenge. He could feel Mahn's need for more control forcing him to relinquish the hold he had over those that fought for him. The Radir paused while the Kreetch, confused by their master's sudden abandonment, moved away from those on the field and converged into a knot of black at the edge of the plain. The Vox were nowhere to be seen but he could sense their presence as they lurked amongst the silent horde on the plains. His gaze rested on a still cloaked and hooded Ramira, pushed to the forefront by a smug Mahn standing a few paces behind her.

"The time has come, boy," roared Mahn so that all within earshot would cringe not only because of his words but also for the reaction he had hoped to elicit from the elf. Neither response took place.

"You will not be victorious." Danyl glared at the monster.

"I have already been triumphant, boy. Look around you. I will spare the rest if you cede to me."

"Never."

"Never is a very long time, boy."

Mahn hissed with satisfaction and ripped off Ramira's cloak. Her blank gaze did not vary as he hoisted her off the ground by the back of her dress, holding her aloft like a shield. If Danyl were to fire his might at the evil, he would have to hit her and Mahn guessed that would be the last thing he would want to do. Sure of his actions and feeling safe, he began to pour himself into Ramira to retrieve the Source. The prince stared at Mahn, showing no desire or attempt to stop him. The bystanders gasped in horror for their worst nightmare was about to come to pass while the only person capable of stopping it stood motionless upon the field.

She felt the vileness burn upon entering her and the pure horror made her squirm with loathing as it oozed down towards the Source. He purposefully raked and clawed his way down, filling the gashes and scratches with his poison. She shuddered and moaned as the venom scalded into her being, refusing to ignite the Source to stop her inner torment. He inflicted every possible abomination on her as he continued to seep into her, the residue of his misery preceding him like detestable heralds announcing his arrival. As offensive and obscene as all of this was, she knew she had to endure it, for once Mahn's appalling apparition was deep within she could trap him, allowing Danyl to destroy him. She could not stop him from taking the Source, a fact Mahn was well aware of, but once he had secured it, there would be little, if any time for the elf to strike. Would he wield his power to annihilate Mahn if it meant he would possibly do the same to her? How could he not brandish it when their end was so painfully evident?

She focused her eyes upon the love of her life, slowly lifting one of her hands to her heart, her finger marking the place he should fire upon. She watched him study her as if it were the first time he had ever beheld her. This response frightened her for this was not the man she knew. What happened to him? Why did he remind her of one of the demons…sweet mercy no! It couldn't be! Please don't let him have been taken by one of the Vox! Panic began to well up deep inside of her, a response that Mahn mistook as a reaction to his intolerable presence. He increased the horrors of his passing, gleefully plunging deeper and deeper into her. For a few precious moments he was oblivious to everything transpiring outside her body.

The only movement on the field caught her attention as she watched Zada ride over to Danyl. She dismounted and walked the last few paces to stand beside him with the same dark look on her face. Mahn was halfway to the Source and both Danyl and Zada wore that glazed-over expression on their faces. Ramira could endure the horror devastating her from within more than those complacent faces as time hastily retreated away from them. All of Mahn was now within and his presence seared every nerve and fiber of her being as he continued to punish her, inflicting as much pain and despair as time allowed. He hovered over the Source, the prize just moments away from being his when he noticed the silver sparkle beside it. He leaned over to investigate what this new thing was, instantly recoiling as he identified the bits of green and amethyst mixed in with the silver. He howled with fury and a tinge of fear, reaching past it and grabbing the Source.

Zada looked over at Danyl, imploring him to use the power. Mahn would only be trapped within her for a short period of time while he took the Source from her. The window of opportunity was small and the elf needed to act immediately or there would be no other chance to do so.

"Danyl, use the magic," she beseeched.

Bereft of his emotions and unable to comprehend what the power had done to him, he stood there like an image carved of stone. He had wielded the power to save Zada from the red mist but there had been a purpose, an enemy he could recognize, but now? Although the evil loomed above Ramira, he could only see her and not what ravaged her from within. He had watched her point to her heart and had seen the pleading within her eyes yet he could not raise his hands to administer the fatal blow. It felt wrong to do so without just cause, even if it meant saving the countless lives waiting upon the bloody plains.

"Danyl…" Zada's voice was filled with panic as she watched Ramira struggle to keep the evil within. She became stiff, the veins and tendons beginning to rise as she tried to restrain the monster within, an evil that, by now, would have realized his mistake. Her face reflected the agony of being forced to endure his presence and that she was nearing the end of her limitations. Mahn was seeking his escape. The tremendous effort it took for her to keep that from happening began to distort her features, sending rivulets of perspiration pouring down her face and neck. Her mouth opened but the soundless scream remained choked down within her throat, her countenance beginning to turn purple with the effort. Ramira could not hold on much longer.

Seven and the others nervously observed the prince do nothing. Gard focused on Ramira, the exertion and pain she endured in order for the elf to defeat Mahn etched on her face. The Khadry located the elven king, the look of dread on his face mirroring his own. Styph's face was unreadable. Gard could well imagine what this torturous wait was doing to him for he, too, felt as if his fate hung on the brink of a massive cliff that ended in a black well of horror.

"Time is running out, Danyl!"

The prince locked eyes with Ramira and she conveyed all she felt for him, their friends and all of the people that lived and died upon the plains. She begged him to drive the Green Might into her and end the nightmare once and for all before the moment passed.

If you have any love for me and all those who wait then you will strike me with your might.

I cannot kill you.

If you do not then the fate you resign me and all the others to would be unimaginable.

Danyl took control of the power then unlocked the door that held all of his feelings and emotions. He steeped the magic in his passions, making it glitter with a ferocity that blinded even him then, screaming with dismay at what he was about to do, let the fire fly from his hands. The brilliant bolt of green shrieked across the plains, its sound like a thousand voices crying out in defiance, forcing those watching to cover their ears and shield their eyes. The concussion from the emerald blast knocked Zada to the ground, her inner sight a maelstrom of images and colors as it followed the power to its intended target. She gasped for air, as the incredible force seemed to suck the life from her breast but was powerless to stop it.

Ramira watched as the green bolt, a gleaming spear bristling with not death but life approached her in slow motion. Those closest to the hurtling power threw themselves upon the soggy ground while many pushed away from the monstrosity that was about to taste its potency. She felt the fire pierce her flesh, then drive deep into her heart but rather than burn and sear her, its touch was cool and comforting. It washed over her like a cooling rain, leaving her at peace for a brief moment. Then the elven magic changed. It began to expand, the refreshing sensation turning into a blistering heat that scalded her before exploding then oozing down to cut off Mahn's escape. Trapped, he had no choice but to stand and wield the Source. The ultimate battle would not take place on the plains outside the city but deep within Ramira, who braced herself as best as she could against the impending clash.

Danyl stood in the center of a glade. Trees and brush surrounded it and he could see glimpses of white dunes beyond their trunks. A slender birch reached gracefully up into the soft light falling through the canopy onto the ground. His gaze drifted toward a pile of rotting wood that had fallen into a heap, the trees around it soon to succumb to the same thing that had toppled their kin. He turned and spotted a vine clinging tenaciously to a tall tree. He could almost hear it grunt with exertion as it sought to reach the top so that its purplish-blue flowers could feel the sun. A hint of white to his left caught his attention: tiny blooms peeked around thick, waxy leaves with the shyness of a small child. Danyl looked down and saw that the ground was composed of sand from which thick patches of deep green grass grew. He noticed a small black ridge poking up through the grains, the curved thorns part of a faint circle nearly lost beneath the sand. A twig snapped somewhere within the streaming light ahead of him. He stared into the half shadows and haze, the Green Might draining down his arms and into his hands until they were consumed with the emerald fire. Danyl's wait was short.

A glittering ball of black screamed toward him from the trees and fell short of its target. The roar of fury following it quickly took on the shape of his adversary. Mahn exploded from the murkiness, firing volley after volley of power at Danyl. The closer he came the more accurate his aim became. Danyl easily deflected the magic, holding his ground as the darkness rushed toward him. The elf sensed he had assimilated the Source with his own energy and braced himself for the worst. The two combatants faced off against each other in the center of the glade. One bristled with death while the other blazed with life. It was time to determine what fate would befall the land and her people.

Mahn surged forward, blasting the elf with his blackness, annoyed by the unruliness of the Source. It weighed down his powers as if forged of lead, missing his target regardless of how accurately he directed it. *Stabilize it, you fool!* The evil concentrated on steadying the two magics but found them even more unwieldy than before. The elf began to move forward, pummeling him with the Green Might. He was initially able to ward them off, but the Source tugged on his arms making it difficult for him to lift them up. He had to discard it…for the time being, anyway. Mahn released the amethyst power, unconcerned that it lay within easy reach of the elf.

Danyl smiled faintly as Mahn discarded the Source. The evil had misjudged not the Source but the person who had housed it all these centuries. The elf began his assault, flinging one bolt of emerald after another at the black shape expending all of his energy to prevent the Green Might from consuming him. Great bursts of power incinerated bushes and blew branches off the trees. Mahn sent a mighty blast at Danyl, who sidestepped it and watched as the tiny white flowers turned to ash. Another discharge splintered the willowy birch, the agonizing cracking and snapping sound it made as it toppled to the ground echoing throughout the dell. The vine wilted beneath the onslaught, hanging limply from the trunk. The gentle light that had illuminated the hollow became lost in the smoke and fire devouring the glen.

Mahn circled around Danyl, absorbing the painful blows as he drove him toward the thorny ridge. The menacing barbs began to twist and bend, pointing toward the elf. Mahn struck the ground behind Danyl, opening up a jagged rift that caught his foot. He stumbled and began to fall backward, rotating to one side and landing inches away from the sinister spines. He rolled away from the black magic Mahn hurled at him, choking on the dust and fine grains of sand stirred up by his hands and feet. They got into his eyes and mouth, and no amount of tears or spit could oust them. He scuttled backward, dodging the blows Mahn rained down on him while never getting a chance to return his own fire. The evil tried to force him toward the crest of spines, their razor sharp spikes pointing at Danyl no matter which direction he took. They hungered for his flesh and blood as much as Mahn did. Mahn stepped into and jumbled up the trails Danyl left in the sand, obliterating the elf's desperate attempts to get away from the evil and stand up to fight back. Mahn had other plans and redoubled his efforts to finish off the elf and take his prizes. The evil hissed with satisfaction, as Danyl's escape route was about to be restricted. The prince never saw the pile of moldering trunks blocking any further escape, the sudden impact his head made on the rough bark cutting open his head just above the brow. Blood seeped from the gash on his forehead but he could still make out the blurry shape looming in front of him. Mahn clasped his hands together and formed a huge ball of energy then raised his arms high over head. *You have lost, boy!*

Danyl shook his head, ignoring the droplets of blood flying away from his face. He rubbed away some of the sand from his eyes, squinting as he coughed and spit out the fine dust from his mouth and throat. Mahn menaced him with the black power spinning crazily between his gloved hands, the triumphant set of his shoulders matching the exultation in his hiss. The evil's gloat left the door open for the elf. Danyl clapped his hands together, concentrating all of the Green Might into a gleaming emerald spear. He plunged it into the center of Mahn's hood, holding on as the evil first shivered then began to convulse. Danyl clenched his jaw, every muscle and tendon visible beneath his reddening skin as they labored to keep the contact. Bits of Mahn's power rained down upon him, the droplets feeling like acid as they dripped on his body. He ignored the pain, concentrating instead on the shuddering form above him. Then, without warning, the spear left his grip and propelled the evil into the middle of the glade. Danyl's chest heaved, his eyes wide as the evil began to break up into pieces. The fragments started to revolve around the green lance, whirling so fast that they kicked up the debris around it. The elf brought his arms up to protect his face from the sharp objects being shot out of the vortex then vaulted for cover behind the fallen trees he had been pressed against. He peered through a gap in the trunks and held his breath.

The Green Might sent out sizzling currents of power, encompassing the blackness swirling around it. Danyl shielded his eyes from the brilliant elven magic then jumped as the whirling mass exploded with a mighty boom.

The glen was utterly silent. He looked through the break and rose to his feet, leaning on the top of the tree and surveying the area in front of him. A smoldering crater marked where the evil had been destroyed. The Green Might spiraled lazily over it like some bird of prey riding the air currents searching for its quarry. Danyl placed his hands behind his head as he looked at the devastation done to Ramira's soul. His arms dropped to his sides and he lowered his head in grief and regret, his blood drip-dripping to the ground. A rustling sound from behind him pulled him from his anguish. He turned toward it and stared in disbelief.

Ramira stood just beyond his reach. Her red-gold hair shone like silk and her bronze-hued skin glowed warmly in the soft light that fell once more upon the glade. Her eyes sparkled with love and the smile she bestowed upon him made Danyl forget about every terrible thing that had transpired. His gaze traveled down to the bundle she cradled protectively in her arms. A tiny hand reached out from the blanket eliciting a choked cry of astonishment from the elf. He cocked his head to the side and moved toward them, his fingers extending out to touch them when the Green Might slammed into his back and began to yank him away. He fought the elven power with an intensity that made his battle with Mahn seem like nothing more than a skirmish. The Green Might was determined to return him to the land of the living but the elf had other ideas. He would rather die here with them than return to the loneliness that awaited him. The elven power desperately clawed at the elf, raking and shredding his essence as it sought to control him. Danyl's substance began to break apart as he strained toward Ramira.

You must go, Danyl! You cannot stay here!

I...won't...leave you!

The danger has not completely passed. You must finish your task out on the plains.

I...

Danyl watched Ramira withdraw into the shadows, the sad look of resignation the last thing he saw. He took a deep breath, swaying unsteadily on his feet as the last of his strength ebbed from his body. He had won and lost at the same time. The Green Might swirled around the complacent elf and transferred him out of Ramira's devastated soul.

Zada was stunned by the ferocious energy radiating from Ramira's eyes and mouth as the Green Might battled the evil. She could not fathom how Ramira was able to survive what was transpiring within her. The Herkah saw the elven magic tear and rip into the black power as it in turn tried to destroy the other, but the elf was not about to relinquish his grip. It began to pulverize Mahn with a retribution that was truly frightening, and as the seconds ticked by, the evil began to succumb to the furious onslaught. She could sense Ramira away from the confrontation, for the woman had done her part and now awaited the outcome just like everyone else on the plains. Rivulets of blood ran from Ramira's nose and mouth, flowing over ugly purplish bruises brought about by the wielders clashing within her. If she died before Danyl triumphed over the evil then Mahn would be set free, Source in tow, to fulfill his dark purpose.

Alyxandyr and Clare, their hands firmly clasped, stared wide-eyed at the terrible scene. They, too, noted that Ramira's body was on the verge of succumbing to the struggle decimating her on the inside. They glanced over at Danyl, his nebulous form burning brightly with the elven might, the ground around him smoking as the power scorched and blistered it. The King and Queen prayed the conflict would soon end, a thought shared by everyone on the plain.

Danyl administered the final blow, concentrating the might before launching it into Mahn. The emerald power erupted with such a blinding force that even he shielded his eyes from it. The demon twisted and convulsed, the magic incinerating its very essence, his feeble attempt to regroup met with another burst of power. Mahn started to break apart; the particles spinning tightly in a narrow column that stretched toward the blue sky. It ruptured, sending bits and pieces of the evil raining down near the forest to the north. Ramira collapsed, the resounding explosion tearing through her and out onto the plains, leveling everyone and everything standing close by. Bodies and great chunks of sod were hurled backward, landing awkwardly on the ground and on each other. Loose sections of the city's outer walls slid to the ground, scattering those who had stood beneath them during the clash of powers. Dust and bits of stone spilled onto the ground, mingling with the shouts and cries of those who weren't fast enough to elude the debris. Silence ruled the land while those who had witnessed the ultimate battle nervously waited to see who had come out victorious. When Zada was finally able to focus her eyes, she saw Danyl standing as still as before, but when she turned to look for Ramira, she saw her lying lifeless on the ground. Mahn was gone.

Danyl recalled the power, collecting it within him once more. Reality began to take hold of him. The essence of who he was, including his emotions, feelings and memories, returned to their proper places, allowing him to become whole again. It took several long seconds for the blank look to vacate his eyes and for the harsh truth of what he had done to sink in. Grief stuck in his throat as he gazed with sorrow upon the woman he loved. She lay in a heap upon the ground, hair and clothing covering her face.

Nothing happened for several moments; everyone was too stunned to move. Almost everyone, because the Vox began to collect what was once Mahn. They, unlike the Radir and Kreetch, did not need Mahn to function, but they did need the dark power to exist. It would take a very long time to gather up the evil's residue but the Vox that had taken Allad's body was unconcerned. He had all the time in the world to do so. The Vox absorbed the details around him then he and the others disappeared from the land of light. Those gathered on the plains began to move and, although a few half-hearted skirmishes erupted, the warriors on both sides simply retreated from each other. Mahn's forces, now bereft of not only their leader but his influence as well, wondered what they were doing here. Many ran away while others simply surrendered. After many days of fierce combat and countless losses on both sides, all felt drained and slightly confused as to what to do. They ended up milling around each other, recognizing friends and foes alike. The resurgent cries of the wounded and dying filled their ears and prompted them into action. They were armed with a purpose and not a weapon, tending to those in need regardless of which side of the battle they had fought on. The area around Ramira's crumpled form began to fill up quickly. Danyl raced toward her but even his swift horse was too slow in getting there. She was gone by the time he arrived. He scoured the area, the panic and loss in his eyes too painful to behold, and even the strong arms of his father and brother could not keep him still.

"Danyl...she's gone, son."

"No! She was just here!" he cried, grabbing at his heart to still the aching sensation knifing through him. The prince knew she had shared in whatever he had done to Mahn. He had killed her. He had slain them both. He stared at the trampled earth, the memory of the tiny hand reaching out to him too much to bear.

Alyxandyr put his arms around his son, holding him tightly for he needed to feel Danyl as much as his son wanted his fathers touch. Styph placed one arm around them, both sharing in their grief. Then each of the other companions joined them in the embrace.

Zada stood alone watching the Vox that imprisoned Allad as it withdrew from the plains. The Vox had managed to acquire a formidable Herkah, one whose intelligence and supreme skills would make him a superior foe. It would, she knew, return to the foul depths from which it hailed and would torment Allad until he was released from its terrible grip. She swore she would fulfill that act. The nomad gazed at the knot of family and friends offering each other solace, her heart wanting desperately to join them. Her legs were unable to make the short journey to where they stood. She had crossed the Great White Desert, this land and the vast between world where shadows lived yet did not have the strength to walk the short distance to them. She crossed her arms and hung her head, crying for Allad and all the others that had been slain.

-14-

Those who survived finally sat down to eat long after the moon had risen. They had refused to abandon those in need on the plains, leaving only when everything was well under control. The physicians tended to the wounded, sewing up both man and elf, a duty that would take them well into the next day. It was impossible to bury all the men and horses that had fallen in battle so they were placed upon huge pyres and burned. The city walls had held, but the damage they suffered would take weeks to repair, maybe longer considering so many able men had died. Cooper spent most of the afternoon trying to convince his confused and fearful men they were no longer in danger, an odd task considering he usually instilled dread into them. Styph and Zada made sure enough food, blankets and other essentials were available to all those that needed them. They walked beside a wagonload of supplies, passing out items to friend and former foe. They replenished the cart several times before returning to the castle long after nightfall. The elf prince and the Herkah freshened up and joined their companions for dinner.

The night was balmy, the balcony doors open to reveal a full moon. They ate out of need, with few words being exchanged, their aching and exhausted limbs barely able to raise their forks to their mouths. Their empty hearts cried out as their eyes stared at the vacant chairs: Lance, Nyk, Allad and the gentle Karolauren were among those that slept the eternal sleep…no, not quite. Allad yearned for that merciful rest. The demon inhabiting his body would surely give him anything but peace. And Ramira? What had befallen the woman with the red-gold hair? Had she also been hauled into that abominable lair or had Danyl somehow managed to release her from this world? Alyxandyr glanced around the table, noting the deep creases running along their foreheads, the dark circles under their eyes and their pale faces and knew that his fared no better. Although Seven had sustained severe injuries, he had insisted on dining with them. He nodded for Clare to pour them all glasses of his concoction after they had eaten, smiling sadly when Zada filled a second set of glasses with Allad's liquid.

"We owe the dead a great debt," began Alyxandyr in somber tones. "May their souls rest in peace and may the spirits of those still alive find solace in their sacrifices."

Strangely enough, not one person grimaced as the strong drinks burned their throats.

"I will, in the future, increase my vigilance and make sure we communicate more often," Cooper stated. The toll this had taken on him was as great as the others.

"We will all have to be more attentive," added Alyxandyr, looking over at the empty seats.

"What will you do now, Gard?" asked the first advisor.

"I don't know, Mason. There is much to do here and I'm sure there is nothing left of my home. I will let my people decide."

"You are welcome to stay in the city or anywhere else on these lands," offered the elven king.

"Thank you, I'll let them know that."

"What about you, Zada? Will you go back to the desert?"

"It is our home," she replied.

"I doubt any of us will be leaving soon, at least not until our wounded are well enough to make the journey home," said Seven, the pain in his voice reflecting more than the wounds covering his body.

"You are all welcome to stay for as long as you need."

"Danyl?" His brother was concerned because the prince had kept his eyes downcast without uttering a single word the entire time.

The prince did not reply but refilled his glass with Seven's drink and went out onto the balcony. The Green Might had withdrawn back into his soul but it did not resume its slumber, remaining awake as if its time was not yet over. He drained the glass and shuddered with the memory and the potency of the liquid.

"Danyl?" Zada approached him and placed her hand on his arm as it rested on the balustrade.

"What?"

"The brown woman, Oma, loved Ramira as if she were her own child and thought the world of you. She wanted me to tell you that the bonds that are created during one's lifetime transcend even death. She also wanted me to tell you what I saw when she took me back to Thebes."

And so Zada did. She revealed everything she had seen and experienced and in doing so told the elf what kind of person Ramira really was and how little the difference was between then and now. Danyl listened absently at first then began to pay closer attention to what the nomad told him, even though her own pain at losing Allad was evident. When she was finished, Danyl could not help but notice her story ended abruptly, without explaining how the first king fit in or how Ramira ended up in the cave.

"Do you know what happened after the Broken Plains were created?"

"No, for some reason Oma did not show me."

The balcony door closed behind them then Zada's inner sight began to pulse. She sensed no danger but shivered nonetheless as the night stirred, washing a peculiar coolness over them both as they watched the shade materialize before them. Oma stood before them, her eyes brimming with understanding as she beheld the distraught pair. There was a great deal of compassion flowing from her shimmering form and both the elf and the nomad sensed it as it eased their tired souls. A small fountain of hope seemed to have erupted from within the dry wells housing their souls at the prospect of the brown woman providing them with some much needed answers. The brown woman's heart ached for them, just as it did for the young woman she had raised as her own child. The responsibility to destroy the evil had fallen upon this elf even though he and his people had nothing to do with its resurrection a thousand years ago. That burden fell upon Ramira's shoulders. Although they had done everything in their power to avert such a catastrophe, she was still the reason for Mahn's existence. Oma placed her hands on theirs and took them through the rest of the journey…

But I will show you now.

Ramira trembled with rage and fear as she watched the total destruction of her home. The King held on tightly. He could feel her straining to free herself and run into the melee taking place about a mile away. Her eyes were wide and wild as they glanced at the fractured city and all she could compare it to was some huge animal, mortally wounded and in its death throes. Mahn, deprived of his prize, skulked away. The terrible sounds began to die down and soon only the flames feasting on Thebes' carcass moved.

"I have to go and see if anyone survived!"

"You will only find your own death within those ruins," he countered as he secured the hold he had on her.

"I can't leave them…I have to help!"

"I will go with you then."

"No, it isn't safe for you to do so. Please, go to your people."

"Come with me…us," he corrected as he gazed upon her with compassion. "There is nothing left for you here."

"I cannot." The intensity of his eyes reflected the deep-seated anxiety he felt for her safety, realizing she would not abandon her people. He nodded and sighed at her decision.

"Be well, then, and if you ever decide to leave, follow the sun as it rises in the east and you will find us there."

"Thank you," she replied, and walked away from him, her bracelet falling into his hand as she pulled her arm away.

The first king dropped his head as she turned away. He doubted she would live to see another sunrise. His magic had reacted to the dark power that had pulverized an entire city, but it would not flare to destroy that darkness. He could not understand why it did not, and as her form merged with the night, he wondered what he could do to assist her and those that remained. He realized there was nothing he could do to help her people. The flames must have found another supply of fuel; they suddenly blasted up into the night sky, threatening to consume the very heavens. He turned to meet up with his kin.

Ramira looked back once but the night hid him from her sight, his face and touch firmly etched into her mind. She hoped he had left and met up with his people, for there was nothing here for him. Every somber step back to Thebes reminded her she was the reason for its destruction. The contorted features of those who had tried to escape glared up at her, the terror of what had befallen them frightening to behold. She approached the boundary of the smoldering city and was nearly overcome by the devastating silence hovering over the smoke and ashes. The evil had spared nothing.

She trod amongst the crushed foundations and pockets of fire, jumping as the incredible heat caused stones to pop and fracture. She followed along the perimeter until she was on the north side where she heard faint cries and whispers and knew there were indeed survivors. She called out to them and heard a distant reply, following it even though it might well be a trap. She spotted nearly a fifty or so huddled figures and approached them, their eyes wide with fright and confusion. She calmed them and asked if they had any provisions, for they would have to find another home. They had nothing more than the clothes on their backs and a few personal items hastily thrown into packs. Ramira told them to head north along the mountains and wait for her there. She and a few others would scrounge for whatever staples they could find. Ramira assured them they would meet up with them no later than the next day.

They moved out while Ramira and the others headed back into the city to look for provisions and, with any luck, more survivors. Ramira picked through the debris, lifting small pieces of rubble to see if she could find any food or blankets underneath. She managed to find several blankets and a few broken vessels of wheat, the latter which she scooped into one of the blankets. She carried her things toward a partially collapsed house, the back wall leaning precariously against a cracked side wall. She dropped her bundle and carefully squeezed her way in. A fire in the house next door illuminated the kitchen area, one that somehow looked familiar to her. A sob rose in her throat as spotted the broken rocking chair strewn on the floor. She wiped away the tears beginning to flow, forcing herself to gather up as much food as she could. She heard someone call out her name and crawled back out of Oma's house.

"Here!" she hailed the Theban. "Take these blankets and food to the others. I'll follow the perimeter of the city in case I can find anything else then meet you later on. Hurry!"

She watched the man disappear into the ruins and turned to gaze at the house one last time before moving on. She wiped away the sweat from her face, conscious of how hot it was getting. Then she detected the far-off rumbling of thunder. No, not thunder. It originated in the ground beneath her. It grew in sound and frequency, toppling whatever still stood. She looked toward the palace, gaping with shock as it began to sink into the sands. She remained motionless, eyes wide as the massive building disappeared, taking with it the avenues and surrounding structures. The ground buckled and shifted; great geysers of sand blew up into the night, blotting out even the full moon. Ramira was thrown onto the sands that were being sucked down into the hole where the royal residence had once proudly stood. She struggled to her feet and ran toward the dark mountains, looking back over her shoulder to watch the desert consume the city.

She reached the base of the peaks and stopped, gasping for air and rubbing her cramping legs. She had to head north to catch up with her people but the spectacle before her would not release her from its hold. The sands began to revolve and form an eddy, dragging everything into the giant maw in the center. She shrank back into the shadows as Mahn soared over her, bellowing with rage at what was transpiring on the desert. He desperately tried to stop the city from disappearing, flinging great balls of power down into the void. The result was catastrophic. Huge chunks of debris and grains of sand were flung for miles around, compelling Ramira to seek immediate shelter. She crawled up the side of the mountain and entered one of the crevasses, intending to wait out the destruction. It wasn't safe near the entrance, either.

She went deeper and deeper into the fissure, urged on by the blasts pounding the passageway behind her. The rocky corridor began to collapse. She hesitated, wanting to get out the way she had come in, but the mountain had other plans. If she waited a moment longer she'd be buried beneath tons of debris. She ran on, her mind never acknowledging her next step might send her toppling into an abyss or she might smash her head on an overhanging rock. It almost felt as if something or someone was guiding her as she sped through the nearly black tunnel. She finally spotted a faint outline directly ahead of her, and as she lunged for the ill-defined opening, the last of the mountain crashed down behind her.

She dropped to her knees, her chest rising and falling while the sweat poured from her body. She swayed unsteadily on her knees then dropped down onto all fours hoping the nausea would pass. She had to find a way to meet up with her people. She finally began to breathe normally and attempted to rise but a gentle yet firm touch seemed to take hold of her.

Lie down and rest, child.

Ramira did as she was told. Just before sleep took hold of her, she sensed a presence, one that collected every shred of memory and tucked it away where it would be safe. The last sensation she had was of being wrapped within a gauzy cocoon…

"She went back…" began Zada, realizing Ramira was the one who gave the Herkahs, once residents of Thebes, a second chance at life.

The Lady of the Sands knew if Ramira stayed, Mahn would have taken what he had so desperately wanted and the only way to avoid that was to compel her to escape. Ramira had no inclination to leave her people, which gave the Lady only one choice: cut off her return.

"Why didn't the first king wield his magic?" Danyl asked, the images he had seen when breaking the beads surfacing in his mind.

It wasn't powerful enough.

Those words stunned Danyl, for he had always believed the magic was most powerful in the first king, weakening or dispersing through the generations. In truth, it had strengthened, making him the most powerful bearer of the Green Might ever, and it still pulsed with power deep within him.

"Oma? Who is Ramira really?" Zada asked tentatively. She saw Danyl stiffen for Mahn had repeatedly told him Ramira was just like him, a lie he was sure, to devastate him and keep him from acting. Danyl swallowed hard; he knew Oma had no reason to utter anything but the truth. What they heard, however, was something they were totally unprepared for, and Danyl could do nothing but stare at the brown woman, as she confessed to them.

Ramira is a child of the darkness, birthed of the same evil that spawned Mahn.

A strangled cry of denial escaped the prince's throat. The mere thought of Mahn being right was a painfully direct contradiction to the unconditional love he held for Ramira. It also began to reveal more truths that answered many questions. He forced himself to keep on listening although Omas' words were like knives stabbing at his heart.

The Lady had already come to me with the news that this child housed the Source, and initially all three of us were nervous and frightened of the monumental task she handed to us. We were all quite anxious when the time came for me to stand as midwife to the ceraphine. My arms were the only contact she had when she was born. The ceraphine had no desire to hold the infant she found pale and homely. Luckily for us, she chose to ignore the child, never realizing what rested within that tiny body. I held the most potent power in the land but instead of blanching with fear I began to coo at the newborn. The newborn smiled back at me and stole my heart. I saw a baby and not a tool of destruction. I cleaned her up and swaddled her in a blanket, grinning as if she were my own child but frowning at her dull hues. I could not imagine her living her life wearing the dismal shades of her heritage. The Lady agreed, and while I held the newborn aloft upon the balcony, the Lady coaxed the setting sun to impart its beautiful hues into the new life. The Lady allowed me one more gift: a name. I chose "Ramira" which means "Child of the Light." For some peculiar reason those acts instilled a sense of optimism into our dangerous task. It signified the first of many victories, both big and small, that we were able to win over the darkness. The Source's unpredictability left us with quite the dilemma: kill her and allow the Source to be set free or try to offset its evil nature. Imhap taught her everything that his scrolls, tomes and maps allowed while Horemb sharpened her skills with the knives. It fell to me to nurture her emotions. The day would come when she would find out that she housed the Source, but we clung to the belief that the good in her would temper the dark power. We had enough faith in her that if she ever brandished the magic it would be for a good, and not evil, purpose. Her life has given us joy while our deaths gave her life. The Source, like your Green Might, will extend your lives beyond all others but the day will come when you leave this land and go to a place the powers cannot follow.

"Ramira is a demon yet your influence changed the nature of what she was…" breathed Zada, not knowing whether to feel relieved or more frightened.

"What will happen to you now, Oma?" Danyl was unsure what to make of the answers to so many questions. Mahn had not lied to him about her yet even now he was able to look beyond what she had been intended to be and what she had become. The intimacies they had shared teetered but did not collapse beneath the knowledge he had just acquired. The elf knew he would sort through this information for a long time yet he would never know the outcome of his introspection until he faced her in the future.

My task is done now and I will finally be able to rest.

"Does she know that she is a …child of the darkness?" asked Zada, the thought of Ramira living with that truth too painful for even her to bear.

No, Zada, she does not. Of the living, only the two of you know.

Danyl and Zada knew the truth they held was a tremendous burden they would carry their whole lives. If they ever saw Ramira again that very truth would destroy her and they both knew that all too well. However, if she were demon spawn, would they not be obligated to bestow that information upon those who had so valiantly fought her kin? Yes, she was one of them, but by the same token she was also part of those that thrived beneath the sun. The three were slain because they loved and believed in her; they had bequeathed that gift to Ramira. The elf and the Herkah exchanged looks, silently vowing to never reveal what Oma had told them.

"Where is Ramira now, Oma?" he asked the shade, the familiar longing strangling his voice.

She is where she is meant to be. Be well and do not forget us.

Oma faded away, leaving Danyl and Zada with many questions. Oma's words and tones indicated she was not within that well of evil but in a place that would grant her some measure of peace. For the first time since the onslaught began, the elf began to weep for all who were lost, the Herkah taking him in her arms and adding her own tears of sorrow to his.

The noxious morass to the north and east of where once an ancient city stood began to bubble and belch, sending long, thin strands of yellowish mist into the night. The sickly fog began to spread outward, carrying with it an awful stench and terrible wailing sounds that echoed eerily across the desert. Ghostly lights flickered within the unhealthy haze pinpointing a cloaked figure walking the well-worn path leading into the heart of the swamp. The brawny form moved with a slightly unsteady motion as if unsure of its footing. Its bearing, however, never wavered. It halted briefly, turning around to stare back at the way it had come, the cowl hiding its features until a pair of gloved hands reached up and slowly pulled it back. The ghastly light revealed hawkish features and a pair of black eyes wild with trepidation and anguish. The being desperately sought help but found only a glittering expanse of sand and a black, star-encrusted sky. He grimaced as he endured the evil thriving within. The Vox allowed its prisoner one final indulgence, the resounding roar of malice echoing across the frigid dunes. It rolled like thunder toward the heart of the desert, dislodging scorpions burrowed within the shifting dunes. The sound grew fainter the farther it traveled until the Great White Desert smothered it. The gloved hands reached up, tugging the hood back over the face before disappearing into the mist, a strangled cry marking the spot where it vanished.

The cold night air stirred and carried the vibrations to the place of the Horii where the vague silhouette of a woman placed her graceful hand across her breast and dropped her head in grief. She stood upon the dais marked by four columns, traces of earlier numerous offerings and an elegant fountain. Translucent curtains undulated in the twilight as they moved to the strains of the winds whispering over the dunes. Stars glittered brilliantly overhead vying with the bright face of the moon as it turned the desert into a sea of silver. The Lady turned her attention to the shape lying motionless in the middle of the platform. A sigh escaped her lips as she looked at the body. She knelt down beside it, placing her slim hand upon the forehead as a tear rolled down her cheek. She rued this task; it was the most unfair of them all, and even with her formidable might she was powerless to avoid it. She rose and descended the step carrying her onto the desert and away from what was about to transpire. She gazed at the form for another moment then raised her arms up to the heavens invoking the Horii to mount the dais. She brought them down then waited.

The sands around the stone pavilion began to shift then roil as if boiling over. Steam rose from the sands, partially obscuring the platform as it sought to blur the very night as well. The columns began to shake while the clay pots and bowls vibrated and danced across the stone platform; the fountain spewed water in every direction. The wind blew in gusts around the dais, stirring up the grains and flinging them everywhere, forcing even the Lady to shield her face. It reached its peak then began to abate until the desert was utterly still. The Lady took a deep breath and backed up a few paces, staring at the subtle movements at the foot of the steps. First one, then dozens of the

Horii began to stream up onto the dais, converging around the motionless form without touching it. They began to circulate around it in unison, changing from white to silver to gray and then black. When all the Horii were completely dark, they surged as one through the wrapping and into the body, the sudden and vicious intrusion making the body lurch and sway. The Lady could hardly breathe as she watched, her heart pounding loudly in her ears nearly blocking out the disturbing sounds the Horii were making from within the linen shroud. She watched with horror as bits and pieces of the shroud shifted and stretched as the snake-like things burrowed into and out of the body. She knew all too well what the Horii were doing.

Forgive me, my child...

Alyxandyr surveyed the plains around the city, absently scratching the scar forming on his forearm. Two weeks had passed since the fighting had ended. Patches of grass sprang up from the torn up earth, the bright green clumps contrasting sharply with the black tents that once again filled the terrain. He glanced over toward the walls, the new rocks and still drying mortar marking the damage done by the catapults. A group of elves and dwarves hoisted up a large slab, painstakingly trying to fit it in a gap on the rampart. Khadry hunters emerged from the orchard carrying deer, fowl and rabbits back to the city. The elven king gathered his courage then looked over toward the blackened pit between the city and the orchard. He remembered every face that had been incinerated there. The wrinkles on his forehead began to abate as he noticed bits of yellow and blue poking up through the scorched earth. The King sighed heavily and urged his horse back into the city. He rode up the main avenue, glancing from side to side. Shopkeepers waited on customers; blacksmiths hammered away on their anvils; children played near their homes and the old sat together on benches.

He crossed the intersection and winked at Sophie as she chatted with a neighbor, Cricket and Anci giggling as they sat on the stoop. He approached the castle and relinquished the reins to one of the guards, walking tiredly up the stairs and into his home. He waved away an assistant trying to hand him a stack of reports and ascended the staircase to his rooms. He dismissed the guard at his door then closed it behind him. He walked over to the balcony and gazed out across the city. He saw Danyl and Styph walk by, the crown prince's hand resting on his brother's taut shoulder. The King's youngest son had yet to shed the guilt for Ramira's death.

Ramira was the magnet that had attracted Mahn but she was also the reason they existed on this plain: if she had not warned the first king this land would surely be a different place. Her resiliency spanned the centuries, manifesting itself in an entirely new world where peace actually had a chance to flourish. It was a shame she could not share in that victory or be allowed to love and be loved by his son. Fate was not always fair or kind, a reality he learned from the moment he lost his queen up until this present time.

He gazed up at the clear blue sky, the warmth pulsing from the bright sun heating his tired face. It began to thaw the layer of cold dread and sorrow within his breast and chased away the shadow of despair hovering around him. He stirred the memories of his loved ones, offering to share the sunlight with them no matter where they were. He spotted a small elven boy crying at the edge of the park then watched as a Herkah crouched in front of him and wiped away his tears. The nomad picked him up, the boy burying his face within the black garb as the Herkah carried him to his mother. She took the child from the Herkah and nodded her appreciation, smiling as he ruffled the boy's hair. A pair of dwarves helped an elf place several pieces of lumber that had fallen off his cart back onto it. If someone had described such a scene to him a year ago he would have thought they were completely crazy. The road leading to such trust had been a long and bloody one that spanned many centuries, centuries one woman's heroic courage had allowed them to live.

"Thank you, Ramira."

-15-

Lanterns strung from brightly colored ribbons illuminated the center of the city. Lamps hung on poles beside tables of food and drink and glowed warmly from the windows of the homes fronting the square. Pots of simmering herbs and spices emitted delicate tendrils of fragrance throughout Bystyn and reminded everyone that spring was not far away. It was a joyful thought shared by the races as they mingled with each other for the final time. They would be returning to their own homes the following day to pick up the pieces of their lives. Spring had not quite yet claimed the land but the surprisingly balmy day and early evening was appreciated by everyone.

Alyxandyr escorted Zada through the throngs dressed in their finest clothing, stopping and chatting now and then as they made their way to Sophie's house. Seven and Clare were already sitting on the steps next to Cooper, enjoying glasses of wine and plates of sweets. Anci and Cricket ran inside to get more goblets and another bottle.

"He looks so old, Alyx," said Zada, watching Danyl approach. His hands were in his pockets and his gaze downcast unless someone spoke to him. He would nod politely and move on, his expression never changing.

"Something other than Ramira's death has devastated him."

"I think you're right, Clare, but I doubt he'll ever tell anyone," stated Seven.

Danyl greeted them then sat down, accepting the goblet from Cricket and smiling as she leaned up against him. He put his arm around her and wondered when her crush on him would diminish. She still wore the little pouch holding the blue stone, a reminder, he guessed, of the hard life she left behind. The musicians started to play a lively tune, goading even the most reluctant individual to at the very least tap their toes. Within moments elves, dwarves and Herkahs clapped their hands and began to dance, integrating the dissimilar dancing styles into one chaotic movement.

"Look at all those fools! Must I teach them everything?"

They laughed as Seven limped over to the dancers, his hands gesturing into the air then toward his feet. He hopped and twirled then grabbed onto the nearest woman and proceeded to waltz unmethodically around in a circle. The dwarf king reeled to his own beat, the woman hanging on for dear life as the crowd clapped their approval.

A nebulous shape, barely discernable in the brilliant rays of the setting sun floated just outside the gate. It hesitated, wavering nervously back and forth then moved forward, timidly moving under the gate and up the avenue. The farther it traveled into the city the more pronounced its appearance became. What had started out as a thin wisp of mist began to congeal into a vague human shape.

Zada's hands froze in mid clap. She turned her head slowly toward the avenue running down to the gate, her gaze fixed on the people sauntering up to the square. Her inner sight clicked on. Bystyn and its denizens' bright colors were replaced by various shades of gray, the lights taking on a dingy yellow cast matching the glow making its way up the avenue. Her face began to blanch and beads of perspiration formed on her brow. She did not see Sophie's hand covering her mouth nor Clare slowly standing up. She didn't hear the elven king speaking to her or notice Anci and Cricket holding on to each other. Cooper brushed his fingers against the back of his neck, trying to shoo away the annoying insects crawling on his skin. Zada slowly rose from the stoop, staring straight up the street as she woodenly made her way to the square, Danyl and the others a step behind.

The indistinct figure continued on, heedless of the crowd pointing before parting and letting it pass. People stopped talking and laughing, unsure of what to make of this person treading up the avenue. They retreated to the walkways, the music ceasing as the figure passed the halfway point. The revelers abandoned the square, replaced by guards with weapons drawn and at the ready. Silence reigned as the figure stopped at the edge of the plaza.

"Zada, is that what I think it is?" Alyxandyr could not look away from the shape.

She took a deep breath and glanced over at Danyl, the mystified look on his face mirroring that of everyone else. Nothing happened for the longest time, and then the haze comprising the form dissipated, leaving behind a slight shape clothed in a tattered and dirty cloak. A limp cowl hid its features while flashes of dull skin could be seen between the rents in the garment along the shoulders and sides. Feet encrusted with dust and grime peeked out from under the frayed hem. This poor wretch would have been tended to without a second thought had it not been for its peculiar entrance into Bystyn.

"Who are you and what do you want? Show yourself!" demanded the elven king.

Zada watched the creature flinch at the King's words, its head dropping down to its chest while taking a step backward. Zada approached the bundle of rags, ignoring the protests erupting all around her. She halted a few paces away from the figure.

"Who are you?"

Zada held her breath as the being slowly extended its arms from within the worn, thin cloak and turned its trembling hands palm up. The Herkah's gaze began at the dirt-caked fingers, down her palms and froze as they noted the tiny slash marks around her wrists. The scars continued up her arms, disappearing beneath the ragged edges of what remained of the garment's sleeves. She swallowed hard, her wrists and ankles burning and itching in response. She inched forward and reached into the droopy hood with an unsteady hand and touched the chin, her fingers feeling smooth though dirty skin.

"Zada! What's going on?" she heard Alyxandyr call from behind her.

Danyl stared at the poor creature trembling before Zada and wondered why the nomad was paying so much attention to it. It had cringed when he tried to go toward it and that had only increased his curiosity. He cautiously closed the distance between them, hesitating every time the creature took a step backward. He stopped and backed away when Zada lifted her arm, ending up between his father and Cricket.

Zada lifted the wretch's chin just far enough for her to see inside the cowl. She bit her lip and fought back the tears as she looked upon the washed out features illuminated by the lanterns. Soft, silver eyes surrounded by skin so bleached it appeared nearly transparent beseeched the nomad. Guilt clouded them over and she tried to lower her head as crimson stains spread across her delicate cheeks. Zada would not let her turn away.

"I had to come back, Zada," she said in a raspy voice trembling with nervousness.

"I know, child." She swallowed hard as Ramira's tear ran over her fingers.

"I'm…I'm one…of them."

"You were one of them, but that changed a long time ago."

"I cannot escape my heritage, Zada."

"You have risen above it and taken us with you."

"I want to be here so very badly, but, by the same token, I'm terrified, too. Maybe I shouldn't have come back…"

"You are where you are meant to be."

The words left Zada's lips before she even realized it, the haunting echoes mingling with the truths before her. The Lady of the Sands had given Ramira a second…or was it third chance? She could not even begin to imagine what the Horii had done to her. The sacred spirits had determined she was worthy and the Lady would certainly not have sent Ramira back into the world of the living if she were still dangerous. Zada glanced over her shoulder at Danyl.

He scrutinized everything that was transpiring, his inquisitiveness metamorphosing into suspicion. His narrow eyes ceased calculating what the creature in front of them might be, becoming more rounded with incredulity at what it really was. The Herkah looked to the west and held her breath. The setting sun was absolutely dazzling, painting the sky with brilliant shades of red, orange, lavender and blue. Oma had held a newborn up to those colors centuries ago hoping they would camouflage her ancestry. The love and devotion of a long dead woman had transformed Ramira from demon to human…could those same emotions by the elf repeat that feat? Zada had precious little time to think about that. She gripped Ramira's hand and held out the other toward Danyl.

Danyl was afraid if he took a step forward the ghost would dissipate into thin air, taking his fragile hope with it. Zada's tense nod for him to join them urged his rigid feet ahead. He walked through the tense silence on shaking legs, not daring to breathe, fearing his exhalations would scatter the shade standing beside the nomad. His arm lifted up and his fingers extended to Zada's, the Herkah's warmth and certainty stilling his apprehensions as she grasped his hand. The nomad brought the two hands together and took several steps away from them. The sunset neared its zenith.

Danyl's hand slowly slipped into her hood and caressed her face, the feel of her skin a balm to his wounded soul. He began to relax as she tilted her head into his touch, looking at but ignoring the scarred arm that snaked up his chest from within the tattered cloak. He inclined her head until he could see into the hood, the overjoyed look on his face chasing away the doubts clouding her features. He pulled her against his body then leaned forward and gently kissed her pale lips.

The elf's uncompromising passion flooded into her being, burning through the shadows and cobwebs of her forlorn spirit. It blazed more brightly than the elven might and ignited her sense of self-worth. It illuminated the faces of all the people she had cherished, their looks of satisfaction and contentment fuel for the fire racing through her. She freely gave all of herself to him, allowing him access to even the darkest corners of her soul. He never faltered in his quest to fully revive her and that energized her even more. Her skin began to tingle and her eyes watered as his strength flowed into her.

Zada stared at Ramira's arms as they wrapped around the prince's neck. The scars shifted then receded, the milky color of her skin replaced by the faintest of bronze hues. The white wisp of hair poking out of the cowl deepened into a vibrant red-gold color. Ramira's hood started to slip off her head in slow motion. Zada watched the edge of the cowl delineate what had already transformed while hiding what had not yet been changed. A cascade of red-gold hair spilled from the hood as it finally fell flat against her back. The nomad had been so mesmerized by the process she never noticed the others approach, watching as intently as she was. There was only one more alteration left.

Danyl reluctantly withdrew his lips and gazed into Ramira's face, oblivious of the circle of friends and family surrounding them. He, like the others, waited for her to open her eyes. She finally lifted her lids, blinking as if waking from a deep sleep. Danyl smiled broadly and Zada clapped her hands with joy and relief at the amethysts twinkling brightly from their sockets. Danyl scooped her up in his arms, the Herkah adjusting the worn, thin garment as he carried her to Sophie's house amid tumultuous cheers and claps.

Seven clutched Clare's hand as they watched the pair disappear into the crowd, surfacing momentarily as Danyl climbed the front steps. Mason put his arms around Sophie, Anci and Cricket. Gard stared at the couple for a few moments then shifted his gaze to the cobble-stoned street, his jaw firmly set within his impassive face. Cooper crossed his arms and looked over at his family, the faint longing in his heart not yet strong enough to compel him toward them. Styph nodded with approval, grateful that his brother was able to find happiness and serenity. He looked over at his father, noting the tiredness slowly diminishing from his features. The unmistakable touch of a slender and graceful hand rested upon Alyxandyr's arm yet he did not glance down to see who stood beside him. He inhaled deeply, the scent of roses bringing peace to his soul as he placed his hand over the invisible one.

The Lady of the Sands stood in front of the stone pavilion and gathered her garments close to her ethereal shape. The quest for the source of darkness had not quite turned out the way Mahn had anticipated. He had overlooked one very crucial truth: the ultimate evil had forgotten how truly powerful the spirit was. The danger was not past for the equally disturbing Vox had, for the most part, survived the battle and lurked along the edges of darkness. The present, however, would allow those who dwelled in the land to replenish their lives and hopefully stabilize and strengthen their futures. With her role complete, the Lady of the Sands burst into a cloud of sparkling brilliance then floated down upon the dunes, becoming indistinguishable from the infinite grains constituting the Great White Desert.

Printed in the United States
58396LVS00019B/120

9 781413 774276